One Last Gasp

Andrew C. Piazza

Copyright © 2012 Andrew C. Piazza
All rights reserved.
ISBN: 1491249080
ISBN-13: 978-1491249086

DEDICATION

This book is dedicated to the quiet ones; the men and women who sacrifice for the greater good, without being asked and never expecting reward or recognition. You are the light standing against the darkness.

FOREWORD

Many thanks to all who assisted in the creation of this book; some with technical and historical advice, some with moral support, all greatly appreciated by me.

For you history experts, I did a great deal of research to try to keep the details correct on the military units, designations, equipment, and all that good stuff. There are undoubtedly errors. Hopefully they are minor enough to escape notice or at least be forgiven in the grand scheme of things.

And finally, for you, Gentle Reader, thanks so much for picking up this book and entrusting me to lead you on a little walk into the imaginary. I hope you find this work worth your attention. I do appreciate, encourage, and enjoy interaction with my readers, so please feel free to stop by my website, www.andrewpiazza.com, and leave your thoughts in the comments section of whatever story you'd like to comment on. I try to respond to all of them.

Now, let's get this ride started.

1

I am the only surviving member of 1st Battalion, 518th Parachute Infantry Regiment, 101st Airborne Division, Army of the United States. My unit was decimated in the Ardennes forest during the winter of 1944-1945, by enemies both human and otherwise.

This account has been a long time coming. I don't really know how to explain that. Part of it is the nature of the beast; my generation is particularly reluctant to dwell on what we've done… or especially how we felt about doing it. We had a job to do and we did it. Over and done with. Maybe it's just the way we were brought up. Maybe it's just me. It's dangerous for one man to speak for a generation.

Part of my delay has to do with the nature of what happened in those snow-covered woods all those years ago. War is surreal by nature; it's hard enough to try to describe what it was like to begin with, much less talk about the things we found and saw and fought in Dom Caern without sounding insane or senile or both. Maybe you won't believe me. Hell, there's already guys who say the Holocaust never happened, and I saw that, too.

Part of it is the nightmares, in which dark shapes huddling just out of sight in the mists murmur warbling commands in a language no human has ever spoken. I don't understand the words, per se, but the meaning is clear: keep your mouth shut.

I guess the reason I'm writing this at all is my fading memory. My memory has become my blessing and my curse. It's getting so that I can't always remember what it is I did today or the day before, or even what I was in the middle of doing. Those days, though, those days I can remember almost photographically; every day from when I signed up for the Army all the way through jump school and the drops on Normandy and Holland and then the Bulge and all the rest, until we ended the war up at The Eagle's Nest, Hitler's mountain refuge in Austria.

Remembering those days at Dom Caern is a curse. It will be a blessing when this Alzheimer's or whatever it is that's eating my memories gets around to lunching on January 1945. For those of you that don't know history, it was the tail end of the Battle of the Bulge... the biggest battle ever fought by the US Army. It involved over a million men stretched along a front hundreds of miles long. Hitler made a last gasp offensive for Antwerp with an army that was already considered defeated. It was a doomed, damn fool gamble and a lot of men got killed for it; but then, old Adolf had a knack for getting people killed, didn't he? Sometimes it's dangerous for one man to speak for a country.

After we held off at Bastogne, the 101st was immediately ordered to assist in pushing the Germans back... there would be no rest for the Airborne. In early January, we were holed up in the woods near a tiny village to the west of Noville. I never did find out its name. It was frigid cold and dirty and terrifying, mostly terrifying because we were waiting for a German counterattack. They always counterattacked.

The war got truly terrifying after the attack came.

It started with an artillery barrage.

2

His screams could be heard even over the explosions, which shook our spines and rattled our teeth and showered us with dirt and snow and spent fragments of shrapnel.

"They're killing us! They're killing everybody! Jesus Christ, we didn't even have a chance, they ran right over us and they didn't stop and..."

"Settle down!" I shouted, shaking him a little bit. It was bad enough with the artillery falling all around us; this guy's panic was like throwing lit matches at a puddle of gasoline.

Already his screaming was starting to have an effect on the men in the foxholes around us. One to the left front of my hole started shouting at the top of his lungs, "Fuck you! Fuck you! Leave me alone, you bastards! I'll kill every fucking one of you, I get my hands on you, you son of a bitch!"

I'm sure the mother of Artie Gorman...the guy shouting in the hole... would cringe at his language or the desperate harshness in his voice as he hurled it up at the shells coming down around us. But you have to understand the situation. An artillery barrage is like nothing else on Earth.

The best way I can describe it is like this. Imagine yourself lying in bed at the end of an exhausting day... I mean you're bone-weary, dead-dog tired. You lie down and close your eyes, and your body seems to sink into the mattress as you dip your toes into the waters of sleepiness to test them. And then, as you're about to drift off, somebody creeps in, kneels down, puts their face a few inches from your ear, takes a deep breath in, and screams as loudly as they can directly into your ear. What happens?

You jump out of your skin, is what happens. Electric bolts shoot from your spine out to the tips of your fingers and toes. Your heart feels like somebody stuck an ice pick into it. Your lungs get stuck momentarily, like they forgot whether they were in the middle of an inhale or an exhale.

And you get pissed. Oh God, do you get pissed. Dogs barking, car horns blaring, any kind of loud noise gets us pissed when we're tired as hell.

So. Take that sensation and try to amplify it, because the shells are a hell of a lot louder than a shout. On every one, every single one, you get that spine-jarring sensation, but now add in the fear of knowing that it's not just a loud noise, that each explosion is also accompanied by a hailstorm of red-hot, razor-sharp metal shards whistling through the air as fast as a bullet. And you're not just tired, you're exhausted, because you've spent all day marching and then the rest digging a hole in the frozen ground that you wish you'd dug even deeper once the 88s start sending over some mail. That, and you didn't get any sleep the night before, for this very same reason.

You can't fight back. You can't get up out of that bed and punch the guy who screamed in your ear. You can't get your asshole neighbor to shut his dog up or turn his incessantly blaring car horn off. All you can do is sit, and take it. For hours. It sometimes lasts for hours.

And guys snap. You can't help it. You scream or cry or pray or do whatever you have to do to release that wildfire of panic. So don't blame Artie too much for his mouth. I've been there myself.

I gave the trooper who was screaming in my hole a little slap across the face to settle him. I couldn't have him setting off all my men like Artie. I call panic a wildfire because it can spread from man to man just like a wildfire.

Instead of snapping out of it, he just snapped. Looking at me with wild eyes, he shouted, "Fuck you guys! They're coming here next! They killed everybody at HQ and we're next! I'm not dying here with you, you bastards!"

He made a move to jump out of the hole. That's suicide. Only madmen, medics, and runners get out of their holes when there's arty coming in, especially as intense as that night. I cold-cocked him with my helmet and he dropped like a stone into the hole.

He'd be okay. By the time he woke up, the shelling would be over, and we could get him to an aid station. And for now, I wouldn't have to listen to his screaming.

A shell hit overhead in the top of a nearby pine tree, showering shrapnel down like the blast from a shotgun. I could hear pieces of metal thud into the tree trunk two feet from my hole. I cursed the bad luck or oversight or both that got my battalion stuck in the woods. It's the worst place to get shelled. Treetop explosions throw death into foxholes like nobody's business.

A quick peek over the top of the hole to get my bearings in the dark, and I psyched myself up for the run. Madmen, medics, and runners get out of their holes during an artillery barrage, and you can add first sergeants to that list. I had to get to the captain, our company commander.

Right after the next shell hit, I launched myself out of the hole and tore ass through the trees, toward where I knew Captain Powell had his foxhole. There was a whistling shriek, and my balls pulled up into my stomach, because long experience at listening to those shells told me it was going to be close.

Only one thing to do. I hugged the nearest tree trunk. The theory is, the shell hits the treetop and blows shrapnel down and out in a cone, so there's blind spot of sorts right at the bottom of the tree. In theory.

Except this time, I heard branches snap above me, sending down a cascade of snow shaken loose from the boughs, and then I saw the shell... I mean I really saw it, in the dead of night in a snow-covered wood... come down right in front of me.

There was no life flashing before my eyes for me. I just shorted out, popped like a burnt-out light bulb, and then when I blinked, I knew I wasn't dead after all.

It was a dud. It stuck out of the ground three feet in front of the tree, a dark shape thrust into the middle of the whiteness. Steam rose with a hiss around its edges from its heat melting the snow.

Thoughts came in a flurried haze. *—Holy Shit did that just happen? — Someone up there loves me! —Move, shithead, the next one won't be a dud!—*

I pried my arms from around the tree and practically leapt the ten yards to the next foxhole. There were two troopers in it already, but I squeezed my way in somehow.

"Holy Shit, Sarge!" one of them said breathlessly. His name was Pelosi and he'd joined the company right before Bastogne. "Did you see that dud hit right in front of you? You'da been…"

"Can it, Private!" I barked at him. The last thing I wanted to dwell on was how close I'd come to getting blown into hamburger.

And then, like a reprieve or a gift from God… it stopped. Well, not stopped, not entirely, there were still shells hitting our front lines about a hundred and fifty yards away, but it wasn't anywhere near what we'd been getting.

"Hey, is it over?" Pelosi asked, squirming underneath me to try and get a look out of his hole.

"Stay in your hole," I said to the both of them. "They'll sometimes give us a little pause, let us think it's over, and once we get up and out to take care of the wounded, whammo, they hit us again."

I didn't want to climb out. The closeness of our bodies drove a little of the frigid cold out of me.

"Right, Sarge… hey, where are you going?"

"Got to get to the Captain," I said, and ran like hell.

The shelling at our front lines petered out to nothing, and then I could hear it again… the sound of tank cannons and machine-guns firing back in the direction of our Battalion HQ. They were really catching hell; it sounded like every Kraut in the woods had one of those Schmeisser submachine-guns we called "burp guns".

The company CP was in a clearing; the Captain knew what he was doing, so he picked a spot where the tree-burst shells couldn't rain sharp metal down on him. His hole was about thirty yards from the edge of the trees, and I think I covered the distance in all of two seconds.

Again, it was like trying to shove five pounds of dirt into a three-pound bag. The Captain was used to visitors, and so his hole was larger than normal, but there was a radio operator in there with him, and the three of us were like wool-wrapped sardines until we figured out whose limb was whose.

"Sergeant Kinder," the Captain said in greeting as we jostled for position. "Did you find him?"

"Him" being the screaming trooper lying unconscious in the hole I'd left. A medic had come into the company CP, yelling about a raving soldier from Battalion HQ, and the Captain had sent me back to find out what was what.

"Sergeant?"

"Yeah," I said, finally getting into some semblance of a comfortable position. "I found him."

"Where is he?"

"Knocked out in the bottom of a foxhole," I said, and after catching a look from him, shrugged and added, "He went nuts and tried to run out of the hole. I had to."

Captain Powell seemed to consider that. "Where's the medic, um..."

"Christainson. Arty round got him."

"Oh. Did you find out anything? Telephone lines to Battalion are out and they're still not responding to radio. The only people I can get a hold of is Baker Company next to us."

Now that the ringing in my ears had subsided, I could pick up the sounds of battle from the area of Battalion HQ more clearly. "Sounds like Battalion's been overrun, big time," I said. "From the reaction of that trooper, and the amount of automatic weapons fire coming from that direction, I'd say they're getting hit by something pretty disagreeable."

Captain Powell frowned and mulled things over for a moment.

"Contact patrol?" I asked.

"And have them get wiped out by whatever's back there?" Captain Powell said, shaking his head. "No. If we go, we go in force."

He kept looking back and forth from our front lines, back in the direction of Battalion HQ, and back to the front lines again. I knew what he was thinking. Do we abandon our prepared defensive positions to help HQ, and maybe get hit in the rear by a German attack on our front, or stay put, and maybe get cut off from the rest of the battalion or even the entire regiment?

"Very well," he said at last. He used the words "Very well" the way most people say "Okay". "We go. Assemble 3rd Platoon and get me two runners to send for 1st and 2nd Platoons."

"I already sent Harvey to contact 1st platoon," I said with a knowing grin.

Captain Powell returned it. We'd been together long enough to finish each other's sentences, much less anticipate each other's actions. "You'll still need one more."

"Runner!" I shouted.

As the runner reported in, along with a few men from 3rd Platoon and a pair from 1st Platoon, the radio operator announced one of the phone lines was actually working. "I've got 3rd Platoon, sir. Diaphragm on the receiver was frozen but I got it thawed by breathing hard on it."

His words reminded me again how bitter cold it was. With all of the excitement, I'd forgotten that I felt like a soldier-cicle.

Within a few minutes, a trickle of GIs had collected around the CP. "This is all?" Captain Powell said. "Where are the rest?"

"Bunch of 3rd Platoon's guys are spread out on the line to close up gaps, and 1st Platoon is taking their damn time getting back here," I answered.

Airborne rifle companies are made up of three rifle platoons (1st, 2nd, and 3rd) of about forty men each and a headquarters section of about another fifteen or twenty men. Spread out among each platoon were our sixty-millimeter mortars (short-range artillery), our bazookas, and our thirty-cal (light and mobile) machine-guns.

However, we weren't anywhere near full strength… it was hard to think of a time when we ever were… so we'd taken a few machine-gun crews from 3rd Platoon and sprinkled them on the line with the other platoons to close gaps. What it boiled down to was, we had about eighteen men rallied at the CP for the spearhead of our counterattack.

But then, Airborne policy has always been to replace firepower with crazy people, and you have to be crazy in order to jump out of a perfectly good airplane.

Captain Powell fidgeted visibly. "We don't have time to wait. We'll have the rest of 3rd Platoon follow us up as they come in. Then 1st Platoon on our left flank and 2nd in reserve. Clear?"

Men shrugged out of their heavy overcoats… those that had them, that is… and worked the actions on their weapons. As soon as Captain Powell saw we were ready, he nodded. "Let's go."

Andrew C. Piazza

3

The firing had almost completely stopped, but we ran like hell all the same… we might still save some wounded or prevent some of our boys from being taken prisoner. The trees in that area of the Ardennes are close rows of pines, so close together that it's like a jungle canopy. You can't see more than ten feet in any direction, and that's during the daytime. It's easy to get lost, and easy to get separated, so we stuck close together as we ducked under branches and fought through the snow.

We made great time, although if you would've seen us, you would've called it crawling. We had to watch our step; if you bumped a pine bough and dumped the snow off it, you've just told every German machine-gunner around exactly where you are. So considering the handicap, we made it back to Battalion in no time.

Battalion HQ, of course, wasn't dug in amongst the dense trees. Major Carey, 1st Battalion commander, was billeted in a farmhouse along a tiny road that wound along the edge of our stretch of woods. There were still trees here and there, of course, but the line of pine trees ended fifty yards shy of the farmhouse.

Captain Powell called us to a halt at the edge of the woods. I could hear voices barking orders in German and the noisy, oily clanking of engines… panzers. A glance showed me Shorty Malone was within arm's reach with his bazooka, and that made me feel a bit better.

HQ was history. The farmhouse and one of its outbuildings were burning, along with a haystack in the field nearby. The roaring of the flames made it seem as if the farmhouse was groaning out its last breath as it was eaten alive. The fires burned high, in seeming defiance of the fat snowflakes tumbling down out of the sky, and turned the area into a frozen level of Hell. Bodies were scattered about like debris tossed by a severe thunderstorm.

Panzers were lined along the road. There were a lot of them; I counted eight stretching from left to right before the darkness beat out the firelight and hid the rest in the gloom. They were leaving. Tracks from their treads were all around the area, but now they were lined up neatly on the road and preparing to move out, to our right, into the dark. Infantry swarmed around them like worker ants. Most of them scrambled up onto the tanks for a free ride. Others herded prisoners into a group in front of the half-track bringing up the rear of the armored column.

They were SS. No doubt about it. Even fifty yards away in the dark, I could read their uniforms and the insignia on their vehicles like a billboard.

"We keep them from taking the prisoners," Captain Powell whispered quickly. "Set the two machine-guns up there and there. They cover our assault. Sergeant Kinder, take half our men. I will attack straight on with the other half. You hit the left flank, the end of the column, with yours, sweep them away from the prisoners. Questions?"

My hands were sweating despite the cold. They slid around inside my gloves as I wrung my hands around my carbine.

The armored column started to move out just as we got our machine-guns into position. The half-track, being last in line, wouldn't be moving for a minute or two, and the dozen or so infantry assigned to it lined the prisoners... maybe twenty or thirty of our guys... next to the road in a neat two-row column to be marched out.

I could recognize our medical personnel and some of our walking wounded. Right in front was Bill Smith, who had taken shrapnel in his leg the day before and refused to be evacuated. He didn't want to leave his buddies. I had to drag him bodily from the lines to the aid station, and even then, I only managed that by promising him he didn't have to leave Battalion if the doctors at the aid station gave him the okay to stay.

Behind and to the left of him was Ryan Filmore, a platoon sergeant from Baker Company. He'd gotten himself a nasty case of trench foot and severe diarrhea to boot. There were a lot of guys on the line with those problems; they only came back to the aid station when it got so bad they couldn't function at all anymore. Some of them waited so long they lost toes or even feet.

The SS had wiped out our HQ personnel and taken over our aid station as well. The guys were visibly shaken; they moved like drugged men or men just woken up. I can't say I blamed them. With eight or more panzers and God knows how many troops attacking from out of nowhere in the middle of the night, I was amazed there were any survivors.

We instinctively split into our two groups, and just as the Captain was about to give the order, it happened. The SS troops cleared away from the prisoners, one chopped through the air with his arm, and a jet of flame erupted from the trailing half-track.

It looked like they were dousing the men with a hose, but instead of water passing over them in a stream that went left to right and back again, it was liquid fire that clung to them like thick molasses. The screams started immediately, as men threw themselves into the snow in a futile effort to put out the fire that was eating them to the bone.

We were all stunned into shocked silence. The SS laughed at their victims, at how they danced and screamed and flailed their arms about. They let it go on for a few moments before raking the group with machine-gun fire.

One of the burning prisoners charged the half-track, unarmed, and an SS officer sidestepped and tripped him easily. It was Bill Smith, charging the enemy even though he was burning alive and wounded so badly in the leg he could barely limp. But then, Bill always had been a tough son of a bitch. I'd known him since Normandy.

Once he fell, the officer put a boot in his back, forcing him into the snow as he writhed and burned, and finally shot him in the back of the head with a pistol. He chatted idly with the soldier next to him the entire time, trading an occasional laugh.

I lost it then. I don't know how to explain it any other way. They called me a hero for what I did next, but I really just lost it, fell into a haze of rage and vengeance.

"Son of a bitch!" I shouted. I wrestled the bazooka away from Shorty and ducked under the last of the pine boughs into the clearing.

The prisoners were still burning, still dancing out their deaths, and the sight of the flames engulfing them began to engulf me in a fire of its own. My body began to burn, with a desire for murder and blood and savagery, and I lost myself to it.

I charged them across the field, straight towards the half-track and the dozen or so troops surrounding it. The frigid air burned the inside of my lungs with bitter frost, but still I screamed a madman's war cry at them all the way.

They spotted me once I'd made it about halfway. The officer took a shot at me with his pistol, and that seemed to be the signal for the fight to begin.

Our two machine-guns opened up from the woods, chattering a stream of lead and tracer bullets into the SS troops. The rest of the men surged forward out of the trees, shouting and firing as they came, but I was oblivious to all of it. All I saw was that damned half-track, and once the officer took his shot, I knelt, took a half-second to aim, and fired the bazooka.

The rocket sailed straight to its mark. There was a small explosion, as the rocket punched through the skin of the half-track, and then a much bigger one, as something inside the half-track ignited. A brilliant fireball sailed up into the air, lighting the battlefield like daytime for a brief moment.

That moment was lost on me. Dropping the bazooka, I unslung my carbine and resumed my charge, firing as I went at the pair of SS troops near the rear of the half-track. They were dazed by the explosion, and I put three rounds into one infantryman's chest before the SS officer shook out of his daze and scrambled around the half-track for cover. Before he passed out of sight, one of my shots punched a hole in his leg.

My weapon either ran dry or jammed. It didn't matter, though; a stray round from an SS rifle caught it in the barrel and spun it out of my hands as if it had been kicked. Like a madman, like a man possessed, I dug the .45 pistol out of my flap holster and ran right up to the half-track.

"Burn, you bastard!" I screamed at it, spittle flying from my mouth like a rabid dog. "You want to burn? Fucking *burn!*"

Up the side of the burning half-track I climbed, in sheer defiance of logic. I had hit the ammo supply on the half-track, which had caused the explosion and set it alight, but there were still the fuel tanks waiting to blow and incinerate anything in the area. But I was lost to the battle and nothing I did made sense.

Two SS troopers were trying to pull a badly wounded comrade from the wreckage, and once I was on top of the half-track and could see them, I emptied my pistol into their faces. There were other SS around the half-track, but by now, the other GIs had almost caught up with me, so the SS were too busy with them to worry about one crazy sergeant with an empty pistol.

The officer I'd shot, the executioner, was hobbling toward the next vehicle in line, a Panther tank, barely visible in the firelight. I threw my pistol at him and then, a trickle of sanity crept into me and I repeated the performance with a grenade from my belt.

The sharp crumple of an explosion went off next to him, throwing snow and metal fragments across his body. He hit the ground hard.

Bullets began to snap the air around me and *ping!* off the metal skin of the burning half-track I'd mounted. The SS troops further up the column were firing on us, especially on me, in an attempt to protect the rear of their column.

Snarling like a wounded animal, I whipped the barrel of the half-track's mounted machine-gun... the same machine-gun that had just been used to murder our men... around and cut loose at them, aiming at any muzzle flashes I saw flaring in the dark.

People were shouting at me from the ground, telling me to get off the burning vehicle before it exploded, but all I knew was the rapid *brrrrp* of the machine-gun as it rattled under my arm and the muzzle flashes that I raked incessantly. The Panther tank was pulling away quickly now, the SS troops along with it, and I was determined to burn out either the machine-gun's ammunition or its barrel before they left.

Someone pulled at my jacket, shouting in my ear, but I shrugged him off and kept firing. In the dim half-light outside the radius of the fire's illumination, I could see the Panther tank's cannon swiveling around toward me.

Come and get me, I thought, spraying machine-gun fire over the tank. *Show me what you've got, you son of a bitch.*

Finally, strong hands yanked me away from the machine-gun and hurled me bodily to the ground. The Panther tank fired its cannon an instant later, blasting the top of the half-track into a mass of twisted metal.

I struggled to my feet, pushing off my savior, and ran after them. "No, don't you run!" I screamed. "Don't you run away from me, you fucking cowards, I'm not done with you yet!"

The Panther tank was swallowed up by the dark, but I threw a grenade anyway, more to throw something at them than to do real damage. I had no weapon but I didn't want it to be over; I wasn't satisfied, I wanted to burn like the farmhouse, consume myself in an orgy of killing until I fell to pieces from sheer exhaustion.

And there was the officer, the executioner, the one with a bullet in his leg and grenade fragments through his body. He was still alive, barely, trying to drag himself in the direction of the already-disappeared armored column.

I was on him in a second, scooping up an entrenching tool… a short shovel… that was sticking out of the earth nearby. It made a good makeshift axe, and he wasn't wearing a helmet.

My memory is kind of fuzzy on the next couple of seconds. All I really remember is the feel of the wooden handle gripped tight in my fist, and the feeling you get in your hand when you've hit too many balls during batting practice. The sound of metal splitting bone, and the soft tearing sound as the blade wrenched free again and again.

Once more, somebody tried to stop me, shouting "Sarge! Sarge!" in my ear, and then finally, he grabbed my arm and my jacket lapel and screamed "Harry!"

I whirled on him. It was Captain Powell.

"He's *dead*, Harry," he said loudly, but evenly. "He's dead."

And like a gust of wind blowing away the summer heat, it was gone.

I blinked my eyes stupidly. My lips were curled back in a snarl; the muscles of my face ached from the frightful mask I'd twisted my features into. They felt like coiled springs being released. Everything on my body drooped. I was suddenly aware that I was panting like a marathon runner.

Captain Powell looked at me with an expression I couldn't quite translate. My right hand hurt, actually ached with fatigue; I looked down and saw with some surprise that it held an entrenching tool covered in blood and tissue. I let it drop to the ground from my exhausted fingers.

Then I saw the SS officer and the mess I'd made of him. I stared at him for a few seconds, thinking *Holy Shit, did I do that?*

"Harry, do you need a medic?" Captain Powell asked with real concern in his voice. All I could do was stand there, numb to the world and blinking rapidly.

Shorty Malone came up, armed with one of the SS troopers' weapons... it looked like a large burp gun... and swore when he saw me standing there like the walking dead. His wide eyes went from the SS officer to the bloody entrenching tool lying on the ground by my feet.

"Goddamn, Sarge," he said. "I'm glad you're on *our* side!"

Andrew C. Piazza

4

Only one of the airborne troopers survived the flame-thrower half-track, and 'survive' can only be used as a relative term. It was Ryan Filmore, the platoon sergeant, and he was dying. The only reason he was alive at all was because he'd been partially shielded from the flame and the bullets by those in front of him, and like the savvy soldier he was, he dropped and played dead as soon as the shooting started.

It only gave him a temporary reprieve. He was burned so badly he looked like a cinder; his clothes were blackened and stuck to his skin, which was so charred and cracked that I could see lines of red surrounding islands of scorched flesh. Most of his hair was gone, but his face was a little better than the rest of him… he must've instinctively shielded himself when the flame-thrower ran across him. Still, his lips were blistered severely and trembling in unimaginable pain.

"What happened here, Ryan?" Captain Powell asked, as he and I waited for a medic to arrive.

Ryan shook his head by minute degrees, as the skin of his neck was charred badly, and he licked his tongue over his blistered lips. "Came… out of nowhere. We heard vehicles, thought it was our guys, this far back and since they were driving like they knew where they were going. I don't know how the hell they did it. No lights. Came on in the dark, like they could see in the dark."

He started to cry, and I got out my canteen to give him some water, but he shoved my hand away before he went on. "You don't understand! It was… he wasn't human. See in the dark, and a skull…"

He stopped again, lost to hysterics. It was unnerving to see; Ryan and I had fought alongside each other in Holland and he and I had seen some of the same terrible sights, and I had never known him to fall apart like this. If it could happen to him, if what hit Battalion HQ could turn Ryan Filmore into a trembling basket case, then it could happen to any of us.

"What are you talking about, Ryan?" I asked. "What skull?"

"Him!" he whispered hoarsely, as if I weren't listening carefully enough. "He had a skull for a face! You think I'm crazy but I'm not! I saw it! With my own eyes, I saw it, I saw *him*, he had a skull for a face and fangs like a... like a damn animal, or a..."

Ryan shook his head again, even though I could see the cracked skin on his neck was starting to bleed. "You can't... he came out of nowhere, out of the dark, and they just ran right the fuck over everything. Then he came riding up on that huge Tiger tank, and they brought one of the prisoners to him, a nurse who'd come up to the aid station from Division, and she was scared and shaking and he laughed and...."

He stopped again, tears running down his scorched face, and he shut his eyes tight against the memory. Captain Powell looked over at me, and I could read his face just like he was reading mine. Neither one of us wanted to hear about a nurse getting executed.

"What happened?" Captain Powell asked softly. "It's okay, Sergeant. You can tell us."

Ryan's body was heaving with sobs now, and he had to force the words out, in a tiny voice that was almost a whine. "He... bit her."

"Bit her?" I said.

"He b-bit her," Ryan said again. "She was crying and scared and he grabbed her and bit her in the face. I c-could see it, I could see his fangs even though they'd clubbed me good with a rifle butt. He bit into her face and she screamed and a piece of it came off and he... he *swallowed* it."

My body shuddered and I felt the pit of my stomach twist upon itself. I might've gotten sick if I'd actually eaten anything in the last twenty-four hours.

Ryan wasn't done, though. "She started to freak out and flail around and he wiped his mouth on a handkerchief and ordered her taken a-away." He looked at me with a sudden, terrifying intensity, and grabbed my arm with a hand that was little more than a twisted claw. "They took a bunch of them, Harry. A bunch. Like ten or twelve. They looted the aid station, and then when they didn't find any kitchen trucks or ration supply, they rounded some people up and marched them off. Before they even had all the prisoners counted or lined up, you know? I thought that they... that they were taking me too..."

The medic finally arrived and neither Captain Powell nor I had the heart to keep morphine from the man just so we could ask more questions. I doubt there was much more Ryan could've told us, anyway. We let the medic take his pain away.

We could see a lot for ourselves. The farmhouse was blown apart, as were most of the outbuildings. There wasn't anything left of a perimeter; HQ was effectively wiped out.

By this time, the rest of the company had arrived to reinforce us, and we set up a makeshift defensive perimeter as quickly as we could. The rest of us searched for survivors.

"Sarge! Hey, Sarge!"

Shorty came up to me with a trooper I didn't recognize. His equipment was brand new, though, and unlike the rest of us, his face was clean-shaven.

"Who the hell is this?" I asked.

"Runner from Baker Company," Shorty said. "Wants to know what's what."

"P-private Weiss, First Sergeant," the private stammered. "I, uh, I'm a r-replace... a new... I just got up here today. Haven't r-really been assigned to anyone, I just... Major Carey told me to be a... I was just... on loan I guess, you know, until they figured out where to put me."

I stared at him for a second. "Weiss?"

"Yes, Sergeant?"

"Do you have a stutter?"

"Um, no."

"Then why are you talking like that?"

His eyes kept shifting around, from the burning buildings to the bodies to the blown-out half-track. "Well, I guess I'm just nervous, what with the attack and all..."

"Forget it. Come on," I said, and led him over to the Captain. "Captain, this is Private Weiss, he's a runner from Baker."

Captain Powell casually returned Weiss's smart salute. He'd been on the radio when we came up.

"Sir, um, Captain Jackson would like a, um, well, he'd like to know what's going on back here, sir."

"If he would've responded when we radioed for assistance, he could've come back here with us and found out already," Shorty grumbled.

I tended to agree, but the Captain said, "I'm sure Captain Jackson felt it best to hold his position in the line. Private, have you had any contact with A company?"

Weiss shook his head, as if almost confused by the question. "Uh, no sir, not that I know of."

"We can't raise them on the radio, either," Captain Powell said, then he nodded to himself, as if coming to a decision, and said, "Very well. Sarge, take a sound-powered telephone and line and get over to A company, see what's going on. We'll contact Baker via radio. Report back here as soon as you find out their situation."

"Yes, sir," I said, and gave Shorty a slap on the shoulder. "You're with me."

"What, um, what should I do, sir?" Weiss asked.

"Go with the sergeant, Private," Captain Powell said, nodding in my direction, and then returned to his radio.

"Come on, let's go, uh…" I said, and then snapped my fingers, trying to remember his name.

"Weiss," he finished for me.

"Yeah, right, Weiss, come on."

I always had a problem with the new guys' names. It wasn't a serious problem; they usually got killed before it became an issue anyway.

"Um, Sergeant, I really think I should go back to Captain Jackson and…"

I recovered a rifle from a dead GI, as I'd lost my carbine, and interrupted him. "I said you're coming with me, Private. You said you weren't officially assigned yet? Now you are. Your official assignment is to carry this telephone, and this wire…"

I handed him a sound-powered phone and spool of wire. "…and reel it out behind us as we go. Davey! Goliath!"

Two troopers waved back to me from the flickering shadows near the farmhouse. After a while, you can recognize people in the dark by the way they stand or walk.

"Why is he called Goliath?" Weiss asked.

" 'Cause he's enormous," Shorty said around the cigarette in his mouth.

"Why do they call the other guy Davey?"

" 'Cause he's short. You know, David and Goliath?"

Weiss frowned. "But you're short, and they call you Shorty."

"Kid," Shorty said, "you keep it up, *your* name's going to be Asshole."

I tried not to laugh. Getting replacements to fit in was a tough job but you needed to do it quickly, so they could become veterans that you could count on like Shorty.

"What's up, Sarge?" Davey asked once they joined our party. He and Goliath really did look like their namesakes, and were inseparable.

"We're going on a contact patrol to A Company, and I want Goliath and his B.A.R. handy in case we need some firepower."

The Browning Automatic Rifle was an excellent weapon that we never seemed to have enough of. It was a heavy clip-fed rifle that fired on full automatic, so it had a lot more firepower than our semi-automatic M1 rifles and carbines. They were usually handed out one to a squad and were used like light machine-guns. After what I'd seen so far, I wanted all the firepower at my disposal that I could get.

It didn't take long to get to A Company's CP. The sky had become overcast, though, and even with the white snow reflecting the ambient light, we couldn't see a damn thing.

"This ain't good," Shorty whispered.

"Why?" Weiss asked.

"We haven't been challenged," Shorty replied. "If there were anybody here, they would've challenged us by now."

Just then, Weiss shrieked at the top of his lungs and fell to the ground. Into the ground, actually, straight into a foxhole, and Shorty nearly shot him reflexively.

"Jesus Christ, you dumbass!" he shouted. "You want to get shot, screaming in my ear like that?"

"Here, hang on," Goliath said, his voice a deep, mellow bass that always seemed to calm my nerves whenever I heard it. "I'll help you out."

"Stay put, Goliath," I said. I wanted that B.A.R. ready to go. "I'll get him out."

"Oh, God, they're dead, I put my hand right in his…" Weiss said, and we could hear him begin to vomit.

"Weiss? Weiss, get up, give me your hand," I said, and waited as patiently as I could. "Come on, make it today."

I felt his hand touch mine and I dragged him out of the foxhole.

"Sorry," he said.

"What should we do, Sarge?" Shorty asked. "Can't see a damn thing. Do we go falling into every hole that A company dug?"

I frowned, and decided to take a chance. "This is First Sergeant of Charlie Company," I said loudly. "Any A company troopers out there?"

No response, except the pine boughs creaking under the weight of heavy snow. The way they criss-crossed over our heads, they felt like a heavy blanket weighing us down. Or wide hands pushing us into the earth.

"Must've pulled back to another position," Davey said, but he was close enough that I could see he had his carbine shouldered and I could hear him chewing at his gum nervously.

We weren't going to get anything accomplished like this, not fumbling about in the dark. I took the phone from Weiss and spun the crank to start it up.

"Captain, we're up around A company's position, but we can't see a thing," I said into the receiver. "If you've found the eighty-ones, could you send up a flare or two for us?"

"Stand by," he answered, and a minute later, we could hear the dull *Thoomp!* of two mortar rounds being fired back at Battalion.

A pair of parachute flares opened up over top of us, floating lazily down and bathing the area in a blood red light. The tree trunks created jittery shadows along the ground that set my mind on edge.

The forest had been blasted into a landscape of nightmares. Trees lay over each other like spilled matchsticks; their splintered trunks were the result of direct hits from tank cannons.

A Company hadn't pulled out. They'd been slaughtered.

Foxholes had been fired into point-blank by the panzers, blowing the occupants to bits. Other troopers had been burned alive with the flame-thrower we'd seen in action earlier. The fires had burned themselves out but the charred skeletons still smoked in their holes.

Other GIs had made a run for it; their bodies were riddled with bullets or smashed into an unrecognizable jelly by tank treads. The foxhole Weiss had fallen into was particularly grotesque: a tank had squatted over the hole and run its treads in place, churning up the dirt until it had dug down deeply enough to grind the foxhole's inhabitants into hamburger. I'd seen it before, but the effects always made me shudder and wonder what that would be like, trapped under forty-plus tons of steel grinding slowly down on top of me.

It looked like a graveyard dug by lunatics, with the foxholes being graves left uncovered and the bodies left lying around as if forgotten by the undertaker. We walked along the open graves and bodies like drugged men, dazed by what we were seeing.

There were tank tracks everywhere. So many, in fact, that it was impossible to estimate how many panzers had come through here.

"How the hell did they do this?" Shorty asked. "I mean, get all these tanks in here, in the dark? And this fast? It's impossible."

Ryan's words came back to haunt me. *They can see in the dark.*

There were bodies that didn't look too bad, either; they probably had been wounded and died from the cold as much as their wounds. As frigid as it was, even a minor wound could tip a man over into shock and kill him. I knew a guy that got hit in the foot and ended up dying from the shock and the cold. There were plenty of bodies that looked just like him, starting to stiffen up and freeze solid.

There was one foxhole with a pair of dead troopers that didn't seem to have any wounds on them. One of them was armed with a Thompson submachine-gun, and I jumped in to get it. It seems macabre, but the Thompson is an excellent weapon and I'd been looking for one for a while.

The dead trooper held onto it pretty hard, and it took some effort to get it out of his hands. As I was in there, Weiss stood staring, turning slightly green.

"What happened to them?" he asked.

"Gassed out," I said, finally freeing the tommygun with a grunt.

"What?"

"Gassed out," Davey repeated for me, always willing to be the font of information. "Remember those guys in the foxhole that got squished by the tank spinning its treads over the hole?"

"A panzer tried to do that here," Goliath picked up seamlessly. "But the ground was too frozen… like concrete. So they sat over the hole, revved their engine…"

"…and choked them to death with the fumes," Davey finished.

"Good God," Weiss whispered.

Shorty thumped him good-naturedly on the back. "Welcome to Belgium."

5

"It doesn't make any sense," Captain Powell frowned, looking over the four eighty-one millimeter mortar tubes dug in near Battalion HQ.

"Sir?" I asked. We'd reported what had happened to A Company and returned to Battalion HQ immediately thereafter. None of us wanted to stick around in that graveyard.

He gestured at the mortars. "They left the eighty-ones. And the pile of ammunition lying a few steps away."

Now that he pointed it out, I had to admit, that was kind of stupid of them.

Captain Powell shook his head and looked around the shattered remains of HQ. "They decimate A Company, roll right over HQ without any appreciable losses… because we didn't find any enemy bodies except those killed next to the flame-thrower half-track. So their losses were minimal enough for them to recover bodies along with the wounded."

"Okay," I said. "I follow."

"They raid our kitchen supply," he said, pointing at the area where we would've kept our rations, "but we haven't been re-supplied for a while, so there isn't much to take."

"Doesn't take them long to scoop that up," I said.

"Right. So then what? They leave the heavy mortars and ammunition alone. They not only don't take them, they don't even bother to destroy them… the mortars which can shell the town from here."

"We could hit the town with the sixties too," I said.

"Maybe. They might barely reach. But these were the big threat. And all of our ammo supply," he pointed again, with another frown and shake of his head, "they don't even bother with."

He took a moment to think before speaking again. "The last two weeks, every German unit we've hit has been scraping the bottom of the supply barrel, making do with next to nothing."

"But these guys," he went on, "are burning up gas and firing ordinance like there's no tomorrow, and they leave our ammo supply untouched. And yet…"

He tapped the barrel of his Thompson against his leg in thought. "And yet they take the time to round up and march off prisoners, and line up the wounded in neat rows to execute them."

I shrugged. "They couldn't take the wounded with them."

"Then why take any prisoners? Why not just kill them all?"

There wasn't any obvious answer to that. I was about to ask him if he'd been able to contact Regiment yet, when an excited GI came running up out of the dark.

"Captain! Captain!"

"What is it, trooper?" I asked.

"We found the Major," he said.

Major Carey's body was hanging upside down from the lower branches of an apple tree about a hundred yards away from the farmhouse that had been his CP. They'd stripped him naked, and by the way the corpse swung in the wind, I could tell he was already frozen stiff. Frost lined the edges of his eyebrows and his parted lips.

The hilt of a Hitler Youth knife and half an inch of blade jutted out from between his teeth. The last three inches of the blade stuck out of the back of his head. Blood was frozen in mid-drop dangling from the tip of the steel.

"Why would they do this?" Weiss asked. He'd stayed close to me ever since our trip to A Company.

"Scare us," I answered. "Or piss us off. Or both. What's that on his chest?"

Something was scrawled on his chest in blood, but it was impossible to read in the red light of the parachute flares. Somebody got out a flashlight and shone it on his body long enough for us to read it.

"What's it say, Shorty?" I asked. "You've got some German."

Shorty looked at the ground, scratched at the week's worth of dirty beard on his face. "It, uh…"

"What does it mean, Shorty?" Captain Powell asked quietly.

"It means," Shorty said, "sort of… well, unfit."

"Unfit?" I said. "Unfit, as in unfit for command?"

"No, Sarge. It means…" he said slowly, then stopped.

He shuddered once before finally spitting it out. "It means unfit as in, unfit to *eat*."

"Sergeant Kinder," Captain Powell said through clenched teeth.

I'd never seen him really mad before. Hell, he almost never raised his voice, except in combat. Even then, it was just adrenaline and fear and battle rage, which isn't really anger in the conventional sense. But what I heard now in his voice was barely contained fury; and like I said, I'd never seen him really angry before. "Yes, sir?"

"I want you to have the men collect every heavy weapon salvageable from A Company and HQ… every mortar, bazooka, machine-gun, everything. Have them arm themselves with any automatic weapons they can find… Thompsons, grease guns, B.A.R.s… including those new automatic rifles all the SS troopers had."

"Sir?"

"There's going to be close contact in that village," he said. "We're going to want every automatic weapon we can get."

"We're attacking." It was more of a statement than a question. After seeing the Major, I think we all knew we weren't going to let this go unanswered.

Captain Powell looked at me at last, and there was a fire in his eyes that wasn't a reflection off the parachute flares. "You bet your ass we're attacking."

"Listen up!" he said, raising his voice so everyone gathered around the body of the Major… about twenty-five of us… could hear. "I know you're all tired, and freezing, and hungry. Probably a few of you are shaken up. So I know it's a lot to ask, to give an order to attack. Believe me, I know, because I'm standing right here with you, freezing my nuts off."

There were a few scattered laughs, along with a few guilty glances up at Major Carey.

"I know doing your duty is enough to make you follow an order to attack. I know the desire for payback… for what they did to Major Carey, to our wounded, for what they might be doing right now to our men taken prisoner… is enough to make you want to attack. But as we get ready to jump off, and the cold and the fatigue and the hunger starts getting to you, I want you to keep something else in mind."

"At dawn, we are going into that village," he pointed back towards our lines, towards the nameless little town we were dug in outside of, "and we are going to kill every SS we find. I don't care how many tanks or burp guns they've got… this time, they've fucked with the wrong paratroops."

Another shocking first. I had never, ever heard Captain Powell use profanity in front of the men before.

"And when we're done, and the town is ours," Captain Powell finished, "there will be warm billets in houses, and beds for some of you, and as much hot chow as I can get up here."

There were some excited murmurs at the mention of warm houses and hot food, and Shorty said loudly, "Shit, Captain! For a warm bed and hot chow, I'll shoot every Kraut in Germany!"

A bunch of guys laughed at that, and Captain Powell smiled and pointed a finger at him as a warning. "You be careful, Shorty. I might take you up on that. Sergeant Kinder?"

"Let's go to work, troops," I barked loudly, and we set out to take our revenge.

6

We couldn't just go charging out of the woods, of course. I don't care how pissed off you are; when you attack a town, you make the proper preparations or you get dead.

In this instance, it started with the artillery.

"We're attacking?" Weiss asked, right on my heels, as always. "After getting the shit kicked out of us, we're attacking?"

I paused in my striding around and giving orders to the men. "Hey, Weiss, are you Airborne or not? You sound like you want to get transferred to Supply."

That may sound like so much chest-thumping ho-hah to you, but there's a reason for it. All kinds of things make men fight: duty, rage, glory, honor, desperation, commitment, jealously, greed… and pride. Pride in one's country and especially in one's unit. More than once, I got a nervous trooper to get up and do his job by thumping him a good one and asking him if he remembered who he was; not just any soldier, but Airborne, by God.

"It's not that, Sarge, it's just…"

"Relax, Private, we're not going in right away," I said, and held up a hand as, almost on cue, the big guns back at Regiment boomed. A couple of seconds later, we could hear the shells exploding far away in the town. Once the first shells hit, the four eighty-one millimeter mortars attached to our Battalion HQ opened up, firing shells with their distinctive *Thoomp!* sound.

"There, hear that?" I said. "We're going to shell the shit out of them for a while, soften them up and keep their heads down before we move in."

"Yeah, give it to 'em!" a voice shouted from off towards our front lines. "Keep pouring it on, boys! Don't ever stop, not until they're all fucking dead!"

It was far away, but I could still recognize it as Artie Gorman.

"Sergeant Kinder!" Captain Powell called out, waving me over. I weaved my way through the flurry of paratroopers readying themselves for the attack and answered him with a "Yes, sir!"

"What is this about a squad of survivors from A Company?"

"Just found out myself, Captain," I said. "Five troopers on the far right flank of A Company survived the attack. There was such a big gap between their holes and the rest of the company that the Krauts must've missed them."

"They stayed in their holes the entire time?"

I nodded. "They figured with all that firepower, this was another full-blown counter-offensive, and that they should hold their flank to give their company a way out."

"They were right," he said. "How are they?"

"None of them are wounded."

"That's not what I meant."

I knew what he meant. "They look like a whipped team in the half-time locker room, sir. They think there's something they should've done, that they let their buddies die."

"That's ridiculous. There was nothing they could've done."

"You know that and I know that. But them…" I raised my hands up, as if it were the only way to end the sentence.

"Right."

And then, he surprised me yet again by digging out a pack of Lucky Strike cigarettes. The pack had never been opened, and Captain Powell tore the top off clumsily and fumbled a cigarette out of the pack.

"Smoke, Sergeant?"

I took it slowly, confused. "Thank you, sir. I didn't think you smoked…"

"Where are they?" he asked, taking a second cigarette out and putting it in his mouth. "Do you have a light?"

"Sure," I said, pulling my Zippo out of a pants pocket. "Squad's over there."

Instead of lighting his cigarette, he took the Zippo from me. "May I borrow this?"

"Yeah, sure." My curiosity was getting the better of me, and I followed him over to the five survivors of A Company, dragging Weiss with me. "Come on, Weiss. You might learn something."

The survivors were sitting on a woodpile, heads down, hands clasped between their knees, none of them talking. If it wouldn't have been so cold they might've been crying.

Captain Powell didn't introduce himself at first; he just stuck the pack of cigarettes under the first trooper's face and said, "Smoke?"

"Thanks," the trooper said, then, seeing the bars painted on the helmet of the guy who gave it to him, quickly added, "I mean, thank you, sir."

"You?" Captain Powell asked the next one in line, all the way down to the end, until all five men had Lucky Strikes hanging out of their mouths. Then he lit all their cigarettes, only lighting his own after all five of them were puffing away.

I noticed he didn't inhale.

"I'm Captain Powell of Charlie Company," he said at last, holding the cigarette well away from his face. "I knew your CO, Captain Barnes. He was a good officer and a good man, and if he were here, he'd tell you what I'm about to tell you."

He paused until each of the beaten men looked up. "You could not have stopped what happened tonight," he said slowly, each word emphasized like a separate sentence. "You couldn't have done a damn thing except get killed. So I don't want to hear one more word about it. We estimate there were over a dozen tanks and two tons of infantry, SS, all armed with automatic weapons. They took out two companies of men, so five guys couldn't have done anything but get killed."

He took a puff on his cigarette... again, a shallow one, not a real drag... before continuing. "You boys want to make a difference, you can make a difference right now. You want payback, now's the time. We're going on the attack, and I need every man I can get. I would consider it a personal favor if you would spearhead the attack for Charlie Company."

And like that, like flicking a switch or snapping your fingers, it was gone. The survivor guilt, the downcast glances, the slumped shoulders, gone. All five of them straightened up and looked at each other like men who were just told they could leave work an hour early.

"I figure I speak for all us guys when I say we'd appreciate a chance to kill us some SS real soon, Captain," one of them said.

"You'll get it," Captain Powell said.

Damn, but I loved that man. Captain Powell was the best leader of men I've ever known. He knew how men fought, how they felt, how to inspire them, and how to make them overcome their faults to do their jobs the best they could. At moments like those, I thanked God I had a CO like Captain Powell.

It seemed God wasn't listening that night. Just then, the shout we'd all been dreading floated towards us from down the road.

"Tanks! Tanks coming in!"

7

We could hear them clanking and creaking toward us in the dark, massive metal creatures waiting to rain doom on us in the blackness. I couldn't see them yet but it was easy to imagine hulking shapes grinding along the road, with cannons big enough to crawl into.

We went toward the sound at a run: Captain Powell, Weiss, the five A Company survivors, and myself. A couple hundred yards from the farmhouse, trees bracketed the road, and for now, the tanks were still lurking inside that cover.

"Sergeant, take A Company and get on the left flank!" Captain Powell shouted, disappearing into the dark on the right side of the road and raising his voice so the other troopers in positions along the road could hear him. "Bazooka teams, left and right side! Move it!"

"C'mon, guys!" I yelled over my shoulder, and sprinted along the left side of the road, angling away from it slightly. The black blob of a thirty-cal machine-gun was visible against the snow in a copse of trees about twenty yards from the road, and I led my little group to it.

Two troopers manned a foxhole that had been dug by HQ's guys earlier. The thirty-cal was loaded, and I noticed the two troopers had already cleaned all the snow and frost off the weapon and its belt of ammunition.

"Are they Krauts?" I asked, breathless streams huffing out of my mouth.

"How the hell should I know?" the gunner answered. "Can't see shit."

The others caught up with me. "Weiss, stay here and man this position, take over if somebody gets hit. You five guys, spread out along these trees, and get ready to raise hell with hand grenades if it's Jerry. Where's the bazooka team?"

After a good five seconds' worth of silence answered back, the machine-gunner said, "Looks like nowhere, Sarge."

Wonderful. The Nightmare Panzer Division was right on top of us and there wasn't a bazooka in sight.

"Anybody got a rifle grenade?"

One of the survivors from A Company answered in the affirmative.

"Get it ready," I said. "What happened to the sentry?"

A frightened voice answered from somewhere further back in the trees in a Kentucky drawl. "I'm right here, Sarge."

I recognized his voice. "Wayne? What the hell are you doing back here? Did you challenge them?"

Here's how it works: when you approach a unit's perimeter, a sentry shouts a word to you... a challenge. You immediately shout back the counter... or password, if you like... and that means you're a friend. If you don't know the counter or you forgot it, then you get shot. I used to rehearse the counter dozens of times to myself when returning from patrol, just to be sure I avoided an accidental hole in my belly.

The flip side is, the sentry has to expose his position to call out the challenge... and those tank treads sounded like a horde of dragons crunching tin cans in their jaws.

"Are you kidding?" Wayne shouted back, to be heard over the noisy clanking. "Challenge *that*?"

We could see them now, vaguely; heavy war machines crushing their way remorselessly into our lines. The machine-gunner ratcheted his bolt to ready his weapon, and the rest of us flicked off our safeties.

Still, the problem was, if they hadn't been challenged, there was no way to know if they were Krauts or not. The sentry hadn't done it, which meant...

...which meant it was up to me. Of course it was up to me. Nobody else would be so damn stupid as to stand in the middle of the road in the dark in front of an armored column with an upraised hand and a command to "Halt!"

I pinched my eyes shut and cursed the stripes on my sleeve. "You got a sound-powered phone in this hole?"

"Sure do, Sarge."

"Get on it. Tell them to send up a flare, and be ready to call arty down on them if they're Krauts. And if they shoot, be sure to get the one who got me."

With that, I was running across the snow and to the road, right into the teeth of those metal-crunching dragons.

Let me tell you something. Infantry are terrified of tanks. You ever stand near a really big animal, like a horse, that was agitated? It's unnerving to say the least, all of that raw energy bounding around uncontrolled.

Tanks are like that. They're huge; I mean *huge*, and heavy, so heavy that they'll crush you to a pulp and never even know it. They bristle with machine-guns, and their cannons can blow a man-sized hole through a brick wall. Fire your weapon at them? You might as well throw rocks for all the good it'll do.

And they're just shy of blind. Which makes them unpredictable. Guys get crushed by tanks all the time, by accident, simply because the driver couldn't see a damn thing.

Imagine standing in a parking lot with an eighteen-wheeler driving figure 8's around you… except the driver is blindfolded. That's what it feels like to be around tanks.

And here I was, running out into the middle of the road, with at least four tanks outlined against the snow in front of me. More might be waiting further back in the trees; the flare I'd asked for still hadn't gone up, so I couldn't see worth a damn.

Usually I forgot the cold when the action was on, but this time, my joints ached and ears felt like they might shatter and split from the cold. I was terrified. It hurts more if you get hit when it's cold.

The huge cannon on the lead tank seemed like a lance aimed for my heart. I could feel the machine-guns on the vehicle following me, feel the gunners take up the slack on the trigger a little more and a little more and a little more.

"Halt!" I shouted, stopping in the middle of the road. "Halt! Whistler!"

I'm sure they were frightfully impressed by a single trooper with his knees shaking almost as much as his voice. The tanks kept coming, to within ten yards now. They seemed bigger than our tanks, but it's hard to tell in the dark.

I started to back up. "Halt!" I shouted as loudly as I could, cocking my weapon. "Whistler! Give me the counter, damn it, or be fired on!"

Run, Harry, I thought, *for God's sake, get the hell out of here*, but to my great surprise, the lead tank lurched to a sudden halt in front of me.

My mouth was dry. The tank stood perfectly still, perfectly quiet, perfectly inscrutable, and then there was the low whine of the gun turret as the cannon traversed slightly... to point straight at me.

I'm fucked, I thought, squeezing my eyes shut in preparation for the blast and simultaneously feeling very disappointed in myself for that being my last thought.

A muffled voice snarled "Son of a bitch!" from inside the steel monster.

My eyes opened and blinked twice as a hatch clanked open and I could hear coughing and cursing.

"God damn oil burning wreck!" it snarled.

I thought about repeating the challenge, but figured there wasn't much point in that. "Identify yourselves!" I shouted, hoping the wind would hide the way my voice cracked and my teeth rattled together.

Just then, a dull *Thoomp!* came from back at the mortar pit, and a red parachute flare opened up high above me. My luck was still good; those weren't panzers spread out on the road in front of me, but four M18 "Hellcat" tank destroyers... *American* tank destroyers.

A helmeted head jutted out of the smoking hatch, a cigar stub clamped in his teeth. "How ya doin'?" he said, then looked around as if lost. "Where the hell are the Krauts?"

8

"Captain," I introduced, as Captain Powell came down to the road to meet our new guests, "this is Lieutenant Frank Tedeski, attached to the 761st Tank Battalion. All Colored unit, sir."

That was the politically correct term in those days for blacks… or African-Americans, whichever you prefer. Back in my war, the Army still segregated combat units; that is, when they decided they would allow black troops to be a part of a combat unit at all. The 761st quickly got a reputation for valor under fire to the point of recklessness. I guess they felt like they had something to prove.

Captain Powell shook hands with the lieutenant, who had dismounted from his TD. "Captain Jim Powell, Charlie Company of the 518th. You're hell and gone from your unit, Lieutenant."

Lieutenant Tedeski shrugged. "That never bothered me much, sir. Just as long as I got plenty of gas and booze and shells that go bang."

Tedeski was a short, stocky guy with hair permanently matted down by his tanker's crash helmet. His dark skin was always streaked with grease and soot, and I could tell he was one of those nutcases who wanted to be out front in a fight, cursing and spluttering and daring the enemy to come and get him. I liked him instantly.

"Who hit you?" Tedeski asked.

"SS panzer unit," Captain Powell answered. "Came up on us in the dark, tore hell out of A company, then came here and did this to our Battalion HQ."

"They lined up our wounded and used a flame-thrower on them," I added, with a nod toward the charred corpses marring the whiteness of the snow.

"No shit?" Tedeski said, walking over to get a closer look at the blackened limbs jutting at awkward, twisted angles out of the snow. "God damn Krauts."

He shook his head, and then slapped his hands on his thighs, as if indicating he had to get back to business. "Well, just point me in their direction, Captain, and I'll…"

"I think," Captain Powell interrupted, with a sidelong look in my direction, "that we would all be best off if you joined up with us."

"What the hell, Lieutenant," Shorty spoke up from off to my right, "are you looking to take on the entire Kraut army single-handed?"

"Not the entire army," Tedeski said a wink. "Half of 'em are off fighting the Russians."

Captain Powell cleared his throat. "All the same, I think… are those our supply trucks?"

Tedeski turned back to look at his makeshift armored column. "Oh, yeah. Ran into them along the way. They decided to tag along in case it got hot for them. We picked up a meatchopper somewheres or other, too."

"Really?" I said, my ears perking up. A meatchopper was a half-track with four fifty-caliber machine-guns set up for anti-aircraft use. The quad-fifties were hooked together like the legs on an upturned table, and the gunner sat in the middle.

The Germans were terrified of our fifties, as well they should have been. A fifty-caliber round is deadly business. While thirty-cals might go through a wall, fifties will go through buildings. And buildings. And buildings. Concrete walls are like tissue paper. A meatchopper fires four of these weapons each at about 500 rounds per minute, and used on ground targets… well, it earns its name.

"Oh, yeah. Haven't had a chance to use it yet, though," Tedeski said.

"Lieutenant," I said, patting him on the back, "have you ever been called a Godsend?"

** *

It took us longer to get Captain Jackson from Baker Company to join us than it did to explain the plan of attack to Tedeski.

"Simple," Captain Powell said, and drew a circle in the snow to indicate the village. "I take Charlie Company and attack head-on. You accompany Baker with the four tank destroyers, swing around the back, and hit from the rear."

"How do I get there?" Tedeski asked.

"Use the same track the SS panzers used. We sent a scout along it; it heads back to the village. The artillery will keep their heads down to cover your movement," Captain Powell said. "They want to see a surprise attack? We'll show these bastards a surprise attack. Captain Jackson?"

The CO of Baker Company nodded. He wasn't a fantastic company commander, but if we pushed him in the right direction, he should be okay. "Sounds good."

"Why don't we go in head on, with the TDs, I mean?" Tedeski asked.

Captain Powell shook his head. "Because that's not where the panzers will be. German defensive doctrine is to put the main line of resistance down the middle of the town... infantry. They keep a large reserve... that's where the panzers will be. The enemy hits the MLR, the Germans counter-attack with the panzers. The saying is 'The MLR is the shield, and the reserve is the sword.' Do you understand?"

"Yes, sir," Tedeski said, staring at the snow map of the town and chewing on his stub of a cigar thoughtfully.

"The shield will be the infantry. We can handle that. But there may be a dozen or more panzers down there somewhere, and we need your TDs to catch the hand holding the sword before it can swing."

"I said, I understand the metaphor, Captain," Tedeski said. "I may smell like gasoline, but that doesn't mean I'm drinking the stuff."

Captain Powell smiled. "That's good to know."

"When do we attack?" Captain Jackson asked.

"Charlie will jump off at 0730, just before first light. The darkness will cover our movement on the village, and by the time we hit the buildings, it will be light enough to see what we're shooting at." Captain Powell checked his watch. "That doesn't give you much time. You'd better move out. Good luck."

It took a few moments before everyone cleared out and I could ask, "Orders?"

"Be sure the platoon leaders understand what's going on, and that the bazooka teams have at least one automatic weapon to guard them. Private Weiss?"

"Sir?"

I almost jumped out of my skin. Weiss was picking up a bad habit of following right on my heels, and I hadn't noticed him behind me.

"You said you were waiting to be assigned," Captain Powell said. "You have a home now... Charlie Company of the 518th. Sergeant Kinder will find you a spot."

"Yes, sir. Thank you, sir," Weiss beamed.

I guess you have to float around without a home for a while in a tightly knit Army unit to understand Weiss's gratitude. The front line is a nightmare, day in and day out, and there's no nightmares worse than those you have to wake up from all alone in the dark. Camaraderie, a sense of family, of belonging, is just as good as having a loved one there when you wake up from a terrible dream. Their mere presence helps to chase away the bogeyman. Having buddies on the front line isn't only important in order to have someone to watch your back; they also help to dilute the crushing sense of terror that builds up in you like a head of steam every day that you're on the line.

"Sir," I said, before the Captain could wander off, "We sure could use that meatchopper. It'd make Charlie Company's job a lot easier, especially if the Germans are all armed with those automatic rifles like Shorty took off of the dead SS guy."

He nodded. "See to it."

"C'mon, Weiss," I said, when Davey came running up to us out of the dark.

"Sarge! Captain! Sir, I..." he paused to catch his breath. "Cappy found a naked Brit in the woods!"

I stared at him. "Davey, did you find some cognac?"

"No, Sarge, I ain't drunk!" he snapped. "I'm serious! Cappy found a Brit in the woods, wearing nothing but an SS overcoat. Cappy almost blew his head off. He says he's an escaped prisoner, took off from that column when we hit that flame-thrower half-track. Used it as a diversion, you know?"

"This night is getting more bizarre by the minute," I said, and nodded to the Captain. "I'll check it out."

Andrew C. Piazza

9

"Hey, Sarge?"

It was Weiss, trailing me closely, as I followed Davey out into the snow-laden pines. The trees quickly swallowed us up; a few steps, and we couldn't see the fires still flickering in the ruins of the farmhouse.

We had to be careful. It was easy to get turned around in those dense pines, easy to lose contact with each other, and once you did lose contact, you could get good and lost awfully quickly.

"What is it, Weiss?"

"Um, my weapon's frozen. The action, it won't… it's frozen stuck."

"Piss on it," I said, ducking under some pine boughs.

"What?" he asked. He didn't duck far enough and hit one of the boughs, dumping snow on top of him.

I winced. It we had been in enemy-held territory, that slip-up could've killed the both of us.

"I said, piss on it. Take out your dick, and piss on the action of your rifle. The warmth will loosen it up enough that once you fire your first shots, the heat from shooting will keep it unstuck. Just be sure to clean the hell out of it once the fight's over."

"And not to leave your dick out too long," Davey added from in front of me. "Might freeze off. There was this one guy, Willy, Chilly Willy we called him, 'cause one night…"

I decided to interrupt him. "Davey. Watch where you're going."

"Yeah, it's right up here, Sarge," Davey said, and then I could see Cappy Johnson pointing his sniper rifle at the head of a half-naked man lying in the snow. He had his arms raised, but that didn't always matter to Cappy.

Cappy Johnson was a fisherman from Maine, a real tough S.O.B. who captained his own ship... hence his nickname. The military decided a man with his nautical experience would best serve the war effort in the Airborne infantry, in a fine display of Army logic. Cappy was a solid trooper, cool under fire, but he had a bad tendency of shooting unarmed prisoners. "He tried to make a run for it, Sarge," he would shrug, and ignore how the bullet hole was in the guy's forehead and not his back.

I'm sure a lot of you cringe at that, and wonder how and why we put up with it. It's kind of hard to explain if you haven't been there. You remember what I did to that SS officer, right? Let's just say that we needed all of the solid troopers we could get, and that we tried to make sure Cappy was never left alone on guard detail.

"Cappy," I said, as soon as I saw the situation, "lower that rifle and take your finger off the trigger."

"No can do, Sarge," he said, his eyes never leaving the shivering man on the ground. "Ain't got any proof this guy is a Brit yet."

"The Germans don't run around with no shoes and only an overcoat on. There's four of us here now, so lower that weapon and ease down. It's an order, Cappy."

He frowned. Man, I could see him wanting to drill the freezing man just to spite me. "Fine," he said, and lowered the rifle at last. "I hear we got a couple of darkies looking to join up with us."

"A couple of..." I trailed off, until I figured out what he meant and fixed him with an angry stare. "A *lieutenant* with four tank destroyers has offered to help us. Unless, of course, you'd like to refuse the armor support due to your discriminating tastes."

Cappy shrugged as an answer and stepped away from the freezing man.

"T-Thank you, Sergeant," the Brit stuttered though teeth chattering so hard I thought he might chip them. I could see two things right away; this guy was about as German as Churchill, and he was quickly freezing to death.

"Blankets, Weiss, and lots of them, fast," I said, pulling off my overcoat so the Brit could use it as a blanket in the meantime.

"Again, I thank you," he said, wrapping the overcoat around him. His SS overcoat shifted a bit and I caught sight of a nasty bruise on his chest... probably the result of a blow from a guard's rifle butt.

"I'm Harry Kinder, First Sergeant of Charlie Company of the 518th," I introduced. I lit a cigarette and put in it his mouth for him.

He puffed on it. "Mmm. Very... very kind of you, Sergeant. Most kind. Major Jonathan Hayward, 1st British Airborne Division. Was a prisoner of war until just a bit ago."

I shot Cappy a glance. "Sir, I apologize for the treatment. We'll get you some proper gear immediately."

"Oh, no bother, no bother," he said, waving me off. He had that British gentleman's air of insisting you not go to any trouble even as he froze to death in front of you. "Situation's quite improved for me, quite improved indeed. Dreadful people, those SS."

Weiss came back with a pair of blankets and we practically cocooned him in them. Now that I could get a closer look at him, I could see he was older... well, compared to us, at least... mid-thirties, and relatively thin, although that could've been a consequence of his imprisonment.

"Market Garden?" I asked, lighting a cigarette of my own.

"Yes, that's when they got me. Dreadful business. Dreadful. Kept me in Holland a bit, then sent me to this neck of the woods."

He was talking about an airborne attack on some bridges in Holland. It was a gamble that failed; the British paratroopers just happened to land right in front of heavily armed German troops and were cut to pieces. A lot of them surrendered. A lot never got the chance.

"I say, Sergeant," he said, as if we were sitting at a dinner party and he'd suddenly had an interesting thought, "I very much need to speak to your commanding officer. At the earliest possible convenience, of course."

I nodded. "That might be tricky right now, Major. We're in the middle of setting up an attack on that town. We're hoping to catch the SS while they're napping."

"There's the spirit!" he said, slapping me on the thigh good-naturedly. "I understand they gave you a bit of a bloody nose."

"Shattered A company and HQ, and turned a flame-thrower on our wounded."

"Good Lord. Dreadful people, the SS. Dreadful."

"Sir, how did you escape?" I asked.

"Well, they had myself and seven other prisoners in a large truck. About the middle of the column, I should say. They kept us quite naked, I'm afraid, under blankets and hay to discourage flight. Towards the end of the attack, there was a flurry of action toward the rear of the column… a counterattack of some sort, I suppose. Our guard was distracted, and I seized the opportunity. Struck him over the head with his own helmet. After that, everyone in the truck grabbed blankets and ran for the woods, including myself, once I'd acquired this coat."

"There are other prisoners in this wood?" I asked.

"Not really sure," Major Hayward said. "The SS shot most of them as they ran… perhaps all of them. As far as I know, I'm the only one who got away."

"Sons of bitches," Cappy muttered. I found that kind of ironic, but I decided to keep my philosophy to myself.

"Well, Major, let's get to back to HQ, or what's left of it," I said. "Davey, Weiss; at his head and feet. Use the blankets as a stretcher."

"No, no, none of that," Major Hayward immediately protested. "I can walk on my own, I assure you."

"Nonsense, sir. I won't have you going back to the 1st British Airborne with stories of dreadful American hospitality."

He laughed loudly at that, and let himself be lifted. "My dear Sergeant. I wouldn't dream of it."

10

The Captain took the time to meet with our new British friend, after we'd found him some odds and ends of clothing to wear, and called me over to him immediately thereafter. I have to admit, I was pretty curious. Major Hayward insisted on speaking with the Captain privately, and when I came over, Captain Powell's face was almost ashen gray.

"We move everything up an hour," he said, sounding almost like he was going to be sick.

I'd never heard him like this before. "Sir, we do that…"

"I know, I know, it's rushed. I have my reasons."

"Are you okay, sir?" I asked. "You look a little…"

"I'm fine. We go an hour ahead of schedule."

"That means the first guys into the town, it'll still be dark for them. Could get messy."

"I said, I know the risks, Sergeant," he said. "I've just gotten some information that… we need to try and get our guys back as quickly as possible, if we can at all."

I wasn't quite sure what to make of all that, but I could tell the Captain wasn't in an explaining way just then, so I simply nodded and said, "Yes, sir."

There were a thousand things to do before the attack, a thousand tiny ducks that all needed to be in a row if we were to give our assault any chance of succeeding. When I first got my stripes, I hated all those stupid little details… this man goes here, this man goes there, enough ammo, enough weapons, etc., etc.… but soon, I came to rely on them. You see, waiting to jump off is a terrible, terrible stretch of anxious quiet. I would much rather be in the middle of a firefight than waiting to jump off. My thousand little details kept me from sitting and dwelling on what might or might not be.

Still, my thousand details ran out eventually and with them, my reprieve. I took my place on the line. Weiss was by my side, as always. We didn't even have the luxury of staring down at the town, our objective. It was still dark and even the light reflecting off the snow wasn't any good at this distance. A fog rolled in, as it sometimes did in that area, and soon I had nothing but a dark gray curtain of blankness to stare into.

I've never been good with quiet times like that. Years later, when I read about psychologists using sensory deprivation tanks to experiment on people, I laughed and wondered who would be such a damn fool as to volunteer for that. Hell, I didn't even like sitting in a room with a person who doesn't talk. Some people don't feel the need to fill the silence with conversation. I never learned that trick.

When you've got nothing to do, nothing to see, nothing to say, your mind turns inward. It searches for some stimulus, anything to keep it busy, and so recent memories get replayed. Potential threats or opportunities are imagined and explored. Anything and everything becomes amplified, including nervousness and fear, in the mind's desperate search for fodder.

I often had a bad habit of looking around and wondering who was going to live and who was going to die. Not in an emotional way, but more like you might wonder who's going to show up at a dinner party. Oh, there's Cappy over there. Wonder if he's going to get it today. That sort of thing.

It was a stupid, useless pastime. The simple fact of life over there was, people got killed doing what we were doing. That was it. It was a part of the job. Dwelling on it only distracted you and put you at more risk, not to mention draining you emotionally.

For that night, though, the introspection started with the cold. When I was busy, I could forget it. It was a distant and unimportant detail. But once I was still, it came back with a vengeance. I was covered in wool from head to foot, but I still felt as if I was lying naked in a snowdrift. My skin had that dry, cracked, almost chalky feel from being so cold for so long that I couldn't remember ever being warm. It felt like I was frozen on the outside. I began to think of myself as a popcicle; a cold piece of wood surrounded by ice. It seemed like my blood might crystallize in my veins. When the wind moaned and blew, it cut through me like a pair of frosty hands pushing open a curtain from the center; it felt like I was being opened up and ice water poured inside. My bones creaked like the swaying pine trees.

That wasn't enough, of course. I stared into that gray mist and daydreamed about what we would find in that village. Hundreds of SS, thousands maybe, fanatical troops all armed with automatic rifles and with enough tanks to give Patton second thoughts.

They can see in the dark.

Now the SS had glowing eyes in my mind. They all had moldering skulls for faces and mouths full of fangs, and bullets wouldn't kill them.

Stop it, I told myself, shaking once to chase away my thoughts. It was stupid, irrational fear, fed by too little sleep and too much quiet.

It had been like this at the siege of Bastogne, when we waited every night for The Big One, that one all-out assault by the Germans that would finally break our tattered lines. Then, like now, my thoughts would turn the Germans into horrible bogeymen beyond fear or death. Then they would come, and it turned out bullets killed their men and bazookas or artillery shells killed their tanks, and they could be beaten just like us.

I reminded myself of that. I reminded myself of the dozen or so SS we'd killed around that flame-thrower half-track. They weren't supermen. They were vulnerable. They were fallible.

It wasn't working. Images of what they had done to A Company and Battalion HQ defied my rational thought and sent me back into dry-mouthed anxiety.

There was one last thing to fall back on. Kate. My wonderful, beautiful Kate, only an imagination away. I closed my eyes and blocked it all out; the cold, the wind, and the occasional rattle of some trooper's equipment as he shifted position. It all melted away, like the world was made of nothing but wax, and the real truth lying underneath it all was in my mind.

It was a talent I'd cultivated ever since my first bivouac with the Army a century or two before. Close the eyes, shut out the world, and there she was; slim, curvy, warm, soft, beautiful, smiling, gentle, and she always, *always*, smelled so damn good. In my mind's eye, we were always in the kitchen on a warm fall day, the end of September, when it's warm but not hot during the day and cool and breezy at night. She stands up from the table and comes to me, smiling, and I hold her in my arms as I look out of the window into the back yard. The sun shines through the glass and falls on her, making her hair shine like brass and gold. I can even feel the smooth skin of her cheek against mine, if I try really hard. Even now, now that she's been gone for so long, I can still close my eyes and see her that way.

Thankfully, my last trick worked that night. Kate's apparition chased the world away long enough for me to catch the last gasp of air I needed before plunging headlong into Death. I could open my eyes and deal with it all now.

I could tell the quiet was getting to Weiss, too. He fidgeted about, never sitting still for a second. He would've been chain-smoking if we hadn't had orders for light discipline. I would've, too.

"Sarge..." he finally whispered.

"You'll be fine, Weiss," I said. There were troopers all around us, and like I said, panic can spread like a wildfire. But sometimes, so can inspiration. "You'll be fine. Just keep your cool and don't pop off. Take things as they come, one at a time, and don't think too far ahead. Let the Captain worry about that."

As if conjured by the mention of his name, Captain Powell came up out of the dark and settled in next to me. "Sergeant Kinder?"

"Everything's set, sir."

He dug in his pockets for a second. "How are you holding up, Private Weiss?"

He said "Private Weiss", but as loudly as he was talking, I knew he was really addressing the entire company; those within earshot, at least.

"I'm... I'm okay, sir. I'll be fine. I won't let you down."

"I know you won't." He finally got his pocket watch out of his jacket, the watch that he'd kept there as long as I'd known him, and checked it with the aid of a flashlight hooded by his helmet. "Very well, gentlemen," he announced. "It's time."

Andrew C. Piazza

11

The old saying goes, "No battle plan survives the first contact with the enemy", and that was just about right for us on that day. 1st and 2nd Platoon trudged their way up the road, dark phantoms outlined against the white snow. The fog and the darkness swallowed them up before they'd gone a hundred yards. Almost sixty men, poof, vanished.

Then, it was a waiting game once again, as we twisted our hands around our weapons and bit our lips and prayed for something to break the thick, silent stalemate… and then we cursed ourselves for praying for that, because that would mean gunfire and nobody wanted to hear that, not really. But we knew it was coming sooner or later, and we wanted it over with.

It didn't take long. A single rifle shot echoed its way back to us from the outskirts of town. The fog distorted the sound so it was hard to tell where it was coming from, but we found out later that it was a German sentry in an outpost right on the edge of the village. That single rifle shot was like a spark to a powder keg. Gunfire rattled and roared in the village, pattering out lethal staccatos at irregular intervals.

Even then, we had to wait. Our reserve platoon, the 3rd, and HQ section, had to wait until we found out where the weak part of the line was, on our side or theirs, and either plug the hole in our weak line or punch through the hole in theirs. The Captain noticed we were champing at the bit like nervous horses and let us move up a hundred yards to give us something to do.

Visibility was awful. It wasn't going to be light for another half-hour, and the fog was thick enough that even daylight visibility would only be fifty-sixty feet. No matter how hard I tried, I couldn't keep

Ryan's hoarse warning out of my mind... *They can see in the dark*. Then there was whatever had the Captain so anxious to jump off.

Finally, we were on the move, as the dull *Thoomp!* of light mortars began to complement the rattle of gunfire. Something tugged on my sleeve and I almost screamed.

"Are those ours?" Weiss whispered.

"You'll know once the bombs start dropping," I said, and gave some orders to keep the soldiers near me spread out properly.

The gunfire got louder and I could smell it now... cordite. It's a smell that to this day fills me with a bewildering array of emotions; fear, mostly, with a good dose of jittery excitement over the prospect of unleashing a little thunder of my own. My mouth got dry and my breathing got shallow. We dumped our overcoats and heavy belongings on the ground.

The fighting was close now. It was like getting close to a fire; first you know there is a fire by smelling the smoke, then you know you're close when you hear the crackle of the flames, and finally you begin to feel the heat thrown off by the heart of the fire. We'd smelled the smoke and now we heard the crackle; soon we'd feel the heat.

I could see our guys huddled behind a handful of buildings set on either side of the road... two buildings on the left and five on the right. Like most of the other buildings in the village, they were two-story and of stone and wood construction. The two closest to us on the right side had been obliterated by artillery fire. Beams and planks jutted upwards like splintered ribs on an old corpse, and bricks and rubble were scattered on the ground like the guts from a split-open body.

A mortar team was set up behind the closer of the two buildings on the left side of the road. They were firing quickly, so quickly that I suspected they had no clue what they were trying to hit.

"3rd Platoon and HQ section on the right side of the road, back by the rubble," Captain Powell ordered, then gestured for me to follow him closer into the buildings.

He took one look and shook his head. "This is not good."

We didn't have time for me to ask him what he meant. He dashed across the road to the mortar crew, and used their telephone line to contact Lieutenant Frost, the 1st Platoon commander. It may seem a little silly to you; Frost was in the next building up, less than twenty yards away maybe, but when a sudden burst of enemy machine-gun fire seemed to fill the air with angry hornets, I was glad we weren't taking any chances.

I took a peek around the house while the Captain talked things over with Frost. It looked like the Captain was right. 1st Platoon was pinned down in and around the two houses on the left; machine-gun fire from at least two positions in the middle of town kept them from moving an inch. It was after I'd seen this that I realized dawn had arrived and the world was now a series of dull grays rather than the black and white of night. The fog was thinning, but still passed through the town like curtains blowing in the breeze.

2nd Platoon was pinned down behind the three houses that were still intact across the road. A low stone wall led from the last house into the center of the village, but it didn't offer any protection from the machine-guns I could hear tearing at the dawn air like angry buzz saws.

I returned to the Captain and told him what I'd seen, adding, "They've got this town pretty tied up, sir."

He nodded his agreement and pointed to the mortar crew. "They're trying to break the stalemate by shelling the machine-guns, but with visibility the way it is, they're just throwing shells around blind..."

A sudden explosion ripped the world in half, throwing me to the ground and filling my ears with a loud ringing. A local hailstorm of dirt and debris fell on top of me; I was dazed and felt like a shaken can of paint.

"Harry? Harry?" Somebody was shaking my shoulders. I blinked a few times and saw it was the Captain. He'd lost his helmet and as soon as he'd seen that I'd come around, he retrieved it from the ground.

I remember thinking in a stupor that it was important for him to do that. He didn't look right without his steel helmet with the pair of Captain's bars on the front. He looked naked. I remember thinking *Now we can get down to business* once he'd put it back on his head.

"Are you okay?" He had to shout it in my ear due to the ringing and the thunder of return fire our guys were throwing at the town.

My senses suddenly returned to me and I dragged myself to my feet, recovering my weapon almost instinctively.

"Harry, are you okay?" he asked again.

An anti-tank gun of some kind had blown a hole through the back half of the second floor of the house we were hiding behind. A thirty-caliber machine-gun that had been set up on the second floor now lay about ten yards from me on the ground, torn up and ruined. Three similarly torn up and ruined troopers, the gun's crew, were scattered around it. I stared at those ripped up rag dolls until the Captain shouted in my ear again.

"Harry? Are you all right?"

I put my helmet back on and snorted once with grim irony. "Hell yes, sir, I'm fine. It's a good day to be alive."

12

"Are you sure you're up to this, Harry?" the Captain asked.

"I'd better be. Who the hell else is going to do it?" I said, giving him a little grin to let him know that I really was okay, and then I waved HQ section... about fifteen men... over to us.

We'd retreated to 3rd Platoon's position behind the rubble after our close call with the anti-tank gun. The Captain had tried to have me sent back to the aid station, but we both knew that he needed every soldier he had. Almost as important, there *was* no aid station anymore... not after what the SS had done the night before.

Lieutenant Barbon ran up and the Captain gestured for the two of us to kneel as he drew into the snow. "Okay. Here it is. The road through town is shaped like a reverse S. We're here at the bottom, pinned down in these houses. Wall along here leads into town at the center of the reverse S, and there's at least three machine-guns with interlocking fire covering all approaches."

"Move the meatchopper up," I said. "Blow the hell out of them."

"No good. That anti-tank gun is set up somewhere near here," Captain Powell pointed, "which means it can cover the road. The meatchopper would be history before it could make a difference."

"Baker Company and the TDs?"

"Pinned down by an anti-tank gun on the outskirts north of the village. The Germans took out the lead TD and now Captain Jackson's terrified to move on them. No, no, we're on our own, and we have to move fast, before those panzers start up their counterattack. They catch us out in the open like this and we're history. In the middle of town we have a fighting chance."

"But machine-guns pinning us down and protecting the anti-tank gun, and the anti-tank gun protecting the machine-guns…" Barbon said, shaking his head. "The Sarge was right. This town is tied up. Maybe we should fall back and wait for some support."

The Captain frowned. "We can't do that. If we are going to have any chance, any chance, of getting our men back… the ones the SS took prisoner… we have to move now."

I wasn't sure what he meant by that. "Captain?"

Captain Powell sighed, as if he hadn't wanted to tell us this. "Major Hayward told me some things… just believe me when I tell you that the clock is ticking on their lives."

"They'll execute them?" I asked.

"Worse than that if we don't get to them soon," he said. "Much worse."

What could possibly be worse than that? I wondered, but the look on the Captain's face told me all I needed to know. "What are your orders?"

"We're going to whip around the right flank to break open the line," the Captain said. "Sergeant Kinder takes a squad and moves up on the right side, behind those buildings here. See this machine-gun on the far right? That's what is pinning 2nd Platoon down. Once we take it out, I can move 2nd Platoon up to take out the machine-gun on the left that interlocks with it. Then we meet in the middle, make it a pincer move to gobble up the first half of the town. After that, we can take out the AT gun. But that machine-gun has to go first. That's the weak spot. Once it folds, we can start taking it all apart."

"And after that, bring up the meatchopper to rain a little doom on them," I said.

"What about me?" Barbon asked.

"Coordinate 1st and 3rd Platoon," Captain Powell said, "to reinforce us once the pincer move is done, to exploit that breach. After that, it's go hunting for the panzers."

"I'll need a thirty-cal set up over there to give me cover fire for the first leg of my run," I said, pointing. "It's twenty-thirty yards of open ground before I reach the cover of those couple of buildings."

"You've got it."

"Davey! Goliath! Shorty! Cappy! You're with me!" I shouted, checking my magazine pouch to make sure my ammunition was within easy reach. "Weiss... you may as well come along, too. You know how to reload a bazooka?"

"Um, yeah, sure do," Weiss said. "But..."

"No buts. You're elected. Stick close to Shorty and his bazooka and do what he says. He's got a bag of rockets for you to carry."

The Captain patted me once on the shoulder. "We'll stop the mortar fire once we see you're on the move."

"That would be nice," I said, and checked to be sure everyone on my newly formed squad was ready. "Wish me luck. Let's go!"

Then, I was off, leading five men into the teeth of an enemy who could see in the dark and whose leader had a skull for a face.

Andrew C. Piazza

13

Crossing open ground covered by a machine-gun is the most nerve-wracking experience imaginable. An artillery barrage is like getting kicked while you're down; crossing a machine-gun's territory is like being chased through the woods by rabid wolves. You can feel the bullets snapping at your heels, until you can almost imagine the hot breath of closing wolves on your skin. Ten yards seems like a mile, and twenty yards like an impossible, impassable, endless gulf.

I led my squad along the row of buildings on the right side of the road, all the way up to the last one. We paused behind it as I peeked around the corner to take stock.

The road was to the left, out of sight due to the low stone wall. Ahead of me was the heart of the tiny village. A line of buildings to the left hid the road. Some of them were smashed into pieces from our artillery. There was an open clearing dead ahead... the firing zone for the machine-gun... and then a pair of buildings, one behind the other, ahead and to the right. They would be our cover... if we could get to them.

The Jerrys in the town reminded me I was not allowed to stay exposed for too long by firing a couple of bursts at me. I ducked behind the corner of the house as bullets punched into its front wall.

"Okay," I said to the squad. "We're going for that house ahead and to the right about twenty-thirty yards. We clear it, move up to the next house, clear that, and take out the machine-gun in house number three past that. Once that's done, we break left toward the road. We're the right arm of a pincer movement; Captain's the left. We envelop the front half of the town like two arms making a bear hug. Got it?"

Nods and murmurs told me they did, and I gave the last instructions. "Look, no matter what, that machine-gun goes down, understood? The clock's ticking; if we stay here pinned down, those panzers are going to roll right up our ass and we're all dead. So take it at all costs, okay?"

Weiss looked back and forth at the others, who all nodded in grim understanding. They knew what that really meant, first hand; for Weiss, it was only a bunch of words. For now.

I rapped on the sill of a shot-out window leading to the first floor of the building we hid behind. Artie Gorman's head popped out. "Yeah, what is it, Sarge?"

"That thirty-cal set up yet?"

"Ready to go," he said.

"Okay. When you hear us fire, you join in. Make it thick," I said, and returned to the corner of the building.

God, I don't want to do this, I thought. *Haven't I done enough already? Haven't I cheated Death as many times as any man can expect to? Why can't somebody else take a turn?*

I shook my head. There was a job to do. It was my turn until the war was won. That simple.

Then, against all expectations, a stroke of luck. A thick tendril of fog snaked across the open space we had to cross. It wasn't as good as a smoke screen, but I'd take what I could get.

"Here we go!" I said over my shoulder, giving my tommygun one last check. "Now!"

My boots thudded across the ground like lead weights. They wouldn't move fast enough; no matter how hard I willed my legs to churn faster, they seemed to plod along at a pitiful pace. The others were right on my heels, spread out a few yards each, firing their weapons as they ran. The thirty-cal inside the house we'd just left opened up, sending tracers into the formless gray of the mist. The return fire was almost instantaneous; tracer rounds reached out of the fog like fiery arrows searching for us.

The cover fire had the desired effect; the Germans shot at the guys firing the machine-gun instead of cutting us down like cattle. Still, it felt like I'd run a thousand yards when I reached the next building, and I wanted to wrap my arms around it and kiss it for standing between me and the German machine-gun.

The rest of the squad thumped their way behind the building, and we immediately set about clearing it. "Davey!" I said, and we both pulled grenades from our harnesses and pitched them in through a window.

As soon as they went off, Goliath and I went in a door around the side... after he'd blown it off of its hinges with his B.A.R.... and sprayed down the interior of the building. Nobody was inside.

We shot upwards through the ceiling and then tossed grenades upstairs. Davey and Goliath went to shoot up the second floor, and Cappy and I checked the cellar.

Again, nobody, but Cappy found a jar of canned cherries and tucked them into a jacket pocket with a rare smile. It may sound odd that we'd take time to do that, but forget all those movies or stories where some asshole says "How can you think of food at a time like this?" Take it from someone who's gone without it for long periods of time... you can *always* think about food.

Once the building was cleared, I had Shorty shoot his bazooka from the outside corner of the house to blow a hole in the next building up. It wasn't as good as a tank cannon... what I would've given for one of Tedeski's TDs at that point... but it would have to do.

Goliath covered our run to the next house out of an upstairs window. Somebody from a building to our left took a couple of pot shots at us with a rifle, but Goliath's B.A.R. drove them off with a pair of bursts.

Once again, we threw grenades in through the windows and Shorty's bazooka hole and went in shooting. No need. Another empty building. After Goliath caught up with us, he and Davey went upstairs, while Cappy and I hit the cellar again.

Cappy almost shot her. Thank God those sniper rifles couldn't be snap-shot very well; as soon as he saw movement out of the corner of his eye, he spun and fired, sending a slug bouncing off the stone cellar walls.

There was a shrill scream and I yelled at Cappy to hold his fire. It took a couple of seconds to dig out my flashlight, and the whole time, I'm thinking *Idiot! Sitting duck! Just shoot and play it safe!*

It was a woman who had screamed, though. I knew it. And once I got my flashlight working, the light confirmed it for me.

She was huddled in the corner, cowering under a tablecloth like a child convinced that the monsters can't get them so long as they're under the covers. I could tell at a glance she was undernourished. Her hair was bedraggled and dirty and unkempt. Still, for all that, she was also a natural beauty.

"Civilian," Cappy shrugged, and turned to go back up the stairs.

"I don't think so," I said, and stepped down the last few steps and crossed the cellar toward her.

She shrank away from me, as if she thought she could press herself into the stone walls and disappear into the earth itself. Her eyes were those of a trapped animal that knows the trapper has come for her hide.

"It's okay, it's okay," I said, in as soothing a tone as I could muster.

You're waving a gun in her face, jackass, a little voice reminded me. I winced at my own callousness and slung my weapon. "There, see? It's okay."

Once I was close enough, I could confirm my suspicions. She was hiding and shivering underneath that tablecloth because she was naked underneath it. Just like Major Hayward in the woods.

"She's another escaped prisoner," I said. "Cappy, tell Weiss to look through this house and find some clothes, a blanket, anything. Fast."

"Is that looting, Sarge?"

I couldn't tell if he was joking or not… I never could with Cappy… so I just snapped, "No more so than your cherries," and waved him back up the stairs.

It was Davey and Goliath who came down to the cellar, though, carrying a man's dress shirt and a heavy overcoat with them. A second glance told me it was actually Goliath's overcoat… while the rest of us sometimes ditched our coats before battle to save weight, Goliath was a monster, so he barely noticed a few extra pounds. It served him well during the Bulge; most of us lost our equipment in that way, but he'd held on to his coat, and so he didn't freeze to death like the rest of us.

"We got one shirt and one oversized coat for her," Davey said, tromping right up next to me and checking her out like she was a novelty. "Think she escaped like the British guy?"

"Here you go, little lady," Goliath said in his smooth, easy baritone, handing her his coat and the scrounged shirt. When she looked at them like she thought they might be booby-trapped, he smiled his big smile and said, "Come on, now. It's okay. Can't have you freezing, now."

She took another hesitant look before reaching a hand out slowly for the clothes. Goliath didn't move a muscle; he was like a big, smiling statue. The girl… I say girl, but she was probably twenty-one or twenty-two… finally took the clothes and murmured something that sounded like "Mercy."

"What was that?" I asked. "Mercy?"

"No, no, *merci*," Davey corrected me. "You know, French for thank you?"

I knew as much French as I did German, which was about two words, so I just shrugged. "Okay."

Davey nodded down at her, as if he'd finally identified a mysterious object. "I bet she's actually French-speaking Belgian. *Parley vouz Francaise?*"

Her eyes brightened up a bit and she nodded, immediately chattering away in French. Davey held up his hands and cut her off.

"Whoa, whoa, whoa, slow down, sister. That's all the French I know."

Goliath was still kneeling stock-still in front of her, as if afraid his moving even now would startle her. "What do we do with her, Sarge? Can't leave her here. Starve or freeze or both."

I groaned inwardly. Yes, Goliath the Gentle Giant was right, we couldn't just leave her, but it was more complicated than that. You can't wander around a war zone trailing civilians behind you; it's dangerous for both parties. And we were in the middle of a damn firefight, on an all-costs attack on a machine-gun nest, for God's sake!

"Sarge?" Goliath said, looking up at me with those huge eyes of his, and I thought of my wife and the puppy-dog eyes trick she uses to get her way.

"No, damn it, Goliath, we're not going to leave her," I said. "The Captain's going to want to talk to her if she escaped from the SS. But we can't take her with us, either, and you both know it."

Both of them wanted to argue, but they traded a glance and held an entire conversation between them in that look. They also knew I was right.

"So what do we do?" Davey asked.

I hemmed and hawed and finally came to a decision. "We leave her here for now, finish our objective. Once we finish the pincer move and link up with the rest of the company, we'll send somebody back for her."

"Not Cappy," Davey said.

"No, not Cappy," I said. "Jesus, Davey, give me some credit for brains. But for now, we have to get up and get our asses back in the war. Understood?"

Davey reached down and patted his other half on the shoulder. "Whaddaya say we go shoot us some Krauts, big man?"

Goliath took one more look at the tattered and terrified Belgian girl before nodding. "Hell, yes."

14

I had a hard time getting the Belgian girl to stay in the cellar. First she's scared to death of me, then she can't stand the idea of being alone. I kept gesturing and telling her to stay put, and she kept jabbering at me in French and pulling on my jacket, so finally I simply turned my back on her and went back up the stairs.

Machine-gun fire suddenly tore through the windows and the shattered front door, chewing up the wooden windowsills and punching holes in the walls. Debris and ricochets filled the air; I dropped and hit the floor in an instant; covering my head with my hands.

Davey and Goliath were already there, pressing themselves flat under the barrage.

"They spotted us!" Davey shouted. "The gun crew in the next house up spotted us!"

"Where's the others?" I asked.

"Upstairs!"

Another barrage raked the house. It was too much to be just one gun, and I said so in a strained shout.

"Sarge!" Goliath said during a lull in the firing.

I turned to see where he was pointing and saw that damn Belgian girl at the top of the cellar stairs, wearing her new shirt and coat, with an expectant look on her face. "Get down!" I shouted, lunging for her, but the machine-guns started up just before I tackled her to the floor and manhandled her back down the stairs.

She was trembling; close calls will do that to you. As if something suddenly occurred to her, she looked down at her long, extra-large overcoat and spotted a neat round hole in the bottom.

I poked a finger through it and wiggled it was her eyes went wide. "See?" I said. "This is why you *stay down in the cellar*."

Without another word, she went back down the steps, and I could get back to my war.

"Cappy!" I shouted upstairs. "Can you hear me?"

"Yeah!" came the reply.

"Can you see them?"

"Yeah!"

"Where are they?"

"Two MG-42's, one right next door, that's the one we came for. Another one we didn't see before, up one building and to the left one building."

Shit! Another interlocking field of fire. The Krauts seemed to have no shortage of machine-guns in this village.

Well, the hell with it. I wasn't about to get pinned down to the floor only to wait for a panzer to roll right over me. Especially not with the entire company depending on me.

I low-crawled over to Davey and Goliath, trying to ignore the way the debris scattered across the floor bit into my arms and legs like a thousand pungi stakes. "Listen up! You two get upstairs. Davey, get Shorty's bazooka, send him and Weiss down. You two put some fire on the close machine-gun with the bazooka and the B.A.R.; Cappy keeps the far gun crew's heads down with his sniper rifle. I take Shorty and Weiss to take out the house with the close machine-gun. Got it?"

"Got it!" they said, nodding simultaneously. It was a little scary when they did that, like twins separated at birth that didn't look an inch alike.

They scurried upstairs during the next lull in the firing, and a few moments later, Shorty and Weiss came down. Shorty was still armed with the automatic rifle he'd taken off the SS trooper from the night before; he'd figured out how to reload it and said he wanted to give them a taste of their own medicine.

I laid out the plan for them and we crawled up next to the front door. It was a risky move, but I poked my head around the doorjamb to catch a glimpse of where we were going. Machine-gun fire immediately blew chunks out of the doorjamb, and sharp shards of stone bit into my cheek before I could duck back.

"Jesus, Sarge!" Shorty shouted. "Don't *do* that!"

From upstairs came the word we'd been waiting for…"Ready!"… and as soon as we heard the bazooka fire, we were on our feet, out the door, and charging the next house like crazy people. My tommygun shook in my fists; I had to make a concerted effort to slow down my fire before I burned up my ammo supply out here where bullets were hard to come by. Goliath's B.A.R. rattled thunder over our heads, and kept the gun crew's heads down long enough for us to reach the building.

Grenades, again, and Shorty and I led the way in, shooting up the first floor like madmen. There wasn't anybody there, though; the gun crew was on the second floor.

I waved Shorty and Weiss over to the stairs and had reloaded my weapon when a German potato-masher grenade came twirling down the stairwell to land at my feet. Once again, I froze, thinking, *I'm fucked*, and simultaneously hating myself for having such a stupid last thought. Shorty was frozen solid as well, staring at the grenade like he could keep it from going off through sheer force of will.

And then, Weiss… of all people, Weiss… bent down, picked up the grenade, and tossed it back upstairs over the railing and onto the second floor. Just like that, casually, like you might pick up a stick and toss it out of your yard.

It went off with a deafening explosion, shaking dust and plaster loose from the ceiling. The explosion shook Shorty and I out of our haze, and we charged up the stairs with a yell, tearing the three dazed Germans to pieces with long bursts from our weapons. One of them survived the onslaught, barely, and thrashed on the floor until Weiss put a round into his chest from his M1 rifle.

I reloaded as Shorty looked Weiss over like he was an alien being.

"No shit," he said.

Andrew C. Piazza

15

The Germans' machine-gun was still operable, if a little low on ammunition, so Shorty and I used it out of a side window to tie up the second machine-gun up ahead and to our left so the others could cross the open space to join us. To my utter horror, the Belgian girl came loping along behind Davey, one hand holding the ends of her overcoat together in front of her.

"Davey! Davey!" I said, pointing at her. "What the hell is this?"

"It's the girl, Sarge," he said, and when I glared at him, Goliath spoke up.

"She wouldn't stay put, Sarge. Honest. She's probably safer…"

"She doesn't even have any *shoes*," I said. "You're letting her run through the snow in subfreezing temperatures, and she doesn't even have any damn *shoes* on."

"We didn't know what to do to stop her," Goliath said with a helpless shrug.

I ground my teeth in despair. 101st Airborne Division, the Heroes of Bastogne, can't control one twenty-two-year-old female escaped prisoner.

"Fine," I said at last. "One of you see if you can pull the boots off of one of the soldiers upstairs. She can use those for now. I can at least get that done, can't I?"

Cappy and Davey went upstairs, and I shouted, "And maybe a pair of pants, if they don't have too much blood on them!" after them. After that, I sneaked a peek at the remaining machine-gun to our front left.

"Okay," I said, pointing at the house in question. "Same drill. We pin them down with suppressive fire, rush the house, take out the gun. We'll go straight on that way…"

The Belgian girl began to tug at my arm, saying, "No, no, no!" and I had to shake her off to continue.

"Knock it off!" I snapped at her. "We'll go straight on…"

She started up again, and I was starting to lose my cool when she began jabbering in French again, pointing off to our front right.

"Look," I said, "We *have* to…"

"No, no, *no!*" she insisted, then pantomimed a pair of guns with her hands and started going "Ba-ba-ba-ba-bap!"

That held me up. "What?"

She pointed again, off to our right front. "Ba-ba-ba-bap!"

"Another machine-gun?" I asked. "Where?"

She looked around, as if unsure what to say, and then headed up the stairs, gesturing for me to follow. After a moment's consideration, I did.

Upstairs, she led me to a window that opened directly to our front. She kept low and pointed to a pile of rubble a bit past another house up ahead.

"Ba-ba-ba-bap," she said.

I didn't see anything. The morning was getting brighter, but it still was nothing but a mass of broken beams and blasted stones. Then, the fog thinned out momentarily, and there, almost indistinguishable from the junk, was the barrel of another machine-gun.

"Son of a bitch," I whispered.

"Sarge?" Cappy was at the window next to us, watching with curiosity.

I waved him over. "Check it out. The pile of rubble. See it?"

He stared through his telescopic sight. "No… yeah. Son of a bitch. Just waiting there."

I nodded. "Ambush."

Cappy looked over at the Belgian girl, then at me. "Sarge… they would've cut us to pieces, and we never would've known what hit us."

I nodded again. "I know."

I turned to the Belgian girl, who was pulling on a pair of boots taken off one of the dead Germans. She was also wearing a tattered blue dress that Davey had found abandoned in a corner somewhere. It was the lowest point of fashion; tattered blue dress with a man's dress shirt underneath, wearing a gigantic Army issue Olive Drab overcoat over top of that, and huge German jackboots that almost reached her knees, but I swear, she was still the most beautiful woman I'd ever seen.

"I guess when you hid here, you saw them set that machine-gun up," I said to her, then realized she didn't understand a word of it.

She shrugged and smiled.

It was infectious. There was something about the utter lunacy of the situation... a pretty, grinning Belgian girl dressed like a carnival worker saving us from being wiped out... that made me have to smile. Or maybe it was seeing a smiling female face after all the shit I'd been through. In any case, I found myself grinning like an idiot, and I decided to complete the insanity and bowed with a flourish.

"*Merci*," I said grandly. "*Merci beaucoup*."

Andrew C. Piazza

16

"Cappy stays here and covers our advance. Shorty, leave the bazooka. We go in twos: me and Weiss first, Davey and Goliath, Shorty brings up the rear."

"I'm always getting the ass end of things," Shorty said, and winked at me.

"Very funny. We rush the next house, go around it to the right and flank the ambush site."

"What about the gun to our left front?" Goliath asked.

I shook my head. "Listen."

We could hear the distinctive bratta-bratta-brat of our thirty-cal machine-guns getting closer.

"That must be 2nd and 3rd Platoon coming up. That gun has stopped firing on us; they must've shifted positions to another window to fire on the others. We rush the next house, flank the machine-gun set up in ambush in that rubble, and that envelops the other gun in our pincer move. Then we wait to link up with the Captain."

I got the nods and murmurs that indicated they understood what I was talking about, so once Cappy went back upstairs to his window, I led them outside. A glance at my ammo pouch told me I was down to one spare magazine. I had to make them count.

Weiss gave me a nod indicating he was ready, and then we were off, hauling ass for the next house. It was really only half of a house; the back half had been blown apart by an artillery shell. I pointed at the ragged edge of the back wall as we got within a couple yards of the house, to indicate to Weiss that he should keep an eye on it.

A pair of rifle shots crackled through the cold air like lightning, and the next thing I knew, I was down with a heavy weight on top of me. *Holy Shit I'm shot! I'm shot!* I thought, but instead of scared, I got pissed. *Son of a bitch, I'm taking you with me!*

Weiss had fallen on top of me, pinning me down, and I yelled at him to move his ass as I scrambled for the tommygun I'd dropped. I'd barely gotten a hold of it when a German soldier ran right up to me, working the bolt action on his rifle. He shouldered his weapon and pointed it at me.

Another rifle shot, but this one punched through the German soldier's helmet with a *Ponk!* sound. The German fell instantly lifeless, like a puppet whose master suddenly dropped its strings. Blood poured out of the bottom of his helmet like milk from an overturned cereal bowl.

I think I've mentioned before that Cappy was a hell of a shot.

"Behind you!" Davey shouted, and I turned just in time to see a young German soldier duck back behind the jagged edge of the blasted wall.

Seven or eight yards away from me, Goliath dropped to one knee and poured heavy fire straight into the wall. Little known fact: armor-piercing ammo was practically standard issue for the B.A.R., and it could punch through a concrete wall.

Holes appeared all along the side of the house, and then we heard a scream that told us Goliath had hit his mark. Goliath hadn't even finished firing before Davey reached me.

"Are you okay? Are you okay?" he asked, trying unsuccessfully to drag me out from under Weiss until Goliath came up and yanked me to my feet with one pull.

"I'm fine," I said, waving them off. "Check Weiss."

"Nah, he's dead," Davey said. I looked down and saw he'd taken a bullet straight through the heart.

I thought *God damn, I'm glad that wasn't me.*

That's what I thought whenever the guy standing next to me bought it. On the line, you get so used to people dying that it's not a surprise someone's dead; it's a surprise that it isn't you. Two soldiers shot at

Weiss and I; one of them hit their mark and one of them missed. I was glad as hell that I got the lousy shot in the group.

Once Shorty caught up, we went around the jagged wall Goliath had shot up to check up on the young German soldier who'd fled into the remnants of the house. We could hear him even before we went inside. He was sobbing hysterically, and when we found him lying on a pile of rubble inside of the shattered house, we knew why.

He'd been gutshot. A pair of slugs had blown some of his intestines out of the front of his belly. He was trying to push them back in, weeping and sobbing and trying to ignore the blood that was pouring out over his hands.

If he was over sixteen, then I'm Betty Grable. He looked up at us with an almost pleading expression, then went back to trying to put himself back together, huffing and sniffling wetly the entire time.

"Jesus Christ, guys! Are you just going to let him suffer?" Shorty snapped, shouldering his way through us. He put a single shot into the kid's forehead, and the boy's body went totally limp.

We stood there staring, the crackling thunder of distant battle in the rest of town seeming like a separate reality. I don't understand it. We knew Weiss, at least a little, but he buys it and we don't miss a step. Then we see this stranger, a shot-up teenager, trying to stuff himself back into place, and we're stunned. I don't know. Maybe it was because Weiss died instantly and the kid was suffering. I don't know.

Shorty was the one who got us going, slapping me on the back and shouting, "Hey! Snap out of it! We still have that machine-gun to take out!"

I stirred and nodded. "He's right. Break time's over."

The pile of rubble serving as the machine-gun's hiding place was only fifteen yards or so from the blown-out house. We could only see the barrel poking out, pointing off to our left. They had no idea we were coming. The pile of rubble that hid them from us, also hid us from them.

The Captain's words echoed in my mind from last night. *They want to see a surprise attack? We'll show these bastards a surprise attack.*

Seeing that dying kid had taken a little fire out of my belly, though, and I had to psych myself up for this next rush. You have to be aggressive in attack, and if you let your edge get dulled, the enemy won't hesitate to take advantage of it.

They killed Weiss, I told myself, clenching and unclenching my muscles to get the blood flowing. *They would've killed me.*

"Grenades," I said, and all four of us pitched hand grenades over the pile of rubble onto their positions.

They went off almost simultaneously, and we charged up over the rubble and right on top of the Krauts. Only one of the three lying there was still moving, and he was really just rolling in agony, but we sprayed them down all the same with our weapons to be sure.

The machine-gun was as blown apart as they were, but they had a couple of Panzerfausts tucked away that were still in working order. Panzerfausts are disposable rocket launchers that I swear look like giant Q-tips. It's a three-foot steel tube about as thick as your wrist with a big warhead stuck on the end… the bulb of the Q-tip. You press the button, it fires, and you throw away the tube. They were great little weapons; easy to use, easy to carry, and a big warhead that could punch through any tank on the battlefield.

"Sarge!" Davey shouted, pointing to our left, and sure enough, there it was.

Next to the road, behind a demolished building, four German soldiers were manhandling a towed anti-tank gun into a better firing position. Just as we spotted them, one of them spotted us, and pointed at us with a shout.

"Shorty! Panzerfaust!" I shouted, and burned the last half of my magazine at the gun's crew. I could see a bullet ding off of the gun's metal carriage and one of the gun crew went down with a bullet in his hip.

Davey joined in; firing his carbine quickly while Goliath reloaded. Another of the gun crew went down and the rest took off, fleeing across the road as Shorty fired one of the Panzerfausts.

He didn't hit the gun. He went one better and hit the ammo supply piled next to it.

It all went up in a sharp crumple of an explosion. The anti-tank gun lifted up two feet off the ground and fell onto its side. Once the dust settled, we ran up to the wreckage to make sure that the gun crew was dead.

As I stooped over one of the bodies, I couldn't help but remember my vision of terror troops with fangs for teeth. I pushed the dead soldier's lips back. Just regular old ivories, if a little worse for wear.

We started to whoop and holler in victory, until Davey warned "Behind us!" and we all spun with weapons at the ready. I remembered I was empty and loaded my last magazine before I saw them.

"Hold your fire," I said, then shouted "101st!" to the shapes moving up toward us out of the mist.

An almost ghostly "101st!" floated back through the air, almost as if it were an echo of my own voice.

"That's Lambourne," I said, identifying the voice. "Those guys are 3rd Platoon."

We waved a squad of our guys up to our position so we could fall back to where Lambourne was directing his platoon's advance. I took the last Panzerfaust with me… they had to counter-attack with the panzers any second now.

I had no sooner thought it than my fears were realized. Sergeant Lambourne had just told me that he was the second half of the pincer, that we now held the first half of the town, when a runner dashed up to us out of the mist, breathless huffs of hot air streaming out of his mouth.

"They're counter-attacking! They're counter-attacking through the cemetery!"

Andrew C. Piazza

17

Everyone looked to me, and for an instant, I forgot I was the ranking non-com. I wanted to say, "What the hell are you looking at me for?", but then I remembered the stripes on my sleeve and forced myself to work through it one step at a time.

"Okay, first off," I said. "Where's the cemetery?"

I didn't really need to ask; I could hear a mass of crackling gunfire off to the left, across the road. It sounded fast and furious.

"It's about twenty yards further up the road on the left side," the runner huffed. His name was Frankie Bickel and he was an excitable kid from Brooklyn. "There's a million of 'em and they're shooting like crazy…"

"Settle down, Frankie! Where's the Captain?"

"He's, uh, he's…" Frankie stammered, and Lambourne answered for him.

"He's back about a hundred yards or so, next to the road on the left side. There's a bunch of buildings, maybe five or six, all smashed up by arty. Then back a little the way we came is an intact house. He's using it as an observation post to direct our mortar fire."

"And that's where they're hitting us," I said. "Cut us in half, take out our HQ… Frankie."

"Yeah, Sarge?"

"Haul ass back to that meatchopper and tell those guys the AT gun is history and to get their asses up here. Pronto. Go!"

Frankie took off running, and I wanted to do the same, to burn off some of the nervous energy that was welling up in me over the prospect of having to face all of those tanks head-on.

"Shit!" Shorty said. "Sarge, we left that girl back there with Cappy!"

I swore and rubbed at my head. "Okay. Shorty, get back there and collect your bazooka and Cappy and get to where the Captain is. We're on our way there now."

"What about me?" Lambourne asked.

"3rd Platoon stays put. You must hold here, Sergeant. You are now our right flank. You fold, we're all fucked. Got it?"

He nodded gravely. He understood what I meant. At all costs.

I put a hand on his shoulder. "If they come at you with tanks, keep your bazooka team well-guarded and mobile, and hit the panzers in ambush from the side or rear. It's the only way you'll punch through a Tiger or Panther tank's armor. Do what you can."

"You got it, Sarge," he said, his voice cracking a little. It was easy to understand why; he had maybe twenty or so guys with one bazooka among them to take on God only knew how many tanks.

"Very well," I said, in an eerie imitation of Captain Powell. "I'll see you when it's over."

With that, I led Davey and Goliath off at a run through the fog and the haze toward where the Captain should be. It was well into morning by now, so there was plenty of light, but the fog still drifted in heavy banks through the town, cloaking everything into a confused mystery.

I was worried that the machine-gun we'd by-passed would give us trouble, but then I saw our guys carrying a thirty-cal into the building where it had been. Some of 3rd Platoon's guys had come up and taken it out.

My eyes picked out Private Wayne, the sentry from the night before who had failed to challenge the TDs, standing sentry in a window with his M1 rifle propped up on the sill. We went into the house and I rolled up next to him to look out onto the street.

"See anything?" I asked.

"Not yet," he drawled.

The half-dozen buildings directly across the street were smashed into junk. To my left, back the way we'd come about eighty yards, was an intact two-story stone and wood house. It must be where Lambourne had said the Captain was.

There was a tremendous amount of gunfire going on behind the rubble, out of sight. Off to our right, deeper into the village, all was quiet, but the fog seemed to hang heavy with malice.

"Listen up," I said. "There's a counterattack coming in on the other side of that rubble. Some of it may spill out into the street. If it does, don't shoot right away. Let a few of them into the street and out in the open, and then take them all at once. Got it? And you be sure to stay out of the open."

"Got it, Sarge."

I was suddenly tired. No, not just tired; I nearly passed out. People who have boxed or wrestled understand that once the whistle blows, just standing in the ring burns up an incredible amount of energy... that's why the rounds are measured in minutes. Fighting is like that. You're revved up to maximum; while you're in the middle of it, you can't feel it at all. You feel like you're in top form, but once there's a lull, you crash.

I was crashing now. I'd been up for forty-eight hours straight. I hadn't eaten in twenty-four, since breakfast the day before, and even then, it had been nothing but a cold block of C-ration cheese. During that time I'd been fighting and running and you name it, and I'd been doing it for weeks prior to this. And now that there was a momentary lull for me, even though I could still hear the shooting nearby, my body shut down.

Things got a little blurry and I swayed on my feet. I was suddenly aware of how bone-chilling cold I was; my teeth rattled together and I started to shiver uncontrollably. My stomach ached. I wasn't just hungry; my stomach *ached* with the need for fuel. It felt like it was a pit of quicksand sucking in the rest of my body.

"Sarge?" Davey asked. "You okay?"

"Yeah, uh, s-stay here," I stammered, and stumbled out of the room and into another one where no soldiers could see me. It doesn't do to break down in front of your men.

Fight this! Fight it, damn it! I screamed at myself. *Snap out of it! The battle's not over, there's no time for this!*

It was no good. I shook so hard my helmet fell off and hit the floor with a clatter. My face twisted and contorted into a grimace, the kind you get when you weep hard and uncontrollably. It felt like I was going to pass out and throw up and sob all at once.

I tried thinking of Kate, but her face wouldn't come to me. I hit myself in the chest, tried to bully myself back into shape, but I couldn't. I was falling apart, breaking down like a lame horse.

Then I opened my eyes.

The mind's a funny thing. All my efforts to keep it steady had failed miserably, and yet, a simple drawing on the wall distracted it enough to keep me from succumbing entirely to my fatigue and terror and weakness.

I say a simple drawing, but truthfully, the artist's skill was considerable. His subject was The Crucifixion, life-size and drawn in charcoal; you could make out thorns on Christ's head and tears coming out of His eyes. His outstretched arms made the drawing seem larger than it really was, but it was His eyes that held me. Whoever had drawn this picture had done an incredible job; it seemed as if Christ's eyes were looking right into me.

I'm not saying I had a religious experience. After all the things I've seen, I'm too much of a skeptic to say that. I'm not saying anything. All I'm saying is that I saw an impressive drawing and it dulled my pain long enough so that I could hold myself together. I was still freezing and terribly hungry and terribly tired, but I wasn't falling apart anymore.

There was suddenly the sensation of someone else in the room, and I turned quickly and saw Goliath looking over my shoulder at the drawing. "Kinda nice, hunh?" he said, speaking softly in his smooth baritone. His voice was the last bit of salve I needed to come back into myself.

"Yeah," I said, wiping at my eyes. I reached over and picked my helmet up off of the floor, like it was the reason I had come in here in the first place. "It is."

He stepped into the room next to me. "Definitely nicer than that one."

I looked where he was pointing. On the wall opposite the Crucifixion drawing, as if to oppose it symbolically, someone had used that same piece of charcoal to draw something else.

To say it was hideous would be an understatement. It was repulsive. Just looking at it made my empty stomach turn.

This artist had far less skill than the first. His drawing looked like a black cloud or fog bank that seemed to swirl with malicious intelligence. Dead bodies were strewn about on the ground all around it. Some of them were impaled on spikes. Other people, soldiers, were burning more bodies on spits over a vast fire. The words BEFOLGEN SIE DEN GEIST were scrawled off to the side.

There was something about it that pushed me away, like it and not Goliath was really the source of that someone-else-in-the-room feeling. I didn't even want to be in the same room as it. The Crucifixion drawing seemed to look inside of me with compassion; the dark cloud in this drawing seemed to shove at me with hate and pull at me with longing all at once.

The feeling must've been contagious; I'm almost positive this painting was the reason the room had been empty in the first place. Nobody wanted to wait for the enemy with that thing staring down on you.

"Let's, uh," I said, backing away from it, now fully back in control of myself, "let's get moving."

Andrew C. Piazza

18

Artie Gorman got shot as we reached the pile of rubble in front of the Captain's new HQ. He and three other troopers were taking cover behind a low pile of stones and bricks, and when Artie got up to a kneeling position and popped off two rounds from his rifle, a slug caught him in the shoulder and he dropped to the ground.

"Medic!" I shouted, diving to cover as a fresh barrage of gunfire snapped the air around us and split pieces of stone and brick from the rubble.

Davey and Goliath and I low-crawled up to the rubble. Artie Gorman was thrashing around and screaming, and I hoped the medic got here soon to give him some morphine. I said before that panic can spread from man to man; the last thing we needed was to break right as they counter-attacked.

Someone came running up from the house. I assumed it was a medic, but when I turned and looked, it was the Captain, carrying a field telephone and trailing wire behind him. Another trooper kept pace with him… his runner… and they both hit the dirt next to me.

"What are you doing out here, *sir?*" I said, saying the word 'sir' much like I might say 'damn fool'. "You should be back in that house. Actually, you should be further back, in…"

"I need to see to direct the artillery," he said. "This fog is cutting visibility too much; I needed to get closer."

"You need to not get shot," I said, then shouted, "Will somebody get Artie a damn medic?"

To my utter horror, Captain Powell crawled to the left along the rubble and poked his head out to get a look.

I crawled closer and pulled him back. "Sir, *stop* that!"

He glared at me and tried his field telephone. "Damn it."

"What?"

"Line's out."

"Could you even see anything?"

He shrugged. "You can see up to the front line of headstones, and that there's some infantry in there using them as cover. That's about it."

I waited until I thought he wasn't looking, and then I poked my head over top of the rubble to see for myself. He was right; the fog shrouded everything past the first line of headstones in a gray blankness. Vague dark shapes huddled behind the headstones and occasionally dashed amongst them.

"Hey!" the Captain shouted, pulling me back down. "What was that all about?"

"I'm more expendable than you are," I said.

He looked like he wanted to argue, but then Shorty and Cappy came up and took their places on our new front line. "Very well. Let's… Sergeant, what the hell is a civilian doing up here?" he said.

I looked over and ground my teeth. The Belgian girl was cowering behind the rubble at the far right end of our line.

"Shorty…" I growled.

"It's not my fault!" he shouted before I could finish my promise to skewer him once this was over. "She wouldn't stay put! I told her to but she kept coming anyway and I didn't know what to do!"

I sighed and shrugged toward the Captain. "I'm sorry, sir. We found a Belgian civilian in one of the cellars; I think she's another escaped prisoner like the Brit. She only speaks French and she won't stay put no matter what we say."

He stared at me for a second, then shook his head. "Mademoiselle!" he shouted in her direction, then to my surprise, followed it with a faltering handful of words in French.

I'm pretty sure he was butchering her language, but she responded in a rapid-fire chatter mimicking the machine-gun bursts directed at us from the cemetery.

"What did she say?" I asked.

One Last Gasp

"I'm not really sure," Captain Powell said. "My French leaves much to be desired, but I think the gist of it was, she'd rather die than be captured by the Germans again."

"She may get her chance," I said, popping up just long enough to lay down a short burst at one of the headstones.

Machine-gun fire chased me back down to ground again, and one of the troopers... his name was Byron, I think... snapped at me, "Damn it, Sarge, don't do that! You're drawing their fire!"

"We can't let them pin us down like this," the Captain answered for me. "Goliath, everybody, get ready to lay down some cover fire so we can move a thirty-caliber up here. Runner!"

"Yes, sir!" said the runner who'd come up with him.

"Get back to the mortars and tell them to drop twenty and fire for effect. Go now!"

The runner was up and off, but he didn't make it ten feet before a machine-gun burst stitched him across his back and he fell heavily. Captain Powell shook his head and pointed back toward a machine-gun crew taking cover back by the house.

"You two! Move up!" he shouted, waving his hand in a come-here gesture. "Cover fire!"

We all rose up and laid down as much fire as we could, even when return fire began to snap the air around us. Another trooper took a round... this one through his side... but by the time we all ducked back down behind the protection of the rubble, our machine-gun was up and in position.

"I'm out," I told the Captain, taking the empty magazine out of my weapon.

He dug in his pouch and handed me two of his. "How'd you do?"

"We took out two MG-42s and the anti-tank gun," I said, loading one of his magazines into my weapon. "Lost Weiss. We completed the pincer move and 3rd Platoon is up there on the right flank now."

He snorted once. "You've been busy."

I shrugged and gave him a grin. "Hell, yes, I've been busy. I'm an enlisted man. I work for a living."

"Very funny," he said, and then, it all got quiet.

We could hear firing in the distance, in the direction of Baker Company, but the cemetery was quiet as a church mouse. I took the opportunity to set the Panzerfaust I'd captured between the Captain and myself. "For when the panzers come," I said.

"Should be any time now," he said.

We waved a pair of medics up to drag Artie and Byron away while there was a lull. Once they'd done so, Shorty muttered, "This can't be good."

It wasn't. A few seconds later, a hailstorm of lead poured over our position, from at least two machine-guns and God only knew how many rifles. Our own machine-gun fired to answer back, but the intense fire killed both gunners almost immediately.

"This is it!" Captain Powell shouted. "Hold the line! Hold the line! Don't let them break through!"

Against our every instinct, we rose up and shot like crazy at the dark forms rushing at us through the mist. They came yelling, shouting a war cry at the top of their lungs, rushing like an oncoming flood around and between the headstones and toward us.

I remember thinking *This is it!* and then *Screw them, I ain't going down easy!* I cut down two men straight away, and was about to pull the trigger on a third when an explosion blew dirt and shrapnel up along the front line of headstones.

"The panzers!" somebody shouted. "The panzers are shooting at us!"

"They wouldn't be shooting at their own men!" Captain Powell shouted back, and when another shell landed in the middle of the Germans, scattering them and ruining their attack, he shouted, "God bless you, Tedeski!"

Our tank destroyers had finally broken through to the north and were blowing the hell out of the cemetery. I shouted at our guys to pour on the fire, make sure the attack was repulsed, but a nearby explosion drove us all down to cover.

A tremendous, thundering rattle exploded right over our heads. It was continuous, unrelenting, and I covered my head with my hands, sure it was the end, before I realized what it was.

The meatchopper had come up behind us and reached our lines. All four heavy machine-guns on the quad-fifty mount boomed like cannons over our heads. The huge slugs tore up the ground, the enemy, and blew headstones to pieces. Chunks of granite and body parts flew through the air.

The Germans weren't fools. They ran like hell into the fog, out of sight, the quad-fifties chasing them with devastating fire all the way.

The Captain lifted his head up from the dirt and snow and grinned at me. "It's a good day to be alive, Sarge."

I grinned back. "So I've heard."

Andrew C. Piazza

19

The last bits of German resistance fell back to the church in the middle of town. Why they didn't give up, I can't understand. Those guys never seemed to understand the meaning of the word 'lose'.

We followed the meatchopper half-track up the road, pausing whenever somebody took a shot at us. The quad-fifties would bark out our response, tearing through walls, blasting apart doors, and chewing up the scenery in general.

Somebody waved a white flag off to our left from one of the buildings near the church. He didn't take two steps out of the front door before Cappy shot him through the chest.

"Damn it, Cappy!" I said, pushing his rifle barrel down. "That was a white flag!"

He looked at me without expression. "And?"

"*And*," I said, "you shoot at guys waving white flags, sooner or later they drop those white flags and start picking up their guns again. The point is to end the shooting, Private."

He looked me up and down before shrugging non-committally. "You're the one with the stripes."

Captain Powell moved up beside us. "I don't want to see that again, Cappy. I need prisoners to interrogate, not bodies. These aren't the troops who hit us last night, and they can't tell us where the SS are if they're dead."

I almost stopped in my tracks right there in the middle of the road. What an idiot I was! I hadn't realized up until now that what Captain

Powell said was true: these weren't SS troops but Wehrmacht, regular German army troops.

How could I not have realized that? The uniforms were totally different. The soldiers who'd shot Weiss and nearly got me too were using the standard bolt-action rifles the regular army used, not the new fully-automatic rifles the SS were using the night before.

Cappy seemed to like the Captain's argument better than mine. "Yes, sir," he said. A nod indicated the TDs approaching from the other end of the village. "Your pet nigger's coming up."

"I don't want to hear that kind of talk again, either," the Captain said. "Clear?"

"Crystal," Cappy growled and moved off to our left to find a good spot from which to cover the church.

"That's why they haven't hit us with panzers," I said.

Captain Powell nodded. "And they're not going to. Because they don't have any. This is a totally different unit."

"So where did the SS go?"

"That's what I intend to find out," the Captain said, waving his arm at a tank destroyer coming down the road the opposite way.

"Sir," I said, nodding back the way we'd come. The Belgian girl was trailing behind us by about twenty yards.

"Oh, for God's sake…" he muttered, then shouted some clumsy French and waved her off. She shook her head and rapid-fired French right back at him.

He looked at me and I shrugged. "See? I told you; she doesn't listen."

Captain Powell waved all of that off. "Oh, forget it."

The lead tank destroyer met our half-track right in front of the church. We stayed on the safe side of the meatchopper; no telling when an overly ambitious sniper might want to take a pot shot.

The front hatch flipped open on the TD and Lieutenant Tedeski's head poked out, cigar stub and all. "I miss anything?" he shouted.

"You might want to keep your head down," Captain Powell said. "There's still a dozen or so in the church, and they haven't given up yet."

Tedeski craned his neck around to get a look at the church. "Oh, yeah? How about I give them a warning shot?"

"That might be a good idea," the Captain said.

"Hey, what is that, a civilian you got with you?" Tedeski said, looking over our shoulders at the Belgian girl.

Captain Powell grimaced. "It's... it's a long story."

"Yeah, well, hang on. One warning shot, coming up."

He disappeared back into his tank destroyer and a moment later, the big cannon swung on its turret with a loud whine of machinery. It seemed to take forever to turn the ninety degrees toward the church, and then the muzzle began to drop.

"Hey," Shorty said from right behind me. "That don't look like a warning shot to me. That looks like he's aiming right at the..."

BOOM! The cannon thundered and the big double doors to the church blasted apart, instantly shredded into splinters. We held our hands over our ears and winced; the cannon's report so close by was like getting your ears boxed. By the time we recovered, Wehrmacht soldiers were stumbling dazed and bloodied out of the hole where the church's front doors used to be. Those that were able to waved white cloths feebly.

"Hell of a warning shot," I said.

"I'll say," the Captain agreed, waving our guys in to take the Germans prisoner.

We walked over to the TD as the hatch flipped back open with a loud clang. Tedeski's head popped up again and he nodded with satisfaction at his handiwork. "There you go."

"Warning shot, hunh?"

He grinned. "You shoot the first sonofabitch in line, makes a good warning for the others."

"Where's Captain Jackson?" I asked.

"That asshole," Tedeski spat. "Thought you Airborne guys were supposed to be tough. First shots get fired, we lose a TD, he's hiding in a barn, frozen stiff, can't decide what to do."

"So where is he?" the Captain asked.

"Dead," Tedeski said around his cigar. "Anti-tank gun missed my rig and hit the barn instead. All we found were his legs. It's like I always say… the best way to avoid getting hit is to grab 'em by the balls before they know what's happening. You hesitate, you die."

"Well, sir," I said, turning to the Captain. "Looks like the town is all yours."

20

We set up our CP in one of the few buildings left untouched by our artillery. There was a working stove, and the Captain ordered it lit immediately. Within minutes, the kitchen was filled with GIs desperate for the first taste of real warmth in weeks. I had to start rotating them through before it got too crowded.

Captain Powell had ordered the kitchen trucks forward as soon as we routed the Germans at the cemetery, and our guys were already lining up for hot chow, the first in days. I cut in line and got a plate and some coffee for the Captain and took a biscuit for myself. It was gone pretty quickly, but I promised myself more was soon to follow.

I found him on the radio in the CP, talking to Regiment. He nodded as I set the food and coffee down in front of him. I noticed he sipped at the coffee, but barely touched the food. He was too busy.

The Belgian girl sat in one corner of the room in her ridiculous outfit, watching him. There was a chair next to her so I sat down, trading a friendly grin with her.

"He won't eat," I said, gesturing toward the Captain.

She looked at me quizzically.

"He won't eat," I repeated, pantomiming eating and shaking my head. "He's been living on coffee and pure willpower. He needs a rest."

She shook her head and shrugged, oblivious to what I was saying.

I smiled again and pointed to myself. "Harry. Harry Kinder."

This time, she understood and pointed to herself. "Rebecca. Rebecca Mampel."

"Pleased to meet you, Rebecca Mampel. What is it, Shorty?"

I could tell Shorty was excited by the way he fidgeted about. "You won't believe it, Sarge! This house, its plumbing *still works!* Toilet in the other room works, and the one upstairs. There's even a *bathtub*. Really!"

You have to understand front line life to appreciate Shorty's enthusiasm. Some of you who've gone hiking for weeks at a time know what it's like to go without a shower for days or weeks, and to have to squat over a hole in the ground to use the facilities. I couldn't remember the last time I had used a flush toilet… months, maybe… and we were so filthy it felt like the dirt would cake up and flake off like flecks of plaster.

I gave him my explicit instructions and returned to the Captain's side. Once he got off the radio, I gave him the news about the plumbing.

"Good," he said, "saves us the need to dig a latrine. Let the men rotate through to use it. Um… uh, get them to… make sure they're fed, in turn, and…"

He took another drink of coffee and pinched the bridge of his nose as if to ward off a headache. "Rotate the men through the kitchen facility. Have any house with a stove or fireplace use that stove or fireplace and have them warm up. Rest, too."

He shook his head and seemed to compose himself. "I want them rotated through getting fed, getting warm, and getting rest, in that order."

"It's already taken care of," I said, picking up his plate of food and handing it to him again.

"Later. First…"

"No, now," I said, looking around and stepping close to make sure nobody could hear us. "Everything's taken care of, Captain. The men are being fed, we've got a perimeter in place, the prisoners are…"

"Prisoners!" he groaned, tapping a hand to his head. "I've got to…"

"You've got to get some rest," I said. "The war can get by without you for the next three hours. Regiment knows our location and situation, and everything's taken care of. You need some rest."

"I don't have time…" he protested, and I shushed him, to his great surprise.

"Captain, you need to eat and get some sleep. You've been up for almost three days straight and I can't remember the last time I saw you eat something. If you don't get some rest you become a liability to this company. You become a danger to your men when your judgment is affected by fatigue. You faded out there a second ago; that should be your wake-up call."

He frowned and looked down at the ground. "But... well, when was the last time *you* got any sleep, Sarge?"

I shrugged and gave him an Aw-shuks grin. "I got some sleep before the war. I'll get some more when it's over."

He smiled and laughed a little, the laugh of someone who's been up too late and now finds everything hysterically funny.

"Now go on," I said. "There's a bathtub upstairs; I had the men fill it with hot water from the stove. There's a mattress, too. Go up there, get a bath, take a shave, eat your food, sack out for a while. I'll come up to get you in three hours. That's what you owe me, three hours."

"Two," he said.

"Two and a half," I countered. "Now get your ass up there. Sir."

He finally took the plate of food away from me and practically staggered up the stairs, nodding. He turned briefly and pointed at me. "Okay, but it's your turn next."

"Yeah, yeah, yeah," I said, waving him off, and once he was out of sight upstairs, drank the rest of his coffee at a go. It was hot and burned on the way down, but I was falling apart myself and needed a jolt.

"Shorty!" I said. "Check the supply trucks and see if you can find some new clothes for the Captain. You know, clean ones for after his bath? Ditto for Rebecca here."

"Who?" he asked.

"Rebecca, the uh, the civilian." I pointed to her in the corner, and she waved at us with another smile. "Shit! And some food for her... wait, I'll take care of that myself. And Shorty?"

"Yeah, Sarge?"

"Nobody disturbs the Captain. Nobody... I mean *nobody*. I don't care if Hitler himself walks down Main Street in his fucking underwear; *nobody disturbs the Captain*. It there's a problem, you come to me. Clear?"

"You got it, Sarge," he said, and scurried off.

Maybe it seems strange to you that I would take things over like that... after all, I wasn't an officer, and maybe you think it would be Barbon, the XO, who would take over. First off, Barbon had become a casualty... took a round through the calf muscle... and second, it was second nature for me. That's what a first sergeant does in a company. He makes sure the machinery keeps going. The Captain ran the company, but I made the company run.

I walked Rebecca over to the chow line, smiling a little at the way her big German jackboots clunked around her little feet as she walked. It's funny; when she was huddled naked and terrified in that cellar, her thinness and vulnerability invoked pity and sadness. Now, though, now that she was relatively safe and on her way to being fed, now her vulnerability and fragility and piecemeal clothing were a part of her considerable charm. Even her inability to speak English... that little handful of French she'd say and then smile and shrug in a sportsmanlike fashion... endeared her to me. To all of us, really.

If you ever were such a fool as to try to cut in on an Army chow line, you'd better have bars on your helmet or a flame-thrower in your hands, or you're a dead man. But those starving and frozen troopers who hadn't seen a hot meal in over a week parted the way for Rebecca like the Red Sea for Moses. She clomped her way up to the end of the line, intending to wait her turn like everybody else, and guys I'd seen punch each other's lights out over a place in line stepped aside and waved her forward with a clumsy grin.

Each time, she protested, but was waved forward more insistently, and the growling in her belly combined with the smiles and nods of the men to propel her forward. I stayed right behind her, following in the wake of her feminine blitzkrieg on the chow line.

Something else was strange about the guys. There wasn't a single comment, whistle, or nudge to a buddy's ribs. None of the usual chatter and nonsense from a group of guys checking out a pretty girl. This was different; the guys were almost... reverent, maybe, standing in mute awe of the female presence that they'd been denied for so long. Maybe it was her frailty that created such a hushed response; maybe the guys saw that she'd been through as much as we had and maybe more and didn't need an ounce of heckling.

Maybe someone had told them about her saving us from an ambush. I think it was the simple magic of her charm and grace in the midst of madness that won them over. She was instantly a precious object to be protected and treasured, not jeered at.

I shook my head at it all, at how even the cook dumped the food on her plate in an almost apologetic manner, as if embarrassed that the quality of the chow wasn't any better. My chow, of course, was slopped on in the usual haphazard manner, but I made sure to take a few extra biscuits to give to Rebecca later, in case our supplies got tangled up. What can I say... even a happily married man like myself couldn't completely resist her humble charms.

After we'd been loaded up, I walked our new demi-goddess off and out of sight of the chow line, in order to wake the grizzled troopers from their dream. She and I ate as we walked, not talking, just enjoying the lack of shooting and the end of hunger pains and the chill in the air paired with the knowledge that we could return to a warm house whenever we wanted to. It was a blissful experience made powerful by its simplicity; my spirit went a long way on moments like those, savoring them like slowly melting chocolate when times were terrible and Death was working overtime.

I've always said that the only good thing about going without is building up an appreciation for when the lean times end.

We wound up at the end of our supply trucks, where Shorty was rummaging around in the back of the last truck in line. Major Hayward stood at the vehicle's bumper, constantly telling him not to bother, no trouble, he was fine in the rags we'd given him before we went on the attack.

He caught sight of us once we were almost on top of him. I got a pleasant nod, but when he saw Rebecca, his eyes lit up and he swept the helmet liner we'd given to him for a hat off his head with a heartfelt "Mademoiselle!"

On any other man, it would've been a gaudy, grandiose gesture, but Major Hayward made it look as natural as me extending my hand for another man to shake. Rebecca cried out and clomped her way to him, throwing her arms around him and almost dumping her plate of food in the process.

"Careful now, dear. You'll lose your breakfast," he said, repeating himself in fluent French as she kissed both of his cheeks.

She looked down at her food and immediately offered it to him. He and I both protested at once, and I handed Major Hayward my plate to keep her from insisting.

"Oh, no," Major Hayward said, shaking his head at me. "No, no, Sergeant. Wouldn't dream of it. Couldn't bear to go on knowing I'd eaten another man's breakfast."

"Not at all, Major," I said. His manner of speech was contagious. "I'm stuffed to the gills. Couldn't eat another bite if it was forced down my throat on the end of a ramrod."

Rebecca said something to him, and he laughed and took my plate away from me. "She says you have a bad habit of giving your food away to officers."

I nodded with a grin. "They have a bad habit of not eating unless I do."

"Quite right, quite right," Major Hayward said, and began to finish off the last half of my breakfast, eating in neat and measured bites, although I'm sure it was at a faster pace than was usual for him.

"You know each other?" I asked.

"Yes, yes," Major Hayward said between mouthfuls. "She was held prisoner with me. When we ran away from the truck last night, I thought the SS had shot her. You have no idea how relieved I am that she was not."

"Here we go!" Shorty shouted from the truck, and his head popped out. "Oh!" he added when he saw Rebecca. "Hang on, I found some stuff for you, too."

A second later, they each had US Army issue sweaters, gloves and wool scarves. Major Hayward kept his SS overcoat, refusing to deny "some fine American lad his coat just for the sake of worn out old me," but Rebecca traded Goliath's coat back in for one more suited to her frame. She sat down on the truck's bumper and I helped her pull her oversize boots off so she could put on two pairs of GI socks before getting back into those ridiculously large jackboots.

Major Hayward climbed into the back of the truck to pull on a pair of pants and boots that Shorty had found for him. I waved Shorty closer, and indicated I wanted him to walk with me. Rebecca followed behind us, eating and shuffling in her boots, as if reveling in the feel of her toes being encased in wool and warmth at last.

"You've got some German, Shorty," I said. "There's something I want you to have a look at for me."

Andrew C. Piazza

21

The house where I'd nearly passed out during the battle was right along the road through the center of town. Like most of the other buildings in the village, it was two stories and made of stone and wood. Also like most of the buildings in the village, it was pockmarked with holes from bullets and shrapnel.

The inside wasn't much better. It's funny; just after the fight, I couldn't have described the interior of that house to save my life… with the exception of the two drawings, of course. I was too busy trying to stay conscious and free of bullet holes. After that second trip, though, I'll be in my grave before I forget that house.

The front part looked like every other shot-up building in that town: splintered debris scattered across the floor, nothing of value that wasn't smashed or hidden or stolen long ago, an occasional splatter of blood on the floor or the walls, that sort of thing. GIs milled about, setting up a defensive position in case there was an immediate counter-attack from a nearby German unit.

Then there was That Room, the one with the two charcoal drawings on the walls. It was why I'd brought Shorty in here, and yet, as I approached that room, a curious apprehension slowed me down to a stop outside its doorway. It was as if the room was filled with a clear, thick fluid that I didn't want to have to force my way through.

"Sarge?" Shorty asked.

A shiver rippled through me, even though I wasn't cold, but I shrugged it off with a derisive grunt and pushed my way into the room. My eyes seemed to instinctively avoid the ugly, crude drawing and drew instead to the finely drawn image of the Crucifixion. The others followed me in; I could hear Shorty grunt at the sight of the hideous drawing, and after Rebecca's over-sized boots clomp-clomp-clomped into the room, there was a strangled cry and clatter as she dropped her plate to the floor.

It had been so quiet, the loud sound seemed to grab me by the belt and shake me. Rebecca's already pale face became positively white; her hands shook as she raised them in front of her mouth as if trying to hold in a scream.

Her wide eyes were locked on the ugly drawing facing Christ from across the room. As thin as she was, as hungry as she still must've been, her dropped plate of food never got so much as a glance of remorse. Instead, once she seemed able to shake herself out of her paralysis, she turned and fled from the room, huffing out incoherent sounds that were almost sobs.

"What happened?" I asked.

"How the hell should I know?" Shorty said. "She took one look at that picture and flipped out."

"Stay here," I said, and went after her. She hadn't gone far, just outside of the building, where Major Hayward held her shaking body in his arms and whispered soothing words in her ear.

Once I saw she was okay, I went back in to Shorty, who was grimacing at the ugly drawing as if he'd eaten something rotten. I took my place next to him, and we both stared in grim silence like two art critics assigned to reviewing a particularly revolting piece.

"That's ugly," Shorty said.

"Yeah," I agreed.

"I mean, even forget about that cloud thing or fog or whatever it is in the middle. Look at the Germans."

"Germans?"

"Yeah, you can kind of tell they're supposed to be German soldiers if you look just right at their helmets."

I frowned, tilted my head, and tried to see what he was seeing. He was right. If you knew what you were looking for, you could see that the artist had intended to draw the soldiers' helmets to look like the German variety. "Okay. What about them?"

"What about them?" Shorty said. "Look at them. They're spitting people on spikes and cooking them for breakfast."

Something clicked in the back of my mind, like a key suddenly lining up all of the tumblers in a lock, snippets of the last twenty-four hours lined up in my memory.

"Whoever drew this was one sick puppy," Shorty said, but I was thinking of something he'd said the night before.

Unfit, as in, unfit to command? I'd asked.

No, Sarge, he'd said. *Unfit, as in, unfit to eat.*

Why were the SS traveling with prisoners stripped naked in a truck?

They executed the sick and wounded, but they took the healthy prisoners with them.

Captain Powell's voice, this time. *They raid our kitchen supply but... there isn't much to take.*

They leave the heavy mortars and ammunition alone.

And yet they take the time to round up and march off prisoners....

The crude drawings on the wall began to look more and more ominous. My stomach began to hurt, as if the tiny bit of food I'd managed to get into it had suddenly turned sour.

The SS had ignored sound tactical doctrine in order to round up healthy prisoners. They kept more prisoners right on hand with them in a truck, like a pile of supplies, stripping them naked to discourage them from running off into the frigid cold. But they'd killed the sick and wounded.

Unfit, as in, unfit to eat.

"Shorty," I said, my voice suddenly dry, "What does that say? The German phrase there?"

Shorty squinted at the wall. "Obey the... Obey the Geist."

"What does Geist mean?"

"I don't know," he said. "My German ain't too good."

"It means 'ghost'," someone said from behind us, and we nearly jumped out of our skins.

"Jesus, man!" Shorty exclaimed. "You scared the hell out of me! Don't sneak up like that!"

Major Hayward smiled distantly but kept his eyes on the drawing, as if expecting it to move and attack us. I noticed he didn't actually enter the room, but hovered in the doorway. It seemed I wasn't the only one with an irrational loathing of that drawing.

"Ghost, hunh?" I said.

He nodded. "Ghost, or spirit, or ethereal presence. That sort of thing."

"Must be what this big ugly thing in the middle is," Shorty said, tapping the wall.

"Don't touch it!" Major Hayward hissed.

We both looked at him quizzically, although I had almost said the same thing when Shorty pawed at the drawing. It seemed to me like he was prodding a sleeping tiger.

"What I mean is," Major Hayward said evenly, "your Captain may want to see that. Best not to disturb it."

I wasn't sure I liked that choice of words... *Best not to disturb it...* but I had other questions I wanted answered. "You speak German as well as you speak French?"

Major Hayward nodded again, almost solemnly. His eyes never left the drawing of the Geist.

I decided to probe the lines, so to speak. "Probably helped to keep you alive."

His eyebrows raised in curiosity and he finally looked away from the drawing and at me. "Sergeant?"

"You know. Kind of hard to eat something when it's having a conversation with you."

Major Hayward's face was granite, but after Shorty looked back and forth between us and his mind had time to catch up, his face fell open in stunned horror.

"God damn!" he whispered. "You mean the SS were..."

"I had rather..." Major Hayward said, looking over his shoulder in the direction of the troopers in the other room. He lowered his voice before continuing. "I had rather hoped we could keep that under our hats for a bit."

"What the hell for?" Shorty said.

"You told the Captain about this?" I asked, but I already knew the answer. Captain Powell had stepped everything up an hour after his private conversation with Major Hayward, even though he'd known it would put us at more risk.

"Yes, of course. He agreed with me that we could keep this… crime… under wraps for now."

"What for?" Shorty said again.

"Because once you report this, you will have staff officers swarming this place asking questions," Major Hayward said. "They will clog up your machinery, so to speak, like nothing else on Earth. Your Captain needed the chance to conduct this attack without those men getting in the way. He still needs some time to interrogate your prisoners before they are whisked off to the rear and so tied up with red tape that you'll never be able to find out what happened to your men."

I almost slapped a hand to my head. What a bumbling idiot I was! The attack had been over for how long now, and I still hadn't arranged for the prisoners to be interrogated. I'd accused the Captain of slipping because of hunger and fatigue; it looked like I was throwing stones from the front yard of my glass house.

"It's only for another two or three hours, Sergeant," Major Hayward said to me. "Then we let the world know."

"Yeah." I shook my head to clear it of the fuzziness I was now suddenly aware of. "Speaking of which, I'd better go find the German's CO so the Captain can talk to him. We need some answers about a lot of things."

I glanced at the drawing of the Geist and the German soldiers when I said that, and I noticed Major Hayward did too.

"Geez," Shorty said, turning away from the drawing with a shudder. "With that shit going on, no wonder that Belgian girl ran out of here like that."

Major Hayward's eyes seemed to concentrate on the hazy drawing of the Geist, however. "Yes. Small wonder, indeed."

Andrew C. Piazza

22

None of us seemed particularly loath to leave that room. As soon as we were outside, Shorty lit a cigarette with a shaking hand and said, "Sarge," nodding up the street so he wouldn't have to point and betray his trembling fingers.

Davey and Goliath were coming at a trot. Shorty shook his head at them and once they came to a stop in front of us, said, "Have you guys ever considered surgery, to remove yourselves from each other's hips?"

"What?" Davey said, confused.

"What is it, Davey?" I said. It was no good trying to explain to Davey that Shorty's favorite way of dealing with anxiety was to joke it away.

Davey looked Shorty over for a second before reporting. "The Krauts' lieutenant wants to talk to the Captain. He said all kind of things, but all any of us could understand was '*sprechen*' and '*officier*'. I know you don't want the Captain disturbed…"

"No, no, you're right." I rubbed a hand over my face to remind myself I was still awake. One good thing about that frigid cold… it helped to keep me at least a little alert. "I'd better go take care of that. Major Hayward, we may need a translator, so if you feel up to it…"

"Certainly, Sergeant. I am at your disposal."

I nodded. "Thank you, sir. Okay; let's go wake up the Captain."

It turned out we didn't have to. Like the stubborn mule he was, he hadn't gotten any sleep. Instead, he spent all of half an hour in that upstairs room, scrubbing himself clean and shaving, and then came back down to start running the show again.

Shorty heard me groan when I saw the Captain downstairs in direct violation of my orders for him to get some sleep. "Hey, I had nothing to do with it," he said, holding his hands up in surrender.

"Relax, Shorty." At least Captain Powell had afforded himself the luxury of a bath and a shave. It may sound weird, but those two things were actually more precious to me than sleep while I was on the line. After all, you can catch little snippets of sleep almost anywhere once you get used to doing it, but you might go weeks and weeks without a shower. Anybody who's been out camping on the trail for weeks at a time knows how going from filthy to clean can change around your entire outlook on life.

And, he'd gotten his new clothes… Shorty had managed to get that taken care of before we went looking at that ugly charcoal drawing. The Captain looked shiny and new in that kitchen, surrounded by grimy GIs whose dirty appearance made him seem all the more clean in comparison. I remember thinking that was very appropriate, that he should look the part of the diamond in the rough. He was the best of us.

Rebecca was floating around the room, looking the radio set over with some curiosity. Mike Wilcox, the radio operator, was more than happy to point out all of the machine's knobs and buttons and whistles for her. I rapped him on the helmet once to remind him to pay attention to his job before I started in with the Captain.

"How did you sleep, *sir*?" I asked, trying to make that last word sound like another, much nastier, word.

He took a drink of coffee and tipped me a wink. "There's always after the war," he said, before returning to the telephone receiver in his hand. "Yes, sir."

"Major Hayward?" he said, hanging up the receiver. "I think it's time you made your report to your superiors. I've already contacted mine."

Major Hayward raised an eyebrow. "I'd thought you wanted to…"

Captain Powell nodded. "Time's up on that, I think. Besides, it'll take hours for them to get here, even if they do come in droves like you think. I can have this room cleared for you if you feel you need privacy."

"Yes, that's very kind of you, but, um…" Major Hayward said, looking over at me expectantly.

I picked up the cue. "Captain, the Germans' CO would like to talk to you, and Major Hayward is the only one around with more than a handful of German."

The Captain seemed to think that over, then nodded. "Very well. When we're done, then. Where are the prisoners being held?"

"In the church," I said, eyeing his steaming cup of coffee with more than a little longing… for the warmth as much as the caffeine.

"Let's go, then," he said, and led us out of the house.

I trailed behind a bit, to the end of the procession, as a consequence of my fatigue. Rebecca was there, following faithfully along, her boots still clomping even though they had her feet and two pairs of socks in them. She handed me one of our metal mess kit cups.

"Coffee," she chirped with a smile. I couldn't help it; she was such an adorable creature, I wanted to pinch her cheeks and kiss her on the lips and give her a big hug all at once.

"Thanks," I said, then corrected myself. "I mean, *merci*."

"I know thank you," she said, and I spit out my coffee in surprise.

She didn't break stride, but smiled wide and kept her eyes front as we trudged to the church.

"Oh, I see, so now you speak English?" I said, with more humor than frustration. You can't stay mad at a girl like that.

She shrugged. "Little English."

"Unh-hunh. Well, you didn't seem to speak *any* English when I was trying to get you to stay down in that cellar where it was safe. You must speak that selective English, the kind that whatever you don't want to hear gets lost in the translation."

She smiled innocently and shrugged, eyes front, tromping along in her big boots. God bless her.

"Great," I groaned, but I was smiling, too. "What will I find out next?"

There were about twenty-five prisoners in the church, give or take. They already had their wounded laid out on pews in one section, with what I took to be a medic going from man to man, doing what he could with nothing.

Upon seeing us, their lieutenant immediately stood and snapped to attention with a salute. Captain Powell returned it casually.

The German lieutenant was about the same age as Major Hayward; mid-thirties, maybe a little older, with prematurely graying brown hair and blue eyes. Even though he was as haggard as we were, maybe more, he still carried himself like he was in dress uniform in the middle of an inspection. As soon as his salute was returned, he lowered his hand to his side and rattled something off in German.

"He says his name is Lieutenant Schmidt," Major Hayward translated. "He would like his wounded looked after."

"Oh, would he?" Shorty said, and I shot him a glance that shut him up, but not before he muttered, "Kraut son of a bitch."

"I'll see to it," Captain Powell said. Major Hayward translated the message.

That seemed to relieve the German officer somewhat, and his stiff posture relaxed a bit. I think willpower was the only thing keeping him up at all.

"Yeah, *we* don't burn our prisoners alive with a flame-thrower or stick them on a spit," Shorty snarled.

The Captain ignored that. "Tell him we need to talk about the SS unit that attacked our lines last night."

"Yeah!" Shorty said loudly, fists clenching at his sides, as Major Hayward translated. "Tell us where the SS are, you lousy bastard! You know what I'm saying!"

"Shorty!" I snapped at him, but Shorty's entire body was trembling with rage.

"Tell us! You know where they are! You know! You understand me! Unh? *Verstehen sie?* Where are the SS? *Wo ist the fucking SS?*"

His voice rose to a fever pitch, and he darted forward and grabbed the German lieutenant by the lapels and shook him. "Where are they, you fuck? You son of a bitch, tell me…"

The Captain and I grabbed Shorty and pulled him off the German with more than a little difficulty. Some of the other prisoners looked like they wanted to stand up and come to their commander's defense, but the two guards we had posted to the church changed their minds by shouldering their rifles.

"Shorty! Shorty!" I shouted, finally getting between him and the German. "Knock it off!"

"He fucking *knows*, Sarge! He *knows*!" Shorty said, his voice cracking. He sounded like he was on the verge of tears.

I traded a look with the Captain and we held a conversation in it. I half-escorted, half-shoved Shorty toward the door. By the time we reached it, he was shaking and tears were in his eyes.

"I'm okay," he said, coming to a stop. "I'm okay, I'm okay now."

I nodded. He'd just snapped, is all. I had my moment of weakness during the firefight in the room with the charcoal drawings; this was his. He was tired and worn out and terrified over what we'd learned about the SS and what they did to prisoners.

He rubbed his sleeve over his wet eyes. "I am, I really am okay now, Sarge."

"I know," I said. "Go ahead and go take your turn in the bathtub. Get cleaned up, get a shave, have a smoke."

"No, I mean it, I can stay…"

"You've got twenty minutes," I interrupted him, "before the next guy rotates in for that tub. So move it."

"Yeah, okay," he said in a resigned tone. "But don't let him trick you. He understands what you're saying. He knows. We gotta find our guys before…"

"We will. The Captain will take care of it," I said, and gave him a pat on the back that was also a shove toward the door.

The lieutenant was straightening his worn and dirty uniform when I returned. He looked as if he were re-arranging himself after an embarrassing fall at a dinner party.

"I apologize for that, lieutenant," Captain Powell said, and the Major translated.

"*Bitte, bitte*," the German waved off.

Captain Powell stared him down for a second. "Major, please tell him to join us in that small room over there." He pointed to a door leading to a side room. "Then you can go ahead and contact your superiors."

Major Hayward balked at that. "Erm, Captain, if I am the only person capable of translating…"

"Oh, I think we'll get along all right without you," Captain Powell said.

23

Rebecca tried to follow us into the back room, but I shooed her off. She shook her head and pretended not to understand me.

"Don't play games with me, Rebecca," I said as sternly as I could. "This is an interrogation. You can't go everywhere we go."

"It's all right, Sergeant," the Captain said. "She can't understand English anyway, so Lieutenant Schmidt here has no reason not to talk to us."

I was a little confused by all that, since Schmidt didn't *sprechen* English and we didn't have a translator, but I'd learned to trust the Captain even when it seemed like he wasn't making any sense. I shrugged my shoulders and led the prisoner into what looked like the priest's office.

Rebecca sat in a chair in the corner of the room, her eyes driving daggers into Lieutenant Schmidt. The German sat at one end of a small table, and the Captain at the other. I stood behind the Captain.

Captain Powell stayed quiet for a good long time, staring at Lieutenant Schmidt with an almost blank expression. I followed his lead. A lot of times, you can get a man to talk, just by subjecting him to the crushing weight of uncomfortable silence. People will jabber away to break the quiet that seems to fill your lungs up with cotton.

It worked, sort of. Lieutenant Schmidt fidgeted for a bit, sweating under three intent stares, and finally rattled off a couple sentences in German.

The Captain sighed, as if bored, and took out the pack of cigarettes that he'd opened for the five survivors of A Company. He took one out, slowly, ran it under his nose to smell it, and put it in his mouth.

"Sergeant? Smoke?" he offered.

It was certainly a day for strange things. "Sure."

I lit up and so did he, but as before, I noticed he didn't actually inhale, he sort of puffed and let it trail smoke from his fingers.

Lieutenant Schmidt looked back and forth between us, and after a minute, I realized that he was actually staring at our cigarettes and not us. German cigarettes were awful, and there weren't a lot of them to go around; everybody in Europe wanted American cigarettes... Lucky Strikes, especially.

"You want one?" Captain Powell said to the German, setting the pack down on the table between them.

The Lieutenant smiled and made as if to take one, but the Captain set his hand over them.

"Ask for one."

Lieutenant Schmidt frowned, looked at me, at the Captain, and then at the cigarettes.

"Ask for one," the Captain repeated.

The Lieutenant seemed confused, then finally pantomimed smoking and said, "*Einen cigaretten, bitte?*"

Captain Powell shook his head. "In English."

Schmidt frowned again in confusion and shrugged. "*Ich nicht kan...*"

"I can understand why someone would pretend not to speak the language if they were a prisoner, in the hands of the enemy," Captain Powell interrupted. "You play dumb, and save yourself an interrogation. Can't interrogate somebody who doesn't speak your language. Even if you've got an interpreter, the guy doing the talking can't hit you hard and fast with questions, on account of it takes time for the interpreter to interpret."

Lieutenant Schmidt stared at him blankly.

Captain Powell tapped his ashes on the floor. He didn't take a drag. "I already know you speak English. You've been telling me you speak English since I met you. Not with words, of course, but with your body language, the way you react, that sort of thing. You see, in a normal conversation, somebody says something, and everybody knows who to look at, because they know who's being addressed even if there aren't any names being used. For example, I say, 'You need some new clothes, young lady', and we all know I'm talking to Rebecca in the corner over there, even though I haven't said her name. And we all look at her, because that's the convention. That's what is polite. You look at whoever is being addressed."

He paused for a second before continuing. "If you can't speak the language, you can't pick up on those cues, and you end up looking around stupidly until you see who everybody else is looking at. But you haven't done that. You've been a fine, polite gentleman and looked at whoever was being spoken to... which means you knew what was being said."

Now the Captain shook a cigarette out and set it on top of the pack. "I'm afraid your good manners have given you away, Lieutenant. I know you understand me. You've shown me far too much intelligence for you to act dumb any longer. If you want a cigarette, you can have one... but you have to ask. *In English.*"

Lieutenant Schmidt looked at the Captain, then down at the cigarette, and I could see the longing in his eyes. He looked at me as I took a long drag. I knew what he was thinking. I'd been there only a few weeks ago during the Bulge, when I ran out of cigarettes and had nearly lost my mind with the craving for a smoke. It had reached the point that I was seriously considering smoking the dirty hay lining the bottom of my foxhole before I finally scrounged up a few smokes.

At last, Lieutenant Schmidt sighed and his shoulders drooped in resignation. "May I have a cigarette please, Captain?" he asked in very good, if accented, English.

"Of course."

Son of a bitch. Did I say Captain Powell was the best of us? I meant the best, period. That whole bit about knowing Schmidt spoke English, and the game with the cigarettes to give him an excuse to admit it... pure genius.

The Captain lit Schmidt's cigarette with my Zippo and let him take a few drags before speaking.

"What do you think of American cigarettes?"

"Mmm," Schmidt said, caught in mid-drag, "I like them very much. German cigarettes are made of newspaper and dust, I sometimes think. And the Lucky Strikes… very kind of you, Captain."

"My pleasure," Captain Powell said, then his smile faded and he looked like a doctor giving his patient some serious news. "Of course, you know that I didn't bring you back here to talk about Lucky Strike cigarettes. I'd like to talk about the SS."

"I do not know what you mean. I am not SS. I am regular Wehrmacht, 370th Panzergrenadiers…"

"No, no, I mean the SS who attacked our lines last night. The ones with all of the panzers."

Lieutenant Schmidt shook his head. "I do not know…"

"Come on, Lieutenant," the Captain interrupted again. I noticed he did that whenever he knew Schmidt was lying, like a parent stopping a child from completing a request before it could turn into a demand. Captain Powell crushed his lies while Schmidt himself still didn't believe in them.

"Come on. That little dirt track they took leads right back here to your village. Even if they told you nothing, you would've had to have seen that many vehicles and infantry. Not to mention the artillery they must've brought along with them."

Schmidt glanced up briefly at that, and I thought, *Jerry my boy, you are one awful liar.*

Captain Powell nodded once. "I understand you feel you have to hold out for your country and your duty as a soldier. I respect that. But this is different. A special circumstance. These SS… they did things no soldier should do."

"What… things?" Schmidt asked.

"They murdered our wounded and medical personnel," Captain Powell said. "Lined them up and turned a flame-thrower on them. Unarmed prisoners, executed."

Schmidt fidgeted in his chair. "I find this hard to believe."

"Believe it, pal," I said around my cigarette. "I was there. They burned them alive and machine-gunned the survivors and they laughed while they did it."

"Yes… well…" Schmidt stammered, his English suffering due to his agitation, "Americans and British fire-bomb our cities many times. You have heard of Hamburg? Fire bombed for five days! Tens of thousands burned alive, a beautiful city gone, for nothing! These are civilians, not even soldiers! You want to say it is so bad to do this and yet you do it yourselves!"

Rebecca suddenly leapt out of her seat with a shriek and would've attacked the Lieutenant bodily if I hadn't caught her first. She bucked in my arms like a wild mare, with a strength surprising to me considering her malnourishment. A profane stream of shrill French poured out of her mouth; she seemed like she was trying to wield the words like a club.

"Whoa, whoa!" I said, and she finally stopped fighting me and spat out one more word that sounded like German.

"What was that?" I asked. "Now you know German, too?"

"Shithole!" she spat at Schmidt. "This is what I call him! And he is worse! He is a liar and killer! Murderer!"

Schmidt fidgeted in his chair again, as if his pants suddenly itched.

"Rebecca, please," the Captain said. He didn't seem surprised to hear her speaking English.

"I thought you said she did not know English," Schmidt said in a shaky voice.

"I know enough to tell you that you are a murderer!" she shouted at him. "My family, my friends! You are animal and killer like SS! Fuck you! Fuck you mother!"

"All right, that's it," I said, picking her up by the waist and carrying her out of the room. She fought me all the way, until I had her back among the pews of the church and the door to the side room had shut.

Once it had closed, she stopped struggling and let me set her down. "You should have let me take his eyes out," she said. "He is a killer. They all are. They come and they kill us and our land and take everything."

"I understand that," I said, "but…"

"Do you?" she asked, turning those terrible blue eyes of hers on me. "Can you ever understand, Harry? Can you know what he has done? Can you ever feel my anger for him and all his kind?"

"I've lost a lot of friends to this war, too," I told her. "I have a wife, and a house, and a life, and they've all been taken away from me by the war and I can't have them back until it's over. Do you understand?"

Her eyes were suddenly wet and she wiped at them. "Your wife is good woman?"

"Well, she doesn't tell anybody to go fuck their mothers," I said, and she burst out laughing. "What was all that about? Did you learn your English from sailors?"

She giggled a little and shrugged. "American GIs."

"Oh, great. My fellow foot soldiers have turned you into a potty mouth. Look. I have to go back in there. Just stay out here and take it easy. Try not to tell the other prisoners to go fuck their mothers."

Rebecca laughed again at that, and as I returned to the back room, she said, "I do not promise!"

24

"Nobody's looking to blame you," Captain Powell was saying when I shut the door and took my place behind him again.

"Yes, but the way she talks it sounds like I am lining the people up and shooting them in the back of the head," Lieutenant Schmidt said quickly. "I do not do these things. I do not kill civilians or prisoners or anything else you accuse me of."

"Nobody's accusing you of anything."

"She is. She is."

I decided now was a good time to speak. "Lieutenant, let me tell you why she reacted the way she did. You may have noticed a large truck in the middle of that SS armored column."

Schmidt stayed quiet and still, still trying to play it dumb about that.

"They kept prisoners in that truck… civilians, military, it didn't matter. They kept them naked and undernourished, under blankets and hay to keep them just barely from freezing to death."

Lieutenant Schmidt shook his head. "This does not make sense. Why would they do this?"

"Supplies," I said evenly. "They kept them as rations."

The Lieutenant shook his head again, not understanding us, then he froze stock-still and the skin stretched tight across his forehead. I could see the shock and horror of understanding creep over him like a spreading pool of blood.

"No," he whispered, almost choking on the word.

"It's true," the Captain said, almost apologetically. "We have other witnesses who confirm her story."

"No, no, God, my God," Schmidt began to moan, burying his face in his hands. "It is bad enough already that all the world hates Germany, now they do *this*? Animals. *Animals.*"

He was quiet for a moment, and the Captain and I traded a long look while we waited for him to speak.

"She was right. The woman. She was right about the SS," Schmidt said at last, tears constantly threatening to break through his words. "Animals. Damn animals. I hate them. I have always hated them."

He took a moment to collect himself before continuing. "Look. I am a German soldier and I love my country and my people. But I am not a Nazi. I am not SS. I have a wife and a family in Aachen. I am a good man. I do my duty. Everyone wants to think all Germans are butchers and killers but this is not true. I am a soldier. My country called. You would do the same. You have done the same. My country says, 'We need you to defend your home.' What do I say? Of course I say yes. I do not apologize for this."

"I understand that," Captain Powell said, "and I respect it. But there are those who don't live up to the same ideals."

"Like the SS from last night," I added.

"SS." Schmidt spat it out like a dirty word. "They are the worst of us. And what makes them the worst of us is encouraged by their leaders until they are savages. They make me embarrassed. I am embarrassed to have them in the same army, embarrassed they fight on the same side as I do. They are not soldiers. They are thugs. I am professional. If I kill, it is because I must, because this is war. It is never for hate. But these thugs in their black uniforms, swaggering around like princes, acting like they are above the rest of us Wehrmacht, they kill for pleasure. They kill because they like it. They kill just to see it happen, for something to do. And when this Kleg shows up, hissing out his orders, I knew he was the worst of all of them."

"Kleg?" Captain Powell asked. "Who is Kleg?"

"Commander of the SS battalion that attacked you. He comes into town yesterday with his tanks and his vehicles and begins ordering my men around, ordering me around, like we were his own troops. Except always there is that contempt, like we were inferior because we were regular army and he was SS."

"You saw him?" I asked. I was thinking of Ryan's description of him... a skull for a face, and fangs for teeth.

"No, no, only when it gets dark does he talk to me," Schmidt answered. "Until then one of his lieutenants relays his orders. He says the commander does not come out much in the day, but prefers the night."

They can see in the dark, Ryan had said.

"But he did speak to you?"

Schmidt nodded and snubbed out the last of his cigarette. He had smoked it all the way down to the nub. Captain Powell gave him another.

"Thank you, Captain. Yes, he speaks to me. When it is dark, he comes to my command post and we take a walk through the town. I can barely see that he is there. His voice hisses, like a hard whisper."

"What did he say?" Captain Powell asked.

"All kinds of things. Crazy things. First he makes me use the last of my mortar shells on your lines. I only keep ammunition for the anti-tank guns by lying and saying I have no explosive shells, only armor-piercing. He has his self-propelled artillery already firing on you. He doesn't need mine. He has so many shells, more than I have seen any unit his size have. Where he gets them, especially now, I cannot say. But still he wants more."

"What else? You said 'crazy things'?"

Lieutenant Schmidt snorted. "Kleg is a madman. He belongs in that old asylum in the woods that he haunts. He talks of God and how he has seen him, actually seen him face to face. How he looks different than we believe. He draws an ugly drawing in a house in this village, where one of my men has drawn the Crucifixion."

"Kleg drew that?" I asked.

"You have seen it?" Schmidt said. "It is ugly."

"Sergeant?" Captain Powell asked.

"It's a drawing of a... black cloud, I guess, with German soldiers spitting their victims on stakes around it," I answered. "In a building along the street not far from here."

"Kleg draws this when he sees my soldier's drawing of Christ," Schmidt said. "He says this is how he sees God, that my soldier is a boy and knows nothing. Kleg says he used to be a painter, but I think he has no talent for it."

I tended to agree. Kleg's drawing was far more crude than the drawing of the Crucifixion.

"A failed painter, eh?" Captain Powell said. "Like Hitler?"

Schmidt shrugged and stared at his cigarette.

"So he didn't draw the Crucifixion?" I asked.

"No, no," Schmidt said. "One of my soldiers does this, before Kleg has come to the village. He has real talent, this boy. Only sixteen years old. He was killed in your attack."

I found myself staring intently at the floor.

"Kleg talks of many crazy things," Schmidt said, his voice becoming very insistent. "But he never talked about what you say, with the prisoners and…"

He trailed off, as if unable to actually say it aloud and make it true by vocalizing it.

"I believe you," Captain Powell said. "What asylum were you talking about?"

Lieutenant Schmidt paused. He seemed like he thought he'd let too much slip. "Look. I only tell you these things because of what you say they did. I will not give away the secrets of the German Army, not even with torture."

"Nobody's going to torture you," the Captain said.

As long as Cappy doesn't get him alone, I thought, but kept it to myself.

"If these men did… this thing, then they are criminals and must be stopped," Schmidt said. "You would do the same if this happened in your army, yes?"

Captain Powell nodded. "I would have them arrested and court-martialed. Or shot, if I thought I could get away with it."

"Yes. These kind of men are a disgrace to the Army. They bring shame to it. Nobody wants these kinds of men in their uniforms. So this is why I will tell you what I do."

"Very well."

Schmidt paused again, as if deciding on the best way to put it. "Kleg is... what do you call it... independent? He does not answer to the higher command as far as I can see. He makes his own orders."

"He's a renegade?" I asked. It seemed unbelievable. Nobody acts without orders from above, especially not in the German Army. American officers were often encouraged to take the initiative in a tough spot, but German officers were raised on the Fuhrer principle... you don't say "boo" unless you get orders from above. No matter what. A big part of the reason the Normandy invasion succeeded was the Fuhrer principle; Hitler was asleep and nobody dared to wake him up to tell him about the invasion. Consequently, no reinforcements were moved up for a counterattack until it was too late. It's how they operated. A renegade in the German Army was inconceivable.

"I do not know if he has authority for this," Lieutenant Schmidt said. "I do not think he cares about authority or orders. I told you, he is a madman, a crazy man. I think he lost his mind and fights his own war now."

"What about this asylum you mentioned?" Captain Powell asked.

"Yes. It is a place close to here, hidden back in the forest. It was a castle many years ago, for a local baron. A brutal man, Baron Caern, famous for the tortures he inflicted on his captives. His family died out a few hundred years ago. Then it was the asylum. It has been rebuilt and added to many times over the years. I have been there once myself, many years ago. Kleg is there. He tells me this is where he comes from."

The Captain and I traded a look. Wherever Kleg was, our captured troopers were. And maybe, just maybe, if we got to them quickly enough, we could save them from a fate worse than death.

Andrew C. Piazza

25

"No, sir, I think this Commander Kleg may very well be a renegade," Captain Powell said into the receiver of his telephone. He'd been relaying intelligence back to Regiment ever since we finished up with Schmidt. "It's a place called Dom Caern."

All big manor houses or estates were preceded with the abbreviation 'Dom.' on our maps. I didn't much like the sound of Dom Caern. It sounded too much like the old word for 'tomb'.

"Yes, sir, Major Hayward and the civilian prisoner were held there. Hayward. The British paratrooper, sir. He confirms what the Wehrmacht commanding officer told us about its location... back an old logging trail about a kilometer or two, in the middle of the forest. Perfect, secluded spot to hide."

I watched him listen to the receiver for a while, and then spent a few minutes scrounging up a cup of coffee in the kitchen of the house we'd made into our CP. As always, the coffee was so boiling hot I had to inhale tiny sips off its surface in order to get it down. It took forever to drink it that way, but amazingly enough, there wasn't a thousand things for me to do just then. In fact, there was a nice, pleasant lull. The Captain and I were the only ones in the kitchen. Well, the only soldiers; as was becoming her habit, Rebecca was less than ten feet away from the Captain. She was dead asleep sitting on a chair in the corner, her head leaned up against the wall. I envied her.

Captain Powell finally said his last "Yes, sirs" about halfway through my molten cup of coffee and hung up his phone. I planted myself across from him at the table and handed him a cup of coffee for himself.

"Let me guess," I said. "We're attacking."

Captain Powell shook his head. "No, actually we aren't."

"No kidding? Are you sure they knew which unit they were talking to?"

The brass had a bad habit of sending us on attack after attack without a rest, especially lately. It was getting to be a bad joke… "Unless you guys hear otherwise, once we're done attacking, we'll be attacking."

"I was starting to wonder," the Captain said. "But really, the orders are, hold in place. A bunch of brass are coming up to see the massacre site, along with some intelligence specialist."

"Intelligence specialist," I said. Our "intelligence specialists" had missed warning us about one of the biggest offensives launched by Germany in the West… whoops, sorry guys, don't know how that one got past us.

"Oh, yes. All the way from Paris, no less. He'll be here by this evening."

"That fast? He'll really be hauling ass. Sir."

"That he will, Sarge," Captain Powell said. "Seems like we've stirred up a hornet's nest here."

"Yes, sir. I don't mind telling you, Captain, I'll be glad when they're long gone and we can get back to our war. Nothing grinds the gears like a staff officer."

"Mmm," was all the Captain said. I'd never heard him speak negatively about another officer unless he didn't have a choice in the matter.

Things got quiet, then. Like I said before, I have a problem with quiet times, so I nodded toward Rebecca's sleeping form and said, "You've made a new friend, I see."

Captain Powell looked over his shoulder at her and smiled. "I suppose I have."

"She's really taken to you."

"Hmm. Well, I'm one of the few people she knows who speaks her language."

"She speaks English, Captain. Some."

"Oh, I know, but hearing your own language in a room full of foreigners is like being in a strange town and seeing a familiar face. It's something to cling to. Now, my French isn't very good, but it's all she's got, with the exception of Major Hayward."

I nodded. "And I guess he reminds her of when they were at Dom Caern."

"That's pretty sharp of you, Sarge. I think you're right. I think they share a bond from enduring that experience together, but I also think the awful memories brought up by each other's company keeps them... distant."

I thought about that for a while. "Shorty said something about her going upstairs while you were in the bathtub?"

"Oh, yes. That. She wanted to make sure I was taking care of myself and not trying to get any work done. You know, make sure I ate, shaved, rested. She said she came directly from you, the... I think the phrase means 'den mother'."

"Den mother?" I said. "Fantastic. My reputation is officially shot."

"I think she meant it affectionately. And like I said, I think she wanted to hear a little of her own language, find a little comfort there."

I thought about how she had fled from Kleg's charcoal painting of The Geist and his murderous followers. She deserved all the comfort she could get.

"So, I told her she had to sit with her back to me, and we talked as best as I could." He dug out his pocket watch and checked the time.

"What's with that watch?" I asked.

"This? This is... my father gave this to me," Captain Powell said, looking at its face as if it were a photograph of his dad. "Right before I left for OCS."

"Your dad is an Army officer too?"

"My father? No, no. No, I am the only person in my family to go Army. The first Powell in the military."

"That's the military's loss. We could use some more Powells."

He smiled distantly. "Well. My father is a banker. Has been as long as I can remember. He didn't understand why I volunteered. Tried to talk me out of it. Tried to bribe me to stay home. And, in the end, he gave me this watch, and I keep it to remind me of the world I knew before all of this."

I decided I could use one of those watches. "Is that what you and Rebecca talked about?"

"What we did before the war? Yes, that was some of it. She was in school to become a nurse. The war interrupted her studies."

"Pretty thoughtless of Adolf to do that."

"She seemed to think so. I agreed."

"What about you, sir?" I asked. "What did you do before the war?"

I suddenly felt like I was trespassing on forbidden ground. Captain Powell never talked about himself, not the real, private stuff that makes us who we are, and I had always accepted that. Most officers were like that, tight-lipped about their personal lives, but it was especially strong with the Captain. I felt like I'd gone too far.

"You go first," he said.

I shrugged, glad to get off so easily. "Bartender."

"Really?" He sounded genuinely surprised.

"Mmm-hmm," I said. "Tended bar in Allentown, Pennsylvania."

"I never would've figured that," he said. He stole a glance over at Rebecca dozing in her chair. "You're married, aren't you, Harry?"

"Yes, sir. Four years."

"Four years." He said those words like he was tasting them as they came out of his mouth. "What's her name? Your wife."

"Kathleen. I call her Kate."

"Kate." Again he seemed to savor the word. "If...if you don't mind my asking..."

He squirmed in his chair a bit, and I have to admit, I didn't like seeing him that way. Captain Powell was supposed to be infallible, unstoppable, in control, on top of things... he always was. So seeing him squirm made *me* squirm.

"Anything, Captain. Go ahead." I said it mostly to end his fidgeting and thusly mine.

He seemed to consider his question carefully. "What is it that you miss the most about her?"

I blew out a long breath. "I don't know. Everything. You can't pick out one thing. There's so much."

The Captain thought that over. I looked at him and thought, what the hell, he's opening up to me, I might as well open up to him.

"I think of her when it gets rough. Thoughts of her... well, I guess they're like your pocket watch. They remind me of home. I concentrate hard enough, and I can feel the warmth of her skin, smell her hair, hear her voice. It feels like home."

The Captain looked embarrassed to have asked. "Thank you, Sergeant."

"Nah, it's nothing," I said. I was suddenly desperate to break the tension. "We met at the bar."

"Oh, yeah?" he said. "What caught your eye?"

I couldn't help a little grin. "Truthfully?"

"Of course."

I shrugged, as if to say, you asked for it. "She has... very large breasts."

Captain Powell stared at me for a second, then suddenly broke out into a surprised laugh. "Really?"

"Oh, yeah," I said. "We're talking enormous."

"Is she... a big girl?"

"No, no, that's just it. She's a tiny thing. But she's got these huge bazooms, and the first time I saw her, I thought 'Holy Cow!' and I knew I had to meet her."

Now we were both laughing and giggling like misbehaving schoolboys.

"I...I guess so," Captain Powell said, at a loss for words. "You're a... you're a lucky man, Sarge."

"Don't I know it. Of course, there's more than that, you know. She's an incredible woman. But I learned all that later. At first it was just Ka-Pow!"

More giggles, fueled by too much coffee and too little sleep, and there was something self-generating about it that made me keep going. "I'm telling you. She puts her bras out on the clothesline, and it's like putting the sails up on a ship. Those babies catch the wind and it's bye-bye to the entire line of clothes."

Captain Powell snickered again, looking around to make sure we weren't waking Rebecca up, and finally waved me off to say he couldn't take any more. "That's something else, Sarge."

"What about you, sir? You have a girl back home?"

The smile drained out of his face and he looked into his cup. "No. No, I never really had much luck with women."

That surprised me. "Really? I don't see why not. You're a good looking guy... for an officer."

He gave me a Kiss My Ass smile. "Thanks so much. I just... I don't know. They don't seem to take to me."

I felt like a jerk for bringing it up. It's never good to have to listen to someone admit a weakness in any aspect of their lives, particularly romance.

"Pennsylvania, hunh?" he said.

"Yep." I couldn't help sounding relieved.

"I was born and raised in Chicago," Captain Powell said. "You wanted to know what I did before the war? Meat inspector. I was a meat inspector. Went from plant to plant, checking sanitary conditions."

He shook his head, as if he didn't believe it himself. "I think back to those days, and it doesn't even seem like it was me doing it. It seems like somebody else's life."

"Was it a good job?" It was all I could think of to ask.

"It was a meaningless job," Captain Powell said. "Utterly meaningless."

"What do you mean?" I asked. "Meaningless? You were watching out for the public's health, right? That's not meaningless."

He snorted and shook his head. "You know what bothers me most about this war, Harry?"

"Sir?"

"It bothers me that I think I'm starting to feel at home here. Oh, not the killing, I'll never be truly used to that. Jaded to it, maybe, but I'll never get used to ordering the deaths of my men, or the enemy, or seeing people get torn up and used up and thrown away. I'll never miss that. But I will miss making a difference."

He met my gaze, and his eyes looked sad. "You see, back home, I show up for work, it's just another day. If I don't show up, nothing happens. If I don't do a good job, nobody knows it. I'm so removed from the consequences of my actions that my actions become meaningless. I quit? So what? A new guy will be there in less than a week, and nothing changes. I can't make a difference."

"But here... here I make a difference. Every day. Every day, I matter. What I do matters. If I screw up, men die. I do my job right, maybe I can save some lives. Maybe I can rescue or liberate civilians like Rebecca. People back home talk about war being unreal, but they're wrong. This is the true reality. What we do here is real, it matters, it makes a difference. Our actions have true consequences. Back home, what did I do? I stumbled through work, and the toughest choice I had to make was what to have for dinner. But here..."

He shook his head. "I knew it even then. Couple of years back, an old friend of mine gets back from Africa, telling war stories, and I thought My God, what a life. You know? It was terrible stories, men dying, but at the same time, you could see that this man had done something with his life. I stumble through life back home, and when I die, what do they say about me? He showed up for work? If I die over here, I'm a hero. I did something worthwhile with my life. So I joined up. Went Airborne. Volunteered for it all."

"I look at this," he said, holding up his pocket watch, "and I don't think of how much I miss home. I think of that other, useless life, and how I dread going back to it. Back home, I'm a useless man who has no luck with women. Here I can liberate towns and flirt with a beautiful woman while I sit in a bathtub. And that's what scares me. Because if I dread the end of the war... what kind of a man does that make me?"

I tried to think of something to say, but I couldn't. There are times when I look back on that conversation and think of a million things I could've told him... about how there was no shame in taking pride in a noble effort, about how we all felt at least a little bit the way he did, about how he always seemed to do the right thing regardless of his fears of becoming a monster. I could've told him how it was noble, not savage, to be at his best when times were at their worst.

The sad truth was, he *didn't* belong in a meat packing plant, checking off lines on a clipboard. He belonged here, in the worst of it, because that was where he was at his best, and better than any other. And I could see why he didn't want to go back to feeling like another cog in the machine. Here, he was at his peak. Where could he possibly go from here but down?

I couldn't think of anything to say at that moment, though. I was just a worn-out twenty-seven year old sergeant, so I tapped out a cigarette and lit it. Suddenly, I realized my reprieve.

"Smoke, Captain?"

"Mmm. Don't smoke."

"I didn't think so," I said. "What was that, then, with those guys from A Company and Lieutenant Schmidt?"

He seemed to think back to remember what I was talking about. "Oh, that. People who smoke share this certain… bond, I suppose. For whatever reason, two men sharing a cigarette break become instant friends. And a light; forget it, you give a smoker in need a light, we're talking friends for life. I don't smoke, but sometimes, I need to create that camaraderie quickly. I don't have the luxury of building it up through time. So with A Company, I wasn't some stranger of an officer spouting off nonsense. I was one of them, one of their kind, at least a little bit, so I could at least get them to listen with half an ear."

"And Schmidt?"

"Schmidt? Have you ever run out of cigarettes, Sergeant?" he asked. "We needed to get him to start talking to us, in English, so he couldn't use ignorance as an excuse or use an interpreter to slow down the interrogation and let him take control of it. The cigarette was a focal point for that."

He had become much more animated and the melancholy drained out of his face. This was what he needed; to talk about something other than himself, to get back into being The Captain rather than plain old vulnerable Jim Powell.

Rebecca stirred and made a little noise. She opened her eyes suddenly and straightened up with a start, as if surprised to discover she had fallen asleep in a chair. Captain Powell cracked an amused grin at her, and she smiled shyly back at him while she rubbed at her eyes.

When I saw him look at her, I realized that what he really needed was time alone with this wonderful, charming woman, and see for himself that there was more to life than leading men in a righteous cause. With her, he might see how a lot could be said for a simple life full of simple pleasures, like warm food and charming company and sitting in a chair at the end of a long day.

"Well," I announced, grunting my way out of my chair and to my feet, "I think it's my turn for the bathtub."

"Don't forget to dry your feet thoroughly before putting your boots back on," Captain Powell said, and then I knew he would be okay. He and Rebecca were chatting and laughing before I reached the top of the stairs.

On the line, a smiling woman is powerful magic.

Andrew C. Piazza

26

God! I could write a thousand books about that bath. The only bathing I'd had for nearly a month had been what we called a whore's bath... face, armpits, crotch, feet... out of a helmet with barely melted snow. Even those were few and far between.

We would get so filthy we'd have to scrape the dirt off with knives or our fingernails. It always felt to me like there was an itchy layer of slime coating my body; you can never truly relax when you're covered in filth for weeks on end. Your body rebels against it, insists you get clean. You're constantly rubbing and scratching and shifting about, trying to shake off that feeling of something crawling all over you that isn't really there.

And it wasn't just getting clean. This bath was warm. Hell, it was hot, but I didn't care. I would've climbed in if it had been boiling. It felt like, for the first time in recent history, I was finally able to get warm, through and through. Standing near the kitchen stove got my skin or clothes or outstretched hands warm, but the hot bath warmed my entire body all the way down to the marrow. It was like re-setting the clocks, re-charging the batteries, winding the odometer back to zero. In a war zone, smiling women are strong magic, and you can add hot baths to that list.

My internal Guilty Pleasure clock was starting to remind me not to hog up the bathtub for too long when a knock at the door confirmed it. Cappy was up next, and it's a further testament to a hot bath's magic that we laughed and joked amicably as I got dressed and he changed out the water. He even let me eat a few of the canned cherries he'd found during the firefight. I whistled my way down the steps once I was dressed, clean and shaved and feeling like a new man.

There was one small side effect. When you're wound tight for as long as we were, once your body feels like it can relax, it goes all the way, trying to make up for lost time, I guess. You can't ease down just a bit; you end up nose-diving into fatigue. When we were off the line, I swear I could sleep for twenty hours a day.

In this case, the bath warming my bones also apparently signaled a sudden, undeniable need for sleep. My eyelids drooped and once shut, I actually had to concentrate to open them. I've mentioned before about crashing during a lull. Well, now I had no firefight to keep me from passing out.

I looked around the kitchen and spotted the chair Rebecca had fallen asleep in. Neither she nor the Captain were in sight, and I told myself to take a seat until this spell of fatigue passed. I gave Mike Wilcox, the radio operator sitting at the table, a smile and a nod, sat in the chair, and leaned back against the wall.

That chair must've had some special sleep-inducing qualities, because like Rebecca before me, I was out before I knew it. The last thing I remembered was thinking *I'll just shut my eyes for a second*, and the next thing I knew, I was dreaming.

The thing is, I never dream. Some people nod off for five minutes and can tell you in intricate detail what they dreamt about. Not me. But there, in that chair, I had a hell of a dream.

The kid, the young German painter we'd killed only a few hours ago, was drawing his charcoal drawing of the Crucifixion. He sang softly while he did it, and I recognized the song as one that Kate used to sing as she hung clothes on the line. He seemed content and I was happy to see him content and engaged in doing what he loved, in doing something for which he had a real talent.

Then, a thick, black cloud began to fill the room behind him. He didn't notice it at first; I cried out for him to watch out, danger was in that cloud, death was in there, but I couldn't make a sound. Finally, he turned and saw the dark mist behind him. His face clouded over with fear, but instead of running, he turned back to his work, singing and drawing more insistently now. It was as if he thought he could escape the black cloud by ignoring it, by singing loudly enough to chase his fear away. It wasn't working; I could hear the strain in his voice and see it in his arm as he scrawled stiffly.

I tried again to shout a warning, but it was too late. A burst of automatic gunfire spat out of the cloud, and a pair of slugs punched through the boy's back and out of his stomach, blowing bits of intestine against the wall.

He fell to the ground, on his back, and now it was a replay of this morning's events. The boy cried and sobbed as he tried to stuff himself back together again.

Out of the mist stepped an SS stormtrooper. He was enormous, nearly seven feet tall, and his face was a skull with glowing green eyes. His black uniform was spotless, perfectly creased and tailored. He walked over to the boy, dropping an automatic rifle to the floor with a clatter as he did so.

The boy trembled with terror as the stormtrooper approached, staring at him with wide eyes, but there was no escape. The skeletal SS trooper reached into the boy's belly, pulled out a handful of the boy's intestines in one gloved hand, and raised it to his mouth. My entire body shuddered as he bit a piece out of them with jaws full of sharp fangs.

The boy began to scream, then, and Kleg... I somehow knew it was Kleg... wiped the handful of bloody guts along the wall like it was a sponge and he was trying to wash away the Crucifixion drawing with it. He turned to look at me with his glowing eyes, and blood dripped from his jaws as he hissed, *"Befolgen sie den Geist."*

I woke with a sudden start and a sharp inhale. Somebody laughed, and I realized why they had when I nearly sucked a cigarette in along with my quick intake of air.

The daze of just waking up kept me from figuring anything out for a second, and I must've looked quite a sight, coming awake quickly and then batting at my mouth, which inexplicably had a cigarette in it. *What the hell?* I thought, pulling the cigarette out and looking at it, and Rebecca giggled again at me.

"Your men play joke on you when you sleep," she said.

I put the cigarette back in my mouth and lit it. "My men play *bad* joke on me," I said, making a mental note to track down the joker who stuck a smoke in my mouth while I was out cold.

Something was off. I couldn't tell what at first; there was a little more activity in the kitchen than usual, soldiers bustling around on one errand or another. That wasn't it, though. I'd given up on figuring it out when I checked my watch and almost jumped out of my chair in surprise.

It was seven o'clock at night. The sun had set some time ago, and most of the light in the kitchen came from a few makeshift lamps constructed of metal canteens filled with gasoline and stoppered with a rag for a wick. They sent up greasy smoke that seemed to coat the lungs, but at least it wasn't the pitch-blackness of a foxhole in the woods.

My first thought was, *Get those lights out before the Krauts see them!*, but the windows were already covered with blankets. Then, I tried to count back and calculate how many hours I'd slept. There wasn't much point; I had no idea what time it had been when I'd fallen asleep. But it was longer than it should've been, I knew that.

Lieutenant Tedeski wandered into the kitchen, carrying a metal cup that I suspected was filled with something more potent than coffee. He winked and raised his cup in salute when he saw me. "So you finally decided to smoke that thing in your mouth, hunh?"

"Very funny," I said around the cigarette in question. "Was it you?"

"No, no," he said. "I don't know anything about it. I always let sleeping dogs lie."

I rubbed my hand over my face to remind myself I was awake and groaned my way to my feet. "What's going on?"

Tedeski snorted once. "Damn brass showed up. Must've really hauled ass to get here this quick. They brought some intel guy with them... Major Webster or Wilcox or some damn thing... who's apparently an expert on being an asshole. There's a big meeting brewing down at the church. I figured I'd have a little refreshment before enduring that shit." He waved with his cup to punctuate what his idea of "refreshment" was.

I nodded and looked over at Rebecca. "I'm surprised you're not with the Captain."

She shrugged. "I want to see you wake up with cigarette in your mouth."

"Oh, that's very nice of you," I said, without any real malice, of course. "Well, come on, let's go. Wait… the church? Where are the prisoners?"

"Marched off," Tedeski said into his cup. "Except their CO. Sprecht."

"Schmidt," I corrected, collecting my weapon and checking it.

"Schmidt," he said, muzzle still deep in his cup.

He followed Rebecca and I out of the kitchen and into the frozen air outside. I didn't need waking up now; the cold was like a slap in the face. Shorty trotted past on some errand or other and I waved him down.

"Hide that meatchopper and whatever other heavy weapons you can," I whispered to him. "You know how the brass likes to commandeer anything decent we scrounge up."

He nodded and started off into the snowflakes that had started to twirl their way out of the sky. "Where are you going?" he asked.

"To the church."

"Confessing your sins?" he said with a grin, and that grin made him Number One on my Joker Suspicion list.

"If you were the comedian with the cigarette trick," I shouted after him, "you're going to need the last rites!"

Andrew C. Piazza

27

"You're not… you're not thinking of having us go back there?"

It was Major Hayward who spoke; he said it as Tedeski and I entered the church with Rebecca in tow. He looked entirely different than a few hours ago. Somebody had brought him a British Army officer's uniform and now he looked more in place chatting with Monty at a dinner party in London rather than freezing his ass off in the Ardennes.

There was more brass in the church than I'd seen since our billets in England before Normandy. Colonel Davis, our Regimental commander, who never came this far front, sat front and center in the pews. An assortment of officers from Division and even further back toward Paris were clustered around him. I tried to pick out the Major…Wheatland or whatever his name was… who was supposed to be the intelligence 'expert', but it was impossible to tell. They all looked the same; clean uniforms, shaved faces, and serious expressions to hide their clueless minds.

"Yes, Major, that is…" Colonel Davis began to respond, when the clomp of Rebecca's boots echoing in the hollow air of the church announced our arrival. He turned, looked right past me, and said, "Captain Powell, who is this civilian?"

Captain Powell stood with Major Hayward on the pulpit, next to a large map resting on an easel. "Colonel, this is Rebecca Mampel, the civilian we found during our attack on this town. She was held prisoner along with Major Hayward by the SS unit who hit us last night."

"And she and Major Hayward are the only survivors of the group?" someone in the front pew asked. To my surprise, he wore a British Army uniform... presumably the source of Major Hayward's new outfit.

"As far as we know of," Captain Powell said.

"There were six others in that truck with us," Major Hayward added. "I personally saw three shot down by the SS."

"And the others may also have been shot or fallen prey to the other gruesome fate you've described to us," the British officer said. "How many prisoners would you say the SS... erm... went through... before you escaped?"

"It's difficult to say," Major Hayward answered. "Some may have simply been transferred. Perhaps as many as thirty or forty, at the rate of two or three a day."

The brass collectively rustled like wheat agitated in the wind, and the British officer spoke for them when he said, "Revolting. Absolutely revolting. I think you see now, Major, why the Americans are anxious to try to retrieve their men."

Major Hayward nodded his acquiescence to that point. "And I think you'll understand then, Colonel, my reluctance to return. Besides, there are other considerations. An attack on Kleg and the SS at Dom Caern will almost certainly claim more lives than it saves."

"I don't leave my men behind, Major," Captain Powell said. "Not to that. Not if I can do something about it. You ask any man under my command, he will be in favor of going to get our boys back. Whatever the cost."

I had to agree. As terrifying as the prospect of taking on Kleg was, I couldn't imagine leaving our guys to be served up to that fate. It simply wasn't an option.

"I understand that," Major Hayward said, "but I believe an aerial assault with heavy bombers, decimating the area, will create the least amount of casualties and perhaps even afford the American prisoners a better chance of survival than an attack with infantry. The SS might simply execute the prisoners as soon as they are attacked. This..."

"Bombing is not an option," one of the majors sitting in the second row of pews said. "You were told this the first time you asked. Nothing's changed."

"With all due respect, Major, I insist…"

"Major Hayward, you forget yourself," the British officer said sternly. "This is an American unit and an American operation; therefore, you are in a position to insist nothing. Since you are the only one here who has seen Dom Caern, you will accompany Captain Powell… *but only as an advisor.* Do you understand?"

"Yes, sir. I apologize, of course," Major Hayward said.

I found myself wondering if this was the same Major Hayward we'd picked up in the woods, the one so stubbornly polite that he would rather freeze to death than ask for a blanket. Now, he was demanding drastic measures from an Army not his own, insisting on courses of action, stepping far beyond his bounds. It was like he was another person.

And why obliterate a target with heavy bombers before you even knew what was there? If Kleg didn't happen to be at Dom Caern when we bombed it, it would just be a waste of ordinance… plus, we would no longer know which rock Kleg would scurry under next.

And heavy bombing, this close to our lines? The word 'risky' doesn't quite cover it. Heavy bombing isn't a surgical tool; our own troops could easily catch hell if those bombers were off by just a little. Whatever Hayward had seen at Dom Caern had sure put the fear of God into him.

"Bombing could never have been an option, John," the American major who had spoken earlier said, ignoring the way Major Hayward bristled at the informal use of his first name. "There are other concerns than the prisoners."

"Other concerns?" Captain Powell asked. It almost sounded like a challenge.

"Captain Powell, this is Major Paul Wexler," Colonel Davis introduced. "He is also going to accompany you."

"In what capacity?" Captain Powell asked.

Colonel Davis looked uncomfortable with what he was about to say. "He will have authority over this operation."

Captain Powell seemed confused. "I thought 2nd Battalion's CO was Lieutenant Colonel…"

"Major Wexler is not the CO of 2nd Battalion."

"3rd Battalion is a bit far away to shuffle them…" Captain Powell began, but Colonel Davis cut him off once more.

"He is not the commander of 3rd Battalion either."

I thought I detected a hollow note in the Captain's voice when he spoke next. "Am I being relieved of command?"

"No, no, Jim, on the contrary. We all recognize your value as a combat officer, and completely approve of your extraordinary efforts to attempt to rescue the prisoners with an attack on this town. Especially after what your unit endured last night."

"So… what, then?"

Colonel Davis settled into a posture common to brass officers, the Now Hear This or This Is How It Will Be posture they always assumed before laying it all out for those of us under their command. "You are to evacuate those wounded or unable to travel to 2nd Battalion's aid station. They will be reassigned to that unit permanently."

I could see the jaw muscles flex on the Captain's face. It's a bad idea to split up guys who have fought alongside each other; both tactically and in terms of morale.

"You will take command of 1st Battalion. As soon as some of the smoke clears and I can get the paperwork done, you'll be Major Powell. 1st Battalion will be taken out of the lines and will temporarily be acting as an independent unit for the course of this operation. Said operation will be under the direct authority of Major Wexler. You've got 1st Battalion, Jim, but Wexler here runs the show on this operation. You're on loan to Army Intelligence. Questions?"

"What is the operation, sir?" Captain Powell asked.

"Go to Dom Caern and subdue any German presence there. Get our guys back if you can. Hold until Major Wexler completes his investigation."

"Investigation? Investigation of what?"

"That's need to know, Captain."

Captain Powell frowned. "Sir, I strongly suggest we take 2nd Battalion along with us, with the additional support of Tedeski's TDs and any other armor we can scare up. The number of the enemy…"

"Should not be a problem," Major Wexler said. He was of medium height and thin build, and had a habit of pushing his glasses up on his nose and raking a hand through his dark hair with the same motion. "You aren't the only ones to be hit by Kleg. It appears he uses Dom Caern as a supply depot and leaves it for days at a time. Intelligence suggests there will be a minimal German presence there."

"Does it?" Captain Powell's deadpan expression belied his doubt.

"Is there a problem?" Major Wexler asked.

Captain Powell stood stock-still, as if in a parade inspection. He was obviously holding his tongue.

"You may speak freely, Captain."

"With all due respect to the major," Captain Powell said, "Intelligence suggested there would be a minimal German presence in the Ardennes forest this winter. And yet, here we are, in the middle of the biggest battle this Army has ever fought."

"Captain, there is no need for talk like that…" the Colonel began, but Wexler stopped him.

"No, no. He's right. We dropped the ball on that one over at SHAEF. Maybe it will comfort the Captain to know that I was not assigned to decoding and troop movements, but to weapons development."

"Weapons?" Captain Powell asked, trading a look with me. "Including small arms?"

"Yes."

"Maybe you can shed a little light on something for us," he said, gesturing for me to come forward.

I stepped up to Wexler's side, carrying one of the automatic rifles the SS had been armed with the night before. The Captain had asked me earlier to keep one handy so we could report it, and Wexler nodded with an "Ah," as if he had been expecting to see it.

"Yes. *Sturmgewehr*," he said, taking it away from me and looking it over.

"Sir?" I asked.

"*Sturmgewehr*, Sergeant, it means 'assault rifle'," Wexler said to me. "Hitler's pet name for it. Cross between a battle rifle and a submachine-gun. Uses light rifle rounds for range and impact, but has the magazine capacity and rapid-fire capability of a submachine-gun. We've been encountering them up and down the line. Excellent weapons, but there's too few of them and they are too scattered around to be a real threat."

"Major," Captain Powell said, "Kleg's entire battalion is armed with those weapons."

"Really?" Wexler seemed a little taken aback. "No wonder your A Company was run over like that."

"That, and they could see in the dark," I muttered. I didn't really intend Wexler to hear it, but he did.

"What was that?"

I cleared my throat, cursing my big mouth. Even in Basic, I'd had trouble learning to shut up and keep quiet when the brass were yapping. "Sorry, sir. Um... something one of our wounded said before he died... that it seemed like they could see in the dark. They ran over that area with fifteen or more panzers, a heavily forested area, like it was broad daylight. They found every foxhole, every slit trench, no matter how well concealed. No way they should've been able to do that."

"Yes, well," Colonel Davis said, "I'm sure you'll find a way to deal with that, won't you, Captain Powell?"

"I can handle anything the 101st asks of me, Colonel."

"That's why you're the man for the job," the Colonel continued, while I retreated back towards the church's smashed doors to stand next to Tedeski. "Besides, like Major Wexler said, you shouldn't hit too much resistance, just a garrison. If you get stuck, call for reinforcements, and we'll see what we can do."

Tedeski snorted derisively into his noxious cup, a bit too loudly for his own good. The Colonel turned in his pew and spotted him.

"Ah, yes, Lieutenant. I'd almost forgotten you."

"Shit," Tedeski muttered under his breath. It looked like he and I shared a bad habit concerning big mouths.

"You're to rejoin your unit and await further assignment," Colonel Davis ordered.

"Sir, if it's all the same to you," Tedeski said, "I'd like to stick with Captain Powell here. He's a good commander to work for and he could sure use the support of my rigs if he has to take on that Kleg guy's swarm of panzers."

"I'm sure Captain Powell appreciates the sentiment, but it's out of my hands," Colonel Davis said. "I spoke to your CO, Lieutenant. Apparently you've been missing from your unit for some time. He was quite interested in your whereabouts."

The skin on Tedeski's forehead drew back in alarm. I almost laughed at the reaction; it was nearly identical to how my eight-year-old nephew reacted when he was caught with his hand in the cookie jar.

"Yeah, well, you know how it is, sir," he mumbled uncomfortably. "Fog of war and all that. Easy to get turned around and lost on these roads."

"I'm sure your CO will want to hear all about it," Colonel Davis said. "Now, if that's all…"

"Not quite," Major Wexler said. "I'll need to take this German lieutenant… Schmidt? He seems to know a bit about the area and we can always use another interpreter."

Colonel Davis shrugged. "I don't see how that could be a problem."

"I'll also need the Belgian woman."

Captain Powell straightened up in shock. "Absolutely not!"

"Surely," Major Hayward broke in quickly, "surely the major does not suggest we take a civilian along on a combat mission?"

"I tend to agree," Colonel Davis began, and Wexler nodded his head.

"I understand your reluctance. But I need her. She's been to Dom Caern, and she may know something…"

"What?" Captain Powell demanded. "Just what is it that you think she can tell you, Major? She was a prisoner. She can maybe tell you about the cell she was in, that's about it."

"Major…"

"Colonel, you know the priority my mission has been given," Major Wexler said, pushing his glasses into place and raking his hand through his hair again. "The information this woman can offer, no matter how inconsequential it might seem, could prove vital to my success."

Colonel Davis fidgeted in his seat for a bit, then finally nodded. "You've got it."

"Sir, you can't be serious…" Captain Powell protested.

"I am deadly serious, Captain! We all have our orders to follow and you will carry out yours or be relieved of command. Am I clear?"

Captain Powell looked like he wanted to spit nails. "Yes, sir."

"Then there it is. You're going to Dom Caern, and the prisoner and the civilian are going with you."

"Harry?" Rebecca whispered, pulling on my sleeve. "What are they saying about me?"

"It's not good, kiddo," I said. "Not good at all."

28

Within moments after the meeting ended, Major Hayward, Captain Powell, Tedeski, Rebecca, and I, all stomped our way through the dark and snowy streets toward our CP. Tedeski summed all of our thoughts up with two words.

"Fucking unbelievable!"

"I... must go back to... that place?" Rebecca asked. Her voice trembled a bit; I noticed she couldn't even say the name of the horror house from which she'd escaped.

"No," the Captain said abruptly, bringing us all to a halt.

"Sir," I said, "you were ordered..."

"To hell with those orders."

"Yeah!" Tedeski said, taking a big swig out of his cup. "Now we're talking!"

"What did you have in mind, Captain?" Major Hayward asked.

"Tedeski, you've been ordered back to your unit."

Tedeski shrugged. "Yeah, but with these roads, you can never tell where you're going to end up."

"Well, wherever you go, you take Rebecca with you."

"Captain," Tedeski said, "where I'm going... it might be just as bad or worse than Dom Caern."

"I doubt that very much," Major Hayward said.

"Wherever you end up going, first you stop in a rearward area," Captain Powell explained. "An aid station, Red Cross, something."

"I will go," Rebecca said, almost as a whisper. She sounded like she was volunteering for a suicide mission. "I will go back to the manor with you."

"Absolutely not," the Captain said.

"You don't want me with you?" Rebecca asked.

The Captain looked a little embarrassed. "Look, it's not that, it's…"

"You want to protect me from what is there."

"Yeah," he said. "I think you've seen enough of that sort of thing."

"He's right, my dear," Major Hayward added, laying a hand on her shoulder. "You've seen more than any person should have to. The important thing is to keep you safe."

She looked at the Captain. "Then how will I see you again?"

Captain Powell cleared his throat, definitely uncomfortable to be speaking so intimately in front of the rest of us. "I, uh, I'll give the… lieutenant… Tedeski here my address back home. We can contact, you know, each other after the, uh… it's over. If I can't find you sooner, that is."

"You'll be fine, dear," Major Hayward said. "Go and get your things… those blankets and what-not we found for you. We'll collect you when it's time to go."

"Okay," she said slowly, and clomped her way into the dark with many a backflung glance toward the Captain.

"Damn, you work fast," Tedeski muttered.

"Shut up."

"She has taken to you awfully quickly, sir," I added.

"And I said shut the hell up, the both of you," Captain Powell said. "And give me that cup. It's been a bear of a night."

"That it has," Tedeski agreed, handing over his cup to the Captain, who swigged the contents and nearly choked to death. "Major?"

"Yes, thank you, it has been a trying evening," Major Hayward said, taking a drink. His face and body shuddered slightly thereafter. "Yes, um… quite… potent, this is."

"Sergeant?"

"No, thank you, sir," I said. "All you officers get drunk, and then us sergeants have to run the show."

They all laughed at that, and Tedeski asked, "So, Major, you've been to Dom Caern; what's waiting for us up there?"

Major Hayward's face suddenly lost all its laughter. Looking down at the snow crushed flat beneath our feet, he said, "At the risk of sounding dramatic… there is quite a nightmare waiting in the woods for us. I hope it is asleep or unaware long enough for us to accomplish our goal and escape intact."

"Kleg," I said.

He shrugged his shoulders noncommittally.

"Yeah, well," Tedeski said, "I'd like to get a piece of that sick bastard. Show him a little about 'terror troops'."

"Just make sure Rebecca gets clear," Captain Powell said.

Tedeski saluted clumsily with his cup and tromped off into the dark, calling back to us, "Don't you worry, Captain! I could never let anything happen to a pretty gal like that!"

"Very comforting," the Captain said quietly, then he turned to me. "Well, Harry. Let's see this drawing."

"Sir?"

"The drawing you asked Schmidt about. Remember?"

For some reason, I found myself trading a look with Major Hayward. I didn't want to be in that room again; I can't explain it, I just didn't.

It took us a few minutes to get to that house and arrange blackout curtains for the windows so we could use our flashlights. As we waited in the dark for the word that the curtains were in place, I became increasingly uneasy. It felt like there were things moving in the dark; soundless, stalking, deadly, in front of me and reaching out with sharp claws toward my throat. I found myself holding my weapon at the ready position, toying with the idea of spraying a burst blindly if only to puncture the pregnant feeling the dark held.

"All clear," the word came, and I sighed in relief as the first flashlight clicked on. There were only the drawings, staring each other down from opposing ends of the room.

"This is the one from the Wehrmacht soldier, the young guy we killed today?" Captain Powell asked, looking the drawing of the Crucifixion over from only three feet away.

"Yes, sir."

"Quite impressive, isn't it?" Major Hayward asked, once again confining himself to the doorway.

"Yes, it is," the Captain said, then turned and crossed the room. "And this is Kleg's?"

"Yes, sir."

"Hmm." It sounded both pensive and dismissive. He reached out a finger to touch the swirling black cloud. "I wonder what this…"

"Sir, don't touch…" I suddenly said, then, after another look traded with Major Hayward, I said apologetically, "I mean, you'll… the charcoal will get on your fingers."

He made a noise that was part laugh and part frown, but he drew his hand away. "Well, we wouldn't want that now, would we?"

I can't explain it. It was like before, when Shorty poked his finger at the drawing… it somehow seemed dangerous to touch it, like you might be tempting Fate or calling attention to yourself from something hideous that you would rather have shamble past you blindly. It was childish and irrational, and when Captain Powell grinned at me, I felt like a stupid little kid asking sheepishly to leave his lights on all night.

It got quiet for a bit, while the Captain studied Kleg's drawing and Major Hayward and I shifted our weight about uncomfortably. I've said before, I've never been good with quiet times.

"You did mean Kleg, right?" I asked Major Hayward, feeling even more childish once I had.

"Sergeant?"

"You know. Earlier, when you said there was a nightmare waiting for us up at Dom Caern."

"Why, whatever else could I possibly have been talking about?" he replied quietly.

His eyes never left Kleg's drawing.

29

"You're in a rather glowing mood today, Sergeant," Major Hayward told me when we moved out the next morning.

He was right. I felt positively re-born, and I told him so as we fell into the long column of troopers marching down the road towards Dom Caern.

"I've had a day's worth of sleep and warmth and hot food," I said. "At this point, I can go for months on that."

He smiled and adjusted the Sten submachine-gun he had slung over his shoulder. "Let's hope that you don't have to."

"Especially since if you're here with me, you'd have to go without as well, Major," I said with a wink.

He laughed out loud at that and I realized I wasn't the only one in a good mood. Everybody's spirits seemed to be soaring; even the weather seemed to smile on us. For the first time in I didn't know how long, the skies cleared and our fighter-bombers swarmed the skies. We could hear them pouncing on exposed German units in the distance.

"I love to hear that sound!" Shorty declared loudly to nobody in particular, when we heard the rattle and boom of their machine-guns and bombs.

It's amazing what a single day of rest can do for a beaten-up unit. And we were definitely beaten up; our "Battalion" only had enough men to staff an under-sized company, so that was how Captain Powell had organized us. What the hell. It was simpler that way anyway.

Under manned or not, we all felt like we could take on the world. Kleg and his ugly drawing were a distant memory; something laughed about in the light of dawn now that he didn't seem half the bogeyman he'd been in the dark small hours of the morning. Had I really been afraid of a silly drawing, so much so that I blurted out a warning to my CO not to touch it?

I laughed and shook off my embarrassment with a twitch of my shoulders. I didn't even think to ask Major Hayward why he had positively overloaded himself with ammunition and hand grenades… he was being prepared, that's all.

Things started turning for the worse once we left the road for the logging trail that led through the woods to Dom Caern. It started with the weather; clouds started rolling back across the sky, and by the time we were deep enough in the woods to feel like we were lost to the rest of the world, it was completely overcast.

The entire company's spirits clouded over with the sky. Shorty stopped his constant joking and kept quiet, occasionally mumbling something about how he could never catch a break. The rest of the men kept their eyes on their boots, slogging forward face down in grim silence. When it started snowing again, some of them grumbled "Swell" or "Perfect" or "Of course", but that was all anybody said.

Even the road seemed to hate us that day. We all slid and slipped and fell heavily on the icy trail. More than once we had to shove our trailing supply truck past slick spots to where it could get some traction.

The column came to a halt after one of these shoving matches. I found myself swearing bitterly, angry that I'd have to break formation and go check out whatever was holding us up. Part of me wanted to say *the hell with it, let the Captain take care of it himself*. Then I remembered the stripes on my sleeve, and I trudged off, waving for Shorty to come with me, and he muttered bad thoughts about me as I muttered bad thoughts about my sergeant's stripes.

The Captain caught up to us as we reached the front of the column. There, seeming to dare the snowflakes to fall on them, were the massive steel brutes of Tedeski's tank destroyers. The Lieutenant himself sat on top of his turret, chewing on a smoking stub of a cigar with his crash helmet on his head.

"Fancy meeting you here, Lieutenant," I said.

"You know, Sarge, these damn Belgian roads," he said, grinning around his cigar, "they get you all turned around until you have no idea where you're going to end up. Where's Wexler?"

"We stuck him in the rear of the column," I said.

"Good. He belongs in the ass end of things," Tedeski said.

"Did you get Rebecca to an aid station?" Captain Powell asked.

His answer came in the metallic clang of a TD's hatch slamming open. Rebecca's head popped out, covered in a GI issue tank crash helmet with straps dangling. "Bonjour, Jiim," she said with a wave.

It would've been comical in another place and another time. As it was, Captain Powell clenched his fists at his side and gritted through his teeth. "Tedeski…"

"Hey, it's not my fault," Tedeski said quickly, holding his hands up in surrender. "I got her in the TD and took off with her last night… you saw me do it. But then she refuses to get out. She knows I'm meeting back up with you and she won't budge from the TD no matter what I say. She acts like she doesn't understand what I'm saying, and I don't know what to do, so I try to trick her. I tell her we have to fix the engines, that she needs to get out so we can do that, and then I try to take off once she goes out into the trees to whiz."

"Then I turn around an hour later and there she is on the rear of the hull. She sneaked up on us when I wasn't watching and climbed on before we could leave. So what could I do?"

"She shouldn't goddamn be here," the Captain said. "Get those TDs warmed up and move out. Sergeant, get the men moving once the TDs aren't holding us up any more."

"Yes, sir," I said, as the Captain stormed back down the road toward the middle of the column.

"Jeez, what's his problem?" Tedeski asked, as I got men to help guide his TD crews forward.

"She shouldn't be here, Lieutenant," I said.

"Yeah, no kidding, Sarge. She shouldn't have been in the middle of that firefight in the town, either, but she was there, wasn't she?"

Even in my foul mood, I could see he had a point. "Look, it's a bad time for this, okay? Everybody's skirts are kind of in a bunch right now."

"Yeah, I noticed," Tedeski said.

"Harry, are you angry?" Rebecca asked, once I got her down from the TD she'd been zipped up in.

"This isn't a good place for you, Rebecca," I said, then added to Tedeski, "I'm going to put a squad or two in front of your TDs to check for mines or infantry waiting in ambush. Leave the meatchopper to fall back toward the rear… we'll put her in that."

"All right," he said, then added before he climbed back in, "It wasn't my fault."

"Yeah," I nodded, and looking at her, I knew it really wasn't. In her own way, she was as unstoppable a force as the early Nazi blitzkriegs.

Still, it was a complication that would have to be dealt with, so I sent Shorty to tell the Captain where she was and then I fell in with the two squads from 1st Platoon that I sent ahead of the TDs. Part of it was simply taking personal responsibility for protecting our armor. Most of it was keeping myself away from the Captain while he smoldered in rage over Tedeski's foul-up.

To my surprise, Major Hayward came up to join me. Maybe it was that he'd run out of familiar faces and wanted to stick close to somebody he knew; in any case, it wasn't any place for a major to be.

"Sir, you shouldn't be this far forward," I said.

"Oh, don't worry about me, Sergeant," he replied. "I've seen a tiny smidgen of action in my time, and should be able to leap into the ditch quickly enough if there's trouble."

It didn't take a genius to figure out he was being modest. If he'd been at Arnhem Bridge, then he'd seen about as much action as any man could handle. Besides, he had a certain calming effect; I felt more at ease with him nearby. So I figured, let him stay.

"I understand our young friend Rebecca has re-joined us," he said conversationally, his eyes never leaving the trees.

"Yep," I answered.

"Strong-willed woman." I couldn't tell if it was a statement, a description, or a condemnation.

"Yes, she is," I agreed.

"Seems to be very taken with your Captain."

"Yeah, I don't really understand that."

"Sergeant?"

"Not that she'd be interested in the Captain," I said. "But they've only spent… what… an afternoon and an evening together? Awfully soon for her to get attached, isn't it?"

He smiled and looked down at my left hand, where my wedding ring was hidden by my gloves. "You're married, correct, Sergeant?"

"Yes, sir."

"Yes. And how long after you met your wife before you wanted to spend every waking moment with her?"

"Long time," I said. "About thirty seconds."

He laughed at that. "It was approximately the same for me with my Janet. Love doesn't make much sense, Sergeant; it's one of the more wonderful things about it. Besides which, they're good for each other; just what the other needs, I'd say."

We left it at that and continued our march toward Dom Caern. A hundred yards behind us, the tank destroyers rumbled and clanked along the narrow road. Snow fell in huge flakes, somersaulting through the air to pile on top of each other, and I started to think that if it snowed long enough, it could bury the war and all of the shit that went with it. So I prayed for it to snow even harder.

It got so still and so quiet that it took me a second or two to react when somebody at the front of our spearhead force shouted "Cover!" and everybody dove into the ditch at the left side of the trail. When I finally did scramble to the ground, fumbling with my weapon, I nearly landed on Major Hayward.

"Sorry, Major," I mumbled, then shouted out, "What is it?"

I recognized Pelosi's voice floating back toward me from about twenty yards ahead. "Don't know yet, Sarge."

Nothing was readily apparent as a threat. Straight ahead was only the thin, narrow ribbon of trail winding through the suffocating, swallowing mass of trees. The tall pines were so close together they were like tunnel walls blocking us in. To the sides, the thick pine boughs concealed anything past the first row of trees.

"Shall we have a look?" Major Hayward asked, his Sten submachine-gun at the ready.

"Well, I guess we have to," I grumbled, and started crawling forward along the ditch. We'd made it about halfway when Pelosi and two other troopers suddenly shouldered their rifles and aimed them into the trees about twenty yards ahead on the right side of the trail.

"What is it?" I whispered loudly.

"Heard something," he whispered back. "In the trees."

I traded a look with Major Hayward and we both readied our weapons as well. The pines were an impenetrable mass of dark green and white, but I stared into them all the same, as if I could peer through them if I stared hard enough.

My mind started to fill in the quiet time with wild speculative images of what was out there. First it was Kleg and his SS troopers, waiting in ambush for us with all of those terrible panzers hidden out of sight in the trees. I could practically feel the muzzles of their cannons pointed at my heart.

Then, I started to think about Kleg's drawing, and I imagined a vast, dark shape amongst the pines, rolling and shifting like water boiling in a pot. It slid between the tree trunks toward us, only occasionally bumping a branch to betray its presence.

A sudden snap of a twig crackled as loud as a gunshot in the still woods. My hands began to sweat inside of my gloves. Whatever it was, it was coming toward us, coming toward the road.

"Hold your fire until they see us," I whispered, hoping that those who couldn't hear me would follow my lead. I snapped the safety off on my tommygun and tried to steady my elbows on the edge of the ditch.

Come on, come out, come out and show yourself, you son of a bitch, I thought, but I didn't know if I was talking to Kleg or to the image in his drawing. As soon as I thought it, I wanted to take it back, I wanted it all to go away and stay quiet so nobody else I knew got killed… especially me.

Things happened quickly. The boughs at the edge of the road rustled and snow fell from them. Everybody shifted their weapons slightly to correct their aim, and our bodies tensed in preparation for the fight. A brown blur erupted from the trees at a leap, and I nearly fired before I realized it was just a deer and not my nightmares come to life.

"Oh, for Christ's sake," Pelosi muttered, as we all dragged ourselves to our feet. "A fucking deer?"

"Well, how's that for action for you, Major?" I said, shaking my head at my own foolishness.

"Sergeant... look," he said, pointing toward the deer.

It still stood trembling in the center of the road, even though a dozen armed men were within ten yards of it. It seemed frozen with terror, then broke the spell by looking back over its shoulder, back along the trail in the direction we were headed. Then at us. Then back down the trail.

Suddenly, it bolted forward, straight at us, and it surprised a few troopers enough that they jumped back into the ditch to get out of the way of a hundred and twenty pound animal's hooves. The terrified deer sprinted right past Major Hayward and I, past the second squad I had in front of the TDs, and around the first tank destroyer and out of sight along the road. I found out later that it ran down the entire length of the column, sometimes coming so close to a trooper that the man had to dodge aside to avoid being run down.

We all watched it run its madhouse dash with our jaws hanging open. I couldn't imagine what could've gotten into that creature to make it run the entire length of a company of infantry rather than go back the way it had come.

It was quiet, and my over-active imagination answered that question for me. *Kleg is up that road.*

I frowned. That was stupid thinking. A deer doesn't know one man from another. It runs from all of them. The idea that it would be more fearful of Kleg and the SS than us was absurd. Believe me, it wasn't any safer around us... we shot as many deer as we could in the Ardennes to supplement our chow line. The only reason we hadn't shot this one was sheer surprise. So it wasn't that it was afraid of Kleg.

My Quiet Time voice wasn't done yet, though.

Kleg isn't the only thing up that road.

I thought back to that black cloud Kleg had drawn, and when I saw Major Hayward staring at the trail leading to Dom Caern, I realized he looked the same as he had when he'd stared at the charcoal drawing. Kleg had called it The Geist, The Ghost, and I suddenly felt the need to say something to shatter the silence before my Quiet Time thoughts got the better of me.

"How about that, hunh, Major?" I said, shivering in the cold to mask my shaking voice. "Damnedest thing I've ever seen."

"Not for me," Major Hayward said quietly.

His watchful eyes never left the road.

30

The snowing got worse as we went, until it seemed to fill the air like sawdust in a mill, clogging our lungs and blinding our eyes. Something was seriously wrong. We should've been able to march to Dom Caern within an hour or less, if Schmidt's report was correct. Instead, we'd been on the road twice that long, lost in our tunnel through the tall pines, and still there was no sign of the manor house.

I had just decided to head back and talk to the Captain about this when we heard the shots. They came from up ahead, rapid-fire bursts from a burp gun or maybe one of those *Sturmgewehr* rifles Major Wexler had identified for us.

Not again, I thought. *Not again, not so soon.* I had just started getting used to feeling like a human being again. Now the last day's worth of normal living felt like a last gasp of fresh air before I plunged deep into darkness. Kleg was up ahead. Kleg and war and death.

It didn't take long for the Captain to show up, with Major Wexler tagging along like a lost puppy. "What is it, Sarge?"

"Don't know yet, sir. Should I move a squad up and take a peek?"

He nodded. "Very well. Watch yourself. Stay out of sight until we can move up the TDs and heavy weapons."

"Don't worry about that," I muttered, looking around for those I wanted to take with me. "Shorty. Cappy. Davey and Goliath. Wayne, you come up as assistant bazooka man for Shorty."

"I'll tag along, Sergeant," Major Hayward announced.

"Not a good idea, sir," I said, and Major Wexler agreed with me.

"You're along as an advisor, Major. I can't risk you getting killed when you're the only soldier we've got who's been inside of Dom Caern."

"Oh, not to worry, Major Wexler," Major Hayward said. "I promise to run away at top speed if we run into the slightest bit of trouble."

He didn't look like he was going to take no for an answer, so I shrugged and said, "Okay, Major, but you stick close to me. Let's go, gentlemen."

Shorty muttered something about always being first in line for everything except chow, but he fell into formation with the others on the road. Wayne didn't look too happy about coming along, either. Those I hadn't picked had that Better You Than Me sort of look on their faces.

"Okay," I said, "we go through the trees, stay off the road and out of sight. Keep your eyes and ears open, and be sure not to bump the snow off of the boughs."

"Once you spot them, contact me by radio," Captain Powell said.

"Should… do you think I should go along as well?" Major Wexler asked nervously. He sounded like he was terrified I'd say yes.

"Not unless you want to get shot, sir. We'll take care of it," I said, and led my little group into the pines.

Once again, it was like being in a jungle, an impossible fantasy of a jungle where the canopy was covered in snow and there wasn't a single bird chirping or insect buzzing. The only sound aside from our heavy breaths streaming through the air and boots crunching through the snow was the irregular crackle of spread-out, erratic gunshots. It didn't sound like a fight; it sounded more like a couple of drunks shooting at tin cans for kicks.

All the same, my heart began a wild staccato beat in my chest, so hard and fast it rustled my wool overcoat. I hated the not knowing, the quiet times when anything could be waiting for you around the corner or in the dark or just past those trees. I wished I could push aside the heavy pines like a thick curtain, just a bit, so I could spy on whatever was making all the noise.

Instead, I was entombed in a green and white coffin that seemed to swallow all sound. My only point of reference for navigating was the gunfire. Visibility was nil... ten feet in any direction maximum.

We could disappear into these woods. The entire company could disappear, and nobody would ever find our bodies, I thought. *You could walk within ten feet of an army and never know it. Anyone or anything could hide forever out here.*

Our little scouting party trudged along, constantly crouched over to avoid knocking the snow off a low-hanging branch and getting us all killed. The gunfire got closer and closer, and the safety of the rest of our company got further and further away, when Davey suddenly brought us to a halt.

I took a look around, wondering how far away the road was and how long it would take for help to arrive. "Davey?"

He was out in front and waved me forward.

"What is it?" I asked.

"Trees end right there," he said, nodding in front of me. Not ten yards away, the last row of trees stood before the forest ended abruptly in a clearing. A careless person would be almost out of the woods and exposed before they even knew it.

"Nice and easy," I whispered, and gestured for the others to lower themselves to the ground.

We belly-crawled the rest of the way, right to the tree line, just far enough to look out into the massive clearing before us. I had to fight the urge to run out into the open; the weight of the woods around me created a crushing claustrophobia that was almost unbearable. If I were in the open, I could be seen, but at least nothing could creep up on me.

"Shit! Tiger tank," Davey whispered, pointing.

It was hard to see due to all of the falling snow, but about two hundred yards away I could barely make out the black outlines of the biggest goddamn tank I'd ever seen. It was one of the King Tiger tank monstrosities we feared so much... seventy tons' worth of war machine, twice as large as our Sherman tanks, and almost invulnerable to our weapons. Bazooka rounds bounced off, leaving a little divot in the hull, and its cannon was big enough to wipe out anything on the battlefield.

Beyond the King Tiger, a vague shadow was all that was evident of Dom Caern. All I could tell was it was big and it was a building; the rest was lost to the swirling snow.

Another burst of gunfire drew my attention away from the tank and the manor house. A group of SS troopers, maybe eight or ten of them, rushed out into the swirling snow and spread out on our side of the Tiger tank. They held their weapons at the ready and looked to be falling back from something; they kept looking around the massive hull of the tank, back toward the hulking shape of the manor house.

They didn't act like stormtroopers. They yelled at each other, in voices that I could tell were strained with terror even at this distance. Occasionally, one of them would fire a burst from their rifle toward the manor house, which would spark angry shouts from some of the other soldiers. Two of them argued over a hand grenade, one of them obviously wanting to throw it and the other insisting he not throw it.

"What the hell are they doing?" Shorty whispered. "It looks like they've gone nuts."

"Or maybe they're drunk," Goliath added.

A sudden explosion threw a cloud of white over the two arguers, and they both fell screaming to the snow. The one had apparently dropped the grenade, and its explosion set off a sudden wave of panicked gunfire. One SS trooper shot up the two wounded arguers, maybe thinking that the shrapnel thrown at him was a murder attempt. Two other troopers cut him down once he fired. Another two killed that pair, and suddenly, it turned into a massive murder-suicide pact, with all of the SS cutting each other down before they even knew why, knowing only that the rules of war had changed and now demanded killing their own.

It was all over pretty quickly. Eight torn bodies lay in the red-spattered snow, and a ninth SS trooper limped away from the scene of the massacre. He came straight at us, dragging his rifle behind him, and even from as far away as we were, we could hear him crying hysterically.

"Sarge," Cappy said lowly, already drawing a bead on the wounded SS through his telescopic sight.

"Hold your fire, Cappy," I whispered. The SS hadn't seen us, and I didn't want to give away our position yet... especially as bizarre as the situation was and with a seventy-ton King Tiger tank within view.

About twenty yards away from us, the limping SS trooper stopped and turned to face the manor house. His sobs were mixed with bursts of unintelligible German, and inexplicably, he raised his rifle and emptied it in a long burst towards the manor house. After the weapon went dry, he threw it back the way he came, screaming at the dark shape of Dom Caern.

I glanced over at Major Hayward, who whispered, "Leave me alone," as the translation.

"Sarge," Cappy hissed, and the SS trooper spun toward us.

"Hold your fire!" I said, drawing a bead on the SS now that we were spotted. Maybe we could order him to keep quiet and surrender, and maybe with the snow we could escape detection from the other SS garrisoned in the manor. The big King Tiger tank hadn't moved at all during all the madness, so hopefully it was empty and not a threat.

The SS trooper looked at us and laughed, dropping to his knees and spreading his arms wide. He said something to us as he began to open his tunic to expose his chest. That was when I realized—none of them had been wearing overcoats. They had run outside, into subfreezing temperatures, in no more than pants and tunic.

"He's asking for us to shoot him," Major Hayward translated.

"I say we oblige him," Cappy said, settling behind his rifle.

"Hold it, Cappy," I said. "Look at him!"

He'd obviously lost it. Blood from the wound in his leg stained the snow at his side, but he was oblivious to it, holding open his shirt with both hands and sobbing and laughing at the same time. He'd lost his helmet, and his blonde hair whipped wildly in the wind, lending him even more of a crazed appearance. He shouted more German at us, shaking his head and weeping.

"What's he saying?" I asked.

"Something about..." Major Hayward said, pausing, whether because of the difficulty of the translation or an aversion to translate it, I couldn't tell. "Something about it doesn't matter, it's all over anyway."

The SS shouted something that sounded like "Alles kaput!" at the sky, and fell forward to his hands and knees, shaking his head. One of his hands snaked back to his boot, and came back with a potato-masher grenade.

"Shit!" I cursed, aiming quickly and putting my finger on the trigger. I'd been so overwhelmed by the strangeness of the situation, I'd forgotten the Germans often kept grenades stored sticking out of the tops of their boots.

"Wait!" Major Hayward hissed loudly, and to my surprise, none of my boys fired.

The SS trooper pulled the pin on the grenade, still laughing and sobbing, and holding it to his chest, he pitched forward face-first into the snow. I had enough time to blink my eyes and wonder if he'd really done that before a muffled explosion lifted the SS trooper's body slightly and blew clouds of snow out from his sides.

"No fucking shit," Shorty whispered.

We sat there in the swirling silence and stared, none of us believing what we'd just seen. Nine SS stormtroopers gone mad, racing outside into the freezing cold without overcoats, firing at nothing, losing their minds and killing each other. And the capper, the icing on this madhouse's cake, was the stormtrooper who had blown his own ribcage open in order to avoid capture.

Capture by whom? crept into my mind, but Major Hayward's hoarse whisper shook me out of my haze.

"Sergeant," he whispered, "perhaps now would be a good time for the radio."

I blinked a couple of times and stirred. "Right. Right. Um… hang on."

By some miracle, the portable radio we'd brought was working… they had a shifty record even under good conditions, and the freezing Ardennes weather made their utility almost nil. It took a few minutes for me to contact the Captain, but at last, his voice answered me from what felt like a million miles of forest away.

I relayed what we'd seen in a faltering voice. When I said the words out loud, what we'd seen sounded so… unreal, I expected the Captain to accuse me of lying.

"Are you sure the Tiger tank is unmanned?" he asked once I'd finished.

A sigh escaped me. I wanted to say, *Yes, sir, one hundred percent sure, watched the crew climb out with my own eyes*, so that we wouldn't have to go down there. My damn, dirty, interfering conscience kept me from doing that, though.

"No, sir. It probably is empty, but I'm not sure."

"All right, Harry. You'll have to check it out. Stay out of sight. If a crew is in there, take them out quietly. If not, disable the thing so we have one less panzer to worry about. Stay out of sight. We're coming up now."

"Yes, sir," I said, switching off the radio. I couldn't help feeling those orders sounded suspiciously like a death sentence.

Andrew C. Piazza

31

"Major Hayward, what's the basic layout of the outbuildings of Dom Caern?"

"Let's see," he said, then pointed to our left. "Off that way is a large outbuilding that was perhaps used as stables at some point. There is a large wooden shed near it. There is another small wooden shack on the other side of the manor; perhaps a tool shed of some sort. Not much else to speak of. Why do you ask?"

"We have to check the Tiger tank."

Scattered groans met the bad news, and part of me wanted to join in. "Hey, cool it, guys! It's heavy snowfall and shifty visibility. We move up to it fast, check it out. If there's a crew, we take them out with knives. If not, then we mess up its works so it can't come back at us."

I checked the distance between us and the tank, which now seemed to me like a sleeping dragon, before I continued. "Davey and Goliath out front. Shorty and Wayne with the bazooka. Cappy and I are rear guard."

"Don't forget me, Sergeant," Major Hayward said.

"Sir…"

"Sergeant, it will get very tiresome for the both of us if you continually try to keep me away from the action," he said. "You need every hand you can get, so let's get on with it, shall we?"

The Captain would skin me alive if anything happened to Hayward, but I couldn't waste time arguing either, so I acquiesced. "All right. We go it at a run, all the way. Any fire comes from the manor, we'll use the tank as a bunker until the rest of the company comes up. Clear?"

I got the requisite nods, and before I could stop myself, gave the word to go. Davey and Goliath charged out of the pines, tearing past the blown-apart stormtrooper, and Shorty and Wayne followed on their heels. The ends of the bazooka waved back and forth wildly as Shorty's legs churned through the snow. Then, I was off as well, sprinting breathlessly through the thick snowfall. The snow on the ground weighed me down like lead boots; it was over a foot deep and heavy with moisture. I remember my overactive mind thinking that the snow would pack into great snowballs, and I almost started giggling hysterically as I pumped my legs as quickly as I could.

Halfway there, I was sure I was going to have a heart attack. My heart beat so furiously, I thought it would tear itself apart; it seemed like it had shaken loose from its moorings and now ricocheted around my chest cavity. All the while, my eyes were on the sleeping Tiger tank, and I prayed over and over again for it to stay still and stay quiet and not move that gigantic cannon an inch toward us.

Fifty yards now, and my fears shifted from the tank to the manor house. How many of those damn MG-42 machine-guns did they have set up in the windows? A half-dozen? More? One would be enough to saw the seven of us to pieces. Visibility was poor, but an alert SS guard would be able to see running men at this distance, and it was too far from the tank to use it as cover.

Davey and Goliath reached the tank, crouching down next to it to stay out of sight from the manor house. Shorty and Wayne reached it a second later, and then it was my turn, my feelings of hate and fear of the King Tiger shifting to gratitude for the protection it afforded us from the manor house. I had to watch my step; the SS troopers' bodies were in my way, and I didn't want to trip on a dead man and go face-first into the steel hull of the tank.

While we re-grouped, Shorty set down his bazooka and recovered one of the dead SS trooper's *Sturmgewehr* rifles. It was empty; he changed its magazine and then nodded to me to indicate he was ready.

I held a finger to my lips for silence as I crept to the front of the tank. This close up, the tank itself wasn't really a threat; but somebody in the manor house… particularly a somebody behind a machine-gun…

certainly was, so I laid down and scooted around the front of the tread so I could sneak a peek of Dom Caern.

My first thought was, *That house is insane.* Not just a house for the insane, but that the building itself was insane, as if the layout of the walls themselves belied a shattered psyche dwelling within the stone.

It was much larger than I expected, more a castle than a manor house, and its architecture confirmed Lieutenant Schmidt's report that it had been built and rebuilt over the years. It looked like a clay model that the artist changed several times in mid-stream, simply slapping on extra material rather than starting over again. Asymmetry seemed its only common theme; a tower stuck here, a wing jutting out there, everything haphazard and just…wrong. It almost hurt to look at it. It disturbed the eyes the way an abstract painting sometimes will with its odd angles and incorrect proportions.

Shorty hissing "Sarge!" shook me from my observation, and I pulled myself to a crouch next to the tank. Drawing my trench knife from my boot, I waved for Shorty to do the same. He did, after a *Why me?* glance, and we crept up the side of the hull like a couple of thieves hoping to murder the dragon before it could wake.

We reached a hatch. I got a good grip on it, nodded to Shorty, and waited for him to nod back. He adjusted his grip on his trench knife, steeled himself visibly for what he was about to have to do, and nodded back.

The hatch came up. Shorty leapt into the hole. I followed in as quickly as I could, not easy because of my bigger size. I was sure I was going to get a knife in the leg or gut before I could figure out what was what in the tangle of bodies in the dark steel confines of the tank.

"Get off me, Sarge," Shorty grumbled, and I knew everything was okay.

The Tiger was empty.

"Why do you think they left it out here?" Shorty asked, sheathing his knife and poking around curiously.

"Probably broke down," I said. "These babies are a nightmare on the battlefield, but they're also a bitch to maintain. It probably broke down here and they couldn't move it."

"Yeah, check it out," he said. "They took the machine-guns off it and there's no ammo for the cannon. This sucker's a seventy-ton paperweight now."

"Go let the others know," I said, "and hand the radio in to me."

I regretted that choice as soon as Shorty climbed out. Hardly any light filtered in through the open hatch, not nearly enough to light up the entire interior of the tank, so I felt once again like I was entombed, this time in steel rather than pine. The wind howled over the open hatch and made it sound as if the dead tank was moaning out its last gasp.

The radio handset came in and I was glad for the distraction of making that piece of junk work. Captain Powell's voice was a welcome sound in that hollow metal shell.

"How'd you do, Sarge?"

"We're at an abandoned King Tiger tank about seventy yards from the manor," I said. "No sign of the other panzers. We haven't seen or heard anything other than the nine SS who killed each other."

"Roger that. We should be up on the clearing any second."

"We'll wait here and link up with your advance elements. I can't see any strongpoints from here but we'll fire on anybody who takes a shot at you," I said.

"Keep your eyes open," he said. "See you soon."

The air seemed to get stale as soon as he signed off, like there wasn't enough oxygen in the Tiger tank to sustain life. The claustrophobia came back, and I climbed out of the tank as quickly as I could squeeze through the hatch, welcoming the light caress of the falling snow on my face. Goliath helped me clamber out of the hatch and drop to the ground, and I relayed the Captain's instructions to them.

Shorty frowned at the dark gray clouds and falling snow as we waited for the Captain to come up. "This is turning into one lousy day."

"Yeah," Goliath agreed. "And it ain't over yet."

32

It only took a couple of minutes for the rest of the company to reach Dom Caern, but for the seven of us huddled behind the carcass of the abandoned Tiger tank, it was maddening. We felt like we were standing on a tiny island in the ocean, one that disappeared more and more with the tide until we were perched together on the last few feet of sand. All around us, the sea of snow swirled in the wind, hiding Kleg and his legion of panzers and covering the nine dead SS in a shallow, frozen grave.

The welcome clank of Tedeski's TDs heralded the Captain's arrival. Our troopers swarmed in little dark shapes across the snow, along the road, moving in leapfrogs toward the manor house, and still, nothing happened. As always, the quiet worked its way into my skin, until I practically begged for somebody, anybody, to shoot just to shatter the silent air into breathable pieces. It never came. A squad from 1st Platoon moved up to our King Tiger tank to set up a thirty-cal without a single shot fired at them. If there was a garrison inside the manor house, they were either napping or waiting until they could see the whites of our eyes.

"Well, Sergeant," Major Hayward said, looking toward Dom Caern, "What do you say? Shall we have a look inside?"

I stole a look myself and decided, what the hell. At least I wouldn't be sitting on my ass fidgeting in anxiety.

"All right, gentlemen," I said, pointing to some stone steps leading to a semi-circular porch. Heavy stone columns held up a roof above it, and wide double doors seemed to dare us to come inside the manor. "That's our next objective. Move fast, keep your eyes on those windows and firing slits, and anything shoots, blow it to hell. Ready?"

There were some grudging nods and grumbles, mostly from Shorty, and we lined up near the rear of the Tiger tank's hull. I waited until the thirty-cal was set up to cover our advance, and the TDs and the meatchopper half-track were within sight of the manor. Then… "Go!"

Another mad dash, this time worse than before, because now we were charging that insane house which watched us with a thousand glass eyes, any of which could spit fire and rain death upon us. My mind kept telling me to turn around, go back, this was a fool's run into a lunatic's castle, and I could only come to a madman's death like the scattered SS who were now freezing solid in the snow behind me.

The closer we got to Dom Caern, the worse the fear became, until I wanted to spray wild, panic fire at the windows like the suicidal SS had done to purge the tension from my body. It became nearly unbearable, until at last we charged up the stone steps onto the wide porch leading to the manor's double doors.

We spread out on either side of it, trying to ignore the dead SS trooper lying between the doors, half-in and half-out of the doorway. His body propped the heavy wooden doors partly open, and I angled my head so I could get a peek inside.

There wasn't much to see; a wide foyer was beyond the doors, with dark red carpeting on the marble floors and tapestries on the walls. As I looked inside, Major Hayward bent down and put a hand on the barrel of the SS trooper's rifle.

"Warm," he said. "But he hasn't been shot to death."

I followed his pointed finger and saw that one of the dead man's legs was missing just below the hip. Once I saw that, I could pick out the blood trail stretching behind him and then disappearing into the red carpeting. He'd dragged himself this far and then died, probably from blood loss.

It was definitely out of the ordinary, but we really didn't have time to sit and ponder the possibilities. Another squad moved up to the front doors with us, and the TDs were close enough to blow the hell out of anything that showed itself in the windows. It was time to go in.

"All right," I said, "guys with the automatic weapons go in first. Be ready for it to get fast and furious."

Goliath and Shorty took their place next to me nearest the doors, along with Billy Ganz from 2nd Platoon, who had one of those 'grease guns' I refused to take seriously as a weapon. Major Hayward joined us, and I didn't have the time or energy to fight him on it. The others crowded in close behind us, ready to pour in through the doors right on our heels. Hands tightened on weapons as I steeled myself for the order, then…

"Go!"

Like a shot, I was in through the doors, which two of our troopers yanked open for us. Goliath broke right, covering the wide stone stairs immediately in front of us, and I went left with Shorty, covering that side of the foyer and the doors scattered along it. There didn't seem to be any rhyme or reason to the placement of the doors; the architect seemed to have thrown darts to pick their location.

Nobody. Not a single enemy met the sudden flood of GIs swarming through the front door.

"What, are they all out pissing in the woods?" Shorty said. He wasn't quite able to hide the cracking in his voice.

"You four, cover the stairs," I said, "and you four, watch those doors on the left. Shorty, Davey and Goliath, Cappy, we're going through that door on the right."

Another squad from 1st Platoon poured through the front door and into the foyer, including Sergeant Ridley, who now commanded 1st Platoon. His former CO, Lieutenant Byatt, had been killed several weeks before by an 88 shell.

"Ridley," I said. "Leave one squad here to hold the foyer and take the rest of your platoon upstairs to clear the second floor. And watch yourself… these SS fuckers are insane. I just watched nine of them shoot each other to pieces."

He glanced up the stairs and nodded grimly, running a gloved hand over his dirty stubble. He was one of the troopers who had missed a chance at the bathtub back at the village. "You got it, Top. Hey, at least it's warm."

Once again, I'd been so pre-occupied that I didn't realize I wasn't freezing to death any more. I ordered my men to ditch their heavy overcoats in the foyer so we could move a little faster indoors. "Where's the Captain?"

"Coming up now, I think," Ridley answered, nodding back towards the double doors before charging up the stairs at the head of two squads. He was a good platoon sergeant... solid, cool under fire, and aggressive... and he was also the most rabid looter I'd ever met.

I turned, and there was Captain Powell, too far forwards as always. A half-dozen troopers crowded into the foyer behind him... I think for warmth as much as anything. I immediately sent them through the doors to the left to clear out that wing of the manor.

"Any resistance?" Captain Powell asked.

"Nothing," I said, pointing at the dead SS minus a leg still propping open the door. "Except the door stop."

"Very well. Ridley's upstairs?"

"Yes, sir. Where's Rebecca?"

"In the meatchopper outside."

"Uh," Shorty said, scratching under his helmet, gesturing towards the door, "you sure about that, sir?"

Sure enough, there she was, stepping gingerly over the mangled SS trooper's body. One grizzled GI held the door open for her and another stood guard behind her with his M1.

"Damn it, Rebecca!" the Captain snapped. "Go back! We haven't cleared it out, and you promised..."

"Is safer in here than out there!" she answered quickly, pointing outside.

"She's got a point, sir," Davey said. "All those windows..."

"Shut up, Davey," the Captain said curtly, then ground his teeth in frustration. "All right, fine. You stay here. You two," he said, pointing at the two GIs who had escorted her in, "had better not let her wander off this time, or your lives will become instant misery. Clear?"

The two grizzled GIs nodded and shuffled their feet, and Rebecca tried to come to their defense. "It is not their f..."

The Captain cut her off with a hissing sound and a cutting motion across his throat, waving us toward the doors to the right of the foyer. I don't know which we were afraid of more at that point; the crazed SS who might be hiding behind those doors, or the Captain and his Rebecca-induced fury.

"She is rather strong-willed, isn't she?" Major Hayward remarked dryly.

The Captain glared at him and started barking off orders. "Shorty, hand off that bazooka to somebody else. 3rd Platoon is clearing the outbuildings and they need it more than we do, so switch over to that *Sturmgewehr*. Goliath…"

A sound came from behind the door on our right, freezing us all for a moment. It was far off and muffled, but all the same, within an instant, all our weapons were leveled in its direction.

Dom Caern wasn't abandoned after all.

Andrew C. Piazza

33

"What is that?" Shorty whispered.

"Shh," Goliath said. "Listen."

The door was thick oak, and made the muffled sound so indistinct as to be almost unidentifiable. It sounded a little like singing.

"Open it," the Captain said. "Goliath up front, Davey by his side with a grenade. You see anything, pitch the grenade, shut the door, and blast through it."

Davey and Goliath crowded side-by-side in front of the door, and Major Hayward pulled it open for them with a yank. There was a half-second of breathless waiting, and then Goliath looked back at the Captain.

"Hallway," he said simply.

Captain Powell nodded. "Go."

Davey and Goliath stepped through the doorway, followed by Shorty and then myself. We kept close to the walls, advancing as carefully and as quietly as we could in our heavy boots.

The sound was louder now, louder and clearer. It was definitely coming from near the end of the hallway, but now I thought it might be crying rather than singing.

I remembered the suicidal SS trooper's hysteria and got a firmer grip on my weapon. "Watch those doors," I whispered, indicating the half-dozen doors scattered along either side of the hallway. "Could be someone behind those."

Davey and Goliath crowded by the first door, on the left, and Shorty and I did the same on the right. I glanced back to insure that Major

Hayward and the Captain were far enough back to be relatively safe, and then nodded to Shorty.

We kicked our door in at the same time that Davey and Goliath did theirs. Another half-second adrenaline burst as the door flew open, then an almost disappointed letdown once we saw it was only an empty study. Shelves full of books lined the walls, some of them spilled out onto the floor like forgotten coins dropped from a pocket.

We backed out of the room as Goliath and Davey came out of theirs. Goliath shook his head. Their room was empty too.

We repeated the process further down the hallway, each time expecting a burst of deadly gunfire from a black-clad SS madman. Each time, we got an empty room in some state of disarray.

The sound was coming from behind the last door on the left. Once the rest of the hallway was clear, we lined up near the door, filled with grim determination now that we knew there wasn't any place left for the enemy to be.

I took a deep breath, let it out, and nodded to Goliath. He stomp-kicked the door in, leveling his B.A.R. as it flew open. I saw his body tense and his weapon rise, dead give-aways that there was trouble. Davey shouted, "Shit!" and fired three quick shots from his carbine.

"Hold it, hold it!" Goliath said, his shoulders relaxing. "Those guys are already dead."

He stepped inside and the rest of us swarmed in to see. The room was a large banquet hall, carpeted from wall to wall with the same dark red carpeting as the rest of Dom Caern. Large candelabras were placed at regular intervals along the room, but most of the candles had been burnt down to the nub. A large grandfather clock stood halfway along the left-hand wall, riddled with bullets.

A massive wooden table stretched almost the entire length of the room. It was set for dinner; it looked like there was service for twenty or thirty people set out. Four dead men sat at random points around the table.

Three were slumped forward, their heads resting face-first on their plates. Davey had shot one of them in the neck, and blood oozed out of the wound to pitter-pat onto the carpeting. A fourth was sitting straight up, but his head still sat on his plate; it had been severed from his body and sat so it stared at us with glazed eyes.

"What the fuck?" Shorty whispered, and then a voice yelled to us from the far end of the dining hall.

It was shrill and in German, and immediately thereafter, we heard the sound that had brought us here. It was laughter.

High, harsh, uncontrolled laughter, hoarse from going on for God Knows how long. It floated to us through an open set of double doors at the far end of the dining room.

"What'd he say?" I asked.

"He said 'Come on in. The kitchen is open'," Major Hayward translated.

"Grenades?" I asked, praying to get the affirmative.

"No," the Captain said. "We need some answers. Alive, if possible."

We stalked along the length of the dining room, weapons at the ready. I couldn't help staring at the headless corpse as I went by it. The wound wasn't clean, like you might expect from an axe. Rather, it looked like the SS trooper's head had been torn off by blunt force.

I pulled my eyes away from the mutilated corpse and kept my eyes on the open doorway leading to the kitchen. As I got closer, I could see the walls and floor were white tile and there were some metal shelves along the walls. The kitchen stretched to the left of the doors, and that was where the laughing was coming from.

God, I wish the Captain had let us pitch grenades in there. They might've torn the room up enough that we wouldn't have had to have seen all that we saw all at once. It might've given our minds a few seconds to process the evil that men can do, rather than endure the tidal wave of horror that we got.

An SS trooper sat on the floor, his back propped up against the far wall. His arms lay slack at his sides, and his right hand held a bloody cleaver limply. A severed human leg, still in its black pants leg and jackboot, lay across his lap.

Blood was everywhere; streaked across the stark white tile in vast puddles, splattered on the walls, dripping off of the edges of a wooden table set toward the far end of the room. There were cuts and divets in its darkly stained wood, implying the impact of the cleaver dangling from the SS trooper's fingers. Some blood had been scrawled into foot-high letters on the walls.

"What does it say?" I asked. My throat felt like sandy floor of the Mojave desert.

"Welcome to the butcher shop," Major Hayward said, his voice choking, and then added, "that one…"

"I don't need a translation for that one," I said, staring at the words DIE GEIST IST HIER trailing streaks of blood below it.

"I have to… I have to get out of here," Major Hayward said suddenly, pushing his way past Shorty and the Captain and back into the dining room. On the way out, he bumped past a startled Major Wexler, whose jaw dropped open at the sight of the kitchen. Wexler had a small hand-held movie camera in his hand.

"Jesus wept," he whispered, eyes going wide.

"Heh, heh, heh," the SS trooper huffed out, his laughter now quiet and weak. It sounded as if he was too exhausted to continue laughing, but he did imitate Wexler as best he could. "Jesus vept."

"The jars," Davey whispered, as if he, like the rest of us, was afraid a loud noise might confirm what we wanted to be a dream as a gruesome reality. "Look at the jars."

The metal shelves were covered in jars filled with a cloudy fluid. Sealed inside each one was either a hand, a foot, or some unidentifiable internal organ.

"They canned them like those fucking cherries I found," Cappy said. It was the first time I'd heard his granite voice waver, and the first time I'd seen those perfectly still hands shake.

The SS trooper said something. His eyes lay lazily on me, and I wished he would turn those glittering blue windows to a madman's soul on someone else.

"Shorty?" I asked.

"It's… something like 'Nothing must be wasted'," Shorty answered, swallowing hard to keep from vomiting.

"Except him," Cappy said, stepping forward and raising his rifle.

"Cappy!" I shouted, pushing his rifle away. He turned back on me with a blaze of anger in his eyes, and for a second, I thought I might have to shoot him just to protect myself.

"You can't tell me he deserves to live!" Cappy snarled, but the Captain intervened before I could answer.

"He'll get what's coming to him," he said, laying a hand on Cappy's shoulder. "I promise you he will. But we need some answers first."

The muscles in Cappy's face twitched in rage, and for a second, I thought he might even go against the Captain and try to kill the maniac who lay on the floor giggling up at him. "All right. All right," he said at last, "you get that son of a bitch Kraut from the village in here, we'll get us our answers. Then we make the both of them clean this up, clean it up and bury it and then we fucking bury the both of them with it!"

"You'll do nothing of the sort!" Wexler said. "These men are prisoners of war, Private! There are laws against that sort of thing!"

"It sounded like a good idea to me," Shorty muttered.

"Both of you, cool it," I said. "It's like the Captain said, this guy is the only witness we've got to what happened here."

A thump from behind a small rectangular metal door cut me off. We whirled on the sound, weapons raised, each of us wondering if we'd really heard it or not.

"What was that?" Wexler whispered.

"Whatever it is, it's in the icebox," I said, nodding to the four-foot square metal door set in the right-hand wall. The SS trooper looked at it and his eyes got wide as he laughed in a parody of an *Ooo, I'm in trouble now!* expression.

"Open it," Captain Powell ordered, covering the icebox door with his tommygun. "Shorty? Open it."

Shorty only took enough time to groan before stepping next to the icebox door. Laying a hand on the metal handle, he took a deep breath and pulled it open.

I couldn't see inside due to his body blocking my view, but I could hear the horror in his voice. "Oh, my God. My God. Medic! MEDIC!"

34

His name was Corporal Freddie Howard, and he'd been a member of Major Carey's Battalion HQ staff when the SS had come calling two nights before. I knew him, a little bit; knew that he had played minor league baseball and was hoping to find a spot in the majors when he got back home. During a quiet time before our drop on Holland, he'd scrounged up a baseball from God knows where and I helped him find a bat-sized stick, and the next thing we knew, we had a pick-up game on our hands. The day had been cool and clear, and like the breakfast walk through the village with Rebecca the day before, that game was one of those few and far-between beautiful moments that I kept close to my heart to carry me through the dark times.

That beautiful moment became a twisted nightmare when I saw them pull Freddie out of the icebox. What the SS had done was bad enough; when it stood in stark contrast next to the memory of Freddie laughing as he pitched inning after inning on that clear, bright day, the evil that men did tore a hole through the center of my soul.

"H-help me, help me," he stammered as they dragged him out, ice and snow spilling in a cascade out of the metal box he'd been entombed in. "Puh-please, please…"

"You're okay, you're okay," Shorty said quickly, but he sounded like he was crying while he said it. "You're going to be fine… Medic! Where's that fucking medic?"

"Shorty, what is it?" the Captain asked. "Step out of the way so we can see…"

Then, Shorty did step aside enough so that we could see, and I wish he hadn't. I wished I'd been killed in action the day before so I didn't have to see what they'd done.

"My arm," Freddie mumbled, or at least, what was left of him. "M-my arm, make sure my arm stays cold."

They'd taken his legs and his right arm off. He clawed at the floor with his left, trying to pull himself around so he could reach back into the icebox. I could see his other arm inside, sitting on the ice and snow, partly wrapped in plain brown paper.

"They might... they might be able to re-attach it if it's cold, right?" he said, shivering uncontrollably. He was trying to cry, too, and when he looked at me, I almost wished he hadn't been able to recognize me. "Harry? Harry? Help me, okay? My arm..."

"Yeah, Freddie, you'll be okay," I said quickly, kneeling down on the floor next to him. Shorty scooted out of the way to give me room, wiping at his eyes with his sleeve.

"My arm..."

"We'll take care of it," I said, picking him up a bit so I could rest his head on my lap. I'm ashamed to say it, but I was revolted to touch him. He looked wrong, incorrect, like a carnival attraction meant to scare children. I hated myself for feeling that way, but deep down inside, I cringed at his touch.

"We'll get your arm back, you'll be fine," I choked off, trying to keep my voice calm to keep him calm. "Medic's on the way. You'll be back on the mound in no time, Freddie."

"How could they possibly..." Wexler said, shuddering visibly. "This is impossible. Impossible. How could he survive..."

"Could you shut up, please, sir?" Shorty demanded angrily, facing away from the rest of us.

"What?" Wexler said, when a sudden scream rebounded off of the kitchen walls.

It was Rebecca, standing ghost-white in the kitchen doorway, face frozen into a scream. Her eyes darted around the room, as if they couldn't take enough of the horrors in at once, and then she bolted out into the dining room and out of sight.

"What the fuck..." the Captain began to roar, when one of the two GIs assigned to watch her broke in.

"Somebody called for a medic and she said she was a nurse..." he said quickly, perhaps thinking the Captain might kill him before he could plead his case.

"Out! Out!" Captain Powell demanded, storming out of the room in search of Rebecca. He bumped shoulders hard with Wexler as he went, snarling, "Aren't you glad we brought her along, *sir*?"

"I didn't know she was..." Wexler began to protest, but the Captain was already gone. In his place, a pair of our medics rushed in, hustling me out of the way and immediately administering morphine to Freddie.

I sat there in the red-streaked ice and snow now melting on the white tile, clenching and unclenching my fists in rage and terror and sorrow. Freddie started crying again as they carried him out the door, and my traitorous mind suggested he'd have been better off if we'd shot him the moment we found him.

Thunderclaps roared in the narrow confines of the room, rattling my bones and setting my nerves sparking with adrenaline. I put my head in my hands. I didn't need to look to know that we'd just killed the SS trooper lying on the floor.

"God damn it! God *damn* it!" Wexler roared, as the familiar smell of cordite stung my nostrils. "Sergeant! Sergeant!"

I pulled myself to my feet and my tired and teary eyes picked out Wexler, red-faced and furious, standing toe-to-toe with Shorty and Cappy. Smoke still curled lazily from the barrels of their weapons.

"Sergeant, arrest these men immediately! They just murdered this prisoner!" Wexler shouted, pointing down at the SS. Sure enough, he had four holes punched through his chest, and his once-glittering, insane eyes now stared sightlessly into nowhere. I shuddered when I saw he was still smiling.

"He went for that cleaver, sir," Shorty said evenly.

"Bullshit! That is a lie and you know it!" Wexler said. "I want these two arrested, now!"

"Better make it three," Davey said, stepping up next to his two comrades. "The only reason I didn't do it is they beat me to it."

"Then you'd better make it four," Goliath added in his smooth baritone, taking his place with his buddies. He dwarfed Wexler, who got even redder than before.

"All right, gentlemen," he said. "You want to play tough guys? You can play tough guys in the damn *stockade!*"

"Major," I said, intending to soothe his ruffled feathers, but he wouldn't be soothed.

"No. No!" he said, whirling on me. "These men are all arrested, now, or you can join them, Sergeant!"

For an instant, I closed my eyes and saw what I wanted to do. In my mind, I stepped forward and knocked Wexler out with one shot to the jaw and said, "Fine. I'll join them, *sir.*"

Then, my eyes opened and I did what was smart rather than what I wanted. "I'll take care of it, sir. But first..."

"First, nothing! I want..."

"Sir, please," I insisted. "With all due respect, perhaps we should go ask Freddie what happened here while he can still answer us."

That slowed him up. "Freddie?"

"The soldier we just found, sir," I explained, nodding toward the still-open icebox door.

Wexler thought about it for a second and then nodded. "Fine. Fine. But these men will be dealt with!"

"Yes, sir," I said, and watched him storm out of the room.

After he'd left, the four of them met my gaze with cold stares. I knew what they were asking with those looks... are you with us, or against us?

"You got a problem with this, Sarge?" Shorty asked, his voice still even and neutral.

I looked down at the SS that he and Cappy had shot and I felt nothing. Part of me... a big part... was glad they'd done what they'd done. After seeing Freddie, another part wished I'd have done it myself.

My stripes didn't afford me the luxury of giving in to such impulses, though. "You should've waited until after we interrogated him," I said, and left to find Wexler.

35

They had Freddie on a table in the book-strewn study which Shorty and I had cleared only minutes before. I think the idea was to keep him out of sight, but if it was, it hadn't worked. The room was practically overflowing, and the hallway was full of curious troopers trying to catch a glimpse.

Captain Powell and Major Wexler were in there, along with Major Hayward and Sergeant Ridley from 1st Platoon. To my surprise, so was Rebecca, helping two of our medics minister to Freddie's needs.

Is she okay? I mouthed to the Captain, and he shrugged.

"She used to be a nurse, remember?" he said lowly, once I worked my way around to him. "I think she was overwhelmed at first, but now she seems to be fine."

"I thought you said her studies were interrupted?" I asked quietly, but apparently Rebecca heard me, because she answered.

"What I do not learn in school I learn living in a war zone for four years," she said, her eyes never leaving her work. She was inspecting the wound where the SS had taken Freddie's arm off.

"Why do this?" Wexler asked. "Carve him up and keep him alive?"

"Keep the meat fresh as long as possible," Major Hayward answered dryly. He seemed much more composed than before, but his face still looked pale and clammy. "They wouldn't want it to spoil now, would they?"

Wexler frowned, then worked his way through the crowd of bodies to get closer to the table. "What happened here, Corporal?"

What the fuck does it look like, shitheel? I wanted to say, but I kept myself from saying it by asking Sergeant Ridley, "Any other prisoners?"

He shook his head. "All dead," he answered, and I couldn't tell by his eyes if they were that way before or after he'd found them. I didn't really care at that point.

"How many?" the Captain asked.

"Six or eight," Ridley answered. "Some of them really torn up. Bastards really went wacko, hunh?"

I nodded. "Looks that way."

He didn't seem able to take his eyes off Freddie, who didn't answer Wexler's question, but wept quietly. "Serves them right."

Wexler gave up and turned back to us. "It's no good. He's had too much morphine. Did he say anything to you guys before he went out like this?" he asked the medics.

"Yes," Rebecca said. She continued inspecting what was left of Freddie's right arm.

"Well?" Wexler asked. "What was it?"

"He said, 'Don't let it get me'," she answered, finally looking up.

"It?" Wexler said.

"Let's give these people some room to work, gentlemen," Captain Powell said, leading us toward the door.

"Excellent idea," Major Hayward agreed.

Unfortunately, Shorty and the others were in the hallway, and seeing them set Wexler off again. "There they are! Captain, these four men are under arrest for murder!"

Captain Powell looked at me, and I explained, "Cappy and Shorty shot the SS guy with the cleaver. They say self-defense."

"Which is a lie," Wexler said. "I saw the whole thing. He didn't..."

A potentially ugly scene was saved by the arrival of a runner from 3rd Platoon. "Captain... Sergeant Lambourne says he found something you gotta see."

"Hold on, Major," Captain Powell said, holding up a hand to hold off Wexler. "What is it, Private?"

"Biggest goddamn ammo dump you ever seen, begging your pardon, sir."

My bones protested against the idea of going out into the cold and the snow and the wind, especially now that they were warm and comfortable inside Dom Caern's walls. I obliged them for a few moments by lingering with Shorty while the Captain and Wexler headed off with 3rd Platoon's runner.

"Found these, Sarge," Shorty said, handing me a handful of metal shards that clinked together on the end of their chains. Dog tags.

"How many?" I asked.

"Seven. Eight, if you count Freddie."

"I don't. Not yet."

Shorty shrugged. "There going to be trouble with that egg-headed asshole?"

"I don't know yet. He's pretty hot for you. Do me a favor and stay scarce for a little while, okay?"

"No problem," he said, leading the rest of his merry men back toward the foyer. "We'll get familiar with the place."

There wasn't really any excuse to stay inside and stay warm any longer, so I sighed and held my overcoat around me tightly as I went for the front door. Troopers were milling around all over the place, most of them smoking, and seeing them made me want a cigarette desperately.

I promised myself one soon and hunched low as I stepped out of the main entrance, as if that might protect me from the cold. As always, the wind bit straight through every layer of clothing I owned, and I felt as if I had dived into a freezing pool of water. The snow stung my eyes, and I had to hood my helmet with my hand to see any further than two feet in front of me.

I followed the fading tracks of the Captain, past the dead Tiger tank and toward a large outbuilding set about two hundred yards from the manor house. Tedeski surprised the hell out of me by popping out of the silent panzer's hatch and waving me over.

"Hey, Sarge!" he called out around the stub of cigar permanently clamped between his teeth. "Check it out!"

He climbed out of the hatch, and was followed by Major Wexler, who was nodding his head in satisfaction. He looked like he'd just solved a particularly challenging crossword puzzle.

"Well, I think we've solved the mystery of your SS who can 'see in the dark', Sergeant," he said, as I climbed up the side of the tank.

"Sir?"

"Some sort of see-in-the-dark night vision do-hickey," Tedeski explained. "Built into the tank. See?"

He pointed out where this equipment was, but the knobs and levers of the tank made about as much sense to me as an airplane's console. "And that can see in the dark?"

"Apparently," Wexler answered. "It's still very experimental, but it looks as though the Germans have got a prototype available."

It should've made me feel better, now that the mystery was explained and Kleg wasn't a super-human bogeyman anymore, but it didn't. If every vehicle in his column was outfitted with a device like that… well, it was no wonder A company had been massacred. It was one more reason to fear the night.

"What's this about an arsenal?" I asked, shivering in the wind now that I was standing still.

"Oh, yeah," Tedeski said. "You gotta see this."

36

As much as I hate to admit it, it looked like Wexler had been right about Kleg. My best estimation was that he'd left twenty men... all currently deceased... behind to watch Dom Caern, and then set out to go hunting. The estate was his supply depot, and this outbuilding, a huge set of stables, was the arsenal.

It was packed, wall to wall, floor to ceiling, with every form of German weapon and ammunition imaginable. Rifles... both the *Sturmgewehrs* the SS carried and some bolt-action Karabiners like the regular Wehrmacht used... and Schmeisser submachine-guns, Panzerfausts, MG-42 machine-guns, tank shells, self-propelled artillery shells, grenades, mines, everything. It was incredible, preposterous; the entire German Army was tightening its belts all along the line, and Kleg had enough ammunition to keep a unit ten times his size in business for weeks.

"Somethin', hunh?" Tedeski said. "Wish I had this much shit for my rigs. Shoot all day long and never put a dent in my ammo supply."

"Where'd he get all this?" I asked, staring around at all the boxes stacked upon boxes stacked upon boxes.

"That's the question," Wexler said, then added, "Ah," as the Captain arrived with Lieutenant Schmidt in tow. "Maybe he knows."

"Unbelievable," Schmidt wondered aloud, as he walked past the rows of boxes towards us. "Where does he get all this?"

"Or maybe not," Tedeski grunted.

"He must've stockpiled it," Wexler said, looking it all over.

"This much?" the Captain said. "And with all of the activity around here?"

"Perhaps he steals it," Lieutenant Schmidt said. "He goes to a supply area in the rear and loads up his trucks without authority for this and comes back."

"How could you possibly get away with that?" Wexler said, pushing his glasses up on his nose and raking a hand through his hair.

"How do I get away with going wherever I want to go and doing whatever I want to do?" Tedeski answered, punctuating it with a broad grin. "Fog of war, my man, all kinds of things can happen."

"Hmm. Well, it's interesting, but it's not why we're here," Wexler said, dismissing it all with a wave of his hand.

Captain Powell shot me a look. "Why are we here, Major?"

Wexler shook his head. "I'm sorry, Captain, I can't discuss that. But I will need Lieutenant Schmidt here and a few of your men to help me search the manor."

"Search it for what?" the Captain asked.

"I... again, I can't tell you much," Wexler said. "Just don't let your men destroy anything, especially documents."

"My men aren't in the habit of destroying things for the hell of it," Captain Powell said.

"Aren't they?" Wexler said. "I think they've proved otherwise."

"What happened?" Tedeski said.

"We found an SS trooper who'd carved up one of our guys," I explained. "Had him stored in an ice box... still alive. He's got no legs and only one arm now."

"Fuckin' A," Tedeski spat out in horror and revulsion.

"Couple of our guys shot the SS."

"Fuckin' A," Tedeski said, nodding in approval.

"It's a war crime, Lieutenant," Wexler said. "Those men must be arrested."

"Hey, news flash, Major," Tedeski said around his cigar, "war *is* a crime. Welcome to the harsh part of reality."

"That's not..." Wexler began, but Tedeski cut him off.

"Sir, do you really want to press this matter? Do you really want every man in this outfit hating your guts when they're the only thing keeping Kleg from turning you into... what was his name?"

"Freddie," I answered.

"...keeping Kleg from turning *you* into Freddie?" Tedeski finished.

Wexler seemed to give up on us and he turned instead to Lieutenant Schmidt. "Lieutenant, I assure you, this crime will not..."

"I have heard of no crime here," Schmidt said simply.

"But..."

"If this man, this SS, did what the sergeant says," Schmidt explained, nodding toward me, "then I am glad he is dead and no longer disgraces the German Army."

Wexler looked like he wanted to pop. There are few things in life more vexing than finding nobody has an ounce of interest in your crusade. Some people feed off being an outsider, though, and I hoped Wexler wasn't one of them.

"Life on the front takes a lot of getting used to," Captain Powell said. "It took me a long time and a lot of stumbling, and I'm still not used to it."

The last part was mostly lie... I couldn't remember the Captain ever having been clumsy at his job... but it seemed to agree with Wexler a little bit. "Well. We'll deal with it later, when it's a more appropriate time," he said. "For now, let's get on with the mission."

"Very good, sir," the Captain said, and we headed back out into the snow to trudge our way back to the manor.

"Sergeant," Lieutenant Schmidt asked, hunching his shoulders against the snow as he fell into step next to me, "is it true?"

"Sir?" I asked.

"What you said about the SS... did he mutilate this man and put him still alive into an ice box?"

I nodded. "I'm afraid so, sir."

He sighed heavily and kept his head down, whether from shame or to keep the swirling snow from his eyes, I couldn't tell. "Horrible. So horrible. Even when I was here, years ago, none of my patients were so twisted as to do this."

I stopped short in surprise. I'd forgotten that he'd mentioned this earlier. "S... you were here? As a..."

"I was a psychiatrist before the war," he explained. "I did some training here, many years ago, while Dom Caern was still an asylum. The manor looks very different from my memory of it, though."

We began walking toward the manor again. "Sir, if you're a psychiatrist..."

"Why am I in the infantry?" he finished with a smile. "I think you know why. This army, the German army, has been fighting so long, there are not enough strong young men left for the infantry. So the Army takes everybody; old men, like myself..." he grinned, "...and young men, too, very young."

"Like your painter," I said, thinking about the magnificent Crucifixion drawing and how we'd torn apart its creator.

"Yes," he said sadly, and shook his head. "I tell you honestly, Sergeant... after seeing so many young men die, on both sides, I am glad the war is over for me."

It was hard to hate guys like Schmidt. There were plenty of German officers who were easy to hate; arrogant bastards who sneered down their noses at you even though you'd just kicked the tar out of them. There was this one German colonel who told Cappy he refused to be taken prisoner by anyone other than an officer. Cappy shrugged and stabbed him in the throat with his trench knife. I had to chew him out for it, but inside, I remember wishing I had that kind of icy fortitude... or maybe plain old abandon.

But Schmidt.... Schmidt was another story. He was too much like the Captain for me to hate him the way a front-line soldier should be able to hate the enemy. He had dignity, not arrogance, in the face of defeat, and he was good at what he did... his stubborn defense of the town with only sixty men proved that. That, and his dedication to his country and his duty made him more of a tragic figure for me than a villain, an unwitting pawn in the hands of an evil force that did not deserve his loyalty. Instead of hating him, I found myself envying him; his war was over, and he could wait out the rest of the conflict in the relative safety and luxury of an American POW camp, while I had to trudge my frozen carcass on towards Berlin.

"Doctor... is it Doctor Schmidt?" I asked.

"If you like."

"Doctor Schmidt," I said, "what... what could drive a group of soldiers to shoot each other, and then themselves?"

He looked over at me quizzically, and I told him about the SS we'd seen from the edge of the pines. Schmidt shook his head sadly.

"All kinds of things can make a front line soldier go mad," he said. "You know this. The shelling, the terrible conditions under which we must live, the lack of food, lack of sleep, the constant fear... it is a wonder more men do not shatter under the strain."

"But... this?" I said.

"Sergeant, with all my experience as a psychiatrist, I have learned one undeniable fact," Doctor Schmidt said, suddenly grinning. "Some people are just fucking crazy."

I laughed at that, and he continued.

"And you must remember, the SS are constantly fighting amongst themselves, every day. Each one looks to destroy his commander so he may step up, and he knows the man below him thinks this too. It is surprising more soldiers do not crack under the stress at the front line, and even more surprising that more SS do not kill each other."

It seemed to me an imperfect explanation, but we'd reached the manor house, and Wexler led the good doctor away immediately, along with a half-dozen of the company who were smoking lazily in the foyer. The Captain and I lingered outside the front door; Major Hayward was shivering himself apart out among the stone columns outside.

"Just... enjoying the brisk air," he said, lifting a cigarette to his lips with a hand shaking so badly that I was surprised it went into his mouth and not his eye.

"After what you've been through, sir, I'd think you would stay as close to a fireplace as possible," I said, tapping out a cigarette of my own.

"Oh, on the contrary, Sergeant," he replied. "I've developed quite a love for open places."

I noticed the Captain staring out at the swirling snow, and I asked him what was on his mind.

"Freddie," he said. "That kid... he really had talent, for baseball, you know? And that young German painter we killed... they deserve better than what they got."

"Well," Major Hayward said. He said it like someone would say 'Yes.' "The world owes us nothing."

"Sir?" I asked.

"Something my father was fond of saying," Major Hayward explained. "The world owes us nothing. Life isn't about what we deserve; it's about what we get. Once we realize that we are owed nothing from Life, then everything we do receive, we become truly thankful for."

My cigarette suddenly tasted stale. I tossed it into the snow, where it hissed out, as if spiting me with its last gasp of effort.

"Yes. I never liked to hear that much myself, either," Major Hayward said with a smile. "He was an overly philosophical bugger, my father."

"Let's check up on Freddie, Sarge," the Captain said. "Coming, Major?"

"No, no thank you," Major Hayward said. "Still enjoying the air, you know."

As we went inside, I thought to myself that it didn't look like he was enjoying the air. It looked like he was enduring it, and barely enduring it, at that. But why would he subject himself to the freezing cold when there was a relatively warm manor house a few steps away?

To stay out of Dom Caern, was the only answer.

37

Rebecca was still at Freddie's side when we returned to the study-come-aid station we'd put together. He was awake, at least barely, but the morphine kept him a little hazy at first.

"How is he?" Captain Powell asked. He didn't sound like he really expected an answer; one look at what Freddie had become was answer enough.

Rebecca shrugged and sat back in the chair she'd pulled up close to the table. She looked exhausted.

"How are *you*?" Captain Powell asked, and she smiled.

"I will be okay. But to see him like this…"

Freddie stirred and suddenly his eyes focused on Captain Powell. "Captain! Captain!" he whispered hoarsely, his arm shooting out and grabbing the Captain's wrist insistently.

"I'm here, Freddie. I'm here," Captain Powell said. "You're okay now. You're going…"

"Don't… don't let it get me!" Freddie said, gripping the Captain's arm tightly enough that I knew it had to hurt. If it did, the Captain didn't let it show.

"Nobody's going to get you," Captain Powell said.

"No, no!" Freddie insisted. "Don't let it get me! You can't, please, it does things to you when you're dead…"

"Listen to me, soldier," Captain Powell said, kneeling down next to Freddie so he could look him in the eyes. "Nothing is going to happen to you. I promise. Nothing can hurt you now. You're going home, you're going to be fine."

Freddie shook his head, his face twisting into a lingering sob. "You can't promise that. Nobody can. It's going to get us all."

He began to cry a little, and Rebecca started whispering in his ear. I flirted with the idea that Doctor Schmidt might be able to help him... I couldn't even begin to fathom what he was going through... but then shook my head at my own stupidity. A German doctor, so soon after Freddie's mutilation at the hands of German soldiers?

Snippets of what Rebecca was whispering reached my ears. "...it can not get you ... are safe with him... nothing can get you..."

Captain Powell nodded toward the door and we both stepped into the hallway. "I would say that he's taking it hard, but how the hell else are you supposed to take something like that?"

"Did you hear what he was saying?" I asked. "Don't let 'it' get me? 'It does things to you when you're dead'? And what's with Major Hayward, hiding outside, and Major Wexler poking around looking for God knows what? We are on strange ground, Captain."

He snorted once. "What else is new?"

He had a point. Even on a good day, the front line was a bizarre place to live.

"All the same," I said, hoping to lighten the air a bit, "it's still a good day to be alive."

The humor drained out of his face. "Not for Freddie."

Davey and Goliath came down the hallway then, saving me from another heavy moment. Davey looked like he was working out algebra problems in his head, and when he saw me, he brightened up, as if happening on me was quite a stroke of luck.

"Hey, Sarge!" he said. "You're Pennsylvania Dutch, right? I was thinking about those jars in the kitchen and it made me remember how I heard Pennsylvania Dutch people eat pig's feet. They keep 'em in jars like that, or that's what I heard..."

"Davey," I interrupted, before he could really get going, "I'm not Pennsylvania Dutch. And that's a little gross."

"Oh," Davey said, but whether he was embarrassed over bringing it up or disappointed I wasn't Pennsylvania Dutch, I couldn't tell. "Did you know that Pennsylvania Dutch people aren't really Dutch? They're

German. They got off the boat and people asked them what nationality they were and they said 'Deutsch', because 'Deutsch' is German for 'German'. So everybody thought they said 'Dutch' and..."

"Davey," I said, cutting him off again, although the Captain was obviously enjoying Davey's antics, "where are the others?"

"Cappy and Shorty are upstairs," Goliath answered for him. It was a habit that went a long way toward Shorty's theory that the two of them were anatomically attached someplace. "Said they found a shower room."

Davey nodded. "A big one, like for ten or more people. And there's barracks rooms, too, with cots. Cots! Each room has exactly fifteen cots. I counted them."

The Captain cleared his throat to hide his smile. Davey's overenthusiasm and love for dispensing "useful" information never failed to amuse him. "Very well, then. Let's get some of our guys some rest. We'll rotate through the showers; first the men who didn't get a chance at the bathtub, then the others. Same with bedding down on the cots. Let's not get too comfortable, though, gentlemen. Kleg is still out there, and if we're here when he comes back, we need to be ready. So pass the word to look sharp... this is not a rearward area."

"Yes, sir," they both said, speaking and nodding in an eerie tandem.

"Real cots, Sarge," Goliath said, punching me good-naturedly on the arm before heading off down the hallway after Davey.

"Tell Shorty to come find me!" I yelled after them, adding, "Separated at birth," to the Captain once they'd gone.

"I think you're right," he said. "I'm going to check over our defensive preparations. Sarge... I want all those bodies, human remains, German, American, whatever, all disposed of. From the kitchen or wherever else they may be. And see if you can get the kitchen cleaned up a bit."

I nodded. Having that stuff around would set everybody's nerves on edge. "Ground's too frozen to bury it. Okay to stack it all out back for now?"

He thought it over and nodded. "Very well. Check in with me later."

He went his way, and I found myself wandering idly back toward the dining room and kitchen. Morbid curiosity, maybe. I knew it wasn't just me; a couple of troopers came out of the door corresponding to that slaughterhouse down the hall, looking a little sheepish when they saw me. Maybe they were embarrassed over their curiosity.

I ordered them to round up some more guys for grave detail, and was a little glad when they left. I felt a strange need to see that room again, see all of that horror up close and personal, to try and make some sense of it, maybe. But I was a little embarrassed of my curiosity, too; when a corporal from 2nd Platoon whistled his way idly down the hall, I froze and pretended to light a cigarette as he went past me and into one of the main side rooms. I felt like I was a teenager trying to sneak into a bordello.

Finally, the hall was empty and I ground out my partially smoked cigarette and walked to the doorway in question. I paused before it, my hands resting on the wood, as if undecided whether or not I really wanted to go in there. Then, curiosity got the better of me, and I went in.

Went in the wrong room, that is. I stopped with a start, frozen with that momentary disorientation you get when you walk into one room expecting it to be another. I laughed at a memory of Kate; she had a funny habit of exclaiming "Oh!" and looking like she'd just been startled when she opened the door to the pantry, thinking it was the bathroom.

"Starting to lose your marbles, Harry," I muttered to myself, but when I shut the door, I didn't feel silly, I felt… out of place.

This door, the one I'd opened, was the right one. It had to be. I'd watched those two troopers walk out of it not two minutes ago. This was the door to the dining room. But when I opened it, there was what looked like a sitting room or parlor, with some sofas and chairs and a large cherry wood coffee table. Some of the furniture was a little broken up, but this was clearly not the dining room.

I closed the door once more on the mystery. This was stupid. I'd obviously picked the wrong door. I'd only come down this hallway once before, and I'd never had that great of a sense of direction anyway. I was famous for it back home, good old 'Get Lost In An Outhouse' Harry.

And just like back home, I was convinced I'd gone the right way when actually I'd mis-stepped yet again.

The door next to me had to be it, then. A cold draft of air passed by me, throwing a shiver into my shoulders, and I wondered where it could have come from as I reached for the next door. Probably an open window in the room across the hall.

A muffled cry and a thump froze me in mid-reach for the door. At first, I thought a clumsy trooper might've knocked over a chair or table, but when the thump came again, immediately followed by a heavier thud, my suspicious mind turned my tired body toward the sound.

Again, beyond the door across the hall, a thump, this time accompanied by what sounded like the combination of a grunt and a choke. They came in tandem, again and again, and I unslung my weapon and stepped over to the door.

I caught myself right before I called out to the corporal... his name was Bradley... that I'd seen go in there a few minutes before. If he was in trouble... and was I ever going to be embarrassed if he wasn't... I didn't want to tip my hand to his assailants.

My mouth went suddenly dry and my heartbeat quickened. When adrenaline hits, it hits like a bucket of water splashed across you; one second you're cool and mellow, the next, you're a crackling live wire.

The door seemed like an insurmountable obstacle, like it would take a Herculean effort to open it, and my body wanted to leave it alone. I shook my head to shrug off that illusion, and before it could return, I yanked open the door with my left hand and held my Thompson steady with my right.

Nothing. Then, I saw the both of them at once; the dead GI torn to pieces on the floor and the tiniest movement of a door on the far wall clicking shut.

"Shit... medic! Medic!" I shouted down the hallway, even though I knew it was too late for Corporal Bradley lying mangled on the floor. It was more a call for assistance than for an actual medic.

My body moved before my mind, rushing across the room to the side door through which Bradley's killers had escaped. A part of me held me up for an instant by the door, screaming at me, calling me crazy for rushing after them solo, but I swept it aside. This was one of my men, my boys, that they'd killed; I couldn't let them get away with it. Not if I could get payback.

I stood to one side of the door and pulled it open, keeping behind the wall and out of the open doorway. Even from this angle, I could tell it was a pitch-dark room, with no windows and no lights.

Perfect, I thought with a groan, trying to decide what to do with my hands first… toss in a grenade or fire a burst or dig out my flashlight.

I decided better safe than sorry. It took me about five seconds to pull the pin on a grenade and pitch it in through the doorway. It took an eternity for it to go off, though… even though I knew that its explosion would be the best call for help possible.

BOOM! It went off like a close, deafening thunderclap, throwing shrapnel out through the doorway past me. I grinned inwardly with grim satisfaction… those bastards would look worse than Bradley did after that treatment… and crossed to the other side of the doorway to get a quick glance into the room.

Still nothing. It was too dark and I couldn't hear anything due to the grenade's explosion, so if they were wounded and moaning or crying out, I wouldn't be able to hear them anyway.

Movement, to my right rear, and as charged up as I was, I nearly cut Rebecca in half before I realized it was her.

"What are you… get back! Get back!" I shouted.

"You called 'medic' and I was just in the room," she began, and I waved her off insistently.

Her eyes got wide at the sight of Corporal Bradley and she suddenly ducked back out of the room, hugging the edge of the doorjamb and only letting her head out so she could whisper, "Harry! Get away from there!"

"Rebecca, stay back!" I said, fumbling in my gear for my flashlight. My ears were starting to clear a little bit, and I decided whoever was in the dark room had to be dead, or I'd hear their groans. Unless by some miracle they hadn't been hit, of course.

"Harry!" Her voice became a strained, shrill shout. "You must get away from there, now. Please!"

Something in her voice stopped me up. She knew I was a soldier, and had to go after the enemy. She hadn't said "be careful" or "wait for the others" or something like that; rather, she shrieked out a warning more suitable to a terrified parent finding their child playing near a minefield.

Her lips were trembling and so was her voice, now. "Please, get away, we have to run away now, we have to go now, quickly, please…"

I'd had enough. The darkness within the room now seemed to seethe with life, and the air itself seemed to swirl with malevolent energy. An image of Major Hayward came to me, when he was standing in the doorway of the room back in the village with Kleg's drawing, refusing to enter. Rebecca looked like that now.

"Fuck all this," I muttered, stepping carefully away from the dark mouth of the doorway. Whatever was in there could wait until some more troopers came up.

Don't walk! Run! my mind insisted, and Rebecca only added to the wildfire of panic now burning inside my skin.

"Hurry, Harry, please, quickly, before it's too late, we have to run, now…"

The doorway seemed to moan, as if the house itself were breathing out the carrion breath of a predator's open jaws, and a chill wind blew out of the doorway and past me. The air tasted foul, stale, spoiled somehow, and as it blew into the hallway and passed Rebecca, the color drained from her face and she sank to the floor, paralyzed with terror, choking out a lifeless cry.

"Rebecca!" I shouted, rushing to her side before I could even guess at what could have affected her this way.

She held her knees to her chest tightly, rocking herself back and forth and trembling like a terrified rabbit cornered outside of its hole. She whispered to herself over and over again in French, and she stared straight ahead, seeing nothing.

The heavy thump of running boots filled the hallway as a dozen troopers ran to us with weapons at the ready. They saw me, saw Rebecca, and murder filled their eyes, murder for whatever had done this to her.

"In there!" I shouted, pointing toward the dark room. "Somebody took out Bradley and went into that room!"

Davey and Goliath were up front and with me in a second, God bless them. They dashed into the room and got on either side of the dark room's doorway in a heartbeat, firing into it as they went.

"One grenade is in already!" I told them, as the Captain picked his way through the troopers staying behind cover in the hallway.

He ducked his head around the doorjamb to glance into the room where Corporal Bradley lay dead. "In there?" he asked, indicating the dark room.

"Yeah," I said.

"Get some flashlights ready," he ordered, then, "Davey. Another grenade."

By the time it went off, a half-dozen troopers had their flashlights out and directed into the dark room. They rushed forward, and Davey and Goliath disappeared with them through the mouth of that black doorway.

There were a few seconds of anxious silence, in which I was sure I was about to hear the screams of my men dying, but the screams never came. Instead, Davey and Goliath came out of the dark room, completely intact, Davey shrugging his shoulders in confusion.

"Nothing."

38

"What do you mean, nothing?" I said, rising to my feet. The Captain knelt down to put an arm around Rebecca, who barely recognized his presence by tilting her head slightly into his shoulder. She still shook frightfully and rocked herself back and forth like a rocking horse.

"I mean, nothing," Davey said again. "Zip. Zero. Some blown to shit furniture and that's it."

"Blood?"

"Nunh-unh."

I traded a look with the Captain and forced my way past the other GIs toward the dark room. "That can't... they must've gone out through another door."

Except there was no other door, as I could see once I stormed into the dark room, which was now criss-crossed by a half-dozen beams of light. I got my own flashlight out, shining it around the room methodically, but there was nothing.

I stumbled back toward the room that held Bradley's body, feeling numb and stupid. This was impossible. There was no way whoever had done that to Bradley got past me in the hall. They came in here, into the dark room, and I trapped them in there. And yet, it was empty. Whoever it was survived two grenade blasts and then disappeared into thin air. In other words, impossible.

"I want four three-man patrols to search the manor. Right now," Captain Powell ordered. "And guards posted wherever troopers bunch up to eat or smoke or rest. Let's keep a sharp eye out, gentlemen. I said this is not a rearward area and I meant it."

Wexler showed up as I got back into the light. He took a look at me, at Bradley's body, and demanded, "What the hell happened?"

I could see the Captain, who was now standing in the hallway practically holding Rebecca up, and he gave me a nod. "I, uh," I began, "I was in the hall and I heard a noise in here."

"What noise? What kind of noise?" Wexler asked.

I had to think for a second to fight through the numbness now surrounding my mind. "Um… it was like a thump. Like a person falling down, and then like somebody getting hit with a baseball bat, I guess."

"You guess," Wexler said. "Be certain, Sergeant."

God, I wanted to crack him across the jaw with the stock of my tommygun. "I heard it and I came in here. Bradley was already dead, right where he is on the floor. The far door, that door, clicked shut, so I ran over to it and opened it up."

Wexler frowned. "Why?"

"Because whoever did this had just gone through it," I said slowly, fighting the urge to add *you stupid shit*.

"I heard explosions."

"That was me," I said. "At least, the first one. I threw a grenade in there and waited for support."

Wexler seemed very upset with me. "Throwing grenades around when you don't even know what was in there. I hope, Sergeant, that there was nothing in there I needed intact for my mission. For your sake, I hope you didn't just destroy valuable evidence on a panicked assumption."

"Excuse me, sir," I said through gritted teeth. "If you take a closer look, you'll notice it's pitch dark in there. Rather than run blind into a room with a flashlight that turns me into a target, to face however many men it takes to do *that*," I said, pointing at Bradley, "I threw a grenade into a probable enemy position and waited until I could get some help."

"And he was right," Captain Powell added, staring down Wexler when he said it. I don't know if it was intended as a reassurance to me or as a lesson for Wexler, but if it was intended as the latter, it didn't take.

"If that's the case," Wexler said, "then where are they? Hmm? Where are these 'enemies'? Where did they go?"

Captain Powell stepped very close to his face. "You're the intelligence expert," he said. "Figure it out."

With that, he led Rebecca out of the room, as she seemed to have her legs under her at last. The rest of the troopers, Davey and Goliath included, filed out after him to search the manor. One of them muttered "Asshole", loudly enough to be heard but not loudly enough to be pinpointed.

Wexler and I were left alone with Corporal Bradley's body. He shook his head, looking at it as if he didn't believe it was there.

"This man is torn to pieces," he said. "Look at his ribcage. It's like somebody took a pickaxe to it. Who could've done this, as quickly as you say, and..."

"Sir," I interrupted, "I know what I saw. They went into that room. They didn't come out. We threw two grenades in there, and nothing. Nothing but..."

Nothing but a cold wind, I almost said, but clamped my lips shut before I bought myself another load of questions.

"But what?" he asked.

"...but broken furniture," I finished lamely.

He sat and stared at Bradley for a while, and the sergeant in me made a mental note that I now had to arrange a grave detail for one more body. Another thought occurred to me during that damn Quiet Time I hated so much. Earlier, when we'd cleared out this area of the manor... I didn't remember the door to the dark room being there before.

"Well," Wexler said quietly, pushing his glasses up on his nose and raking his hand through his hair. "I suppose I'll have to figure it out."

Andrew C. Piazza

39

A hot shower has a way of washing some of your troubles away along with the dirt and grime. I don't really know why that is; I just know that some of the fear or fatigue or whatever it is plaguing me swirls down the drain, so I had Davey and Goliath walk me up to the third floor, where this everyday treasure was located.

"Shorty found a door behind one of those curtains on the wall," Davey explained on our way up.

"Tapestries," I said.

He shrugged as if to say, good enough of a name for it. "Tapestries. Anyway, he figured we should check it out since we hadn't seen it before, so we did, and there it was… big tiled room with shower heads everywhere. Wonder why they hid the door behind a cur… tapestry?"

"Keep the steam in, maybe?" Goliath guessed aloud.

"Yeah, maybe," Davey said. "Steam's supposed to be good for you, you know? Opens up the pores and helps your breathing and all that."

"That so?" I asked, without real interest. When we'd finally reached the hallway in question, after a series of winding turns, I muttered to myself, "Shit, I'm already lost."

"Yeah, it is easy to get turned around in here, isn't it?" Davey said, as if unhappy he couldn't figure that one out. "Me and Goliath got lost twice already, ended up wandering around for God knows how long."

The interior of Dom Caern was as insane as its exterior. I hadn't had a chance to really look around the manor yet, and now that I did, I didn't like what I saw.

Nothing seemed to be built with any sort of rhyme or reason. Hallways erupted from the main passage at random intervals; they canted and twisted and meandered through the manor at anything but a right angle. Some of them sloped upwards or downwards slightly. Some came to a dead end of stone and brick. Some of the floor was marble, some looked more like granite, some was wooden. Some hallways looked like those you might find in an opulent mansion; well-lit, fine detail etched into the columns and woodwork, that sort of thing. Others looked more like a dungeon than anything else.

Stairways were scattered around haphazardly. Some rose up two floors with no way to get from the first to the second floor; it was up to the third or nothing. Some led to a single room that had no exits. Some were spiral, some were straight, none were identical to any others. It was a wonder we ever found the shower room at all.

The aforementioned tapestry was lying in a crumpled heap on the floor. Where it had been, however, was nothing but a blank wall.

"What the hell?" Davey demanded of nobody in particular, rushing up to the wall and running his hand along it. "Where'd it go?"

"Where did what go?" I asked.

"The… door, the shower room door, it was right there," Davey said. "What…"

"Maybe we took a wrong turn," Goliath said, looking around.

"No, no, this is the right place. There's that lamp thing on the wall, and there's the chair and end table next to it with all the candles," Davey said.

"Davey," I said slowly, "is there really a shower room?"

He looked at me open-mouthed like I had asked him if there was really a God. "Honest, Sarge, there was a door right here…"

I rapped my knuckles on the solid wall and raised an eyebrow toward him. It wasn't that I really cared about the shower, I just always took a perverse delight in proving Davey, our constant source of questionable trivia, absolutely dead wrong.

"Very fucking funny, Sarge," he said. He glared at the wall with his hands on his hips, and it was all I could do not to laugh out loud.

The tapestry hanging a few feet to the left of Davey's missing door suddenly bulged outwards. It gave me a bit of a start, until I heard Shorty's familiar voice cursing at the fabric which blinded and enveloped him.

A few seconds later, he struggled out from behind it like a lost stage performer, and I caught a glimpse of a door beyond the swirl of the tapestry before it fell back into place.

"Hey, genius!" Shorty snapped at Davey. His hair was wet and he was only wearing his T-shirt and trousers, carrying the rest of his gear under his arm. "You were supposed to take down the one in front of the *door*."

"I did!" Davey insisted frantically, gesturing at the tapestry folded up on the floor. "I did! I took it, and there was the door, and I... oh, the hell with it. The hell with you both," he said, waving us all off, as I couldn't hold back my laughter any longer. "Especially you, Sarge."

"Hey, don't get pissed at me," I said, holding up my hands in declaration of my innocence. "I just got here."

Davey stomped off down the hall, muttering to himself, and Goliath lingered a few seconds so he could let out the laugh I knew he was holding in. It's funny; Goliath's laugh was usually a childish giggle; not at all what you'd expect from a six-foot-five monster like him.

"I really did think there was a door there too," he confessed between his giggles.

"Yeah, well, go find Davey something important to do," I said. "You know, make him feel better. I know... you two look in on Doctor Schmidt."

"Who?" he asked.

"Doctor Sch... I mean, Lieutenant Schmidt. The German. He used to be a psychiatrist. Keep an eye on him... for his protection, Goliath. That SS bastard in the kitchen had it coming, but Schmidt doesn't."

Goliath nodded. "You got it, Sarge," he said, and went off after Davey.

"There go a couple of university professors," Shorty said, shaking his head as he watched them go. "Help me get this thing down, will you, Sarge?"

"Who else is in there?" I asked, as we took down the tapestry hiding the shower room door. The candles on the small table across the hall flickered as the heavy folds fell to the floor, and for a second, I was worried they would splutter out and leave Shorty and I in darkness. The feeling left as quickly as it came.

"Bunch of guys from 2nd Platoon," he said. "And that British guy."

"Major Hayward?" I was surprised he wasn't still chain-smoking his way to a frozen death outside.

"Yeah. Him."

"Where are you off to now?"

Shorty glanced around quickly, like he was looking for lost keys, which I knew was his way of stalling for time so he could make up some fictitious task to save himself from getting a real one. "I, uh, I have to…"

"You have to go check on the grave detail. Make sure they get all those bodies and other remains outside and taken care of," I said.

Shorty's shoulders drooped in resignation. "Great. Graves detail. Great. You know, the ground's frozen, Sarge. We can't bury them."

"Just…" I waved my hand toward where I guessed was the back of the manor. "…stack them up out back. Keep Bradley separate so the Graves Registration people can tell him from the Germans."

"Graves Registration, right. Thanks, Sarge," Shorty muttered, as he headed down the hall and out of sight.

Ought to get him some stripes, I thought idly as I went through the previously hidden door. *For all his bitching, he takes a lot on himself.*

There was a small antechamber of sorts before the shower room, littered with piles of discarded GI issue clothing. I added my gear to the pile and stepped into the steam, immediately drawing welcomes from the eight or nine dogfaces soaping up under the showers.

"Hey, Sarge!" Private Wayne said. "Ain't this great? I can't remember ever being this clean!"

"And warm," added another dogface, a private from 1st Platoon named Shaffer.

"Yeah, well, don't get too used to it, guys," I said, starting up my own stream of hot, muscle-thawing water and stepping underneath it.

"We're still on the line. Besides, hustle it up and let some other guys enjoy it. Some of you are starting to prune up... *Wayne*."

"Ah, come on, Sarge. This is the first my balls have seen the light of day in weeks," he said.

"Yeah, well, it doesn't make them grow, so you're out of luck," I said, drawing a couple of laughs from the other GIs. "Rinse off and go tell Sergeant Ridley that it's his turn. His platoon has first shot at the cots in the barracks, as well. They're going to need somebody to stand guard after what happened to Bradley."

Does it seem strange that we should concern ourselves with such mundane details when one of our men had just been killed? It's all part of the bizarre nature of front line life; namely, that life doesn't end just because you're on the front line. You still have to deal with eating and sleeping and pissing and shitting and staying clean and all the rest, even though bombs are dropping and bullets are flying. It's a strange situation, to say the least. I've known guys who got killed because they had the runs... they got caught out in the open squatting over a latrine when the shells started to hit, and couldn't get their pants up fast enough to get into a hole in time. Killed because of the shits. It would be funny if it weren't so real.

And after a while, you get used to the idea of people getting killed on a regular basis, not just during an official "battle", but also from the far more common shellings or plain stupid accidents. You get used to it, and you get on with getting food and getting sleep and getting clean around it... because those needs don't stop just because you're in a war.

"I got no kind of luck," Wayne grumbled, shutting off his water and trudging towards his pile of dingy clothes. "It *was* good to see you, Sarge."

"I'd say he's a bit disappointed," Major Hayward commented dryly from beneath the shower head next to mine. The bruise on his chest was turning an ugly yellow around the edges.

I shrugged, closing my eyes and letting the water spill over my face and hair. "Life is cruel. I am a little surprised to see you here, Major."

"Well," he said, "in all honesty, although my balls *have* seen the light of day recently, they haven't been this *warm* recently."

There is something about a British gentleman quipping about his balls that makes a man laugh. "What I meant, sir, was you seemed pretty adamant on staying outside of Dom Caern as long as possible."

He shut off his water and turned to leave. "Some lures, Sergeant, are so irresistible as to override the deepest fears."

After he'd gone, his comments made me think of Rebecca, and I made a mental note to arrange a shower visit for her as soon as I was done. Then, I indulged in a few minutes of nothing but the sensation of a warm cascade of water over my face, which blocked out the world and the war and everything else, including the idle chatter of the other troopers in the shower room.

Once the world was gone, Kate could come through; beautiful, sweet-smelling Kate, shining like gold in the late September sun of my memories. The heat enveloping me made it easy to imagine that it was her body pressed to mine that provided the warmth and not a simple stream of water falling on me from overhead. It was the strongest image I'd had of her yet; I could hear her whisper in my ear and feel the curve of the small of her back under my fingertips. Her slight fingers stroked the back of my head in that certain, special way she did it, the way that made me tingle from top to bottom. Her subtle hint of perfume made the air taste like honey and seem as if the only thing required to sustain my body with life was an inhale of her scent.

After far too little of that interlude, the repeated call of one of my men pulled me back down to harsh reality with an insistent "Sarge!"

It was Shorty, fully dressed now and shouting my name from the antechamber. He looked downcast, defeated, and once he saw he had my attention, his eyes fell to the floor.

"Freddie's dead."

40

"What happened?"

It had taken me about ten minutes to get dressed and get down to our makeshift 'aid station', counting an extra five minutes for Shorty and I to find the right way once we got ourselves good and lost. Something about the winding passageways of Dom Caern clicked with my terrible sense of direction to create innumerable possibilities for me to get turned around and lost. It was as bad as the snow-covered pines outside; I kept thinking that the entire company could be swallowed up by the manor, never to be seen again.

"Morphine overdose," Captain Powell said, sitting near Freddie's head. He stared at the body as he spoke as if he were studying it.

"When?" I asked.

"Don't know," he said.

"Twenty minutes ago," Rebecca said. When the Captain glanced quickly up at her, she said, "I know because I helped him."

"Helped…" the Captain began, and then his entire body sagged. "Damn it, Rebecca. You helped him kill himself."

"He begged me," she said defiantly. "He begged me to help him and I could not say no."

Major Hayward, standing off to the side and out of the way, looked down at his feet. "Oh, dear."

The Captain held his face in his hands. "You shouldn't have done it."

"It was what he wanted, Jiim, and he was right."

"How can you say that?" Captain Powell asked. "Just because he was crippled doesn't mean his life was over…"

"It was more than that!" she insisted. "What happened to him is only part of it. He told me many things and then begged me to help him end it."

"When was this?" I asked. My throat was a little dry and it came out as a rattle.

She glanced at me and then looked down guiltily. "After the soldier was killed. The one called Bradley."

And after a cold wind terrified her into a fit of hysteria, I thought, but kept it to myself.

"You don't understand. You were not here like us," she said.

"We're here now," the Captain replied.

"It is not the same. You have not seen… what we have seen."

I looked over at Major Hayward, but he was busy shaking his head while staring at his shoes. An ugly thought crossed my mind… that maybe Freddie hadn't wanted to die, that maybe Rebecca's own fears had been amplified upon returning to this place until her judgment was distorted. Maybe she had been the one to decide Freddie was better off in the hereafter, not Freddie. She was a nurse; she'd know how much morphine would be fatal.

It wasn't really possible. What I mean is, not Rebecca. Not clomping through the snow in her big boots Rebecca. It wasn't possible.

Anything's possible in this place, I found myself thinking. *In here, I think all bets are off.*

"Maybe you can try to explain it," Captain Powell said.

She looked at Major Hayward expectantly. "John?"

Major Hayward looked up only briefly before clearing his throat and returning his stare to his shoes. "Yes, well. I think their imaginations can fill in the details, yes?"

Rebecca looked stunned by his answer. Not just stunned; more like betrayed. She looked like her only alibi in a murder case had suddenly pled amnesia.

She looked about to speak when a voice came from the doorway. "Perhaps I can shed some light on this."

"Jesus Christ, Jerry!" Shorty snapped, nearly jumping out of his skin. "Don't sneak up on me like that! You looking to get shot?"

"Sorry," Doctor Schmidt apologized. "But I have found something... may I speak with you, Captain?"

Captain Powell nodded and waved him in. I noticed Doctor Schmidt hadn't entered the room until invited, and even then, he walked with measured steps and watched Rebecca with a wary eye. I couldn't blame him. It never hurts to mind your P's and Q's when you are a prisoner of war.

"What's he doing here?" Rebecca said with undisguised hatred.

"He's been doing translations for Major Wexler," the Captain answered. "What do you have there, Doctor?"

"Doctor?" Shorty whispered under his breath.

"He used to be a shrink," I whispered back.

"Major Wexler asked me to translate this," Doctor Schmidt said, holding up a small packet of paper held together with string, "and some other things. He says not to discuss them with anyone, but after reading it... I think you should know this."

Captain Powell nodded. "Very well. What do you have there?"

"This a series of letters written by a Wehrmacht soldier who was stationed here before Kleg came," Doctor Schmidt explained. "There was a small group of Wehrmacht left to guard the scientists who worked here. Then Kleg came..."

"Hold on," Captain Powell said, holding up a hand to stop him. "Scientists?"

Doctor Schmidt looked from the Captain to me in confusion. "You did not know?"

"Know what?"

"This was a research facility for the German Army," Doctor Schmidt said. "Major Wexler did not tell you this?"

Captain Powell ground his teeth in frustration. "No, he did not."

"This 'doctor' is a liar," Rebecca said. "This was a house for murderers, like him. There was no research. Only killing."

"That was after Kleg came," Doctor Schmidt said, almost apologetically. "It is in here, or at least, some of it."

"Very well," the Captain said, settling back in his chair. "Let's hear it."

41

"13th December, 1944," Doctor Schmidt began. "This is when the letters begin having relevance to our situation."

"Go on," Captain Powell said.

"13th December, 1944," Doctor Schmidt repeated, finding his place in the small journal before continuing. "Dear Mother; There is a great offensive underway. The Fuhrer tells us it will throw our enemies off the continent. I look around at my fellow soldiers and see, for the first time, pride in who they are. For the first time I can remember, we do not slog through the mud with our faces downcast, but march with our heads held high. I do not even feel the cold. Peter Meuse from our church is here with me, although now he is Corporal Meuse. The 'old men' no longer joke about me being the youngest in the company; someone younger is here, a seventeen-year-old named Fritz. He is nervous and excited about seeing combat, and it feels nice for me to act like an old hand and give him advice. He shared some chocolate with me as we marched. It is a good day."

"17th December, 1944. Dear Mother; We have come to a place in the woods, a castle that was used as an asylum many years ago. Our commanding officer has been ordered to take control of it and hold at all costs. It apparently is important, although what strategic value it could possibly hold, I cannot tell. There is no resistance. The manor house is empty. My friend Peter says we will have fine accommodations tonight. He sees me writing and says to say hello and to tell his family he is doing well."

"19th December, 1944. Dear Mother; A group of scientists arrived today, along with a large unit of SS... an entire battalion, I think. The scientists immediately declared the lower levels of the manor, the basement levels, off limits. They are very excited or very nervous, I cannot tell which. My platoon sergeant tells me this was a research station, and these men are excited because they had to abandon their work when the American army came through here a few weeks ago, and now they have it back.

There are some men missing. The SS commander, a sinister man named Kleg, thinks they are deserters and threatens to shoot any man not at his post. I cannot wait to leave this place. Kleg and his SS make me nervous. Others feel this way as well. Fritz hides from them whenever possible. I do not blame him. There is something wrong behind their eyes."

"So Kleg was sent here as protection," Captain Powell said.

"It appears so. But let me continue," Doctor Schmidt said.

"21st December, 1944. Dear Mother; Things have turned for the worse. More men have disappeared, and I fear we will find their torn bodies as we found those of Captain Wuhrer and his headquarters personnel yesterday. There is much friction among us; the missing are SS and Kleg is furious. He took a squad of his soldiers and demanded at gunpoint that the scientists show him the lower levels.

I was not assigned to any duties just then, so I lingered near the stairs leading down to the basement after they left. The handful of SS he left behind shared my cigarettes and let me stay. At one point we thought we heard gunshots below us, but the sound was so muffled and distant, it could not possibly have been gunshots. But then, a long while later, the men came back up… but not as many as went down. Kleg looked like he had seen a ghost; he was shaking and unfocused and disconnected. He ordered that nobody be allowed to leave the manor. Fritz asks me if we must obey him, and I remind him of the guns and panzers under Kleg's command. This is enough of an answer for him."

Captain Powell held up a hand to stop Doctor Schmidt's translation. "Sergeant Kinder, have we checked out the basement?"

"Yes, sir," I said. "1st Platoon went through it. Nothing. Wine cellar, storage rooms… nothing much. There were a series of passages leading off to God knows where. Wexler took over the search."

"Very well. Please go on, Doctor."

"The next day," Doctor Schmidt said. "22nd December, 1944. Dear Mother; Kleg is worse than ever before. He makes trips into the basement often, each time taking a different group with him; first his officers, then their sergeants, then their men. Each time, the men come back looking terrified, but Kleg begins to look more and more pleased. Perhaps not that... obsessed is a better word. There has been another killing, three men this time, but Kleg does not seem to notice. He will not let us Wehrmacht leave to return to our division. He will not even let us contact them by radio. We are told we will be shot if we try. I am beginning to worry what he plans for us.

"23rd December, 1944. Dear Mother; We have not had contact with another unit for almost a week now. Our food supply is rapidly dwindling. I try to hoard what I can, to save my rations for lean times, but someone looks through my things and takes whatever I save.

Peter and Fritz were ordered to accompany the SS down into the basement. At first, I worried what might happen to them, but later in the day, they returned and said that they helped to move a vast amount of weapons and ammunition from the basement to a large stable that is located near the manor. Where these weapons come from, they did not know. Fritz, in his youthful innocence, had the brashness to ask Kleg. The SS commander only smiled and said, 'Divine providence'. Fritz and Peter guess that the munitions must have been stored there long ago, and the Americans simply missed them in the short time they controlled this area. Or, perhaps the Americans were never here. I doubt that explanation. This much ammunition would not have been left behind. I can't imagine where it comes from, and frankly, I don't care. I am more concerned with our dwindling food supply. Someone needs to tell Kleg that we cannot eat bullets."

"That explains the stockpile," I said.

"Does it?" Captain Powell asked, and asked Doctor Schmidt to continue.

"24th December, 1944. Dear Mother; There will be no Christmas this year for Peter. The SS took him away, down to the basement, and he did not come back. All of the Wehrmacht soldiers who left with him have disappeared, except Fritz, who keeps to himself and rejects all human contact. He says they killed Peter to hide what he saw in the basement, and soon they will come for him. I ask him what he saw down there that would be such a secret as to kill for, and he shudders and says, nothing but a tunnel and some boxes of ammunition. Four more men died today, and some of the soldiers whisper about things that move soundlessly in the dark, things that come up from the basement to kill us. Kleg still doesn't care about it. He laughs and says not to worry, that we are doing God's work. He is getting worse. He never eats or sleeps and his trips to the basement are so often he practically lives down there. Why won't he let us leave? He doesn't need us here, and soon we will starve.

I tucked away a loaf of bread a few days ago but it is gone now. We are all scared; of the SS, of Kleg, of what is killing us and leaving the strange messages on the walls. I think it is all Kleg, murdering us as a part of his insanity.

P.S. Do not tell Peter's family how he died. If they ask one day, tell them I said it was in combat.

"27th December, 1944. Dear Mother; There are only fifteen of us Wehrmacht soldiers left. Seven were killed last night, along with a few SS. Kleg has the bodies taken somewhere, I do not know where, but he says they will be stored carefully, that he has plans for them.

I don't know what to do anymore. There is no food. I can't think straight; too little sleep and no food and constant fear have made me weak. Many of the SS seem better fed than us. I think they hide food from us. Every day, one or two of our number is taken away. They took Fritz yesterday. He was too tired to struggle; he cried and hid in the corner, but they dragged him to his feet and hauled him away. When they come for me, I hope I have enough strength to fight them."

"28th December, 1944. Kleg's battalion left today on a raid of some sort. He says he has a war to fight, but I do not think it is our war. Thirty of his SS stayed here to watch us. Kleg said it was for our protection, but I know the truth. They are here to watch us. There hasn't been any sign of the scientists for days."

"29th December, 1944. Kleg is back, with trucks full of prisoners. I feel sorry for them, for I am now a prisoner as well. The SS have taken our weapons away. Lieutenant Richner tried to resist them when they demanded his pistol. He was right to do so. They are a badge of office for the officers, but when Richner resisted, Kleg wordlessly drew his Luger and shot him in the head. One of Kleg's staff officers laughed and said he shouldn't have ruined the brain.

Everything is so crazy now. I hear things moving in the dark and know it is not a man. We find messages on the walls, crazy things left by someone with a sick imagination, but nobody admits to them. There is talk among the SS guards of something alive in the manor house, something of horrible power that Kleg speaks to and obeys. There is talk about the 'new rations', as the SS calls them, and how they are not as bad as they thought it would be. I don't understand any of it. All I know is I am frightened and starving. I wonder if you will ever read these words. Sometimes I feel guilty over telling you of such horrible things. Perhaps it is better if you never read this.

"1st January, 1945. For New Year's we were allowed some soup, but I lost my appetite when I felt something in my mouth and spit out a shard of bone. I asked where the food comes from and the SS laughed and said, 'Courtesy of the Wehrmacht'. On the way back to the barracks room that is now our prison, I felt a cold draft of wind pass through us. We know now what that means, and soon, there were the now-common screams of men dying. We didn't even stop walking. Death has become so common we don't even notice it anymore. I am dead already."

My ears perked up at the mention of a cold wind, and when I looked at Rebecca, I could see she was now sitting in a chair with her arms wrapped tightly around her knees. Her eyes stared ahead at nothing; she seemed like she was in a trance. Major Hayward stood at the window, staring outside while resting heavily on the windowsill.

"The last entry," Doctor Schmidt said, clearing his throat. "3rd January, 1945. I was mistaken. Peter Meuse lives! I saw him through my window, standing out by the tree line in the distance. I had to use field glasses to be sure it was him. Why he is allowed out there, when we are prisoners, and why he stands and stares at us like a statue, I do not know. But it is good to see he is alive and allowed to leave the manor. Maybe the others have been allowed to leave as well. Maybe the SS keep us separate for some other reason.

My time has come. The SS are here, with Kleg, and they demand we come with them. If this..."

Doctor Schmidt closed the book slowly. "The words end in mid-sentence."

"Sounds like they killed him," Shorty said matter-of-factly.

"Yes," Doctor Schmidt said. "I think they killed them all."

I couldn't stop staring at Rebecca and Major Hayward. In their minds were more clues to the mystery before us; but as tight-lipped as they both were about their ordeal, I wondered if we'd ever know. Frankly, I didn't care. After hearing those letters, I wanted Wexler to find what he was looking for so we could get the hell out of there. Nobody wants to end up as a bone shard in a bowl of soup.

The silence in the room was a palpable force, and the Captain cleared his throat to break its spell. "Has Major Wexler seen that?"

Doctor Schmidt shook his head. "He is searching the basement, and he tells me to translate some books and the scientists' journals."

"You've read other things, then?"

He nodded. "Some I think you need to see. They were too big to bring them all."

Captain Powell nodded. "Let's go. Sergeant, hang on to those letters."

"Yes, sir," I said, taking the small packet of worn paper and tucking it into a pocket. I still have those letters to this day.

"I will come to," Rebecca said quietly, pulling herself to her feet and standing next to the Captain.

"Major Hayward?" I asked.

Major Hayward only looked away from the window for a second. "I think I'll have a cigarette instead, Sergeant. Outside."

42

"I thought this was supposed to be the library," Captain Powell said.

"It... I thought it was," Doctor Schmidt said slowly, frowning. He'd led us to the third floor and had opened a door to usher us into the large library where he said the books and journals were kept. Instead of a library, there was a long, wide passageway with doors scattered along either side of its length. I found myself trying to mentally draw a map of Dom Caern, as it seemed a passageway this large shouldn't be able to extend as far as it did. Of course, my sense of direction being what it is, it was a completely useless exercise.

My thoughts quickly turned to Corporal Bradley and the cold wind that had terrified Rebecca, and, truth be told, had terrified myself as well. It couldn't be coincidence that the nameless Wehrmacht soldier's letters mentioned the same thing.

There were all kinds of things wrong with those letters. Why did the Germans stay when they were getting picked off? What was Kleg doing down in the basement? Why was he letting his own men die in this place without taking action against it?

Because he's nuts, I answered myself, as Doctor Schmidt led the Captain, Rebecca, and I down the hallway to the door at the end. I was starting to feel a little fuzzy; it was evening now and my body wanted to eat and sit and smoke and maybe drink a little coffee, but it definitely did not want to search through Dom Caern for a bunch of books.

I suddenly didn't like being in that hallway. It was too big, I was sure of it. As far back as we'd already come, there was no way it could stretch as far as it did... especially with a library behind it. Dom Caern wasn't large enough. And the hallway didn't look right; it was as if the architect had been off a couple of degrees when measuring his angles. The walls and the floor and the doorways seemed canted slightly, even awkwardly, or maybe it was a trick of the light and my overactive imagination. My paranoia couldn't be helped. The candles in holders along the walls and in candelabras set on small tables along the passageway provided largely insufficient lighting. There were too many shadows with too many possibilities hidden within them.

"Here it is," Doctor Schmidt said sheepishly, after opening the door at the far end of the hallway. "I forgot the way, I suppose."

I was last in line through the door and I turned to look back down the vast hallway Doctor Schmidt had "forgotten". It was too big; the air in it was too still. It swallowed up our sounds like it was hungry for more. I felt like I was walking into a mausoleum.

The library wasn't much better. Two long wooden tables stood next to each other in the center of the huge room; several dozen books were stacked on the far end of one of them. Along the walls, massive bookshelves stuffed with old tomes stood silent sentinel over those two tables. Those heavy bookshelves seemed like living entities. They seemed like they were waiting for us to sit down and settle ourselves at the tables so they could tip over and crush us to jelly beneath them. I have always loved books, loved their wise feel, their reassuring weight, but now, those books felt like a thousand cells composing the body of a predatory creature.

Doctor Schmidt led us over to the stacked-up books on the second table, sifting through them for the ones he wanted to show us. For some reason, my unease spiraled into a mild form of panic; I found it suddenly became a chore to breathe. My heart trembled like the bouncing knee of a nervous test-taker. My skin didn't fit right; it stretched too tightly in some places and hung too loosely in others. Even the atmosphere here seemed forced, fake, a sham; unreal air for an unreal place.

"There are many books I do not understand," Doctor Schmidt said. Instead of his voice breaking the spell of the library's atmosphere, it made the feeling worse. It was like being at a funeral on the verge of tears; someone's well-meaning assurances and support actually end up tipping you over the edge of grief by forcing home a cruel reality you needed to recognize more gradually. The library air made me feel I might suffocate, my breathing became so shallow. My weapon, normally slung over my shoulder, was in my hands, and I wrung it like a wet towel, to remind myself it was still there.

"What do you mean?" Captain Powell asked. "Aren't they in German?"

We should've brought more guys, I thought, suddenly torn between going in search of a half-dozen armed troopers to keep us company and the knowledge that doing so would leave the Captain alone with a prisoner and an unarmed civilian. It was an illogical thought; what could possibly be so dangerous in a library that it required an armed escort?

Ask Corporal Bradley, I answered myself.

"They are German books, yes, but they are advanced texts of physics and this sort of thing," Doctor Schmidt explained. "I am not familiar with such subjects. But in the scientist's journals, there are some passages which caught my eye... here is one."

He read through it silently before translating it for us. "There seems to be a self-generating nature to the phenomenon. Since day one, the measurements have become stronger, even though no more energy has been expended through the device."

"What phenomenon?" Captain Powell asked.

"I am not sure. It is referring to something done, perhaps an experiment of some kind. There is talk of an intelligence... here," Doctor Schmidt said, skipping forward several pages. "The deliberate nature of the phenomena and the reaction to stimuli suggests an intelligence at work, although what form such intelligence would take is impossible to say."

Captain Powell shook his head. "I don't see what this has to do with us. There isn't much to go on..."

"Here," Doctor Schmidt said, holding up a hand once he'd leafed far enough ahead to find what he was looking for. "The entries become less scientific and more bizarre: It stretches the mind to consider the realities of what we have seen... a definite control over inanimate matter… a determined, if entirely unpredictable, intelligence. Something looks in on us."

"What does it say it is?" Rebecca asked quietly. She looked like she already knew the answer.

Doctor Schmidt shrugged. "Here it says: We must consider abandoning the facility and leveling it. Destroy it totally. The violent and deliberate nature of the murders causes me to label this so-called 'spirit' as a malevolent entity…"

"Spirit?" I asked suddenly. "What word is used for spirit… I mean, what's the German word used?"

Doctor Schmidt appeared confused. "The G… of course. Of course!"

"What is it?" I demanded, but like Rebecca, I already knew the answer.

"The word used," he said, "is 'Geist'."

43

"Geist?" Captain Powell asked. "You mean, like Kleg…"

"Exactly like Kleg," Doctor Schmidt said. "I am a fool for not recognizing it. I was so used to translating the words into English that I did not realize what I was reading."

"What does it say about the Geist?" Rebecca asked. "What is it?"

I noticed Rebecca had set aside her intense dislike of Doctor Schmidt for the time being.

"The journals do not say," Doctor Schmidt answered. "There are descriptions, though, scattered throughout them. It appears each time they encountered the Geist they documented it."

"What does this say?" Captain Powell asked, pointing to a portion of text Doctor Schmidt was scanning through. "Un… Unbekannter Funchburer Geist?"

"Unbekannter means unknown, never seen before, that sort of thing. Funchburer is… dangerous, scary, frightening, like that. This passage is a description of the Geist, but like the others, it makes no sense."

"What do you mean?" Captain Powell asked.

"It contradicts itself," Doctor Schmidt said. "It says the Geist has no form, or more accurately, that it is without form, and yet, it is deadly. It has tremendous physical strength, but no shape. It is referred to in both singular and plural forms. There is only one Geist, but there are many of them. It has many shapes, but no shape. It is massive in size but it is completely ethereal. It…"

"It can travel without being seen," Rebecca whispered, tears suddenly filling her eyes to spill down her cheeks. She stared straight ahead at nothing and gripped the edge of the table as if it were her lifeline to sanity. "It changes the walls. It kills for no reason. It leaves crazy messages all over. It is everywhere and it is nowhere. It can move like a wind and tear people apart. It can…"

She pinched her eyes shut, shaking her head slowly, unable to go on. My mild panic took a step up. I suddenly didn't want to be here anymore, trapped in this tomb with all these books staring down at me. I felt like a trespasser; like the books and shelves were the guardians of a dread secret I was foolishly trying to dredge up.

"What do you say," I said, "what do you say we take these books downstairs and tell Wexler?"

Captain Powell frowned. "Rebecca… you don't think this 'Geist' is an… an actual thing, do you? I mean, this whole thing is too…"

He stopped cold, staring up over my shoulder back the way we'd come. I turned around and there, above the door we'd come in, were scrawled the words THIS IS NOW MY HOUSE.

"That was not there before," Doctor Schmidt said as evenly as he could.

"You must've simply missed it," Captain Powell said. "It was probably left up there by the SS."

"I don't think so, sir," I said quietly. My hands gripped my weapon more tightly to keep from shaking.

"Why is that, Sarge?"

"Because it's in English," I said, and this time, I couldn't keep my voice from trembling.

"Very well, listen up," Captain Powell said slowly and calmly. "Everyone seems a little spooked by what's been going on around here, so let's call it a day and go down and get some chow. Anything seems possible up here in a shadowy old library with just the four of us and some books we can't figure out… yet. But believe me, once we're downstairs with the others, in the light and smoking a cigarette, we'll all feel a little silly for buying into any of this. Just keep your cool. Let's go downstairs, and you'll see it's nothing more than a case of the jitters."

"No," Rebecca shook her head. "It is not."

"Yeah, well, either way, I like the idea of getting out of here," I said, leading the way back to the door. I held my weapon level with the doorway as I opened it, finger on the trigger, but it was only the long, wide hallway and its dark stone floors waiting for us. "Let's go."

We were almost halfway down the hallway when the door at the far end suddenly opened. Nobody was on the other side. It eased shut slowly.

"Oh, God," Rebecca whispered.

The candles closest to the far door sputtered out, then those closer, and then, I froze absolutely solid as a cold wind, much stronger than before, blew past me and towards the library. Every candle in the passageway blew out with its passage, leaving us in total darkness; behind us, the library door slammed shut.

I couldn't move. It was like when that dud shell fell right in front of me; I had the sure feeling that I'd ducked Death's scythe by inches.

Just like before, I thought. *Just like Bradley.*

There was a sound from behind us, muffled by the door. Something had knocked over one of the tables in the library.

"Run!" Rebecca's voice whispered from the darkness somewhere behind me. "We have to run!"

"Run where, we can't see anything..." Captain Powell said, then... "Rebecca!"

Something hit me hard and I shouted in sudden panic and fear. Luckily, my terror paralyzed me for a second, so I had time to realize it had been Rebecca rushing blindly down the hall and not my nightmares come to life. I stumbled after her, one hand waving out in front of me, the other gripping my weapon tight as I plunged through the pitch blackness. Every step felt like the next would send me careening into a bottomless pit, but a nameless fear of whatever was in the library kept me moving.

There was a cry in the blackness in front of me, followed by a thump, and my feet suddenly tangled up and I fell hard to the stone floor. It was more luck than presence of mind that kept me from accidentally pulling the trigger.

Panic squeezed my heart in an iron fist. I was completely disoriented; the feel of the stone floor beneath me was the only reference point I had to my place in the world. Everything was a blank, black slate; it was like being immersed blindfolded into blood-tinged water, with sharks swimming all around me.

"Jiim? Jiim!" Rebecca called out right next to me, and when something grabbed my arm, I nearly screamed. I found her by feel and dragged myself to my knees, when a sudden light opened up on us.

"Are you all right?" the Captain asked. Thank God he'd had the presence of mind to dig out his flashlight before running into nothing. If he would've bumped into us in the dark, I might've shot him.

"We're fine, she just fell," I said breathlessly, pulling her down the hall as soon as she was on her feet. We ran to the end of the hallway, Captain Powell's flashlight leading the way, and I had my hand extended for the door well before we reached it.

Except there was no door. At the end of the hallway, there was just a blank, stone wall.

"What the hell?" Captain Powell said, putting a hand up against the wall to convince himself it was really there. "What the... where's the fucking *door*?"

Hearing terror in that voice, I mean real terror, the terror of an impossible reality coming true right before your eyes, set off the final blaze in the wildfire of our panic. Captain Powell's voice never showed fear... strain, maybe, but never fear... and if he was afraid, then I was terrified.

The words ICH BIN DIE GEIST were written where the door used to be, in foot-tall, white letters.

"Help!" Rebecca suddenly screamed, pounding on the wall with her fist. "Help us! Please! Somebody help us!"

Doctor Schmidt joined her in pounding on the wall and shouting, and in my whirlwind of panic, I almost did as well, until the skin between my shoulder blades pinched together. The darkness behind us was alive... and intent.

I had just found my flashlight and clicked it on when a small sound froze all four of us into silent statues. It was the library door at the end of the hallway clicking open.

"No." Rebecca's body shuddered out her whispered plea. She shook visibly, worse than Major Hayward had when we had found him out in the cold. "No, no. No... please! Help us! Help! Get us out!"

She began pounding on the wall again, screaming, pleading, and Doctor Schmidt grabbed her by the arms and whispered urgently for her to be quiet.

The beam coming from my flashlight wobbled in the air from my hand shaking so badly. Captain Powell's was a bit steadier. We stood with our backs to the wall, facing the dark with our flashlights in one hand and our submachine-guns in the other. I couldn't help thinking of the crazed SS shooting like madmen at the house, at each other, anywhere. It hadn't done them any good.

The flashlight beams probed the hallway, but they seemed swallowed up, constricted into completely useless fingers of light feeling around in the dark. As far away as the library door was, all we could see were the vaguest of shapes and forms that our memories re-constructed into the doorways and walls of the far end of the hall.

Something moved, or maybe it was my eyes playing tricks with my swirling mind. It was impossible to make anything out; I wasn't even sure I could see the outline of the open library doorway. Still, I was convinced something huge and broad was stalking slowly out of the library and into the hall.

Shoot! I thought, but I couldn't; I didn't know if it was really there, and if I fired, the close gunfire would render me deaf, and I needed my ears as much as I needed my eyes right then.

"Do you see it?" I whispered, swallowing hard on a dry throat.

"I... I don't know," Captain Powell whispered back.

Rebecca let out a sort of shuddering moan, and then began whispering in urgent, sobbing French. Doctor Schmidt tried to comfort her, but his voice was as uncertain as the light.

"What's she saying?" I asked.

"She's... she's saying she wants me to shoot her," Captain Powell said. "Don't you lose it on me, Sarge. Keep steady. We've seen worse."

It was a lie and I think we both knew it. We were pressed back against the wall, staring into the dark as if it were spring-loaded and pointed at our hearts.

Finally, there was a sound for my straining ears. A short series of dry, rapid clicks tapped in slow succession from the end of the hallway. My mind immediately ran down every sound I had catalogued in my memory, trying to identify it, but to no use.

"What is that?" Captain Powell asked.

For a second, I thought I saw the reflection of light off of an eye where the clicks were coming from, and suddenly, I knew what the clicks sounded like. Years before, in what seemed like another lifetime, my old German shepherd Wolf used to make sounds exactly like that... with his claws, tapping on the hardwood floor of my living room.

The sounds stopped, and all I could hear was Rebecca whimpering terrified words to herself in French. Then, they came again, t-t-tap, t-t-tap, and then faster, t-t-tap t-t-tap, t-t-tap t-t-tap, and faster, and I couldn't take it any longer, I knew it was coming at us like a cannonball and I fired blindly into the dark, my flashlight dropping from my hand so I could grip my weapon better, and I didn't stop, I blazed away, screaming at the unseen thing rushing at us, clenching myself around my rattling, thundering weapon to try to hold a lid down on my panic to keep from flying into a thousand pieces.

Somebody shoved me from the side and I dimly realized it was the Captain, shouting for us to get through the door. *There isn't a door anymore, Captain, the Geist took it away*, I thought distantly, but when the others herded me to my right I realized he meant one of the doors lining the sides of the hallway. My weapon went empty before I'd moved two steps, and I only had enough time to remember I'd left my flashlight lying behind us on the floor before the Captain had us in the side room and the door shut on the hallway.

"Block it!" he shouted, and he and Doctor Schmidt struggled with a heavy table, sliding it towards the door. The room we were in was small, and just as dark as the hallway; no candles were kept burning in here. I shook myself out of my haze and joined Rebecca in helping them slide the table in front of the door.

No sooner did it bump up against the wood then the door banged open against it. I could feel the impact of it travel through the table and into my hands. With a shout, I leaned into the table, as did the others, forcing the cracked-open door shut once more.

"It's trying to get in!" Doctor Schmidt shouted, leaning hard against the table.

WHAM! WHAM! A heavy weight hit against the door, each time harder than the last, as if something was testing how hard it needed to push in order to shove us aside. I dug my heels in, pushing back with the desperate strength of a drowning man, but each time, the door pushed open a little further before we shoved it shut again. Rebecca was next to me, her back set against the table's edge. She was screaming at the top of her lungs as she pushed against the unseen force trying to get the door open.

Captain Powell let go of the table and raised his tommygun, firing an entire magazine point-blank through the door. There was a momentary pause in the impacts, and in that pause, light suddenly flooded into the room from our left.

I spun, scrambling for my weapon, but it wasn't the Geist. It was Shorty, God bless him, standing in an open doorway leading to freedom.

"What the fuck…" he began, brow crinkled in confusion at the sight of us holding a barricade in place in front of a door. I was on him in an instant, shoving him back into the lit hallway from where he'd come.

"Go! Go! It's in here! It's in here!" I shouted, pushing him clear of the doorway. Rebecca was right on my heels, but I still pulled her into the hall, and then Doctor Schmidt and the Captain as well.

He slammed the door behind us and we ran like hell down the hall, straight into a half-dozen troopers who had come running once they'd heard the gunfire. We stopped short, pushing Rebecca through to the safe end of the mob, and then Captain Powell and I turned on our heels to face the doorway we'd left behind.

We both realized at the same instant our guns were empty. "Shorty, get a thirty-cal here, fast," I said breathlessly, as I changed magazines with trembling fingers.

"A thirty-cal?" he said.

"God damn it, Shorty, I said get a fucking thirty-cal up here right fucking now!" I screamed, and Shorty blinked once in surprise.

"Do it, Shorty," the Captain said, far more steadily than I had. "The rest of you, lock and load!"

The re-assuring rattle of a half-dozen weapons being readied steadied my nerves somewhat. I was able to recognize the hallway we were in as the one we should've been able to enter if the Geist hadn't taken our door away.

"That door Shorty came through," the Captain said, slapping a new magazine into his tommygun, "it wasn't there before, was it?"

"No, sir, I don't think it was," I said.

"What happened?" Davey asked from the group behind me. "How many of them are there?"

I was about to tell him that 'them' wasn't really the right word, when a crash came from behind the door we all guarded with the muzzles of our weapons. The table, our barricade, had been knocked over.

"No matter what you see," the Captain said loudly, "open fire with everything you've got."

"Get outta the way," Shorty's voice called out as he pushed through the crowd, "Get outta the way!"

He lugged a thirty-cal machine-gun to the front of the group, tripod and all, and set it down with a clatter next to me. "There was one set up in a window a few doors down, so here it is."

I handed him my tommygun wordlessly and sat down behind the machine-gun. Putting my hands on its grip made me feel a bit better. When Cappy knelt down next to me, aiming his sniper rifle at the door with his steely calm, that helped a bit too. My nerves still crackled with energy, but now it was the kind I got in a firefight, the kind that made me want to dare Death to a wrestling match.

Come on out, you son of a bitch, I thought grimly, clenching my jaw in anticipation. *Come and get it.*

The door clicked open and swung wide slowly. I worked the bolt on the machine-gun, taking comfort in the metallic clatter of it sliding home. I had a hundred-round belt ready to go, and I was just fine with using every bullet if I got the chance.

The seconds ticked by, slowly in singles, then stretching out into fives and tens, and nothing. Nothing showed itself. The guys started to fidget about, and finally Shorty said, "So what do we do now? What was it?"

I was wondering what the Captain would say when a strong, cold wind blew over me, coming from the open door and past us and down the hallway. Once again, my nerves shorted out from terror, paralyzing me, and the only thing that broke me out of it was remembering that the cold wind was blowing in the same direction Rebecca had gone.

I leapt to my feet, pushing my way through the crowd of confused GIs, but she was there at the rear of the group, huddled behind Goliath's massive body. My shoulders sagged as I let out a sigh of relief.

Then, the screams began.

Andrew C. Piazza

44

It had been in the shower room and it had been a massacre.

The guard posted outside the room hadn't done them any good; his mauled body lay next to his unfired rifle in the corridor. We weren't the first friendly troops on the scene; there were about fifteen soldiers already there by the time we arrived. Tedeski and Hayward were among them. Major Hayward looked like every drop of blood in his body had been drained.

"I'm afraid we were too late," Major Hayward stammered, purposefully looking away from the shower room.

"Too late for what... Holy *Shit*," Shorty whispered in awe, jaw dropping at the carnage strewn about the room.

It took us some time to sort out the pieces, but we determined it had been nine men in there. Now, it was just scattered scraps. It looked like a bomb had gone off in the close confines of the shower room. Some bodies were missing limbs, some were split in half, and others were crushed flat.

The hard part was, most of the victims didn't have only one sort of injury. Sergeant Ridley's head had been cut neatly off by what must've been a sharp blade, but his upper legs and pelvis were crushed flat like they'd been run over by a tank. A body we had to identify by its dog tags had its face so pulverized that Shorty threw up when he accidentally crunched a dozen knocked-out teeth under his boot. However, several others had only a small hole punched into their chests, right where a man's heart is. One body was impaled on a shower head, its stomach and guts spread out in a gruesome, loopy mess; others were left where they lay.

That was what bothered me the most. Men die in war, and no death is either easy or pretty, but at least it's usually predictable. Gunshot wounds look a certain way, artillery and bomb shrapnel wounds look a certain way, and so on and so forth. But no one weapon could do what we saw in there, kill in so many ways. It was as if all the forms of Death imaginable came into that room at once.

Scrawled on the wall in some sort of black ink were the words I MISSED YOU REBECCA.

"What happened?" Captain Powell asked. His face was set in stone, thank God; I couldn't have handled a wavering tone in his voice just then. "Did anybody see anything?"

Tedeski shook his head and chewed idly on the stump of his cigar. "I was outside talking to Major Hayward when we heard the screams. Ran like hell but the bastards were gone by the time we got here."

"Must be escape artists," Shorty said. "We came the other way and we saw nothing."

Captain Powell only looked for another moment before speaking. "Shorty, take charge of everybody here and put them on cleanup duty. Bodies go out back with the others. Set them aside from…"

"…from the German bodies for when Graves Registration gets here," Shorty said with a look at me. "Got it."

"Sergeant Kinder, Lieutenant Tedeski, Doctor Schmidt," Captain Powell said, and then stopped to look at Major Hayward, who was still standing beyond the doorway with his eyes averted. "And Major Hayward. Come with me, please. You too, Rebecca."

We all headed off in a line down the corridor, Major Hayward trailing in the rear. There were a lot of soldiers in the hall now, all drawn by the commotion or the rumors already flying around the manor at the speed of light, so we had to wind our way through them like a segmented snake.

Wexler bumped into us before we'd made it twenty feet. "What happened?"

"Take a look," the Captain said, gesturing back the way we'd come. "Then join us downstairs in the study, if it's not inconvenient, Major."

Captain Powell led us off again, and Wexler wondered aloud, "What was that all about?" as I passed him.

"He's wondering what took you so long to get up here after hearing gunfire and screams," I said.

"I was in the basement," he said, but I left him behind me and followed the others. I wasn't in a forgiving mood; Ridley was a solid non-com and I doubted I could find someone who could take his place. The others killed in that shower room ranged from old veterans to brand-new replacements, but they were all my men, my men, and something strange and terrible and worst of all senseless had destroyed them. The Captain had been right; it was a damn fool idea to come here all alone under the orders of some intel weenie who played his cards so close to his chest that we had no idea what we were doing. We should leave this place, first thing in the morning, and I intended to say so once we were in private.

"What's going on, Captain?" Tedeski asked once we were in the study. He sat in a chair and leaned it precariously back; Doctor Schmidt sat in another, back straight, with his hands resting in the arms of the chair. Major Hayward stood staring out of the same window as he had when we'd been in this room earlier, staring into dark nothingness. The rest of us stood.

"That's what I'd like to know," Captain Powell said firmly. I'd heard this tone of voice before; it was his I Will Accept No Bullshit tone.

Tedeski frowned. "I don't understand."

"There's been some strange shit going on around here, sir," I said. It was the best explanation I could think of. "The four of us here were just witness to it, and if I may be so bold, Major Hayward, my bet is you've been witness to it at some point as well."

His eyes dropped from the pane to the floor. By saying nothing, he admitted everything.

Captain Powell looked like he was trying to figure out what to say, but Rebecca broke in. "You would not believe it if we told you, Frank. It would sound too crazy."

The Captain nodded, setting a hand on her shoulder. "Which is why you never told us," he said. "You were worried we would think you were crazy."

She smiled and took his hand from her shoulder, squeezing it inside her own and keeping it there. "And you would have, Jiim. How could you not?"

He couldn't help a guilty smile as he looked into her eyes, but it faded when he asked, "So you've seen it?"

"I think you know you cannot see it. If you see it, you are already dead," she said. "But yes, what you mean, yes. It has been near me before."

"What?" Tedeski asked. "What is this 'it'? What are you people talking about?"

Nobody wanted to answer that, myself included. Even though five of the people in the room had been exposed to the terror nobody wanted to describe, language seemed unable to the task of explaining it to the sixth.

It was Doctor Schmidt who finally spoke, his voice measured and precise, as if he were describing a particularly violent patient. "There is something living within the manor house, Lieutenant," he said. "From what we have seen, although it is intelligent, it is not human."

Tedeski's eyebrows arched. "Beg pardon?"

"The scientific researchers quartered here called it 'the ghost', the 'Geist', but even they did not know exactly what it was," Doctor Schmidt continued. "All we know is it is extremely powerful and extremely deadly. It attacked the four of us who went to the library and then somehow got past a squad of soldiers to do what you saw in the showers."

Tedeski looked around at us like he was waiting for a punch line. "Is this a joke?"

Wexler burst into the room, a permanent grimace on his face. "What the hell happened in there?"

"It's apparently quite a story," Tedeski said.

"I think it's about time you told us what we are doing here, sir," Captain Powell said.

Wexler shook his head. "No, I can't Captain, it's classified..."

"Ten of my men are dead, Major," Captain Powell said. "Orders be damned, I am not going to keep my men exposed to some... thing... that is nothing but a gust of wind one second and is something that can tear apart nine men the next. Now what is going on here?"

Wexler stopped cold and scratched idly at his face, lost in thought. "You... that was what... who saw it? What did it look like?"

"Nobody saw it," Captain Powell said. "We were up in the library..."

"Library?" Wexler asked, pushing his glasses up on his nose and raking his hand through his hair. "What were you doing up there?"

"Doctor Schmidt was showing us some journal entries that mentioned this 'Geist', this thing that..."

"*Doctor* Schmidt?" Wexler asked, turning suddenly and severely on the man in question. "*Doctor* Schmidt was instructed not to report his findings to anyone but *me*."

Doctor Schmidt seemed to wither under Wexler's accusing stare, and of all people, Rebecca came to his rescue.

"It was a good thing he did. If he told nobody, then we would still be wondering what is killing the soldiers and making the walls change."

"Making the *what* change?" Tedeski asked. "Have you people been in my liquor stash?"

"It's not a joke, Lieutenant," I said. "Ask Major Hayward. What is it, sir, that's keeping you freezing yourself stiff outside 'smoking cigarettes' and keeping your mouth shut when you obviously know something?"

"Sergeant!" Wexler snapped.

"And what made you try to demand an air strike that would demolish this place before we'd seen a thing?" I said.

"Sergeant! That is enough!" Wexler said. "Major Hayward is under orders not to discuss that with anyone."

"Under orders from whom?" Captain Powell asked.

"From me," Wexler said defiantly. "Listen up, all of you. I know you don't like me. That's your choice. But you still work for me. This operation is under *my* authority, and you will do as I say, Captain, or I will remove you from command."

I'd like to see you try it, I thought, but kept it to myself.

"Very well, sir," Captain Powell said, making that last word sound vile. "What do you propose we do? We have ten dead men already."

"Okay," Wexler said, pushing his glasses up and raking his hand through his hair once again. "Okay. We need to, um... I need the bodies preserved. We'll need to take them with us when we leave."

"They're being stored out back," I said. "They'll freeze solid out there in no time."

He nodded. "Good. Good. Then, um, I'm going to need a group of soldiers, who can go on a, um, scouting mission for me. Reconnaissance."

"You mean a patrol, sir?" Captain Powell asked.

"Yes, a patrol," Wexler said irritably.

"Where are they going?" Major Hayward asked, breaking his self-imposed silence.

Wexler frowned and looked annoyed that he had to slow down to explain it to us. "I... I mean, me and the soldiers that went with me, found a stairway behind a false wall in the basement. It leads down to a tunnel..."

"Major Wexler," Major Hayward said quickly, "I strongly suggest you do not send anybody down there."

"John," Wexler said, shaking his head. "I told you before, I need to *see*..."

"Major, please!" Major Hayward insisted. "You asked me to come along as an advisor, this is my advice. Do not send a patrol down there."

"My mind is made up," Wexler said, holding his hands up to stop any protest before it could begin. "Now, before we go, I want each of you to tell me exactly what happened to you tonight. Don't leave out any detail... not one."

We told him what happened, then, but I could tell it was running off of him like rain off a tin roof. He didn't look scared at all. In fact, the more he heard, the more excited he seemed.

"Sir," I asked, before he dismissed us, "when you found that stairway, you didn't happen to notice a cold draft of wind blow past you, did you?"

"As a matter of fact, yes I did," Wexler said. "Why? Do you think that's important?"

I traded a look with the Captain. This idiot had no idea how close he'd come. There's nothing more dangerous than a careless or clueless leader, and ours was about to lead us straight into the lion's den.

Andrew C. Piazza

45

Thankfully, the Captain convinced Wexler to let us post a platoon-sized force by the stairwell for when our patrol went down it. While we were waiting to get all the necessary men and equipment together, I stepped outside for a smoke and to see how the grave detail was getting along.

"Hey, Sarge," Tedeski said, stepping outside into the dark with me and hunching his shoulders against the cold. "All that stuff you guys said in there... no bullshit?"

"No bullshit, Lieutenant," I said. "I'll tell you one thing; I don't even give a shit what's going on here. I just want to get out of this place now, even if it means sleeping in a snowbank with Kleg."

"Yeah, well," he said, uncharacteristically at a loss for words. "I think I'll get my TD crews to lend a hand with watching this stairwell Wexler's talking about."

"You're going to want more than that," I said, with a nod toward the .45 pistol in his flap holster.

"Yeah, right," Tedeski said, heading back inside without another word.

Shorty trudged up the steps out of the dark with the last of the grave detail as snow began to fall. He looked up at the sky and made a face.

"Oh, great! More snow!" he said. "I'll tell you, Sarge, when I get home, I'm moving to fucking Florida or some place where it never gets cold."

"And then you'll bitch about the heat," I said, hunching my shoulders against the wind.

"Ha, ha," Shorty said. "Big comedian."

"Everything taken care of?"

"The best we could," Shorty said. "Somebody moved Freddie outside."

"I thought I said I didn't want him outside."

"I know, I know. I didn't do it. Somebody took the initiative."

I grunted. "Who?"

"Don't know," he said, "but they did a lousy job. Looks like they took him out the front door and dragged him all the way around to the back and just, pfft, left him a couple yards shy of the rest of the bodies. No respect for the dead."

I handed him a cigarette and lit it for him. "Shorty... I want you to take over 2nd Platoon."

His face went almost white. "But... Ridley..."

"Ridley's dead, Shorty. You moved his body, remember?"

"But I'm just a PFC. That's a job..."

"For a sergeant," I said, "which you're going to be. I'm sure the Captain will agree with me. For now, you're acting platoon sergeant of 2nd Platoon, until we can make it official."

He shook his head. "I don't want no stripes, Sarge."

"I don't remember asking you, soldier," I said. "You will take command of 2nd Platoon. What's left of it."

I understood Shorty's reluctance to accept a promotion. I'd been there myself, each time a new layer of stripes was added to my sleeve. It seems strange, but when you're in the middle of it, it makes perfect sense. As a private, you have no responsibility other than to yourself. Sure, you eat dirt from those above you, but that never changes with rank. And the higher you climb, the more responsibilities you have, the less carefree you can be, and the more men you have depending on you. As just another private, you can shrug a lot off. As a corporal or a sergeant or God Forbid, an officer, you have to take more and more of it on your shoulders. In a war zone, day-to-day life is stressful enough; nobody needs the weight of command on top of that.

"Hey, Sarge?" Shorty asked. "What did the Captain mean? When we were all in front of that door, when you guys were yelling and screaming for help? He said 'No matter what you see, open fire with everything you've got.' That's a little weird, you know?"

I knew, all right. "You... you kind of had to be there, Shorty. But I think you'll get your chance."

"What do you mean?"

"Wexler is setting up a patrol to go down a tunnel he found," I said. "2nd Platoon is going to set up a strongpoint, a fall-back position, right where the stairwell meets the tunnel."

"Oh, fuck me," Shorty groaned, then frowned in confusion. "Wexler?"

"Major Wexler. The intel asshole."

"Oh. *That's* his name." He took a drag on his cigarette and smiled bitterly. "And I bet that patrol is getting put together right now."

"Safe bet. Report to the Captain," I said.

"Where are you going?"

"I have to talk to someone first," I said. "I'll see you down there."

He went off to round up the remnants of 2nd Platoon, and I left in search of the man I needed to see. I found him in the dining room, sitting at the table and cleaning his rifle, completely unperturbed by the bloodstains on the tablecloth.

"Cappy," I said to get his attention.

"Sarge." He never looked up from his weapon.

"I have a job for you."

He didn't respond; his eyes stayed intent on his work, scrubbing the dirt out of the working parts of his Springfield sniper rifle before putting them back into place. I waited for some sign to indicate he'd heard me, but it never came.

"Cappy."

Still nothing.

"I said I have a job for you."

"I can hear you," he said, his attention still on putting his rifle back together.

My jaw clenched but I swallowed down on my frustration. "I want you to keep an eye on Rebecca. The civilian."

That seemed to get his attention. His eyes glanced up at me for a second before returning to his rifle. "Keep an eye on her?"

I figured if anybody could accept the notion of the Geist quickly enough to react to it instantly, it would be Cappy. He seemed to take the insanity of war pretty well in stride; the same should go for the insanity of the situation here at Dom Caern.

"The Captain... she's important to him. With all the strangeness going on... I want you to be her shadow. Nothing touches her. Nothing. You are personally responsible for her safety. Understand?"

Cappy seemed to think about it, then nodded as he slid the bolt back into place and completed his rifle's re-assembly. "Where is she?"

A safe bet was that she was with the Captain, which was where I was headed anyway. "Follow me."

46

"I said, I come with you."

"And I said, no," Captain Powell told Rebecca.

They were standing by the stairs leading down into the cellar, along with the remnants of 2nd Platoon, which was now led by a scowling Shorty. Davey and Goliath were there as well, guarding Doctor Schmidt, as well as Wexler and Major Hayward. Tedeski and four of his tankers, all armed with the .45 caliber grease guns I disliked so much, rounded out the group.

The gang's all here, I thought grimly.

"This is such a bad idea," I muttered once I reached the Captain. Cappy dutifully took up a discreet position near Rebecca and away from Tedeski.

"We have our orders," the Captain said, nodding toward Wexler, who was deep in conversation with Doctor Schmidt concerning one of the journals he'd shown us. "And yours, Rebecca, are to stay up here where it is safe. There is no way…"

"You may need me down there," she said quickly. "If someone gets hurt…"

"We have two medics," he said, pointing out two GIs with red crosses on white backgrounds painted onto their helmets.

She seemed defeated for a second, then said, "There are more soldiers here than anyplace else in the house. Where is more safe?"

Rebecca had a point. 2nd Platoon still had about fifteen men, and along with the rest of us hangers-on, we had better than two dozen men collected together in one place, most of them heavily armed. We also had two thirty-cal machine-guns, a bazooka, and a backpack flame-thrower... which was more firepower than on any other spot in Dom Caern's vicinity, unless you counted the territory directly in front of Tedeski's tank destroyers.

Wexler decided the matter for us. "She comes along. I want to talk to her about some things we found in the basement."

"What things?" Captain Powell said.

"My cell," she answered quietly. "My cell is down there."

Major Hayward nodded. "It's where they kept all of us."

"Well, everyone is here, so let's get moving," Major Wexler said, with an expectant look at the Captain.

Captain Powell glared at him briefly before cocking his tommygun and nodding to Shorty. I felt the old butterflies start up again, the kind that always came right before a battle.

My eyes closed and Kate came to me, just for a second, to stand and smile in the warm September sunlight of my mind to tell me everything would be okay. For that second, everything was warm, and soft, and beautiful.

Then one of the GIs moving toward the stairs jostled me, breaking the spell, and I was back into the cold, harsh, stony reality of Dom Caern. My shoulders twitched once to shake off the last remnants of my fantasy, and after dumping my overcoat near the mouth of the stairs next to the rest of the platoon's heavy gear, I cocked my own weapon and fell into the flow of GIs heading down into the basement.

The stone stairs were wide enough for two people to walk abreast, and Rebecca fell in next to me. Just before she spoke, I could hear Wexler behind me say to Major Hayward, "Hey John, are you coming or not?"

"Harry," she whispered to me, fumbling with a flashlight to switch it on. The Germans had nailed a string of electric light bulbs along the stone walls of the stairwell, but we had trouble with the small generator they had set up, so for now all we had was our angle-headed flashlights.

"What?"

"I want you to show me how to shoot a gun."

One Last Gasp

She stopped me short before I could protest. "Please, Harry. Jiim will not show me. He says we will be leaving soon, and that I will hurt myself. But I see that Wexler man, and I know he wants to stay. He doesn't understand what is here."

"What is here, Rebecca?" I asked.

She shrugged her shoulders. "The Geist."

At the base of the stairs, a plain gray stone hallway led straight ahead into the darkness. The weight of the soldiers in front of and behind me was re-assuring, until I remembered the crazed SS and their lunatic flight from Dom Caern. Numbers and firepower hadn't helped them.

The electric lights suddenly clicked on, punctuating the cold stone walls with occasional spots of harsh light. I imagined I could hear the generator finally starting up upstairs, but it was probably wishful thinking. My ears weren't that good, especially after all the close explosions and gunshots hammering them over the last six months.

Those GIs who had their flashlights on clicked them off to spare the batteries. Rebecca kept hers on, though, holding it tightly with both hands, as if she was afraid someone might try to take it from her.

She caught my look and said, "It was always so dark down here."

Perhaps Rebecca held it so tight to keep her hands from shaking, as well. She kept looking behind us, left and right, all around, as if afraid the Geist might be able to sneak up on her through a dozen troopers either way. Each time we passed a door, she grabbed tightly on to my arm with one hand, staring at the wood until it was at least five feet behind us.

Passageways started to open up left and right, dark tunnels with the smell of a musty cellar about them. The electric lights in those tunnels were not lit; only the string that led to Wexler's secret tunnel was lit, in order to guide us through that maze.

The further we went, the more I felt like a trespasser, like a thief sneaking into a sleeping dragon's lair. It seemed each step took me further away from relative safety, and closer to a terrible monster who may be shamming sleep in order to lure us in. The life-line of electric bulbs seemed far too flimsy and tenuous for me.

I gave an order to spread out; the guys were really bunching up, like herded cattle, and soon it seemed like *we* were the scattered lights strung along the hallway, not the bulbs tacked on to the unfeeling stone. Each one of us was just a single spot of light in the dark, kept shining by a surge of electricity going through our wires, easily breakable, destined to burn out. It made me feel tiny, inconsequential; the light of one bulb compared to the vast gulf of dark space in the universe.

I had to shake myself out of all of that. On patrol, you can't let your mind wander; it's no time for introspection and philosophical investigation. If you let your mind get caught up in the great questions of the cosmos, your distraction will allow the enemy to make you one *with* the cosmos. And this little jaunt into the bowels of Dom Caern felt more like a combat patrol than anything else.

"This is it," Rebecca said quietly, as Wexler called the column to a halt. "The cells are here."

Spread evenly on either side of the hallway were heavy iron doors set into the stone. There was a small window, perhaps a foot long by eight inches high, set at eye level. A metal shutter could be slid into place to close it.

Doctor Schmidt joined us with Wexler at his side. "I never liked this place," he said. "When I was here, they kept the most violent patients here, those furthest from reality. Their screams would echo through these halls at all hours of the day and night."

I pulled the bar from one of the doors and opened it. The inside was filthy, covered in dirt and grime and debris. A straw mattress lay in one corner, partially torn open and nearly black with streaked dirt. Its insides were spilled onto the floor and crushed into the dirt.

"It was like this when you worked here?" I asked.

Doctor Schmidt shook his head. "I did not say I approved of the conditions. I left very quickly, mostly because of these cells. Too many nights, I came down here, and I felt so… nervous. It felt like the air was too thin. It felt like there were always eyes watching me, even if the shutters on the doors were all closed. I felt…"

He shook his head again, as if embarrassed of the thought. "I felt like I was about to fall into a deep pit. One whose edge was close but could not be seen."

"Hey!" Shorty called back from further up ahead. "There's blood in this one!"

The next cell up didn't have a door. More accurately, it had only part of a door; the upper three-quarters was gone, torn off by some incredible force. My guess was plastic explosives of some sort, the way the lower part of the door folded inwards at the point of breakage, but when Rebecca spoke, I found out what it really was.

"Her name was Edie," she said quietly. "She grew up in a village not far from my home. She would cry every night, all night, and beg for the SS to turn the lights on. Then she found out one day the lights were on, but her shutter was closed. She was always so scared. We all were. I tried to talk to her but it never helped."

Rebecca took a long breath before speaking again, and her eyes avoided ours. "The Geist came for her a week ago today. I was lying in my cell…"

"That was your cell?" I asked, looking back at the filthy room we'd looked into.

She nodded. "I was lying in there with my hands over my ears to shut out her crying. I tried to say something to calm her but it didn't help, she kept crying, so I held my hands on my ears to shut out the noise and keep my mind safe. Then I hear it… banging on her door, the iron clanging like a bell. She screamed, again and again, and each time she screamed, the door was hit harder, until I could hear the metal rip with a scream of its own. Edie did not scream for long after that."

"Jesus Christ," the Captain said.

"After a while, I hear a knock on my door," she went on. "At first, I almost faint in fear, because I think now it is my turn. But is it just normal knocks, like a person, and then I hear her. Edie."

"The Geist let her go?" I asked.

Rebecca shook her head. "I thought so at first. She says my name and says she wants to talk to me. But it is not her. I know because there is no fear in her voice. I know because her accent… she talked like a country girl... is gone and now her speech is perfect. There are none of the little mistakes we all make when talking. So it cannot be her."

"So who was it?" Wexler said. "Another prisoner?"

"There were no other female prisoners then," Rebecca said.

"So who?"

"I do not know. All I know is, she pleaded with me to talk with her like I used to, then the shutter opens. I do not look because I am too scared. I hug my knees and cry and beg to be left alone. And finally it ends.

"The next day, the SS let me out of the cell. I think it is to be killed, but..." she shook her head. "...it was to remove her body."

"They killed her for leaving her cell," Wexler said.

"They did not kill her. She was... torn apart," Rebecca said. "Her insides were torn out."

"Then who..." Wexler began to ask, but a call from up ahead cut him off.

It was Shorty. The Captain, Wexler, and I moved up the line of troopers, past the last of the cells to a stone archway leading to a set of spiral stone stairs leading down. The word *Wilkommen* was written in white, foot-high letters across the arch.

"Who wrote this?" Wexler demanded. "I said, who wrote this?"

There wasn't any answer.

"That wasn't there before?" Captain Powell asked.

"No, it was not. I want the man responsible for this, now. I don't know what kind of sick joke you people think you can pull on me, but let me tell you that you are sadly mistaken. Tedeski?"

Tedeski raised his eyebrows and looked around. "What?"

"Where have you been since our little talk in the study?"

"Where..." Tedeski began to repeat, confused, then his eyes narrowed. "Hey, fuck you, *sir*. I was pulling half the crews off my rigs to help your ass out down here."

Captain Powell spoke up. "Remember what we told you, sir. The writing on the walls."

"I think it's far more likely, Captain, that this is the work of one of your men playing a little trick, trying to throw a scare into me so I call off this patrol," Wexler snapped, turning on Shorty. "Mmm? Sound familiar?"

Shorty snorted once and returned Wexler's stare without flinching. Wexler broke first, looking around at all of us with undisguised suspicion.

"Well, whoever it was, it didn't work. We are going down there, and we are going down there now."

Andrew C. Piazza

47

We set five men at the top of the stairs to cover our retreat if we needed it. The rest of us swirled down those spiraling stone steps like water down a drain.

They were narrow, only wide enough to go one at a time, and while the Captain and I waited for Shorty to push a squad down the stairs, I noticed Major Hayward standing near Tedeski and his tankers. The Major's face was clammy, and although the temperature in the basement was chill, a fine sheen of sweat glistened on his forehead. He held on to his Sten submachine-gun like he was trying to hold something buoyant underwater.

"This is as far as we got in our search before those screams started in the shower room. Now we'll see what's what. Come on, John," Wexler said, moving for the stairway, but Major Hayward stopped him with a hand.

"Major Wexler, please," he said.

"John, it's like the girl said," Wexler said, nodding toward Rebecca, who stood as close as she could to Captain Powell, "where else is safer than with us? All these men, all this firepower..."

"Useless," Major Hayward said. "If we go down there..."

"We are going down there. All of us," Wexler said, and practically shoved Major Hayward down the steps.

I couldn't resist a look upwards at the word written on the wall. *Wilkommen.* Welcome.

It was the Geist, and it knew we were coming.

The Captain and I traded a look and followed Wexler, with Rebecca set safely between us. Cappy followed, along with Doctor Schmidt, Davey and Goliath, and the rest, and I remember feeling better about being in the middle of the group with a cushion of armed men in front and behind.

The stairway wound down to a depth of about twenty feet below the level of the basement. The air got colder and thinner, and the electric bulbs did not extend this far, so we were in darkness. Flashlight beams pierced the air with insufficient light.

"This was the escape route for the Baron, when Dom Caern was a castle," Doctor Schmidt said, his voice floating down to us from further back along the column. "It led to a small tunnel going to the surface."

"Led?" I called back. "What happened to it?"

"Yes, it was destroyed in the experiment," came the reply. "The journals mention this."

We reached the bottom of the winding stairwell and came into a wide, plain stone room. Most of it, the close two-thirds, was empty and plain. The floor at the far third of the room dipped down into a wide, shallow basin, and it was only once I got closer that I realized it wasn't the same room at all, but a tunnel that intersected with it. "Intersect" isn't really the right word; it looked as though the engineers had dug a tunnel that enveloped the far third of the room.

"That's it," Wexler said.

The tunnel ran at a right angle to us, both left and right, and sloped down toward the right and ascended towards the left. It was huge; perhaps half again as wide as a two-lane road and as high as it was wide. Once I got closer, I could see it was almost perfectly smooth; only the effects of time and wear and tear had marred the surface at all. It looked like the holes cut by a post-hole digger; a perfectly symmetrical circular plug pulled out of the earth, only sideways at an angle. A large wooden platform sat in the middle, presumably to provide a surface level with the stone floor of the room.

"This is where they did it," Wexler explained, stepping from the stone floor to the platform. His camera was back in his hand.

"Did what?" Shorty asked, looking at the walls of the tunnel with his flashlight. "What the hell dug this? It's perfect."

"And we're going to find out where it goes." Wexler said, pointing his camera down the slope of the tunnel. "That way."

Once again, the Captain and I traded a concerned look and held a conversation in it. Whatever this tunnel was, it was not natural, or even naturally made; and wherever it led, the Geist called home.

We didn't waste much time in setting up a defensive position. Both thirty-cals were set up on tripods on the wooden platform, aimed down the tunnel to the right, down into the earth. The bazooka man sat between them. Just to be on the safe side, the trooper with the flame-thrower watched the ascending portion of the tunnel.

"Tedeski, have your tankers guard the base of the stairwell," Captain Powell said. "Make sure nothing comes down behind us."

"We've got those five guys at the top," Tedeski reminded him.

"And if they get taken out?"

Tedeski nodded thoughtfully. "Okay, so how about I put my guys at the base of the stairwell?"

"Good thinking. Sergeant Kinder, I want three men on each machine-gun, and one rifleman each to guard the flame-thrower and the bazooka. Davey and Goliath, Cappy, Sarge and I, on the platform as well. Shorty and the rest of 2nd Platoon stay out of the tunnel and in this room as reserve."

"I'll, um, I'll stay with them, if it's all the same to you," Major Hayward said, settling into the midst of the seven troopers designated as our reserve.

There were some strange metal fittings set into the middle of the platform, that looked like they might've been a stand for a heavy piece of machinery. If that was so, the machinery was long gone, but we used one of the fittings to mount a spool of telephone wire.

"They must've set the equipment up here," Wexler said to himself, looking over the fittings. "Damn! I wish they hadn't destroyed it."

"Destroyed what, sir?" I asked.

"I'm afraid that's classified, Sergeant, but as you have probably guessed, it built this tunnel," he said, never looking at me as he spoke.

He only had eyes for the depths of the tunnel. "Have they run the... yes, here they are."

While we were setting up the weapons, some more GIs ran the electrical line down the stairs and across the stone room to the platform. We didn't have any electric bulbs to string up yet, but we had found a pair of small floodlights left behind by the Germans, so we set those up pointing either way along the tunnel. The stone room, on the other hand, was lit only by scattered candles and makeshift canteen-lamps.

I couldn't get those floodlights set up quickly enough. Even with the candles in the stone room and a dozen or more flashlights shining about, the darkness always seemed overwhelming, like it might wash over us like a flood and drown us all.

Then, the floodlights clicked on, and my mounting dread eased for a second... long enough to remember that now we'd have to go down that tunnel and find out what waited for us at the end.

"Nothin'," Shorty said, peering down the tunnel as far as the floodlight allowed. "Just keeps going."

"All right," Wexler said, pushing his glasses back into place on his nose and raking back his hair. "We send a group down to see how far it goes and where it leads. Then we'll know how long of a string of electric bulbs we'll need."

"Where will we get them, sir?" Captain Powell asked.

"We'll strip them from the other cellar passageways, the ones that weren't lit when we came down here," Wexler said. "And anywhere else we can find them. But first, I'll go down there and..."

"Um, sir?" I interrupted. "Why don't you leave that part to us? No need for you to go sticking your neck out, especially with only that for company," I said, pointing toward the .45 pistol holstered on his belt.

More evil stares than I could count were directed at me from the troopers. Those looks were easy to translate... *you should've let the asshole get himself killed.*

Maybe a part of me agreed, but that just wasn't the way things were done. Majors do not pull solo patrols armed with a pistol; the idea is ludicrous. Just because he was a jerk didn't mean we could get rid of him.

Wexler seemed to think it over and nodded. "Okay. Captain Powell, what do you think?"

I immediately regretted my speaking up. No, no, Wexler, don't ask me what to do, I'm only a dumb-ass sergeant from Pennsylvania. Ask the Captain what to do.

Captain Powell shook his head in mild disbelief and immediately returned the ball to me. "Sergeant Kinder, pick three men for a patrol."

"Yes, sir. Warnal, Peterson... you two go with Shorty."

Shorty glared at me with wide eyes. I shrugged my shoulders and gestured towards the tunnel, and he gritted his teeth as he locked and loaded his rifle.

"So this is what stripes do for me, eh, Sarge?" he hissed as he passed me on the platform.

"Warnal," the Captain said, "you carry the sound powered phone. We'll pay out the wire up here. You should have plenty of slack. All of you, turn your flashlights on and clip them to your gear to keep your hands free."

"Last thing," he told them. "Keep your eyes open and your wits about you. You see anything, anything at all, you high-tail it back here."

"How far do we go?" Shorty asked.

"Until you find where it goes," Wexler said.

"Suppose it goes nowhere?"

"Start with two hundred yards," Captain Powell said. "I know we have at least that much telephone wire. If you don't see anything, leave the phone there and head back."

"Yes, sir." With a last baleful glance in my direction, Shorty switched on his flashlight and hooked it onto his gear. "Come on, guys. Just two hundred yards. Nothing to it."

Andrew C. Piazza

48

Shorty and his patrol hadn't gone twenty yards when Major Hayward abruptly joined us on the platform.

"Major?" I asked.

"Sometimes the not seeing anything is worse than seeing everything," he said, settling in next to me.

The spool of wire unwound slowly, helped along by Davey so that the wire wouldn't snap under too much tension. Each turn of the spool was another step closer to the patrol being over, so I counted them off, one, two, three, praying with each turn to get just one more, and one more, and one more. When I reached fifty, Shorty and his patrol started getting difficult to see, and at seventy, I had to squint and use my imagination a little to pick them out.

"Call them on the phone. Check the line," Captain Powell said.

I spun the crank and put the receiver to my ear. "Shorty? Shorty, can you hear me?"

There was a moment of silence filled with a sudden fear that there would never be any response, then Shorty's voice crackled over the receiver. "Hey, Sarge, have I thanked you lately for promoting me, you lousy S.O.B.?"

I grinned and turned to the Captain. "Phone's working fine, sir."

"Very well. What do they see?"

"What's down there, Shorty?" I asked.

"Nothin'. Tunnel just keeps going."

"How far have they gone?" Major Hayward asked.

"My guess is, close to a hundred yards by now," Davey said, still unreeling the wire.

"One hundred yards," Major Hayward said, looking like he was doing calculations in his head.

Wexler tugged on my sleeve like an anxious child. "What do they see? What do they see?"

"Nothing, sir," I answered. "It's just the tunnel."

I looked back at the spool and realized I'd lost count. It seemed like a bad sign, like the only thing that had kept Shorty safe this long was my dutiful counting of the spool's rotations.

The seconds seemed to pass reluctantly, as if time had become a stagnant pool of water, and I began to agree with Major Hayward. The not seeing was much worse than seeing. Shorty and his patrol were no longer visible, and the only proof of their existence was the slowly turning spool and the long telephone wire stretching off into the dark.

The silence became too much to bear and I had to shatter it with a little talk. "How are you doing, Shorty?"

"I'd lie and say we've already gone our two hundred yards," Shorty's voice said into my ear, "but that little know-it-all Davey is probably counting the turns of the spool and measuring each one to calculate it all out or some damn thing."

Almost on cue Davey said, "One hundred twenty-five yards."

I smiled despite myself. "You keep your eyes open."

"Don't worry about that."

To my left, Rebecca leaned toward the Captain and said softly, "Jiim, bring them back. They have gone too far, we can not see them."

"One hundred fifty yards," Davey announced.

"Maybe we could move some guys down there, you know, a little closer?" Goliath said. "That way, help would be closer if…"

"Gentlemen, Shorty has been on patrol before," the Captain said loudly. "He knows how to take care of himself."

"Hey, I got an idea," Tedeski said. "This tunnel is wide enough for one of my rigs. If the other end of the tunnel goes all the way to the surface somewhere, we could drive a TD down here and all the way to the end."

"And if it doesn't?" Cappy said, frowning at him.

"We don't have time to find out," Wexler said. "Anything yet, Sergeant?"

"Nothing yet, sir," I said.

For some reason, all of the nervous chatter stopped, replaced by the still silence I hated so much. There was only the clicking of the turning wire spool to let me know time was going by at all.

"One hundred seventy-five yards," Davey announced.

"Come on, Shorty," Goliath whispered. "Almost home."

Out of the corner of my eye, I could see Major Hayward fidget about restlessly. He seemed on the verge of panic; his hands never stopped wringing around his weapon and the cold sweat was now beaded on his brow.

Come on, Shorty, I thought.

"Hey, Sarge," his voice crackled over the receiver, "are we about done here?"

I looked over at Davey, who dutifully replied, "Maybe one-eighty or so."

"Shorty," I said, "go about another twenty or thirty paces and that's it."

"Hell yes, Sarge," came the reply.

"They keep going until they find something," Wexler said.

"Two hundred yards and that's it," Captain Powell said in response. "Then we pull them back and figure out our next move. Tedeski may be on to something with that idea about his tank destroyer rolling down here."

"We don't have time..." Wexler began to say, when Shorty's voice cut in yet again.

"Hey, uh, Sarge?"

"Listen up," I said loudly, to cut off the burgeoning argument before it began. "Go ahead, Shorty."

"Have they found something?" Wexler asked.

I held up a hand. "Hang on, sir. What is it, Shorty?"

"It's a... it's a door," Shorty said.

"A door?" I repeated.

"Damn," Major Hayward whispered to himself, closing his eyes. "Damn and bloody hell."

"Yeah, it's a big wooden… gate, I guess," Shorty said. "There's a little stone and mortar making a square frame for it inside of the tunnel, and then a big set of wooden double doors totally sealing the tunnel off."

"All right, stand by," I said, and relayed the information to the Captain and Wexler.

"Maybe it's another storage room," Davey said.

"It is not," Major Hayward said. "Major Wexler, pull those men back."

"I will not!" Wexler said. "We finally find something, and you just want to turn back? No way!"

"Major, I implore you…"

"Forget it, John! Give me that!" he said to me, snatching the receiver out of my hand. "Hello, P… what's his name?"

"Shorty," I said.

"Shorty, this is Major Wexler. I order you to go through that door and report what is beyond." He listened for a second, then frowned and handed the receiver back to me. "That… that soldier and I are going to have to have a little talk when he gets back."

I ground my teeth in frustration and looked over at Captain Powell. "Captain?"

"Hey, I am in command here, Sergeant, not Captain Powell," Wexler said. "Now tell him to do it."

The muscles on Captain Powell's face twisted in barely contained anger. "Do it, Harry," he said.

I put the receiver to my ear. "You heard the man, Shorty. Open the door."

"Great," Shorty muttered in response. "Hang on."

Just then, a strong draft of cold air blew across us, coming from the stairwell and heading down the tunnel. It froze my blood solid and for an instant I couldn't speak, I could only tremble in sudden, terrible realization of what had happened.

One Last Gasp

It was up in the manor this whole time, I thought. *Waiting. And now, now it's going back down the tunnel to its lair, where Shorty is... and now, Shorty's got no way out.*

Major Hayward was the first of us to break his paralysis. "Oh, God. Oh, God, Sergeant, pull them back. Pull them back!"

"He's right, Harry, get them out now!" Captain Powell ordered. "Everybody lock and load!"

"What's going on?" Wexler asked. "What's..."

"Shorty," I said into the receiver. "Get out of there, now."

"Oh, my God!" Shorty's voice whispered back. "You've got to see this, Sarge!"

"Shorty, listen to me," I said, struggling to keep my voice even, struggling even harder not to drop the phone and sprint down the tunnel to drag him back up myself, "get your ass out of there, right now. Do you hear me? *Right now.*"

"This can't *be*," Shorty whispered back. "It just can't..."

"SHORTY!" I shouted, suddenly losing my cool. "GET YOUR ASS OUT OF THERE, RIGHT FUCKING NOW!"

"Are they coming? Are they coming?" Major Hayward asked.

"Okay, Christ, Sarge, we're coming," Shorty said. "But you've got to see this... Hey... did you guys cut the lights up there?"

"What?" I asked, my throat suddenly going dry.

"I can't see the floodlights... oh fuck!" Shorty's voice rose to a shriek, and then cut off suddenly.

"Shorty?" I whispered hoarsely into the receiver. "Shorty?"

"What happened?" Wexler said. "What did they see?"

"Are they okay?" Goliath asked.

The wire spool suddenly spun with explosive speed, startling Davey so much he tripped backwards and fell to a seat. The wire paid out like a deep sea fisherman's line, whirring as the spool spun, and it finally got so fast that the spool itself toppled off its flimsy stand and tumbled off the wooden platform to the tunnel floor. It spun around in place a few times like a top, then its revolutions couldn't keep up with the pull on the wire and the spool itself skidded off and away, down the tunnel and out of sight. As it went, the end of the wire attached to my phone suddenly went taut and yanked the receiver out of my hand. It, too, slid down the tunnel and into oblivion.

"Holy Shit!" Tedeski said, waving his men over and cocking his grease gun. "Let's go!"

"Don't bother, Lieutenant," Major Hayward said.

"What?"

I noticed Rebecca had her hands to her face and was crying silently. Major Hayward looked down at the ground, almost guiltily, and then raised his eyes to meet Tedeski's.

"Those men are already dead," he said.

49

"We can't just do nothing," Tedeski said.

"You can," Cappy said.

Wexler nodded. "I'm going down there."

"Major, forget it," Captain Powell said. "We should check the other end of the tunnel, find where it reaches the surface, and bring one of Tedeski's TDs down here."

"We don't even know if it goes to the surface," Wexler said.

"Captain, if any of them did make it," I said, "they may be hurt and running short on time."

"You're not going to help them by getting yourself killed," Major Hayward said. "Did you see what just happened here? Believe me when I tell you, Sergeant, there is nobody to save."

"Hey, this isn't a democracy!" Wexler said. "I'm in command, and I say we go. Captain Powell, pick your men to accompany me."

The Captain looked at me with real regret in his eyes, and I realized it was the same look I'd given Shorty a few minutes ago when I tapped him to lead the patrol. I let out a long sigh. In a way, I was relieved to be going. At least there wouldn't be any not-seeing to drive me nuts.

"Davey and Goliath," I said. "Cappy... trade out with someone."

Cappy frowned and looked at Rebecca.

"I know," I said. "I need you with me."

"Here, take mine, Cappy," Goliath said, handing over his B.A.R. and ammunition.

"Goliath, you're going to need that," I said. "We need the firepower."

"We'll have it," he said, and bending down, removed one of the thirty-cal machine-guns from its tripod and held it on his hip.

I'd seen it done before; if a thirty-cal's mount was wrecked or the trooper needed to move fast, he might carry the machine-gun and fire it from the hip. It wasn't particularly effective at any sort of long range; that's why we always had them on mounts. The recoil made it jump around so much, that at any kind of distance, the bullets scattered so far and wide you might as well have been firing blind-folded. However, at close range, it could be devastating, and with a hundred-round belt ready to go instead of a B.A.R's twenty-shot magazine... well, you get the idea.

"It's going to be close up if it happens, Sarge," he said.

I gave him the nod. Davey scooped up an extra belt of ammunition and draped it over his shoulders. Cappy handed off his bolt-action sniper rifle, which was too slow for close-quarters work, and checked Goliath's B.A.R. over before indicating he, too, was ready. We would have plenty of firepower... if that could make a difference.

"I'm coming with you," Tedeski said.

"We don't need you," Cappy said, but I was too tired and too scared to turn down an extra hand.

"Okay, Lieutenant. Major Wexler, let's get you something a little more vigorous than that pistol."

Wexler looked down at his .45, as if surprised he had to carry a weapon at all, and accepted a carbine from one of 2nd Platoon's troopers. "I, um," he stammered, looking it over blankly.

I shook my head in disbelief. "I thought you were a weapons expert, sir?"

"Well, weapons development, mostly strategic... I never had to fire one, I mean, a rifle."

I pointed to the action on the side of the carbine. "Just pull that all the way back and let it ratchet forward. You've got fifteen shots. After that, push that, the magazine comes out. That sleeve on the stock has two extra mags in pouches... that's it. Stick the new one in, rake the action again, and go."

"Okay. But I doubt I'm going to have to use it," he said, slinging the carbine and keeping his small movie camera in his hand. "This is what I'll be wielding."

"Suit yourself. Just remember to take the safety off before you try to fire that carbine," I said.

"Oh. Right."

"Tedeski, have your tankers head the other way up the tunnel," Captain Powell ordered, then turned to me. "I'll send the TD as fast as I can. We'll move our strongpoint down an extra hundred yards behind you. We'll probably have to rip up this platform before a TD can make it down here. Other than that…"

"Other than that, there isn't much you can do," I said, then shrugged. "Hey, at least it isn't freezing cold and snowing, right?"

"Doctor Schmidt," Wexler said. "You're coming with us."

Doctor Schmidt looked at both the Captain and I in alarm. I didn't blame him. To go down there, after what we'd seen, and unarmed? However, it was obvious that Wexler wasn't going to budge on the issue, so he slowly stepped forward and into our group in silent resignation.

Captain Powell shook his head and snorted. "It's a good day to be alive, Sarge."

I flashed him a grin. "Isn't it always, in the Airborne?"

With that, I stepped off of the wooden platform and onto the floor of the tunnel. "We go in an inverse V. Goliath on the point with his thirty-cal, Tedeski and I on either side, and Cappy and Davey on the flanks. Major, Doctor, stay behind Goliath."

"What does this thing look like, anyway, Sarge?" Tedeski asked.

Davey shot him a look. "Thing?"

I groaned inwardly. How was I going to explain this one without sounding like a lunatic? They had a right to know something… but what?

"Just…" I began awkwardly. "Things might get a little strange down there, okay? Just shoot first and keep your cool. We're going down there to get Shorty and the others back if we can."

"Then let's go, Sarge," Goliath said. "This ain't our first time at the dance, you know."

As always, Goliath's baritone smoothed me out, and I gave him the nod to move out. We fanned out into our formation, weapons held at the ready, and headed down the tunnel.

Two hundred yards, I thought. *That's all we have to go, is two hundred yards.*

It seemed like a hundred and ninety-nine yards too far. I counted off our steps, to measure our progress, and it wasn't long before we'd gone far enough that the light from the floodlight began to fade.

"Flashlights," I said, and we all clicked ours on and hooked them onto our gear to keep our hands free. The beams wobbled and waved with the movement of our bodies, and I couldn't help thinking they marked each one of us as a target.

"Should've brought that flame-thrower with us," Tedeski said, as my pace count neared one hundred.

"Sergeant, what exactly did Shorty say before the phone cut out?" Wexler asked. He held the camera to his eye as we walked, filming the tunnel walls.

"The phone didn't cut out," Davey said. "It was pulled off the goddamn platform, remember?"

"Something about, it can't be, that I had to see it to believe it," I said.

"So what does that mean?" Wexler asked.

"You'll find out in another hundred yards," Goliath said.

It got quiet after that, quiet enough that I could hear Captain Powell giving orders far off in the tunnel behind us. They were moving the heavy weapons up closer and taking the platform apart.

They won't be far, I thought. *One hundred yards away. For all the good it'll do.*

My count reached one hundred and fifty. I tried to calculate how far under the earth's surface we were... fifty feet? A hundred? It was impossible to tell. The tunnel kept on going, still perfectly circular, still flawless and inscrutable.

One hundred seventy-five yards.

"Hang on," Goliath said, bringing us to a halt.

"What is it?" Wexler asked.

Goliath adjusted his flashlight so it shone straight ahead. "I think I see it."

"Okay," I said, feeling the butterflies and the old tingle of nervous energy once again, "nice and easy."

It was exactly as Shorty had described it: a massive, solid wooden gate set in a framework of stone and mortar. It was big enough that Tedeski's tank destroyers could fit through it, and a look at the lieutenant told me he was thinking the same thing. Wexler had us pause so he could get a good shot of it on his camera.

"There's blood on it," Davey said.

Not just blood, splashed in a spray across the wood at shoulder height, but a lumpy scrap of tissue as well. I could hear Cappy snick the safety off on the B.A.R. His eyes never left the stain.

"Cappy and Davey, on the rings," I said, gesturing toward the pair of two-foot iron rings set into either door as a handle. "Goliath back ten yards, Tedeski and I on either side of him."

Goliath knelt on the floor and steadied the thirty-cal. The belt of ammunition hanging from the side of the weapon swung and jingled reassuringly. I stood on his right and aimed my tommygun at the center of the door.

God, I don't want to do this, I thought, but there wasn't much point in putting it off. It was my turn, and besides, Shorty was on the other side of that door.

"Once it's open, we move in fast," I said, and nodded toward Davey and Cappy. "Do it."

They pulled, the doors creaked open, and we stepped into madness.

Andrew C. Piazza

50

I've seen all kinds of things, terrible things, but all of them up to that point were at least real, if horrifying. When you see a soldier crushed flat by a tank, you say, well, I guess that's what it looks like when a man is run over by forty tons of steel. Or when you see piles of emancipated bodies and groups of walking skeletons at a concentration camp, even though at first the sight seems to defy reason, your eyes eventually accept it as reality.

But this... this was *impossible*.

There's no way to create the impact of the first glimpse of what lay beyond that door with only words. Words take time to read, and can only describe one piece of the puzzle at once, giving the reader time to assimilate the information bit by bit. But this came all at once, in a tidal wave of lunacy.

There was an entire village laid out past those doors; fieldstone houses, two-story shops and buildings, everything you might find in a mid-sized village in the Ardennes. The ground was covered in three or four inches of snow, and worst of all, a gray light filtered in through a hazy sky overhead.

This can't be.

Too true, Shorty.

"How did we come back up?" Davey said, looking around at the empty buildings. The village was perfectly still and quiet, like a cemetery in the small hours of the morning.

"We didn't," I said. "We never stopped going down."

"Sarge, we had to have come up," Davey said, gesturing at the village.

"The sergeant's right," Wexler said slowly. His camera hung limply in his hand, momentarily forgotten. "My guess is we are over a hundred feet below ground level. The terrain around Dom Caern does not have any cliffs or drop-off topography that we could go down a tunnel and still come out on ground level."

"And there are no towns this close to Dom Caern," Doctor Schmidt said. "This is not possible."

"Wait, wait, wait," Davey said. "What are you saying?"

"Davey," Doctor Schmidt asked. "What is the time?"

"The time? It's four in the morning... 0400 hours."

"Then why is there daylight?"

Realization hit Davey like a shock wave then, as it hammered home inside all of us. We'd traveled one hundred feet deep into the earth in the middle of the night... and we found a snow-covered village bathed in daylight. My mind whirled and tilted in a crazed attempt to reconcile what I was seeing with reality. It simply couldn't be, and yet there it was, in plain sight right before our eyes.

"The snow's wrong," Goliath said, shifting it around with his boot.

"He's right," Davey said, bending down and sifting through it with his hand. "It's too dry, almost like sand. Hey! Maybe it's fake snow, you know? That would mean the Krauts could've built this whole thing, right?"

"Davey," I said. "This place is enormous. An entire village."

"Yeah, but maybe it's a refuge for Hitler, like an emergency bunker."

"And how would they create artificial sky, Private?" Wexler asked, looking up at the blanket of low-hanging clouds.

"Maybe... maybe..." he began, but Tedeski cut him off.

"Whaddaya say we find our guys and get the hell out of here?" Tedeski said. "There's tracks leading into the village, let's follow them and get gone once we find our boys."

"Good idea," Wexler said, pointing in the direction of the village and putting the camera back to his eye. "Let's go."

There was only one set of footprints leading off into the silent buildings. They didn't look right. Snow prints have a sort of punched-out look to them. These were more shuffling, like tracks made in the sand. Goliath had been right on the money... the snow wasn't right.

"Does the air seem thin to anybody else?" Wexler asked.

"Yes. It is like the air at a high altitude," Doctor Schmidt answered.

Every cell in my body screamed for me to turn and run from this terrible, alien place, run before I became a permanent resident here. Bad enough that the village was even here; knowing that the Geist roamed its streets made my knees tremble as I walked.

In defiance of standard street fighting doctrine, we stayed smack dab in the center of the street, mostly because we were too numb with shock to do anything else. Even Cappy... stoic, unflappable Cappy... wasn't immune; his feet occasionally stumbled over themselves as he eyed the buildings and alleyways as if looking for the one flaw that would prove this was all an elaborate hoax like Davey wanted to believe.

I felt myself falling into a daze of bewilderment and knew that the others must be as well. "Look sharp, guys. We're on the clock here, remember that."

Goliath paused for a second and turned back to look at me. "Thanks, Sarge," he said.

I returned the nod, which felt like a lie, and we continued, following the shuffling snow tracks through the silent village. In spite of my own warning, I too stared in bewilderment at the buildings we passed. They were absolutely perfect, complete down to the slightest detail, except for one thing... they were *too* perfect. Every village, no matter how well-maintained by the residents, has its share of broken windows or dirty front porches or whatever other little bits of entropy normally creep into an orderly state.

Not here. The entire village was immaculate; the only scratches on its perfect surface were the tracks in the snow that we followed down the street.

There was something else wrong with the village other than its immaculate nature. All of our architecture is based mostly on right angles and level surfaces; when I looked at the houses and buildings, every line and angle and plane seemed a little *off*. Everything was skewed or twisted or torqued the slightest bit off-kilter. It almost hurt to look at it, and the effect was amplified in my peripheral vision. I constantly twisted my head this way and that to get those weird angles out of the corner of my eye.

"There," Wexler said. Like all the villages in the Ardennes, a large cathedral dominated the village. This one was enormous, easily twice as large as what a village this size could support.

"Ten to one that's where the tracks lead," Tedeski said. The cigar tucked into the side of his mouth wobbled about almost constantly as he chewed at it.

The snow didn't crunch the right way under our boots; it grated like ground seashells, and the feeling went through me like running my nails along a chalkboard. Nothing about this place was right; it was like a plastic version of reality.

"I wonder if the houses have, you know, things in them," Davey said. "Like food, or furniture, or…"

"We're not finding out," I said firmly, praying that Wexler wouldn't contradict me.

As we drew closer to the cathedral, I could see that sure enough, the tracks led up the wide stone steps and to the front doors. One of the doors hung open on its hinges, as if to invite us in.

"Sarge?" Goliath asked.

I glanced at Wexler, but I already knew the answer. He wouldn't miss this for anything. His camera was already trained on the door.

"Go ahead, Goliath. I'm right behind you."

I followed Goliath's huge form up the steps, staying slightly to his right so I could cover that flank if necessary. Our V-shaped formation began to break up, now that we were forced to squeeze through a door, but Cappy and Davey at least had the presence of mind to watch our backs.

Goliath paused for a moment before going through the doorway. I wished he'd say something, smooth out my nerves with that baritone of his, but none of us were feeling particularly talkative just then.

Then, he went inside, and I followed.

One Last Gasp

Like the rest of the village, the cathedral was perfect... too perfect. The floor was spotless, there wasn't a speck of dust on the pews, and everything was immaculate. It was also empty, with no trace of the footprints we'd followed through the snow. There should've been at least some streaks of water left by wet boots, but there was nothing.

Wexler shrugged his shoulders. "Well, let's have a look, now that we're already inside."

I groaned inwardly. My instincts were screaming at me to turn tail and run, but this bastard with his secrets and his orders was forcing me to stay. The clock had to be ticking for us; it was only a matter of time before the Geist came and did to us whatever it had done to Shorty.

"Hymnals," Wexler said, stepping behind a row of pews and pulling a book off the rack. "They're in German."

"Let me see," Doctor Schmidt said. He opened the book and then shook his head. "This is not a hymnal. This is a German military manual."

"And this," he continued, picking up another, "is a textbook on physics. It is a copy of one of the books in the library upstairs... one you said you had studied in the English translation, Major."

"Well, what are they doing down here?" Wexler asked. As he spoke, he methodically ran his camera's eye over the entire cathedral, capturing it for posterity.

"A better question is, what are those supposed to be?" Goliath asked, nodding toward the stained glass windows lining either side of the church.

Images each more grotesque than the last were immortalized in those windows. Some of them were so bizarre, I can't really describe them; they looked like cubist renditions of a nightmare come to life. Arms, legs, limbs, eyes, teeth, claws, none of them human, in all variations imaginable, jutted out at bizarre angles with no rhyme or reason. One of the windows showed a mish-mashed jumble of appendages which slowly dissipated into a mist as the image went from left to right.

Some of them were identifiable. An SS trooper in full battle dress stood staring at us, with a *Sturmgewehr* rifle in one hand and a severed woman's head held by the hair in the other. It looked like a piece had been bitten out of her cheek. Another was a King Tiger tank, and another looked to be a line of prisoners marching from the cells toward the village we were in now.

"I'm glad I brought a camera. This is unbelievable," Wexler said, shaking his head. He was looking at a window that seemed to depict a large mass in the air splitting into several smaller ones below.

"I think this one's supposed to be a scientist working on a machine," Davey said, waving us over, then turned back to the window in question. "Whoa!"

The image was that of the Crucifixion, identical to the charcoal drawing left on the wall of the village we'd attacked the day before. Davey shook his head and pointed at it.

"That was not... that. I swear, that was a different picture a second ago," he said.

"Sarge," Goliath said, gesturing toward the other side of the cathedral.

Kleg's drawing from the village was duplicated in stained glass, exactly opposite the Crucifixion. BEFOLGEN SIE DEN GEIST was in script above it.

"That was..." Davey said.

"A picture of a Tiger tank," Goliath finished for him. "Only a few seconds ago."

Doctor Schmidt glanced at me in alarm. He didn't have to say a word; we both knew what this meant.

"We're leaving," I said. "Now."

"Hold it," Wexler said. "There's still more to..."

"Sir, you can stay here and die if you like, but if these windows are changing..." I wasn't sure how to finish that. "We don't have much time."

The others followed me down the main aisle, Wexler finally falling in once he saw we weren't kidding about leaving him behind. Goliath double-timed it to catch up to me before I reached the door.

"Sarge, what is..."

He stopped dead in his tracks just outside the cathedral's main doorway. So did I.

Standing in the middle of the street, with no weapon and absolutely no expression on his face, was Shorty Malone.

"Shorty?" Goliath asked uneasily. "You okay?"

Shorty might've been a statue for all he moved. There was a dinner-plate-sized bloodstain over the left side of his chest, and his jacket had a small hole in it.

"You're hurt, Shorty," I said, stepping a few steps down so the others could exit the cathedral as well. "You need a medic?"

He didn't say a word, but simply stared straight ahead while the rest of our group filed out into the street in front of him. There was something wrong with his eyes; he looked dazed or drugged, perhaps. Finally, after an eternity of silence, his eyes rolled toward me and he spoke.

"Sarge." It was spoken slowly and uncertainly, as if it were a word in a foreign language spoken for the first time.

"Yeah, that's right, Shorty, it's me," I said. "Are you okay?"

The ache in the pit of my stomach told me there was nothing okay with Shorty, that everything was extremely *wrong* with Shorty. No weapon, no expression, glazed eyes... it was like I was looking at a stranger.

"What's wrong with him?" Wexler asked from the rear of the group.

"Sergeant, ask him what happened to him," Doctor Schmidt said.

"I... missed Rebecca," Shorty said slowly.

I frowned at that. Men in shock sometimes speak pure gibberish, though, so I ignored it and went on. "What happened here, Shorty? Tell us what happened."

"Tell you," Shorty said. "Tell you."

His face suddenly contorted and twisted in pain. He looked as if he were struggling to draw air into his lungs.

"Shorty?" I asked.

"No," he spat out. "No... I don't... want to..."

His fists clenched at his sides and his whole body quivered. "Don't... make me..."

"What the hell is wrong with him?" Tedeski asked.

Shorty's arms raised to his head slowly, trembling and shaking the entire way, as if straining against a heavy weight. He finally got his hands up to his helmet, which he lifted off his head and dropped to his feet in front of him. It landed upside-down like a bowl.

"What are you doing?" I asked. "Shorty, come on, quit screwing around and let's go home."

"Home," Shorty forced between quivering lips. "No... stop..."

He seemed to lose control of himself for a second, grimacing horribly, then he tried again. "Stop... don't..."

His hand slid down and drew the trench knife from his belt.

Five weapons immediately trained on Shorty, including my own. Wexler aimed the camera at him.

"Shorty, put that away, right now," I said. "Put it away. You don't need it."

"Don't... make me," Shorty gasped out, still struggling with himself. "Not... *me*..."

I shook my head. "Nobody's making you do anything, Shorty. Put that away."

His free hand raised once again, shaking its way up to his mouth. "S-stop..." he began, and then his free hand reached into his mouth and grabbed his tongue. Hand still shaking, he pulled it out until it looked like it might rip loose.

"Stop..." he stammered around his captive tongue. "Stop... me!"

"Oh, fuck!" I shouted, lowering my weapon in preparation to tackle him, but it was too late. With a quick slash, he sliced his own tongue off at the root.

51

"God *damn!*" Tedeski said, cringing back and away from Shorty, whose mouth now drooled long strings of blood. The rest of us stared in horror as Shorty unceremoniously dropped his tongue into his upturned helmet.

The trembling in his body had stopped and he turned to face me once more. "Tell," he mumbled, blood pouring out of his mouth as he spoke.

"He's gone nuts," Tedeski said. "We gotta get that knife away from him."

The trembling began again, and Shorty now turned towards Cappy. His face contorted in pain and effort once again, and he said, "Cappy. Kill me."

Cappy didn't move. He simply looked down the barrel of his weapon at Shorty.

Shorty's free hand raised again, turning to point a finger at his neck. His thumb pointed up... he was making a gun with his hand. "Is... not... *me!*" he forced out, then more insistently, "Do... it, Cap-*PY!*"

For a long second, I wasn't sure he was going to do it. For a long second, I wasn't sure if I should stop him or not. And then, that long second was over, and Cappy's weapon bucked once with thunder.

His aim was true; the bullet plowed straight through Shorty's open mouth and out the back of his head. Shorty's body crumpled to the ground unceremoniously.

"You shot him," Wexler whispered, lowering the camera. "You actually shot him."

A long, low moaning rose up from the village, out of sight and all around us. Along with it, came the wind; I couldn't feel it, but I could see it kicking up the dry snow and hear it whistling through the alleyways.

"We must go," Doctor Schmidt said into my ear. "Now."

"How could you shoot your friend like that?" Wexler said, but Cappy had nothing to say.

"He asked him to," Davey answered for him. "Didn't you see?"

"Sarge," Goliath said in a warning tone, and I turned to look.

"But..." Wexler began to protest, and I cut him off.

"Major," I said, nodding toward the street deeper into the village, "now is *not* the time."

Out of the alleys on either side, Warnal and Peterson dragged themselves into the street. I say dragged, because in their condition, walking was an overstatement.

"How can those men still be alive?" Wexler asked in a hushed tone.

"Sir," I said as evenly as I could, "I don't think they are."

Warnal was the worse of the two. His guts hung out of his stomach and dragged in a loopy mass behind him as he staggered forward. Most of his face was gone, along with a large chunk of his thigh, enough that I could see the white of exposed bone even from here.

Peterson's only wound was his left arm. It was torn out at the socket and hung by a flap of skin and combat jacket, swinging around behind him and slapping against his back as he walked.

"Let's go," Wexler stammered. "Let's go, let's go, go now..."

He started to bolt and I grabbed his arm and held him tight, my eyes never leaving the two mangled troopers who shambled into the center of the street.

"Are you nuts?" he said, struggling against me. "Let me go! You're the one who wanted to go, let's go!"

"We don't run," I said.

"The hell with that, we run and we run now," Wexler said. "We have to get the hell out of here!"

"We are," I said. "But if you want to live, you do as I say."

His struggles petered out a bit, and Goliath's baritone said, "Sarge, I'm not sure what I'm seeing here, but I'll back your plan."

One Last Gasp

God bless you, Goliath, I thought. "Keep your cool. We back off nice and easy, back towards the tunnel. No aggressive moves. Cappy?"

"I hear you, Sarge," Cappy replied.

"What do you mean, nice and easy?" Wexler asked. He seemed to have forgotten his camera for now.

Warnal and Peterson came to a stop in the center of the street, facing us. I was glad they weren't between us and the tunnel; I don't know if I could've found the strength to walk past them.

"Do you know what you do when you see a bear in the woods?" I said.

"Is this some sort of a joke?" Wexler said.

"No joke. Just good old back woods know-how. When you stumble on to a bear in the woods, the last thing you should do is turn and run… because he'll only chase you down and tear you apart. No, you back off, nice and slow, to let him know you're going, and to keep him where he is. It keeps the situation neutral. A predator sees something turn tail and haul ass, it will chase it every time."

"So we go slowly, and perhaps the Geist is confused or disinterested long enough for us to get away," Doctor Schmidt said. "A very good idea, Sergeant."

"Yeah, well, it hasn't worked yet, so hold the applause," I said, backing away toward the tunnel.

Warnal and Peterson didn't move; they stood there in the street and stared at us with their dead eyes. The quiet started getting to me; I found myself glancing left and right along the alleyways we passed, sure I would see the Geist and that it would be the image I took to my grave.

"Yep," I said as we all walked backwards towards the tunnel, guns raised, "Sometimes on the line, we'd see some Germans and they'd see us and nobody would shoot. Live and let live. Even if they seriously outgunned you, if you stayed quiet sometimes they'd leave you alone. Not worth the bother."

The seashell snow crunched slowly under my boots, and it took every ounce of energy I possessed not to turn and run in a panic for the gate. How I kept it together, I'll never know. I should've broken; in a situation as foreign as that, how could somebody not break? The human mind is a strange thing, though. It can take a lot more than we give it credit for.

"What do you think made Shorty do that?" Davey whispered.

"I don't know," I said, glancing back toward the tunnel. The gates were getting steadily closer.

"Maybe he was... like those other two," Tedeski said. "You know."

"This doesn't make any sense," Wexler whispered harshly. His camera was back in action now. "The dead can't...walk. It's impossible."

Cappy finally broke his silence. "As impossible as all this?" he said, gesturing with his weapon toward the village and the gray sky above.

"That's different," Wexler said. "There's... it's just different."

"We are perhaps twenty-five yards from the gate," Doctor Schmidt announced.

Warnal and Peterson were almost out of sight now. The others kept looking back at the gate more and more frequently, and I could feel them wanting to break and run.

"Steady, boys," I said, but then, Warnal and Peterson started to stumble toward us.

"Shit!" Davey shouted, and that was all we needed. We spun on our heels and sprinted like madmen, terrified to look back and see what was on our heels and even more terrified not to. We covered the distance to the gate in no time, but my legs still wouldn't move fast enough; they seemed rubbery and heavy and weak.

I stole a glance back and saw something huge and heavy emerge into the street near the cathedral. It was a King Tiger tank, exactly like the one in the stained glass window, and its cannon swiveled toward us.

"Go!" I screamed, shoving Wexler through the open gates to make him run faster, and the boom of the cannon came seconds after our feet hit the tunnel floor.

I tackled Wexler to the ground, as the left half of the gate exploded behind us under the impact of the shell, showering us with wood and other debris and ringing our bells for us.

Where the hell did it get a tank? I thought, but I forced my way through my stunned haze and dragged Wexler to his feet. The others were already running up the tunnel. Doctor Schmidt held a hand clamped over a wound in his arm. Goliath slowed briefly to look back at us and I waved at him to keep going.

"Don't stop! It's right on us!" I shouted.

I noticed that even without my flashlight, I could see, and that's when I realized Captain Powell, that magnificent S.O.B., had moved his strongpoint even closer than promised. The light was coming from the floodlight.

The floodlight which was mounted on top of one of Tedeski's tank destroyers, to be exact. We swarmed up to and around that big, beautiful behemoth, and I wanted to kiss it for standing between me and the Geist.

The Captain saw our panic and gestured towards the machine-gunner on top of the TD, who dutifully raked the action of his fifty-cal machine-gun.

"What is it?" the Captain asked me, as I finally huffed my way up to him, still dragging Wexler with one hand.

"Tiger tank," I gasped. "Don't ask me how."

"The patrol?" he asked.

I traded a look with Wexler and finally let go of his sleeve.

"Dead," I answered. "All dead."

Andrew C. Piazza

52

Our waiting for the Tiger tank or our walking dead or whatever other insanity the Geist could offer turned out to be anticlimactic. For all its earlier showmanship, the Geist seemed content to sit and wait in its village for now. We left the TD in place with a squad of troops to watch the tunnel, and the rest of us got back upstairs where the light and the warmth offered us at least an illusion of comfort.

Wexler was shattered. What we'd seen down in the Village of the Geist was bad enough; that blast from the Tiger tank's cannon sealed the deal for him. You can't underestimate the effects of concussion shock on a man, nor can you predict it. Some guys brush it off like a bump on a crowded street; other men die from it.

We had to carry him, the Captain and I, one of Wexler's arms flung over either of our shoulders. Major Hayward took the camera out of his hands before he could drop it. Wexler stumbled along, dazed, occasionally mumbling to himself.

"What the hell happened down there?" Captain Powell asked.

I nearly burst out into unhinged laughter. How exactly does one relate what I'd just seen? Especially knowing how it will sound? Even though I knew Captain Powell had been witness to some strange events, the words still didn't seem to want to come out.

"How did you get down the tunnel?" I asked rather than answer him.

"It comes up about a hundred yards away from the manor," Captain Powell said. "The Germans covered the hole with plywood. We're lucky one of the TDs didn't drive over it by accident; it would've fallen right through. Anyway, we pulled the cover off and drove one of Tedeski's rigs down here."

"The platform?" I asked.

"Twenty-odd tons of steel crushed whatever we couldn't move out of the way fast enough," the Captain answered.

We dragged Wexler into the dining room, sitting him at the head of the table with the Captain and I on either side. There was quite an entourage with us: the entire patrol, including Doctor Schmidt, and Rebecca and Major Hayward as well.

Wexler shook and stared straight ahead at nothing, so I said, "Lieutenant. Maybe you should get a bit of that liquor stash, sir."

Tedeski snorted and dug a hip flask out of his jacket pocket. "Already here."

I took it from him and held it uncapped under Wexler's nose. He shrank away from it at first, but drank some and seemed to come around a bit. It think it was more the smell than anything else, acting like smelling salts to bring him around; in any case, he was lucid now and that was what we needed.

"Major," Captain Powell asked with surprising concern, "are you okay? Do you want a cigarette?"

Wexler blinked a few times and looked at the offered pack. "Don't smoke," he said, but took one anyway.

I lit it for him and watched as he took a drag and nearly coughed his lungs out. When the fit passed, he shook his head and said, "It's really real. It's really... real."

We all sat silent as he finally raised his eyes and looked around at all of us. "Look. I... I know you all think I've been a real... asshole. But you have to believe me, I never thought any of this would happen. I never... I didn't believe it was really real."

He shook his head and tried to explain. "Up until now, this thing, this Geist, was nothing but a theory. Just a story in a book, you know? It's like you read about something that happened, but it doesn't really hit home that it's real. It's just words on a page."

"Even when I saw this place, saw the bodies in the shower room... it still wasn't real for me. I mean, a bomb could've gone off in there, or... I hadn't seen it happen, so it was all so removed from me. Can you understand what I mean?"

"I think we can all understand what you mean," Major Hayward said.

"It was like that for me on my first combat drop," Captain Powell said. "We spent forever and a day training, and every day we were told this was to prepare us for combat, that we were going to war, that sort of thing. But it was all just training until the first time I pulled the trigger on a man. It was all just words until the first bursts of artillery fell around me."

Scattered nods and murmurs around the table added their assent, and Wexler seemed about to cry in relief. "I know I'm out of my depth here. I'm not a combat officer. I don't know anything about... I guess what I'm saying is, I'm asking you for your help. I'm asking you to help me get us out of this alive."

There was silence all around the table. Even in the face of an earnest plea for help, sometimes people need some proof that the request is genuine.

"Paul," Major Hayward said softly. "Perhaps the time has come to tell them. Tell them everything."

Wexler nodded and stared at the cigarette burning between his fingers.

"I'll go first if you like," Major Hayward said.

"No, no," Wexler said. "No, I'm the one who's responsible for all this. I should go first."

He took a deep breath and dove in. "I'm not a career Army officer. Not by a long shot. Three years ago, I was an assistant professor of physics at Stanford University."

"Three years." He sounded as if he couldn't believe it himself. "The war came along, and soon thereafter, I was volunteered to join the Army. It wasn't really a choice. Besides, it was an opportunity I couldn't pass up... a chance to work with the greatest scientific minds in the country."

"Work with them on what?" Captain Powell asked.

"Strategic weapons," I answered for Wexler. It was what he had said right before we went down into the Village of the Geist, when he explained why a weapons expert couldn't fire a carbine.

"That's right," Wexler said. "Every country in this war, every one, is taxing their scientific limits to come up with new weapons. Especially Germany. Hitler is obsessed with the notion that new super-weapons will pull his fat out of the fire and win the war for the Nazis. *Sturmgewehr* rifles, jet-powered fighters, V-2 rockets, you name it. It's a fool's errand; even though these weapons might give the Germans a local, tactical advantage, they can't be produced quickly enough or in large enough numbers to make a strategic difference. Unless."

"Unless what?" I asked.

"Unless his scientists find a way to create a weapon of mass destruction. A weapon that even in small numbers could create a strategic effect."

"What, like poison gas?" Davey asked. "Even Hitler hasn't used that stuff yet."

"Not quite poison gas," Wexler said. "Worse. We're talking weapons that might be capable of destroying an entire city at once."

There were a lot of unbelieving stares around the table. You have to remember, nobody had even heard of the Manhattan Project yet, with the exception of Roosevelt and a handful of top brass. It would be eight months before Fat Man and Little Boy would show Japan and the rest of the world what a strategic weapon was. In January 1945, the idea of an atomic weapon was as ridiculous to a ground soldier as ray guns and space ships.

"Are you serious?" Tedeski said.

"Are we working on these weapons too?" Captain Powell asked, then shook his head. "What am I saying? Of course we are."

Wexler nodded. "Everything involved is beyond Top Secret. I'm not even allowed to know anything about it. All I know is, there is an effort in that direction. Knowing what I know about physics, I can make some guesses, but that's about it."

"So what does this have to do with us?" I said.

One Last Gasp

Wexler paused for a moment, as if deciding on the best way to explain it. "A few weeks ago, a pair of B-17 bombers disappeared during a run over this area. Poof, right out of formation, gone. One made it back... barely."

"Their story, you might imagine, sounded ridiculous to say the least, even though the details from each witness matched those of the others. The surviving crew have all been committed, Section 8 cases, but now, after what I've seen... I know they aren't crazy after all."

"For all its strangeness, portions of the crew's story lined up somewhat with some intercepted intelligence concerning experiments conducted in this area. Later intercepted communications mentioned this Kleg, and when I heard that name again, from Captain Powell's report, I knew there might be some truth to it. So my superiors sent me here top speed to check it out."

"Some truth to what?" Captain Powell asked. "What is it that's happened here?"

"The bomber crew reported something very similar to what just happened to us," Wexler said. "One second, they were in formation, and the next, they and the other bomber... the one that didn't make it back... were alone and flying above cloud formations that weren't quite right. You see, that day, there was no cloud cover over their target. And then, in a second, there was.

"They came under attack, by things they found difficult to describe. Only one of them got a good look at one, out of the open bomb bay doors. It was too far below them to see much detail and in the midst of clouds, but he described it as being as large as a zeppelin."

"Holy Shit," Tedeski said. "As big as an airship?"

"They also said the creatures appeared and disappeared at will, and that... one of their crew who was killed spoke to them. After he was dead."

"Like Shorty," I said.

"Like Shorty," he said.

"What?" Captain Powell asked. "What are you talking about, like Shorty?"

I ran down what had happened to us in the Village of the Geist. The words came out a lot more easily than I thought they would, mainly because of their juxtaposition with Wexler's story. The incredible seems more reasonable when it sits next to the impossible.

Wexler took a few more pulls on Tedeski's flask and tried the cigarette once more before I finished, and then he continued.

"You can understand why I didn't believe the story. That's why I didn't believe the Geist was real. I came here looking for a weapon, one which could make two bombers disappear off radar and affect the minds of their crews enough to create those hallucinations... what I thought were hallucinations. After I heard about Kleg and how his SS were... with what they were doing here... I assumed their minds had been affected as well. When I got here, I found references in those scientific journals to something deadly that had no form.

"At first I thought, radiation. Radiation has no form; it can't be felt or seen or smelled or heard, but enough of it can kill. And like a fool, I ignored all the evidence to the contrary. I saw only what I wanted to see, only that which supported my theory of a radiation weapon of some sort."

"So what do you think now?" Captain Powell said.

"Well, it isn't radiation," Wexler said with an uneasy laugh. "From what I could gather from the experimental records, the Germans were tinkering with reality on a sub-atomic level."

"Um," Tedeski said, and held up his hands.

"Everything is made up of molecules, and molecules are made up of atoms, and atoms are made up of protons, electrons, and neutrons," Wexler said. "But those particles are made up of even smaller components... we think. And once you start messing around on that level, you see strange things, which can lead to some strange theories."

"Like what?" Tedeski asked.

"Like space is really bent, or time is not linear," Wexler answered. "There's also theories... it has to be."

"What? You're killing me, here! Out with it!" Tedeski said.

"There are theories concerning alternate realities, alternate universes. You can't walk to one or fly to one, because each one is already here, all around us, inside of us, co-existing in the same space and time, but separated from us."

"How?" I asked. "How can that work?"

"It's sort of like... think of a room that is in the dark. It's a dark room; it looks a certain way. You can't see anything but dark, vague shapes. Then you turn the light on, and it looks another way. But imagine that the dark is still there; you just can't notice it because of the light. Two separate rooms, perceptually speaking, in the same space at the same time. I think the Germans found or made a doorway to an alternate reality... a dark side of our own, if you like."

"Is that what that big wooden gate is?" Davey said. "Easy. We brick it up or something."

"It's not that simple," Wexler said. "Remember that tunnel goes in both directions. That bomber crew stumbled into that alternate reality as well. Perhaps... think of the entire tunnel as the door. It's, uh, it's like an overlap, between the two worlds, so it's not just a tunnel through the dirt; it's a tunnel through the air as well. You follow it far enough in one direction, you go into that other world... like we did with the village."

"Sky overhead when we're a hundred feet under the earth," I said slowly. "So you're saying we walked into another reality, one in which we were no longer underground?"

"Oh, please," Tedeski said.

"No, that's pretty close," Wexler said. "The Germans picked this place for a reason. They called it a place where... 'the fabric is thin'. Is that right?"

Doctor Schmidt nodded. "Yes, the journals state that Dom Caern is a place where the fabric of the universe is thin. They say this is so because of the intense emotions released here over the years."

"Because of the inmates," Wexler said. "And the people this Baron Caern tortured."

I remembered what Doctor Schmidt had said earlier. *I never liked coming down here... the air seemed too thin...*

"I believe this may be starting to make sense for me," Doctor Schmidt said slowly. "What is it the scientists named this thing? The

Geist... the ghost, the spirit. And what are ghosts traditionally associated with?"

"Haunted houses," Davey offered helpfully.

"Exactly. And those who study haunted houses... not the amateurs, I mean those who truly, scientifically study them... say that haunted houses are like storehouses of energy, either positive or negative, created by the emotions experienced by those who dwelled within. Emotional batteries, if you like."

"So? So how does that fit in?" I asked.

"I think I see where you're going with this," Wexler said. "Maybe the truth is the opposite. Instead of filling a house full of energy, maybe the haunted house is a place where emotions wear the universe thin."

"And this allows the ghosts to get through," Doctor Schmidt said.

"That might be close," Wexler said. "I don't think they are ghosts, and I don't think they get entirely through. You see, another weird part of subatomic physics is this... it's unpredictable. You look at something on a small enough level, and all of a sudden, it's nudged a little to the side... metaphorically speaking. A particle appears out of nowhere and then disappears a billionth of a second later. An electron's path acts strangely, for no apparent reason."

"So these same theorists who talk about alternate realities say that this is the effect of those alternate realities; that maybe something happening over there affects what goes on over here, and vice versa. A thousand pound bomb goes off over there, it jostles the path of an electron over here. And if there is a place where the boundaries between our realities wear thin..."

"The effects would be more pronounced," Captain Powell finished for him. "Doors slamming shut, feelings of being watched, that sort of thing."

"Right. Emotions are just electrical activity in the brain, and that sort of activity creates an electromagnetic field, so maybe the effects are that ethereal; something happens over there to create a change in an EM field over here, which we perceive as fear or unease."

"So the experiment here found a thin spot and... what? Punched a hole through it?" Captain Powell asked.

"Exactly," Wexler said.

"It's a rabbit hole," Cappy said.

"What?" Wexler seemed startled by the normally silent Cappy actually speaking up.

"It's a rabbit hole," Cappy repeated. "Rabbit digs a hole in the ground. Above ground, is one world. Below it, another. Hole leads between the two. That tunnel is a rabbit hole."

Wexler made a sour face. "I don't, uh, that doesn't sound like a good way to…"

Cappy looked at him with his face set in stone.

"Yeah, okay, I guess," Wexler quickly said. "A rabbit hole, sort of."

"That still leaves a hell of a lot of questions," Tedeski said. "Like what is this thing, the Geist? And why does it do what it does?"

"The easy answer is that it's a natural resident of this other reality," Wexler said. "An alien being, alien in every sense of the world, completely foreign to this universe. Perhaps these wondrous abilities it's shown are as commonplace to that universe as sight or hearing is here."

"Alien beings," Tedeski said. "We found a rabbit hole to another dimension, and little green men are coming through it to destroy us all. Come on. You really believe that?"

"I don't believe in little green men or alternate realities, but I believe in what I see," Cappy said. "And what I saw was an entire village a hundred feet underground with a sky above and three dead men walking. You saw it too, *sir*. Do you doubt your eyes?"

Tedeski frowned down at his hands.

"I do not think the Geist is an alien as you say," Rebecca said, surprising us all a bit. I'd almost forgotten she was there. "Maybe it really is a ghost, and this 'other world' is where you go when you die. Maybe that place is Hell, and the Geist is what you become when you go there."

The room got quiet after that. My skin felt itchy; I couldn't shake the image of grotesque creatures co-existing with us, in our space, inside my body, right now. I had a sudden, almost uncontrollable urge to dig my nails into the skin of my chest, rip myself open to let those misshapen horrors out of me.

"The thing with the walls," Wexler said suddenly, I think to break the silence as much as anything else. "How it can change the walls... that explains the village. If it can change its own physical make-up, maybe it can have the same effect on its surroundings. Create things, buildings..."

"Yes, yes," Major Hayward said. "But I think the most important question to ask is, what do we do about it?"

"Nothing," the Captain said. "We get the hell out of here. First thing in the morning, as soon as it's light."

Wexler looked up at that.

"We can't fight this thing, Major," Captain Powell said. "We can't stay here. We have to leave."

Wexler looked down at the table, and nodded slowly.

"Thank God," Rebecca whispered.

53

Our little meeting began to break up on a rather disappointed note. I had been hoping for all the answers, but what Wexler had told us only created more questions.

It was easy to tell I wasn't the only one who felt that way. As everyone began to mill about before shuffling towards the door, Goliath worked his way close to me and said quietly, almost conspiratorially, "Hey, Sarge?"

"Yeah, Goliath?"

"There's something bothering me... well, honestly this whole thing bothers me, but something especially."

"What is it?"

"Shorty," Davey said from behind me, scaring me half to death. The inseparable duo's hand-off conversations sometimes really got to me.

"What about him?" I asked.

"If this thing can make the dead walk, and Shorty was dead when we saw him... well..." Goliath began.

"Did it seem to you like he didn't want to do what it made him do? Like he was fighting it?" Davey picked up seamlessly.

Now that they mentioned it... "Yeah. You're right. And at the end there..."

"He got control," Goliath said, terrifying me in that now I was a part of their shared conversation, "sort of. A little."

"So if he was dead... how did he know what was going on?" Davey asked. "Do you think that when it makes you do things, that your mind comes back to life too? Do you think you feel and think and everything, even though it's making you do things?"

"That'd be worse than being dead," Goliath said with a shudder, the first time I'd seen him do that. "I mean, when would it ever end?"

I thought about that. "When Cappy shot him, he dropped. The bullet blew out the base of his skull."

"Then that's it," Davey said.

"Sarge, if I go down," Goliath said, "you be sure to take care of that for me. I don't want to be walking around like that forever."

With that, they left the room along with the rest, leaving me to sit staring at the dinner table. My eyes picked out a stain in the wood left by a blood-soaked portion of the tablecloth that we'd removed from the table to cover the bodies stacked behind the manor house. That was some person's blood on the table. They had a life; a mother, a father, a job, dreams, faults, failures, victories; and now, all that was left of them was a stain on a dinner table in a house of waking nightmares.

"I suppose you think I'm quite the bastard."

My heart skipped a beat as Major Hayward's voice jolted me out of my reverie. I hadn't even realized he was still in the room; I turned and saw him leaning against the doorjamb with a guilty look on his face.

"Sir?" I asked, mostly to give me the time to process what he'd said. "No, sir. Not at all."

"Oh, of course you do," he said, leaving the doorway to join me at the table. "I held back information that might've saved some of your men's lives. You knew him well?"

"Who?"

"This Shorty person."

"Yeah," I said. "Since jump school. Before Normandy."

"Yes," Major Hayward said, making it sound like a guilty plea in a court of law. "And it gets worse."

"Sir?"

"Well, Sergeant, it gets worse," Major Hayward explained, "in that I've become quite the coward."

I blinked once in surprise. "Coward, sir? I don't think so."

"No, no, you were right about me," he said, "hiding out in the cold, smoking cigarette after cigarette to stay as far away from the house as possible. The only reason I was in the shower room at all was because I'd lost the feeling in my hands and feet and needed to warm up.

"And there's more. When Lieutenant Tedeski said we came running up to the showers after hearing those screams, he meant *he* came running. I stayed behind, frozen to the spot, paralyzed with fear."

"The worst part about that was, when I finally did move, it was because I convinced myself I would be safe since I would be several yards behind Tedeski; the Geist would kill him first, and I would have time to get away. That is the horrible, honest truth."

He stared at his hands folded up on the table. "So you see, I'm very much a coward."

"A coward wouldn't have volunteered to come along on our patrol through the forest," I said. "And who was the one who first suggested we go for the manor's front door when we got here?"

"Well," Major Hayward said with a distant smile. "At first, I was fine, because the only danger I faced was from men… and after what I've seen, men will never frighten me. Getting shot would've been a blessing. Killed or wounded, either way, I could avoid Dom Caern. And I suppose I got carried away in my exuberance, charging up to the house in a foolish display of bravado, daring the Geist to come and face me. That bravado disappeared once we found poor mutilated Corporal Bradley. Now, in its place, is cowardice. I simply cannot face my fear."

"You're facing it now," I said. "Sitting here with me in the house you're so afraid of."

"If you only knew, Sergeant," he said. "If you only knew what it is taking for me to keep myself from bolting out the door. I feel as though my defenses are a thin string that might snap at any time."

He shook his head. "I have been a soldier all my life, Sergeant. I don't know anything else. And now that I have lost my nerve… I have nothing."

"The world owes us nothing," I said. "You said that, right?"

"My father does all the time, but yes."

"Well, I think he's right, at least when it comes to things like bravery," I said. "There's no guarantees on that; it can be here today and gone tomorrow. I've seen guys who did stuff in combat that I swear should've earned them a Medal of Honor; and the very next time we saw action, that same guy would be cowering in a hole, pissing in his pants. I've been there myself. Bravery, or fear… these aren't permanent states of being. They come and they go. Just because your fear made you stumble today doesn't mean it will forever."

Major Hayward sat silently for a bit. His eyes didn't meet mine; I think he was holding back tears.

"I've never told anyone about what happened to me down there. I knew how it would sound, and that it would never be believed, so I told what I could and tried to do what needed to be done with that. That's why I tried to insist on bombing this place into oblivion rather than coming here. And that is why I tried to delay the reports of Kleg and what the SS have done here… so I could slip a request for a bombing mission through before anyone noticed."

It all made sense now, and quite frankly, I was impressed. I doubt I would've been clever enough or had enough presence of mind to come up with that plan. I probably would've kept my mouth shut and hid in a hole somewhere.

"What did happen down there?" I asked.

He stirred, as if coming out of a dream. "Mmm? Oh. Most simply put, they fed us to the lions. Just like the Romans who pushed unarmed Christians into an arena so they could watch them be torn apart by predators for amusement, the SS… well, it appears that form of entertainment hasn't gone completely out of style."

"They forced you down the Rabbit Hole?"

He nodded. "Yes."

"And into the village?"

"Yes."

I had to wait a few minutes for him to go on.

"They came for me one night. I think it was night. The basement was in a perpetual state of darkness, and as you know, the time of day in the Village of the Geist is not our own."

"They didn't tell us what was happening, but when a dozen soldiers herd six prisoners at gunpoint... we knew it couldn't be good. And we had heard about the kinds of things the Geist had been doing."

"Was Rebecca with you?"

He shook his head. "They only took some of us. I suppose they didn't want to deplete their ration supply too much. Kleg was there, somewhere toward the back of the SS, laughing and urging his men to get the show on the road.

"They led us down the tunnel and to the doors. At that point, panic took hold of the prisoners and they began to struggle with the SS. The guards shot one of them and shoved the rest of us through the door. There wasn't any way to fight them; we were so malnourished and exhausted, it was like trying to wrestle a giant."

"Once we were through... I think you can imagine the reaction. A clear, starry sky overhead... except we were underground and the constellations were not those I had grown up with. Two moons shone down on us, occasionally blotted out by the passage of something massive floating by high overhead. I think that's what hit me the hardest; no matter what insanity we humans perpetrate upon ourselves, the sky never changes. It's impervious, impassive, beyond worldly concerns by its very nature. Except now, even the unchangeable sky had been changed."

"Most of the prisoners scattered and fled, refusing to believe their eyes. They thought we'd somehow come back up to the surface and were being released, so they scattered into the buildings like madmen to escape the SS."

"Where were they?" I asked. "The SS?"

"They stayed in the Rabbit Hole. They closed the gates at first, so we couldn't try to get back in, and then, once they were convinced we'd run off, they opened back up to enjoy the show."

"You were still there? By the gates?" I asked.

"Yes. A captured American pilot named Passeur and I stayed close to the gates. They opened them and stood there, laughing and chatting, taking bets on what would happen next."

"They weren't worried about the Geist coming for them?"

Major Hayward shook his head. "Apparently not, although they did keep their weapons handy. Perhaps they assumed the Geist couldn't pass us up."

"The screams began about five minutes after we'd entered the village. Far off, and to our right. They didn't last very long. Passeur, the American, said we'd better try to hide or find something to press into service as a weapon. I agreed.

"We ran down a side street and into an alley. I told Passeur we needed to stay out of the streets, stick to the houses and out of sight, so that's what we did. We found an open back door to a two-story building that looked to be what passed for the village inn. It was mostly a bar with a room or two upstairs, but you get the idea. In the kitchen, Passeur found a cleaver and I found a butcher knife. We crawled out to the front windows to keep an eye on the street."

"It was only a few minutes before one of the other prisoners came into view. It was an older man, and Passeur wanted to call out to him, to get him inside with us. I stopped him."

He smiled distantly. "In my own defense, I stopped him because I'd heard something. Behind us."

Major Hayward paused for a moment and twisted his hands together before continuing. "So far, everyone has been talking about the Geist as a single thing, which Wexler's bomber crew says was the size of an airship. But when it came for us… there were many of them. They were nowhere near the size of an airship."

"They?" I asked.

He nodded. "I crawled to the door to the kitchen; that's where I'd heard the noise. I waited behind the bar, next to the kitchen door, to ambush whoever came through. I was expecting the SS. Even then, having heard all of the whispered rumors and having seen with my own eyes how real the unreal had become, I still pictured my enemy as human."

"What was it?" I asked.

"It was the Geist," Major Hayward said with a shrug. "You must remember, we were inside an unlit inn during the night time. There was light from the pair of moons shining overhead, but not much filtered into the inn. Everything was varying shades of black and dark gray."

"When it happened, it happened quickly. Something came through the door. Again, all I saw was a large, dark shape, and even though it was considerably larger than a man, I stabbed at where a man's neck should be."

"Larger than a man? How large was it?" I asked.

He hemmed and hawed before attempting to explain. "I could say approximately eight feet tall by perhaps four or five wide, but you have to understand… it changed its shape almost constantly. Even in those few brief moments that I saw it, even in the dark, I noticed that. It changed its shape constantly, like… like oil poured into water. It moved with an insane logic, flowing over the ground and through the air, extending its mass in some places, retracting it in others… It's almost impossible to describe.

"My knife hit something rubbery but yielding, and something hard punched me in the chest. It was a hard enough blow to knock me onto my back and take the wind right out of me."

I remembered seeing the ugly purple bruise on Hayward's chest when we first found him in the woods. I had assumed it to be from a savage hit with a rifle butt.

"So, you can imagine I was dazed for a few seconds. I didn't even have the presence of mind to wonder why it wasn't finishing me off. All I knew was, I was lying on my back on a hardwood floor behind the bar, struggling to get air into my lungs."

"I heard Passeur shout and then scream. The front door to the inn flew open, and there was a sound of shattering glass. It was at this point that I recovered my wits somewhat and pulled myself to my knees behind the bar."

"It was easy to make out the form of Passeur lying in the broken window. He was bent backwards over the sill. The Geist… the dark form we now call the Geist… was killing him. A… limb, I suppose is the best word… held him in place, and in the spilloff of moonlight, I saw another part of it form a… weapon. But unlike any earthly weapon. This was…"

He shook his head again, clearly at a loss for words. "Again, there isn't much I can tell you. It was dark enough to see only outlines and vagaries. I can't tell you what color the Geist is, or its texture, or any specifics. And the shapes it took are difficult to describe... too irregular for typical geometric terms. The best way I can describe its weapon was as a metal snowflake; thousands of sharp shards of metal that all whirled on themselves to create a grinder. It forced that swirling machinery... which was not merely held by the Geist, it was most definitely an extension of its body... into Passeur's chest."

"It tore him apart. Parts of Passeur... hit me... in a spray. Some of it was sharp enough to sting; fragments of bone, I suppose. Another dark form came through the door and a long tentacle jutted out from its mass to grip Passeur around the waist. They pulled him apart."

"There was nothing I could do but stare in numb terror. I didn't cry out, thank God. The two forms flowed out of both the door and window... I say flowed because that was how they seemed to move. Have you ever seen an eel swim through water? They moved like that through the air and along the ground. They flowed out of the window and the door, and joined the others outside."

"Others?" I said. "There were more outside?"

Major Hayward nodded. "They had the old man surrounded. It was easier to see them in the twin moonlight, but distance and the restriction of watching through a window still took away much of the detail. They shifted around, changed their shapes so constantly that it hurt to watch. Eyes that are used to watching the movement of solid, fixed shapes are offended when a part of the universe violates that sensibility. And it wasn't simply that some looked like jellyfish and others like perfect spheres and others like an elephant or rhinoceros or some other large mammal; it was that part of each of them took one shape and other parts took other shapes.

"One of them might be an oblong sphere with a crab-like claw on one side and a pair of antler-like legs on the other, with the main body appearing metallic. Then the claw changes into a tentacle and the body into that of a massive hound or similar animal, with the legs spreading out onto the ground like they just turned to water. Or other forms and shapes, some of them meaningless, some of them similar to earthly objects, some of them nothing but fluid extensions of the Geist's form, but all of them constantly shifting with no pattern whatsoever."

"Except one. Although they flowed and ebbed about... two of them even joined together to make a shape twice the size of the others, and another split into three unequal portions, each of which shifted about like individual creatures... they never allowed a hole to exist through which the old man could escape."

"Two more shapes flowed into and joined with the large one and it flattened out into a wide... sheet, I suppose. It bent over itself... think of a bulldozer blade or a vast wave of water... and the edge slammed down onto the old man, cutting him in two."

"I hid for a long time behind that bar, watching as the smaller shapes pulled the body's halves away and attacked them. The large shape... it was perhaps a little larger than a truck and briefly held the shape of a vaguely ovoid and bumpy lump of clay... suddenly slid along the ground and out of sight in search of other prey. Just before it slid out of sight, it vanished into thin air... as if it evaporated. It seemed to break into a thousand pieces, each of which broke again, and then each of which simply winked out of existence."

If he had been standing on the street at that point, he probably would've felt a cold gust of wind blow past him.

Major Hayward let out a long breath. "It took me a while to force my legs to work. I was trapped by the illogical notion that I was safe so long as I hid behind the bar. Even though my logical mind reminded me over and over again that it was merely a temporary reprieve, that if I didn't get up and move, sooner or later I would be found and caught, still I couldn't leave. I hugged my knees and trembled in the dark behind that bar."

I understood that. It was the hardest thing in the world to get men to leave cover, even when the Krauts had zeroed in on your position and staying put was certain death. Our base, animal instincts don't understand any of that; they want us to crawl into a hole and hide.

"Then, some screams drifted to me from another part of the village, and they galvanized me into action. I scrambled into the kitchen and out the back door, and rushed back towards the gates and the tunnel you now call the Rabbit Hole."

"What about the SS?" I asked.

"They let me go," he said. "They let me go back to my cell, that is. I ran up to the gates, and Kleg slapped one of the other SS on the arm good-naturedly and said something about winning a bet. The other SS guard paid him some money and they led me back to my cell."

"The entire time, they talked about what great fun that little excursion was, and how it was a shame they didn't have more prisoners with which to have their entertainment. Kleg promised them they would have some more soon."

Hayward sighed. "And then they put me back into my cell and I waited to be carved into steaks like everybody else."

I didn't know what to say to all of that, but I couldn't take the silence that lay heavily over us either, so I said, "We'll be leaving soon, sir. Couple of hours."

"And thank goodness for that," Major Hayward said. "Do you know what really frightens me, Sergeant?"

"Sir?"

"I'm terrified that God or Fate or Destiny might've brought us here for the express purpose of fighting the Geist, and that all of our attempts to cut and run will be so much wasted effort."

He shook his head. "We... the Allies, I mean... tried to avoid a confrontation with Hitler. We gave him room to maneuver, turned a blind eye to his annexations of Austria and then more of Europe because we were so loath to see the horrors of the Great War repeated. We cut and run until we realized too late that there must be a stand taken against him, and now our hesitation has cost us dearly. I'm afraid, Sergeant, that we were meant to face the Geist, that we must face the Geist eventually, and that when we do, there will be a terrible cost."

"Try not to worry, sir," I said. "We *are* getting out of here, and once we do, we will bomb this thing straight back to Hell."

Major Hayward smiled his distant smile again. "Let's hope so, Sergeant. For all our sakes."

54

Captain Powell looked up from the radio once he'd seen me walk into the room. "Trouble."

My entire body sagged with a groan. Bad news was not what I needed just then.

Major Hayward and I had mutually decided that it was far too quiet in the dining room after his story, and so we'd searched out the Captain and found him in one of the many studies scattered throughout the manor. This one had been converted into our radio room, and from the look on Rebecca's face as she stood close to the Captain, he was understating the situation when he said, "Trouble."

"What is it?" I asked.

"Kleg."

My eyes pinched shut. "Please tell me he hasn't probed our lines."

"Not yet," Captain Powell said. "But he's headed our way. 3rd Armored reports that an SS unit matching his description hit them earlier tonight."

"How bad?" I said.

"Could've been worse," he said. "3rd Armored took heavy casualties, but apparently they gave Kleg a bit of a bloody nose as well. It looks like he bit off more than he could chew with this raid. In any case, he's going to be hot-footing it back this way."

"Why is that, Jiim?" Rebecca asked.

"If the skies are clear when the sun comes up, his column will be a sitting duck for our fighter-bombers out in the open like that," Tedeski said around his ever-present stump of a cigar.

"But the snow is coming down more and more," Rebecca said.

"He can't take the chance. He'll sprint back here, and once he finds us... I doubt he'll let us leave," Captain Powell said.

"How long have we got?" Major Hayward asked.

Captain Powell gave us his humorless smile that said he hadn't thought we'd have this long. "I send out a ten-men patrol to keep an eye out, but with the dark and the snow..."

"Does Wexler know about all of this?" I asked.

The Captain shook his head. "He's holed up upstairs somewhere, reading through the journals like the world's about to end and reading is the only way to stop it."

"May I suggest, sir, that we keep it that way for now?" I said. "He won't get underfoot that way for when things get fast and furious."

I only realized after I'd said it that I had used the word "when" instead of "if". I guess that, like Major Hayward, I had a sinking feeling we weren't just going to waltz out of Dom Caern.

"Actually, I don't think that's going to be a problem anymore," Captain Powell said. "I had a talk with him after our little pow-wow in the dining room. He's not such a bad guy; he just got caught in a situation beyond his depth."

"If you say so, sir," I said. "What's our next move?"

"Everything gets packed up and ready to move. If Kleg comes back and catches us here, we fight our way through him and out of here. If the sun comes up and he's not here, we make a run for it. Either way, we're gone."

"What about a bomber mission?" Major Hayward asked.

"Already put the call in," Captain Powell said. "But it'll take some time to get the resources in place. Late today at the earliest, maybe tomorrow, but Dom Caern will be wiped off the map."

"Let's hope we're not still here when it happens," Tedeski said.

"Amen to that," I added.

"Tedeski, get your rigs ready to move," Captain Powell said. "Major Hayward, would you stay here with Private Wilcox and monitor the radio? Sergeant Kinder and I need to make some arrangements."

"Of course," Major Hayward said, settling in next to the radio operator.

The Captain and I left the room to begin organizing our withdrawal from Dom Caern. We hadn't gone far before Captain Powell said, "What's on your mind, Sarge?"

I hadn't realized until then how quiet I'd been... an unnatural state for me. "It was pretty rough down there, sir."

He nodded. "That's not it, though."

Damn Captain Powell and his savant-like understanding of the human soul. "You're not going to offer me a cigarette and then fake-smoke one of your own, are you?"

"Well, not now that you know that trick," he said.

I was quiet again, letting the clump of our boots be the only conversation for a bit. He let me have the quiet time, knowing it would eventually push me to speech.

"I sent him down there, Captain."

There was no need for me to tell him who I was talking about. The Captain knew. He always knew.

"I see," he said, and stopped briefly to address the throng of soldiers we came upon in the main foyer of the manor. "You men, get ready to move out. We leave at first light. Pass the word."

He led me down a hallway and away from everyone else before he spoke again. "So who should you have sent instead, Harry?"

I came to a stop in the middle of the hallway and so did he.

He nodded again. "It's a hell of a thing to ask, isn't it? Who should you have sent to die rather than Shorty? Should you have sent Cappy? Wayne? Davey? Who?"

I didn't have an answer for that, of course, because there was none. The Captain let me mull that over for a while before he went on.

"It's a lousy situation, Harry. Deciding who goes, who stays, who takes the tough job, who gets the easy one... it bends the mind after a while." He shook his head. "It's not your fault that Shorty's dead, Harry. It's not your fault there's a war on. It's not our world. We're just living in it."

"I don't know how you do it," I said. "Make these decisions, every day."

"Sure you do. You've been doing it yourself for a long time, now. You simply never realized it until today."

He paused and seemed to think things over for a minute.

"Harry... when this is over, I'm putting in a request for you to receive a field commission."

"A field commission?" I asked. "Oh, no sir, I don't want that."

"I don't remember asking you, soldier."

"But, Captain..." I began, acutely aware that Shorty and I had traded this conversation not too long ago, "...that would mean my leaving the company. I don't want to leave..."

"Want has nothing to do with it. We need junior officers who have combat experience. That's you. You've been doing the job of an officer for a long time now. Frankly, I should've gotten you some lieutenant's bars a while back. I apologize for that. I needed you here. But once this is over here at Dom Caern, you become an officer as soon as I can arrange it."

"But, Captain..."

"No arguments," he said firmly, and checked his pocket watch. "Very well. We've got a little less than two hours until it starts getting light. Let's get the men ready."

There wasn't anything else to say.

"Yes, sir."

55

The weather has always hated me. The war taught me this through many repeated lessons.

In this particular case, the weather decided that now was the perfect time for a white-out. Not just a blizzard, a white-out; the snow came down so thick and fast it was more like being in the midst of a swarm of insects rather than in snowfall. The wind whipped it around so the snowflakes stung our skin, and the whistle and moan of the wind sounded much like buzzing in our ears.

"We're fucked," Tedeski said, and that pretty much summed up the situation for us.

"We can't stay here," Captain Powell said, looking out the front door at the thick wall of white blanketing the entire world out of existence.

"No shit, sir, but look at that," Tedeski said. "Visibility is less than ten feet. If we go tromping around out there, we'll get lost and wander around in circles until we freeze to death."

"Speaking of which," I said, "that patrol still hasn't come back in yet."

"I know," Captain Powell said. "They have orders to get out on their own on foot if they haven't joined up with us by daybreak."

"They're still out there?" Wexler asked, crowding onto the massive stone front porch of Dom Caern with the rest of us.

"Yes," the Captain said. He stared out into the snow for a bit, and then finally said, "Rope."

"Sir?" I asked.

"Rope, Harry. We'll have a couple of guys scout ahead on foot, pounding stakes into the ground at regular intervals and stringing rope between them. Then the rest of us can follow it like a guideline."

"If the scouts don't get lost," Tedeski said.

"We'll tie the rope off here. If they get too cold or turned around, they'll follow the rope back to the manor and start again," Captain Powell said. "If anyone has a better idea, I'm all for it."

"What if we bump into Kleg?" Tedeski said. "Kind of hard to fight like this."

The Captain shook his head. "We won't. Kleg has the same problem we do; worse, actually. We've got three TDs and a half-track to move. Kleg's got fifteen or more Tiger and Panther tanks to slow him down and bottle him up, not to mention any support vehicles. His strength is now his weakness."

"Besides," the Captain added, "if we have to tangle with Kleg, we're better off doing it in the middle of all this."

"We are?" Wexler said.

"No visibility negates a lot of his advantages," I explained. "His tanks are vulnerable because we can easily get to within bazooka range because of the poor visibility. He can't maneuver his men for shit. The odds get a little more even."

"Oh," Wexler said.

I found myself thinking about Shorty as I stared into the blank whiteness with everyone else. I kept seeing him in the village, staring at us with his dead eyes, mutilating himself under the control of that thing we called the Geist. Davey had wondered if he was aware while he did it; the way he had struggled with himself, I think he was.

A look around the porch showed me the same thing, the same damned image, on the faces of each of the soldiers staring out into the snow as if they were able to clear the sky though sheer force of will. Each one of them, any of them, all of them, could be headed for the same fate. I had sent Shorty straight into the hands of the Devil himself. I couldn't do it again. No matter what the Captain said, no matter what platitudes he offered about Shorty's death not being my fault, I simply couldn't offer up another of my friends to the slaughter... or worse.

"I'll go," I said. It was the only way to avoid sending someone in my place.

The Captain saw right through me, of course. "Sergeant…"

"I'll need three more men. Volunteers," I said loudly, before the Captain could stop me. "I'm only going to take volunteers."

"I'll go," Major Hayward said.

"Sir…"

"It's about time I started pulling my weight, Sergeant," he said, then he smiled. It was a real smile this time, and not a distant one filled with guilt or remorse or bitter irony. "Besides, if it gets us away from Dom Caern, I damn well want to be a part of it."

I nodded and waited for two more. Davey and Goliath traded one of their telepathic glances, and I saw Davey start to shift his weight forward to volunteer.

"Not you two," I said, before he could move. "I have another job for you."

"I'll go," Wexler said. He looked around at the GIs raising their eyebrows at him. "What? We're all in it here, me the same as anyone else. I'm going."

"So will I," Doctor Schmidt added. "It will be good to do something, especially something that might make a difference in our situation."

The Captain started to shake his head, but I cut him off before he could say anything. "There's no time to argue, sir. Kleg may be trying the same trick to get to us. We have to get moving."

His eyes were sad and full of remorse, but at last, he nodded. "Very well."

"All right, gentlemen," I said, addressing the GIs assembled in the foyer of the manor. "Rope, and as much of it as you can find. Go."

It took a little while to get what we guessed to be enough rope together, during which time I took Davey and Goliath aside. "Listen up, guys. You two stick close to the Captain. No matter what, he's got to make it out of here, okay? I don't just mean here, Dom Caern. I mean the whole shitty mess, the whole war. He takes too many chances coming up front the way he does. You watch out for him."

"Sarge," Davey said, "why are you telling us this? You can do that yourself."

I looked out into the roiling mass of white that seemed to churn and fold upon itself like a heaving sea during a storm. "I don't think I'm going to make it back from this one."

They looked at each other in alarm. It was true, though; I somehow knew in the pit of my stomach that my time was up, that soon I'd be nothing but a spirit, a ghost, *ein Geist*, and frankly, I was okay with that. I was so damn tired and miserable and full of mourning and loss that I wanted it all to end. I didn't want to have to think about anything anymore, feel anything anymore, or especially fight anything anymore. My heart hung like a heavy weight in my chest. I just wanted it to end.

"Don't talk like that, Sarge," Goliath said.

I shook my head. I wasn't in an arguing mood. "Just do it, okay, guys?"

They never had a chance to answer me. Troopers came up with armloads of rope and my doomed little party had to get on its way.

I took my share of the rope and double-checked my weapon. Doctor Schmidt had the lion's share of the load; since he didn't have a weapon to carry, he got the sticks we'd use as stakes as well as a good length of rope.

The rope slung around my shoulder reminded me of the spool of wire down in the Rabbit Hole. It was easy to imagine the same thing happening to me. The GIs here would look out into the stark whiteness, seeing nothing, and suddenly, the rope would go tight and snap off the stone column around which they were now affixing it.

The Captain stared at the end of the rope wrapped around the stone column. I knew he was thinking the same thing as I was.

"Hey, it's like you said, Captain. It's not our world," I said, shifting the rope on my shoulder so I could keep a better grip on my Thompson submachine-gun, "we're just living in it."

He nodded. "It's a good day to be alive, Sarge."

I gave him a weak smile that we both knew was mostly a farewell. "We'll find out soon."

56

Ten steps into the buzzing cloud of white snow-insects and we could barely see the manor anymore. Twenty and it was gone.

It was surreal. I'd never been in a white-out before; I'd heard stories about the lack of visibility, but they always seemed so extreme as to be impossible. But now, in the middle of it, the reality of the situation was all too apparent.

We had to walk with our heads down, our eyes focused on our boots and the two or three steps in front of them. Any more than that, and the snow stung our cheeks and eyes, foiling any attempt to look up and around for more than a few seconds at a time. The wind cut through our wool layers until it felt like we were swimming in ice-cold water. My teeth began to chatter and my muscles began to shiver almost immediately.

It was slow going. We would trudge fifteen yards ahead, plant a stake, tie the rope off to it, and take a compass reading for our next leg. Once we moved again, I took another compass reading to make sure we hadn't veered from our course. It was that bad. Navigating through the white-out was worse than moving at night with no moon. I'd heard stories about the Navy frogmen who swam ashore before Normandy and marked the beach for landing. I guess that might've come close to our situation; trying to feel your way around with no visibility and no reference points with which to anchor yourself.

All we had was the tenuous life-line of rope stretching further and further behind us into the white. It made me feel like we were scaling down a cliff on a long rope, and the further we went, the more likely the rope would snap and we would plunge to our deaths.

"Do you think that patrol is okay?" Wexler asked loudly, to be heard over the swirling wind.

"In this? Probably frozen solid by now," I said, holding a hand out to stop Doctor Schmidt from pounding a stake in. "Hang on. We're a couple of degrees off. Move it over here."

"Good *Lord!*" Major Hayward said, as we made our correction and began tying the rope off to the stake. "This is so terribly wrong! It should never be allowed to get this cold!"

I tended to agree. "Major Wexler?"

"Yeah?"

"How about telling us what you found out about the Geist? In the journals you were reading. It'll help to pass the time."

"Like what?" Wexler asked.

"I don't know," I said. I checked the compass for our next leg, keeping my chin tucked as far inside my coat as possible to conserve warmth. "How can it appear and disappear? Change shape, make the walls change, all of that?"

"Well," he began, nearly shouting now to be heard over the wind, "the Geist obviously has a lot of control over mass and energy. They're related, you know; in fact, some people say they're the same thing. There is energy stored in mass and all mass is made up of energy."

"Like a bomb?" I said.

"Sort of," Wexler said. "Except most matter is so tightly bound together that all of the energy doesn't get released at once. But, on a big enough scale... the sun, for instance. Classic case. It's not just burning its mass, it's detonating it, in a constant, prolonged explosion. Sort of."

"Wait a minute," I said. "Does that mean it can burn out?"

"Run out of fuel?" Wexler said. "Sure. But not for a billion years or so."

"So we have some time, then," I said. "That's good to hear."

"Anyway, the point is, the two are made up of each other, closely related. So maybe the Geist is able to manipulate its energy/mass make-up, and become a solid shape or dissipate."

"Into nothing but energy?" I said, bringing us to another stop. "Another one here, Doc."

"Actually," Wexler continued, as Doctor Schmidt pounded another stake in. "My guess is a gaseous form. We felt a cold wind, remember? I think the Geist is able to instantly transform the physical make-up of its being, anything from solid to liquid to gas, and still maintain a cohesion that keeps it a single entity."

"So that Tiger tank we saw... it might've been the Geist itself?" I asked.

"Sure, why not?" Wexler said. "It's seen enough of those around here, what with Kleg and all, so why can't it mimic what it sees?"

"The arsenal," Major Hayward said.

"Sir?"

"The arsenal," he repeated. "That soldier's journal mentioned Kleg's troops bringing loads of munitions up from the cellar. We assumed they were simply stored there, but perhaps they were created there."

"Right, right," Wexler said. "If it can create the walls or passageways, it can create objects as well."

"You mean the Geist made all that shit?" I said.

"Possibly," Major Hayward replied.

"But why would it do that?" I asked.

"Who knows?" Major Hayward said.

"Kleg worships it," Doctor Schmidt said. "Remember what I told you about him, in the village? He said he had seen God. And his words over that ugly drawing of his."

"Obey the Geist," I said.

"Yes."

"But the Geist killed his guys too, right?" Wexler said.

"I am out of rope," Doctor Schmidt said, and our conversation came to a halt as we tied our second length of rope to the last stake and moved out again.

"What about... what about Shorty?" I asked. "You know..."

"Right," Wexler said. "I had a thought about that. Think of the human body as an electrical system... in many ways, it is. The nerves are basically wires going to muscles or organs or whatever, providing the energy or 'juice' to make them work. Simply put, of course. And neural signals are essentially electrical in nature."

"You can make a frog leg jump if you shoot electricity into it," I said. "Davey won't shut up about that."

"That's right. And I think that's what the Geist is doing, on a much more sophisticated level. If it can manipulate mass, it can probably manipulate energy as well. So it creates an electrical force to re-animate the dead. It uses our own built-in circuitry and simply adds the juice."

"Warnal's arm," I said. "The one that was almost torn off. It didn't move."

"Because the wire was cut. The nerve was severed," Wexler said. "No way for the signal to get to where it needed to go. I bet the Geist could've made it twitch, but any sort of coordinated movement has to come from the brain."

"When Cappy shot Shorty, he dropped."

"Because he was hit at the base of the skull. Destroyed the connection between the brain and the body. Cut the master switch, so to speak. Broke the circuit," Wexler said.

"He seemed like he was aware of what was going on," I said.

"Yeah, he did, didn't he?" Wexler said. "So maybe a little consciousness and awareness come back with you. Jeez."

He shivered, and not from the cold. We stayed quiet for a few minutes after that, slowly stringing out our thin life-line into the blankness of snow.

"The tunnel is shrinking," Wexler said abruptly. "Not the tunnel through the earth, I mean the real tunnel, the Rabbit Hole, the one that goes through the air as well. Some of the journal entries I reviewed mention measurements of the size of the tear in the fabric… so to speak. It's getting smaller. Slowly. So maybe the holes are self-sealing."

"How do you measure something like that?" I asked.

He just looked at me.

"It's complicated, isn't it?" I said. "Never mind."

"It really is, though. You…whoa," Wexler said, bringing us to a sudden halt. "Did you hear that?"

Our eyes squinted against the stinging nettles of snow and our ears strained to pick up anything over the howling wind. There was nothing; the white-out obliterated any sensory input past a few feet.

"What was it?" I asked.

He shrugged. "Sounded like somebody dropping a rifle."

We waited a few more moments, barely breathing, terrified to move in the slightest lest we miss the tiny sound that would confirm or deny what Wexler had thought he'd heard. I had to clench my jaw tight to keep it from chattering, and then, the wind died down for a second and I heard it.

It sounded like ropes straining on the rigging of a large sailing ship. A sort of tense creaking, up ahead, off to the sides, from more than one place.

"I hear it again," Wexler said, then the wind started back up. "No, wait... I did, though. Like old floorboards creaking. Right up ahead."

"I heard it to our right," Doctor Schmidt said. "From several locations."

"And over here," Major Hayward added. "To our left. Whatever it is, it's all around us."

The butterflies came back in an instant, fluttering and flapping their way around in my stomach. Gone was any sensation of cold; terror covered it up the way the wind covered up the creaking sounds hidden by the swirling snow.

What now? my jittery mind asked in a trembling voice. *What the fuck could it possibly be now?*

"What do we do?" Wexler asked, and then, a voice came out of the snow.

"Harry. Harry Kinder."

The part of me that hadn't been frozen by the wind now froze from terror. The words were spoken too evenly, familiar yet a bit too formal. Worst of all, the voice seemed to come out of the ground itself, low and perhaps twenty yards away.

"It's the patrol," Wexler said. "Thank God. Hey guys!"

"Shut up!" I hissed sharply, grabbing him by the arm.

"What?" Wexler said. "What the hell is wrong with you?"

"Just shut up!" I said, and now, I couldn't stop the shivering in my limbs. My entire body began to shake visibly.

"Sergeant," Doctor Schmidt asked softly, "do you recognize the voice?"

"Yes," I said, and the words felt like an admission of insanity. "I recognize the voice."

Everything clicked into place in my mind, like the tumblers of a lock on a door leading to madness. The way some GI had apparently dragged poor Freddie's corpse around the back of the manor. The creaking noises all around us. The missing patrol, lost and presumably frozen stiff. The voice which seemed to come out of the ground itself.

"It's Freddie Howard," I said at last.

"Freddie..." Wexler began, then his voice dropped to a harsh whisper. "Oh, *shit!* The Freddie you found in the damn freezer?"

His carbine shook visibly as he aimed it out at the snow in front of us. I didn't have the heart to tell him the rest; to tell him what the creaking sounds were all around us. He'd figure it out soon enough. It didn't take much imagination to speculate on what a frozen muscle would sound like if it were forced to strain and contract involuntarily.

"Harry," the voice came again, still flat and emotionless. "Let's play, Harry. Let's play some ball."

"Shut up." The words coming out of my mouth had no force behind them. They came out like a wheeze, like the final wisp of my last gasp.

"Hayward," another voice came from our right; different but still emotionally flat. "John Hayward. The kitchen is open, Hayward."

I could see the muscles of Major Hayward's face moving involuntarily as he struggled to stay in control of his panic. "The SS trooper. The one with the cleaver," I said.

He nodded. "But he's speaking perfect English."

"All right, the hell with all this," Wexler said. "This rope patrol thing is over."

"Harry," Freddie's voice called out to me from ground level. "Harry, let's play some ball. I should be in your garden, Harry Kinder."

"Let's go," Wexler said, tugging on my sleeve. "Back along the rope. Fast."

I couldn't move; my mind was too fixated on creating an image of Freddie, lying in the snow close by, propping himself up with his only arm. A long trail would wind behind him, a track left by dragging his body along with that one arm. The final injustice had been done to him; he'd killed himself to escape the torment of living, and now the Geist was forcing him back into his tattered body.

"My weapon's frozen. The action is stuck," Wexler said.

"Shut up," I whispered quietly, not to Wexler, but to the broken puppet Freddie Howard's body had become.

"Hayward!" the other voice called out, louder now, closer, and more insistent. "The kitchen is open!"

There was laughter then, high-pitched, insane laughter, and I thought I could see a dark figure dressed in a black uniform coming towards us in the snow. It could've been my imagination, but the glint of a cleaver's blade seemed to wink from where his right hand would be.

"No!" Major Hayward roared, shouldering his weapon and pouring a thundering rattle of gunfire into the snow where the dark figure stood.

"Go! Go now!" he shouted, shoving me toward the rope with his left hand before firing another long burst at the dark phantom in the snow. "Go, Sergeant!"

I stumbled along the length of the rope back the way we'd come, one hand trailing along the line to make sure I didn't lose it. Behind me, Major Hayward shouted as he fired at the phantoms shambling towards us through the snow, and Wexler pushed me forward as fast as my numb and trembling feet would allow.

"Come on, Sarge, let's go!" he shouted.

I couldn't help it. I was lost in a haze, a swirl of horror as thick and as blinding as the snow that stung my cheeks. It was too much for me to take at once; I was overwhelmed and crushed under the weight of the frozen terror stumbling towards us out of the blizzard.

I lost track of time and space. All I knew was the feel of the rope in my hand and the knowledge that I had to keep going forward, as fast as I could, or I would become one of those animated corpses staggering through the white blankness with muscles creaking from the cold.

And then, as my numb mind dully began to think that we must be close to home, the lifeline came to an end. A broken tassel of rope hung from the last stake, nowhere near the manor, but stuck out in the center of whiteness instead.

"Why'd you stop?" Wexler asked, then he saw it, too.

Jittery, insane laughter came up from the depths of my soul, quickly turning into sobs of rage and fear. "I give up. I give up!" I shouted, breaking the last stake over my knee and throwing it out into the blizzard.

"Don't say that," Wexler said.

"Why not?" I said, whirling on him. My body felt separated from my mind; it was like I was drunk or about to pass out from lack of sleep. "Don't you see what it did? It ripped up our rope and stuck it back in another place to lead us out into the middle of nowhere."

"So, what do we do?" Wexler said. "How do we get back?"

"I don't know," I said.

"Come on, Sarge, there has to be…"

"I said I don't know!" I screamed at him. "What the fuck do you want from me? I don't know!"

"Perhaps our footprints," Doctor Schmidt said.

"We lost the trail going back to the manor," I reminded him. "And how do we know if we backtrack that we'll pick up the right set of footprints? The Geist could make a fake trail leading straight into nothing, like it did with the rope."

I dropped to a seat in the snow.

"Sergeant," Major Hayward said. "Get up."

"I don't think so, sir. You want to go, you go. I've had it."

It was simply that I'd reached my breaking point. I'd run out my entire reserve of patience and endurance and downright stubborn will to live. The world was full of nothing but misery and death and destruction, and I didn't want to fight anymore. I didn't want to hurt anymore. So I sat down next to the frayed end of the rope and waited for the Geist to come for me.

"Sergeant," Major Hayward said more insistently, "get up this instant."

"I said, no. You want to go, go on. Go."

Doctor Schmidt looked down at me and then sat down next to me with a thump. I had a feeling he felt much the same way I did. I couldn't blame him. All the shit he'd gone through, and now to find out he was on the losing team, and stuck out here, lost, with Death all around.

"So that's it? You're giving up?" Major Hayward said.

"It appears so, sir," I said.

"There's got to be something we can do," Wexler said. He didn't sound like he really believed himself.

"Like what?" I said, gesturing at the snow burying us under. "Look around you, Major. Where are we going to go? We're lost. You want to get up and get going? Which way? We could start walking and end up going away from Dom Caern and out into the woods... or even better, in circles, until we freeze to death or the Geist decides to take us out. Forget it. It's hopeless."

"It is not hopeless!" Major Hayward said. "There is always hope!"

"What hope?" I shouted up at him. "We're fucked! It's only a matter of time before Freddie and the others catch up to us!"

"Only when you lay down to die is there no hope," Major Hayward said. "Until that time, so long as you keep drawing breath, you have a chance. You have hope. If you give up, you have no chance. If you fight on, even though you may still fail, you still at least have got some chance. And the longer you can hold on, the more chances you get."

"This is the real world, Major, not a fucking fairy tale," I said. "There aren't any miracles that are going to save us. It doesn't happen. No miracle saved Ridley and the others in the shower room, no miracle saved Freddie, or Shorty, and no miracle is going to save us. There's no such thing."

"There is," Major Hayward said. "I've seen them. You want a miracle? Dunkirk. A beaten army, a broken army, driven up against the sea with no escape. Outnumbered, outgunned, outmatched... we should have dug our graves on that beach. Certain death surrounded us and closed in for the kill.

"And then, Sergeant, a miracle. Boats. Hundreds of boats. Thousands! Boats of every kind, from ships of the line to fishing boats to sporting yachts, all from England, came pouring to that shore and whisked us away. It was an absolute miracle, Sergeant. Against all expectation, we were plucked out of the jaws of death; but we never would've seen that miracle, if we'd have given up and laid down to die."

"But that's not all. More miracles were to come for me. Captured, tortured, kept as a pack of rations by a maniacal SS commander, and then, against all odds, against any conceivable expectation, I got salvation. You, Sergeant. Your attack on Kleg's column gave me the diversion I needed to escape. And yes, it was out into the cold, with no chance of survival, except I was found by your unit and lived on. Another miracle, Sergeant."

I shook my head and stared at the ground. "Just luck."

"Just luck comes to everyone eventually. Luck, or miracles, or a second chance or whatever it is you call it, will come to us eventually, but we must hang on until it does. Never, never, never, give up. If I had given up, I never would've hit that SS guard and escaped from that truck, and even now, I would be sitting in one of Kleg's cauldrons. I went on by asking, *praying*, for one more day, and one more day, and then one more hour, and one more, and finally one more breath, and one more, and one more. I was like a shipwreck victim begging for one last gasp of air, and then another, and then one more until I reached land. So long as you are given that one last gasp, again and again, you can hold out for your miracle. You can survive. You can go home. You do want to go home, see your wife again, don't you?"

Something stuck in my throat. I didn't want to vocalize the truth of my feelings; even though I was giving up, to say aloud what I felt would ram home my worst fears, put them in front of my face and force me to stare at them until I died.

"Sergeant?"

"I'll never see her again," I said. My eyes never left the ground. "Not for real, not really. I mean, who the hell am I kidding? I'll never make it home. I've been beating the odds for too long. No, the only way I'll ever get to see her is in my dreams. In my mind. That's all she is anymore, Major… she's a fantasy, a phantom. She isn't even real. This is the only reality. This," I said, waving out at the snow.

"That's pain talking," Major Hayward said. "That's misery and fatigue and sorrow talking, and they can do nothing for you. Your wife is real, Sergeant. She and a better life are waiting for you. Perhaps you will die. Perhaps there is little chance of your making it home. Perhaps if you keep fighting, you will still be killed. But if you give up and lay down to die here, than you have no chance at all."

He knelt down next to me and laid a hand on my shoulder. "Come on, Harry," he whispered into my ear. "One last gasp. It's all you need to ask for, all you need to do, and then worry about the next when it's time. One last gasp will get you through this. One last gasp will get you back to your wife. One last gasp will get you home."

I sat there for a few seconds, breathing in and out, staring down at the frayed end of the rope that had led us out into the middle of nowhere. Some distant part of my mind wondered why the dead men we'd run from hadn't caught up with us. Maybe they moved too slowly. Maybe the Geist had lost interest. It didn't matter, really. All that mattered was, they hadn't.

All that mattered was, they hadn't.

They hadn't. They hadn't gotten me yet.

And then, faintly at first, our miracle came to me. It rose and fell, barely there, but at the first sign of it, I straightened up and held a hand out to Major Hayward.

"Help me up," I said quickly. "Help me up!"

Far away in the distance, carried through the blinding swirl of snow, came the faded roar of fifty men shouting together in unison: "101st! 101st! 101st!" Rifle and then cannon fire immediately followed it; not the crazed, sporadic crackles of a firefight, but steady, even shots, calling us home.

"That's enough of a miracle for me," Wexler said. "God bless you, Captain Powell!"

Energy rushed into my body, and I headed off toward the noise at a run, stopping only long enough to turn back and shout, "What the hell are you guys waiting for? Come on!"

Thank you God, for my one last gasp, I thought. *Now if I could only get a few more.*

57

Captain Powell's miracle hadn't led only us back to the manor. It had drawn less welcome attention as well.

When the first shots came, about an hour after our frozen rope patrol staggered into Dom Caern, my first thought was that the Geist had struck again. But then, the volume of fire increased, and a runner from our radio room dashed in with the bad news.

"3rd Platoon's getting hit."

The Captain rose to his feet. "Kleg?"

"Sergeant Lambourne didn't say, sir. They're taking an awful lot of fire, though."

"Tedeski," Captain Powell said on his way out of the room, "we may need your rigs."

Tedeski jumped to his feet and scurried after the Captain, and I followed in close pursuit. "Don't know how much good they'll do you in this weather, Captain," he said. "This much snow, we'll have to get so close that the damn infantry will open us up with panzerfausts."

None of us said anything else until we reached the radio room, which also had our sound-powered phones hooked up for communication with the arsenal.

"Sergeant Lambourne?" Captain Powell said, picking up the receiver for the line to the arsenal. "Report."

He listened for a minute, nodding gravely to himself. "Very well... Lambourne? Lambourne?"

"Cut out?" I said, holding a blanket tightly around my shoulders.

The Captain nodded. He scratched at the stubble growing on his face. "I'm going to need a contact patrol."

"They're just going to get lost out there like the Sarge did," Tedeski said.

"Not if they follow the telephone wire to the arsenal," Captain Powell said, leading us out of the radio room and back to the foyer. Davey, Goliath, and Rebecca joined the small throng of GIs gathered there.

"All right," I groaned, easing the blanket off of my shoulders, "I'm going to need two…"

"Hold it, Sarge," Captain Powell said. "You're not going anywhere."

"Sir…"

"You're half-frozen and half-dead with exhaustion. You're sitting this one out. Davey, Goliath… and Fisher. You three run a contact patrol out to the arsenal. The snow is lightening up, but take no chances. Follow the telephone wire out to the arsenal. If it's broken, splice the break and return. If it's intact, follow it out and tell Lambourne to hold if he can. If they roll in on him with panzers, or he feels he will be overrun, tell him to rig the arsenal to blow and to fall back to the manor. Understood?"

"Yes, sir," Davey and Goliath said in sync.

"Sir, I think I should go along," I said.

"Negative, Sergeant. You men, on your way," Captain Powell said. "Good luck."

"So what should I do, then?" I asked.

"Wait. Along with the rest of us," the Captain answered.

"Come, Harry," Rebecca said, tugging at my arm. "Let's get you some food."

The prospect of yet another hot meal should've sent me scampering toward our kitchen, but Rebecca practically had to drag me there. I ate listlessly, staring at my plate, never tasting my food.

"They will be fine, Harry," she said. "You need to eat and get warm. You can not be everywhere. You and Jiim are both the same way with this."

"I just... feel like I have to do something," I said. "The sitting and waiting and not knowing, the not doing anything... it's the worst part. You wouldn't understand."

"I would not understand?" she said. "I am a civilian caught in the middle of the biggest war the world has ever seen. Every day I am forced to sit and wait and not know and not do anything. You can pick up a gun and fight, or call in your friends to bomb with planes or artillery or hide in tanks. I have none of this. I must be pushed around, by whatever army comes through, and I can do nothing. All I can do is pray, and hide, and hope that nobody hurts me or kills me or rapes me. So I understand."

She shook her head. "I would give anything to be able to pick up a gun and fight like you do. To be able to actually fight the Germans, the Geist, whatever threatens me. I am sick to death of being a victim, of being passive and helpless. I want to be able to fight back. Then at least I can choose how I live and how I die.

"You are lucky, Harry Kinder. You carry that gun with you everywhere. Could you imagine not having it? Could you imagine living here, in this place, with no gun, no weapon, no army of friends to protect you from Kleg or the Geist or any other soldier who might suddenly decide to hurt me or somebody I love? Can you imagine living like that when you hear gunfire all around you?"

I let out a long sigh. "All right. Come on."

There was a collection of weapons left over by the victims of 2nd Platoon killed in the shower room which we'd piled up near the rear entrance to the manor. I recovered Ridley's pistol to replace the one I'd thrown away two nights before and looked the other weapons over to choose one for Rebecca. The M1 rifles seemed a little too big, and I didn't like the idea of giving a grease gun to a novice, so I picked out a carbine identical to the one Major Wexler now carried.

"Watch closely," I said, and ran over the basic operation of the weapon as I had done with Wexler.

When I was done, she ran her fingers over the stock of the carbine, as if wanting to get her hands used to the idea of holding a weapon. "Thank you, Harry."

"Just be sure of who you're aiming at before you pull the trigger," I said. "It's easy to get nervous and excited and then shoot before you look. And that weapon is for emergencies only, Rebecca. You let us handle the heavy stuff."

She straightened up stiff and gave me a salute. The combination of her sloppy salute and the goofy grin on her face created a strange and foreign sensation on my face... a smile. A real, honest-to-God, unabashed smile, and I even got a little laugh to go with it. It felt like I hadn't had my smile around in ages. I was glad to have it back.

Then, the volume of gunfire outside picked up and started getting closer. My smile faded. Some shouting from the front of the manor made me unsling my tommygun and check its magazine.

In an instant, everything changed. Instead of a far-off and remote firefight, now there was a furious eruption of small-arms fire right at the front of the manor house. The sharp crackles echoed through the halls and drew me toward them; first at an uncertain walk, then a trot, and finally a full-out run.

I could hear machine-guns opening up and then cannon fire from the tank destroyers. It all melted together into a roar of weapons fire, the way individual raindrops pattering onto a roof will combine into a thunderous roar when it comes down in a torrent. The old tingle was back, the crackle of nervous energy, and I had to remind myself to glance back and make sure Rebecca wasn't following too closely behind me.

Is it Kleg? I wondered. *Or worse?*

The gunfire died out by the time I reached the foyer. GIs crowded in through the front double doors, carrying a downed trooper between them. Outside, the meatchopper half-track blasted a stream of tracer rounds into the whiteness almost as an afterthought.

"What is it?" I asked the GIs coming back into the manor.

Smoke still rose from their weapons and the smell of cordite filled my lungs as they brought the downed man through. It was Davey.

58

"What happened?" I asked, once we got Davey to our makeshift aid station.

"Not sure yet," Captain Powell said. "All hell broke loose out there, and then a little later we heard Davey screaming inside of that abandoned Tiger tank. I took a squad to recover him and ordered the others to cover us."

"Cover you?" I said. "Every GI with a weapon was unloading it into the countryside."

I looked down at Davey, who was curled into a fetal position and trembling uncontrollably. His eyes were pinched shut.

"The guys got a little excited thinking the Geist was out there," Tedeski said.

"Davey? Davey, what happened?" I asked.

Davey didn't acknowledge me in the least. All he did was shake and cry, his tears leaking out between clenched eyelids. The Captain stared at him for a moment and sighed.

"We need to find out what happened out there," Captain Powell said. "We have to know if Kleg took the arsenal or not, or if we can send a patrol out there."

"I could send out a rig," Tedeski said.

Cappy snorted and turned to leave the room.

The Captain shook his head. "Let's not take any chances, Frank. We need some intelligence before we make our move."

"Captain, he's not telling anyone anything," I said. "Look at him."

Anyone could see Davey wasn't going to say much for quite some time. Whatever had happened out there had shattered his psyche like a pane of glass.

"Where's Goliath?" I asked.

The Captain shook his head.

Now it was my turn to pinch my eyes shut in muted pain. Not Goliath. Not big, steady Goliath, whose voice kept my buzzing nerves smoothed out enough for me to make it through the day.

First Shorty, I thought. *Now Davey and Goliath. Soon I'm going to have nobody left.*

"What about... what if we tried some blue 88's?" Wexler asked.

My eyes opened. "Sir?"

"Something a doctor in a rearward hospital told me about," Wexler said. "What they use on shell-shock cases."

"What is a blue 88?" Rebecca asked.

"It's a drug," Captain Powell answered. "A blue pill."

"Why is it called an 88?"

"The 88 is the best artillery piece the Germans have," Tedeski said.

"The idea is to give the soldier a cathartic release," Captain Powell said. "They take a battle fatigue case and drug him up with blue 88s. It knocks him out, puts him in a trance."

"Like being hypnotized," Wexler added in.

"And then they force the soldier to re-live his fear. They make whistling noises like shells falling, and tell him he's under attack, that sort of thing. It's supposed to purge the soldier of his demons," Captain Powell said. "I personally think it's a little sick."

"Like it or not, it may be the only way to get through to him," Wexler said. "Do we have any blue 88s?"

Captain Powell sighed again, a heavy one this time, and laid his hand lightly on Davey's head. "We might."

Wexler shrugged. "Well, then?"

For a second, I wished the Captain would say no, and order me to take a patrol out to the arsenal to see what was what. If the only way to get Davey to talk to us was to drug him and make him re-live whatever had shattered him, then I preferred to put my body at risk rather than his soul.

"Get Doctor Schmidt in here," Captain Powell said softly.

"Sir?" I asked.

"He was a psychiatrist. If anyone can do this, it's going to be him."

"Yes, sir," I said.

We ran down what we wanted to do once I brought Doctor Schmidt to Davey's side. The doctor didn't seem to like the sound of our plan, but he didn't say no, either.

"This drug," he said, once we'd finished, "do you know what its effects are aside from the hypnotic effect?"

"He'll be unconscious for about 24 hours," Captain Powell said. "I had a few guys go through this and then come back to the company."

"And they were cured?" Doctor Schmidt asked.

The Captain shrugged. "They were patched back together. If it had been up to me…" He shook his head. "But it wasn't. And it isn't now, either. We have to know what happened."

Doctor Schmidt seemed to think it over for a second and then nodded. "Give him the drug. Let us begin."

We had to force-feed him the pill. It took a little while for the blue 88s to take effect, but once his body started to relax and uncurl, Doctor Schmidt sat down near Davey's head and began speaking to him in a soft voice.

"Davey. Davey, can you hear me?"

"Yeah," Davey said loudly. As quiet as Doctor Schmidt was, Davey's voice was almost startling in the still air of the room.

"Davey, do you recognize my voice?"

"Unh-hunh. You're that Kraut lieutenant we captured in the village."

Doctor Schmidt smiled at Davey's innocent use of an ethnic slur. "Yes, that is right. I am also a doctor. Did you know that?"

"Yeah, a shrink," Davey said. "Did you know that Sigmund Freud was a German, too? Or an Austrian, maybe. He's the guy that started psychiatry."

Normally I would've smiled at Davey's habitual dispensing of trivia. Somehow, though, without Goliath there, it wasn't funny anymore. It was sad, like I was watching an animal missing half of its body trying to drag itself along like nothing was wrong.

"That is very good, Davey," Doctor Schmidt said. "Doctor Freud was indeed an Austrian."

"Just like Hitler," Davey said.

Doctor Schmidt paused for a moment. "Davey, I would like to talk to you about what happened today."

Davey's face, which had relaxed into neutrality once the blue 88s had taken effect, now clouded over. "I don't... I don't really want to do that, Doc. Is it okay to call you Doc?"

"Yes, of course, that is fine. I am afraid we are going to have to talk about that, Davey. It is very important. It may help save the lives of your friends, like Sergeant Kinder and Captain Powell."

"The Captain?" Davey said.

"Yes."

"And Rebecca too?"

"Yes. It might save us all."

"But not Goliath," Davey said, and his face clenched into a tight fist, trying to hold in the sob. "Not Goliath. Shit. *Shit.*"

"Davey, I want you to think back," Doctor Schmidt said quickly to change the subject. "Back to before your patrol."

"Yeah, yeah," Davey said, sounding eager to please. "You and the Sarge and that British guy and that asshole Wexler went to string a rope up so we could get out of here."

Wexler shifted his weight and frowned at Davey's drug-induced candor. Again, I might've laughed, but the circumstances swallowed alive any humor that tried to show itself.

"Yes, Davey. Do you remember that?"

"Oh, yeah. That rope we tied off got tight and snapped off the column, or, a few feet down the rope, at least. Then it slid off just like it happened to Shorty in the Rabbit Hole, and I said, 'Holy shit, that's just what happened to Shorty in the Rabbit Hole.' Then Captain Powell tried to run off after it to find the Sarge, and Goliath and I had to hold him back."

"Good. You're doing very well, Davey," Doctor Schmidt said.

"Thanks. Am I hypnotized? I've never been hypnotized before. Did you know there was a guy named Mesmer who invented hypnosis?"

"Yes, that is correct. His name was Anton Mesmer and he did discover hypnosis. His name is where we get the word 'mesmerize'." Doctor Schmidt said.

"Really?" Davey said. "I'll have to remember that one."

"Please go on with what happened today, Davey."

"Well, we heard shooting way off and the Captain said 'Damn it, they've got no way to find their way back' and Lieutenant Tedeski started swearing and asking to drive a TD out after them. But instead the Captain got everybody together and said we were going to shout all at once to get you back. And I said, 'What do we shout, sir?', and he said, 'What do you think we should shout, Davey?' So I said 'Well, we're in the Airborne, so we might as well shout "101st" so they know it's us'. So we did."

"Yes. We heard you," Doctor Schmidt said.

"Boy, when we saw you guys… I thought you were goners. The Sarge freaked me out earlier saying how he knew he was going to die and stuff like that, and then when the rope got pulled away, I swear I thought you were goners, that the Geist was gonna get you. But even though you guys got frozen pretty good, you made it. Which is good, Doc, even if you are a Kraut. You're okay. You know about haunted houses and all kinds of stuff."

I purposefully ignored the stares of everyone in the room who had heard Davey spill the beans about my earlier sense of doom. It sucks to be pitied and frankly, I knew most of them had felt the same way at some time or another.

"Thank you, Davey," Doctor Schmidt said. "Now let's move on a bit. There was gunfire at the arsenal."

"Kleg. We knew it had to be Kleg," Davey said.

"Yes, and communications were lost with that unit."

"We had to go," Davey said. His voice lost all of its former eagerness and volume, and became wispy and hollow, almost apologetic. "We had to. Somebody had to go find out what was happening."

"Yes. You had to go. So you left the manor," Doctor Schmidt said.

Davey's lips moved soundlessly at first, like he was trying to warm up to what he had to say, and then finally, he continued. "We, uh... it's kinda hard, Doc."

"I understand. Please try."

"We, uh, we went out into the snow, and..." He shook his head. "I don't know if... I can."

"All right, Davey," Doctor Schmidt said. "Do you like movies? Moving pictures?"

"Um, yeah, sure."

"Yes. So do I. What we're going to do is this. We will watch your memories like a moving picture. You will see it again like you were sitting in a theater, and then you can tell us what is happening."

"Will that work?"

"Let's try it and see. You left the manor..."

"We left... we left the manor and started toward the outbuilding with all of Kleg's guns. Hey, this really works, Doc!"

"What do you see?"

"It's snowing a lot, so I can't see much. There's a telephone wire going to the arsenal so we're following that. I can hear a lot of gunfire up ahead. I'm a little scared."

"Of getting shot?"

"Yeah," Davey said. "But I'm also worried about that Geist thing getting me. You were there when Shorty... well, you know. I don't want that to happen to me."

"Please go on."

"I've got the wire in my hands. There's ice on it. Goliath is on my right, watching for trouble. Fisher is on the left. He's chewing tobacco and spits every now and again. It's gross."

"What happens when you reach the arsenal?"

"Whoa!" Davey shouted, ducking his head even though he was lying down. His voice suddenly became tight, as if he were exerting himself.

"There's a lot of small arms fire out here! We're running like hell to get behind the arsenal and under cover! Some snow is kicking up where the bullets are hitting. Fisher's yelling and shooting. Knock it off, Fisher! They can't see us but if you shoot they'll fire at the noise!"

"Please continue."

"Okay. Okay," Davey said, breathing heavily and sighing with relief. "We're behind the stables. They aren't shooting as much at us now; I think they can't see us back here. We duck inside quick."

"There's a lot of guys in here. 3rd Platoon. Sergeant Lambourne's down, wounded. Oh, shit, his hand is all messed up. He got shot in the hand. That's it, he's definitely going home. He's telling the other guys to break open the boxes and set up some of the machine-guns that the Krauts had stockpiled."

"Can you see who is shooting at you?"

"Not yet. I'm not near a window. Sergeant Lambourne? What's going on?"

Davey paused for a moment. "Lambourne says a couple of his men have been hit, that some SS troops fired from the tree line and then charged. They fought off the first wave but he doesn't think they can stop another."

"There's a couple of wounded guys. One of them is Allen Shoemaker. He's from Ohio. He's hit pretty hard; I don't think he's going to make it. Oh, and Pat, Pat Fitzgerald, he got it too. We found some eggs together once.

"Goliath is over by a window and he's yelling for me to get over there. I don't know why he's yelling. We can't see a thing. There's trees a little ways off, and sometimes I think I can pick out a muzzle flash, but... Holy Shit!"

Doctor Schmidt straightened up. "What is it, Davey?"

"There... there's something ripping up the trees!"

"What is ripping up the trees? What do you see?"

"I can't... you can't see it, all you can see are... damn, whole trees just... ripping up and getting tossed around like a tornado was going through. Did you know tornadoes can rip up buildings and throw trucks and stuff around like they were nothing? That's what this looks like.

Something big is crushing its way through the forest and the trees are getting ripped up by its going through. Oh, man, do you hear that? It's killing the SS."

"What do you hear?"

"Screaming. They're screaming, and there's a lot more shooting. Goliath's looking at me. He wants to get out of there before it comes for us. He doesn't want to end up like Shorty, either.

"Lots of guys are at the window now, trying to see what's going on. Oh, here they come! Get 'em! Get 'em!"

"What is it?"

"The SS are running out of the woods. We're shooting them and… come on! Come on, Goliath!"

"What is happening?"

"We're running to the front entrance of the stables so the SS can't get in there. It's a much bigger doorway and… where's everybody going? What the hell is going on?"

"Davey?"

"They… everybody is running. All of our guys are running like crazy out of the outbuilding. What are you guys, nuts? Get back under cover! They're not listening to me; even Lambourne is running away, and he's screaming… it's coming for us! It's coming for us!"

"Davey…" Doctor Schmidt began, but Davey kept going.

"Oh, Christ, the Geist is coming, Goliath, let's go, let's go! Forget them, they're not even shooting at us anymore! Half of them have dropped their rifles, let's go!"

"Davey, slow down," Doctor Schmidt said. "Slow everything down in your head. Tell us what is happening."

"We're all running away," Davey said, his voice trembling like a taut wire threatening to break under too much load. "Everyone. GIs, SS, everybody. Me and Goliath are running into the snow. I shot two SS guys but I didn't have to; they don't care about us. They're not even looking at us. They aren't charging the arsenal; they're running away from the Geist."

"Where is the Geist? Can you see it?"

"No." His voice sounded almost mournful. "Oh, fuck. I'm so fucking scared. Everybody's going crazy; there's a big mix of GIs and SS all running into the snow, right alongside each other. They don't care. I see them and I'm thinking this is it, this is the end. It's gonna get us all."

"There's something... I can hear it! Holy shit, I can hear it! I can hear it coming up behind us!"

"What do you hear?"

"Sledding."

Doctor Schmidt frowned. "What was that?"

"Sledding," Davey repeated. "Did you ever go sledding, Doc? You know the sound a really heavy sled with a lot of people on it makes as it goes through the snow? The Geist sounds like that as it goes through the snow... *Boooosh!*... like when you belly-flop onto a sled and go down the hill. It hit the snow and it's coming right at us! Run! Run, go Goliath, go! Don't look back, run!"

"What's happening, Davey?"

"Goliath looked back and now he's screaming. I never heard him scream before and it's scaring the shit out of me. I'm grabbing his arm and pulling him so he'll run faster. The Geist is killing everybody. I can hear them yelling and screaming and some crunching sounds and wet sounds when it gets them. Don't look, just go! We can make it! We can make it! You and me, Goliath! You and me!"

Davey shook his head. "Fisher stopped to turn and shoot at it. That was dumb. He only got two rounds off before it got him."

"What does it look like?" Doctor Schmidt asked. "Can you see it?"

Davey scoffed at him, like he was crazy. "*I'm* not looking back. Are you nuts? I'm running like hell. We're all running, but it's killed a lot of us."

His face began to contort and grimace. "It's coming right up behind us, I can hear it. It's like if you laid down on a hill and closed your eyes, you could hear a heavy sled coming at you right before it crushes your skull. This is it! This is it! Come on, Goliath, you go, I'll slow it down!"

"It's gone. No, not gone. It turned to get some other guys who ran in a different direction. Four or five of them; two SS and two or three GIs. It's killing them. It's crunching them and ripping them up."

"What is happening now, Davey?"

"Just keep running," Davey huffed breathlessly. "Just keep running, Goliath. We can make it. You and me. There. *There!*"

"What?"

"It's coming for us, but the tank, the Tiger tank is right up ahead!"

"The abandoned Tiger tank?" Doctor Schmidt said. "The one near the manor?"

"Where we found them," Captain Powell whispered in my ear.

"Yeah, yeah! Go, Goliath, go! It's coming up on us, it's coming up and it's going to catch us and crunch us and I don't want it to make me do things like Shorty..."

"Davey, try to relax. It is just a moving picture," Doctor Schmidt said, but Davey kept barreling on.

"Go, go, go, in, in, in!" Davey rapid-fire shouted, then his body relaxed and he blew out a breath. "Okay. Okay. We're inside. Goliath helped me up and we got into the Tiger tank. The hatch is closed. We're safe... fuck!"

"What has happened?"

"The... tank, it's hitting the tank!"

"What do you see?"

"I can't see anything. It's pitch dark. The metal, the whole tank, it's gonging like a bell from it hitting the outside so hard! No. No!" he cried, holding his hands against his ears in a useless attempt to keep out the memory of the sound.

"Davey, I want you to slow things down..."

"No, no, no!" Davey said, but he wasn't talking to Doctor Schmidt. "No, leave us alone! Leave us alone! I don't have my carbine! I dropped it climbing into the tank. The whole... tank is moving, it can't, it's too big! I'm bumping around inside and I can't see anything and I can't stop screaming... it can't... it can't... seventy tons. Seventy tons. Seventy tons. Seventy tons."

Davey kept repeating that, "Seventy tons," over and over. I caught Wexler's confused look.

"It's how much one of those King Tiger tanks weighs," I explained. "Seventy tons of steel."

Doctor Schmidt looked up at us, and his eyes pleaded to let this end. The Captain looked to Wexler, the same hopeful look on his face, but Wexler gestured at Davey and said, "Well, go on."

"Davey," Doctor Schmidt said with a sigh. "Davey, I want you to try to relax. Nothing can hurt you. It's just a moving picture."

"Fuck just a moving picture, it's not just a moving picture!" Davey said. He was crying now, tears leaking out between his clenched lids and his entire body trembling with sobs. "It's banging a fucking Tiger tank around like it was a tin can, it is definitely *not* just a fucking moving picture."

Doctor Schmidt held his face in his hands for a moment, and looked like he was already feeling remorse for what he was about to do. "Davey," he said at last. "Davey, you have to look."

"No."

"Davey, you have to. You have to tell us what happened."

"No, I don't want to."

"Tell us, Davey."

"No, I..."

"Tell us," Doctor Schmidt insisted. "Tell us."

"It got in the fucking tank!" Davey shrieked at last. "The hatch just ripped off and light got in and it poured into the hole. It poured in like molasses or something and it's in here and I can't move and I can't and I just shit in my pants and I can't and I'm screaming and screaming and I can hear Goliath screaming too but I can't help him there's no way to help him it's too big and I can feel him bang up against me as it rips him up and I can hear it I can hear the sounds it's making as it kills him and I can't... fucking... *move*."

He broke down all the way then, crying hysterically to the point of becoming almost unintelligible. "I wanted to help, he was my friend, but what could I do? What could I do? It's too big and it's too strong and I was so fucking scared that I couldn't move. I couldn't move."

Doctor Schmidt's voice was very soft. "What happened next, Davey? The Geist killed Goliath. What happened next?"

"It killed him," Davey whispered, clenching his arms around himself. "It killed him. It got quiet and he didn't scream anymore but I closed my eyes shut. I closed them shut, I didn't want to see it. I didn't want to see him. I wanted it all to go away."

Make it stop, Doc, I wanted to say, but the silence of everyone else in the room kept me from it.

Davey let out a long, low moan that didn't even sound human. "Oh, no. *No.* He's talking to me."

"Who?" Doctor Schmidt asked.

"Goliath. He's saying my name but he's saying it all weird. He says 'Open your eyes, Davey', but it's not him. I know it's not him. He's dead. He's *dead*, you fucker, leave him alone! Leave him alone! But he keeps saying it, and he keeps saying it, and then I feel his fingers brush my cheek... Please... Please don't make me... Please don't make me see. Please don't make me see. Please don't make me see."

He repeated that, over and over, rocking himself as he hugged his knees tightly to his chest. Doctor Schmidt stood up. Tears were streaming out of his eyes, and when he spoke, his voice wavered and trembled.

"This is finished," he said. "I will not subject him to this torture for a moment longer."

"What are you talking about?" Wexler said. "We have to find out what happened. We have to know why the Geist let him live."

"He does not know!" Doctor Schmidt said. "How could he know what the Geist is thinking? I will not break this poor man's mind just to satisfy your curiosity!"

"He's right," Captain Powell said. "Doctor Schmidt, is there anything you can do for him?"

Doctor Schmidt wiped at his eyes. "I do not know. I will try."

He sat back down next to Davey and put his arms around him. "It's all right, Davey. It's over. You can rest, now."

"No."

"Yes. The moving picture has ended. It is all over. You are safe. You are safe."

"No," Davey whispered. "It's not over. Nobody's safe. Not ever. Not even when you're dead. Not as long as that thing is out there."

I caught Major Hayward's eye. He looked sad. He was probably thinking the same thing I was.

I'm afraid, Sergeant, that we were meant to face the Geist, that we must face the Geist eventually, and that when we do, there will be a terrible cost.

Around the room, I saw a lot of faces... The Captain, Rebecca, Doctor Schmidt, Tedeski, Major Hayward, hell, even Wexler... and for a moment, all I could see was their deaths at the hands of the Geist. Not just death, though, but worse; that damn devil's puppetry that the Geist inflicted on its victims, making them jerk and twitch and walk and talk even after they were gone.

That'd be worse than being dead, Goliath had said.

I suddenly had to leave the room.

Andrew C. Piazza

59

Grief is sometimes like a thief in the night, stealing up to catch us while we're unaware. One moment, we are safe and stolid, and the next, our purse is cut and our soul spills out like cold copper coins.

It doesn't always hit us the same way, either. Sometimes it dulls the senses until you're drunk with it, sometimes it enrages until you're ready to murder God himself, and sometimes it hurts so much you feel as though you're collapsing in on your own heartbeat.

That day, I left the room feeling a little tingly and dissociated, but otherwise okay. Seeing Davey go through that had choked me up a little, but now that I had left, I was mostly preoccupied with carrying out the mission that had suddenly occurred to me.

You be sure to take care of that for me. I don't want to be walking around like that forever.

I reached the foyer where a dozen or so troopers were lounging near the manor's front door. "Where's Goliath?" I asked. "Where's the body?"

"He's mostly out back with the others," Pelosi told me. "I mean, most of him is. As much as we could scoop out of the Tiger tank."

"Pelosi, you and..." I pointed out two more troopers, "you two, come with me."

I led them toward the back of the manor, picking up another half-dozen guys along the way. Once we reached the back door, I pointed out the bodies stored out back... those that hadn't walked off earlier, that is... and ordered the GIs to stack the bodies in a pile away from the house.

"Where are you going?" Pelosi asked.

I didn't answer him. There wasn't much point in it; he'd see soon enough.

Backpack flame-throwers are heavy, much heavier than they look. Not only have you got the actual machinery, but you're also hauling ten gallons of diesel fuel in the tanks. I barely felt it, though. I was kind of set outside myself.

The guys were finishing up when I dragged the flame-thrower outside and set it on the snowy ground. They all looked at it and then each of them nodded slowly.

"Those starter cartridges are tricky," Pelosi said. "Cold makes 'em go bad sometimes. You got some spares?"

"Yeah," I said. "George. Phil. Go get a couple more cans of gasoline."

"You got it, Sarge," they said, and went back into the manor.

The rest of us looked at the pile of frozen bodies for a while before Pelosi broke the silence. "You know, Sarge, when Cappy and Davey and… Goliath… told us about what happened down in that village, none of us could really believe it."

"Believe it," I said. "Believe it."

"Yeah," he said. "We do now. We are on some strange ground here."

"I know it."

"Look, Sarge, if it happens to me…" he said.

"I'll take care of it. If I'm still around. If I'm not, a bullet to the base of the skull ends it. I'm assuming if you completely burn the bodies, that'll work, too."

"Here you go, Sarge." The two troopers returned and sat three jerrycans of gasoline on the snow with a sloshing thud.

"Thanks. Can I have a little privacy here, guys?" I said.

"Sure thing, Sarge," Pelosi said, patting me on the back as he led the others inside.

Goliath's body, from the waist down, was on top of the pile of bodies; maybe fifteen corpses or so in all, including the handful the guys had brought in from the Geist's latest attack. The troopers hadn't had the time or inclination to go search for the others.

The rest of him was on the ground. He was still there from the ribcage up, but his abdomen and its contents were gone. I sighed heavily and trudged over to him. They'd set him face down, and a little too far from the others for my liking. I wanted to be sure his body was completely burned.

I guess a part of me wanted to see his face, see for certain that he was dead. That's why we have viewings at funerals, after all... so we can see for certain that those we knew were gone, that there is no chance of a mistake having been made.

Even half of Goliath was heavy. I got a hold of one of his arms and flipped him over. Frost covered his face and some snow was in his mouth. His eyes were still open, clouded over and staring at nothing. I hated that. Somebody should've closed his eyes for him. It at least affords us the illusion that the dead are merely at rest.

He's really dead, I thought. The words were hollow in my mind.

I took a second to steel myself, and reached out to shut his eyelids. His clouded over eyes rolled toward me and he said, "Harry."

"Fuck!" I shouted, recoiling backwards. I tripped over my own feet and fell on my ass into a little snowdrift.

Goliath lazily spat the snow out of his mouth and said again, "Harry."

I let out a moan that turned into an angry snarl. "You fucker! You mother... let him go, you fuck! Let him go! For Christ's sake, he's dead, let him go!"

"Harry," he said. He spoke a little like a drunk, with no emotion on his face. "Harry Kinder. I should be in your garden."

Shorty had said that earlier and I still had no idea what it meant. I didn't really care. I could feel myself falling apart; cold and fatigue and fear and loss were beating me down yet again, and I didn't have any reserves left to draw on. I curled my knees up and tightened into a ball, clenching tight fists in front of my face. "Why?" I whispered. "Why are you doing this to us?"

There was a flurry of motion through Goliath's face, the same way as had happened with Shorty when he seemed to get control of himself. "Sarge?" he asked. It sounded like he was begging. "Sarge? It hurts. It hurts."

It was what I needed to get me moving. I dragged myself to my feet, fumbling with my flap holster to draw the .45 pistol I had taken from Ridley's gear to replace the one I'd lost.

"It's okay, Goliath," I said, cocking the pistol and flicking the safety off. "I'm taking care of it. I'm taking care of it right now."

All of the expression left his face and the Geist spoke through him again. His baritone voice, so often a salve for my damaged soul, was now a hollow, twisted facsimile, an insult to what the man had meant to me. "Harry. Do not shoot. Do not shoot me."

I stepped close and pointed the pistol at his head, aiming carefully to be sure the first shot would finish the job. Goliath raised a hand up to ward off the shot; the fingers were snapped off halfway, and my spine shuddered when I thought of how the exposed bone must've scratched Davey's cheek when they brushed up against him.

"I should be in your garden," he said. "Tell me about your wife, Harry Kinder."

"You'll never meet her. I'm going to see to that, you bastard," I said, and shot him through the mouth. I shot him twice more to be sure.

I could feel the shakes coming back on, and I had to tighten up my entire body to hold them off. Not now. I wasn't done yet.

A look at Goliath verified that. His arms twitched, again and again. It wasn't death throes. He was already dead. It was the Geist, trying to play its puppetry game with a broken doll.

His muscles twitched against my hands as I dragged him up against the other bodies. It made me want to vomit. It made me want to scream and pull out my hair and run like a lunatic out into the snow.

I didn't have that luxury. I had a job to do.

It was easier once Goliath was propped up against the other bodies. I pulled open the caps on the gas cans and poured them over the pile of frozen and half-frozen corpses.

"Sarge," one of the corpses said. "Please don't burn us, Sarge."

It's got the hang of contractions, now, I noted distantly.

He was too deep in the pile to shoot, so I pulled the flame-thrower onto my shoulders and worked the starter cartridge. It didn't light on the first try, but on the second, it caught fire and extended its little finger of flame in front of the nozzle.

"Don't burn us, Sarge."

"Shut up," I whispered. Tears streamed out of my eyes. "Just shut up."

Flame leapt out of the nozzle and across the bodies, setting the gasoline ablaze in a whooshing inferno. I hit it with another two-second burst and then another, making sure Goliath was thoroughly covered, and then once more before the tanks ran out of fuel.

I sat the flame-thrower down on the snow and dropped to a seat beside it. The fire threw off an enormous amount of heat, even as far away as I was sitting, but I took no comfort in it. It seemed like a dirty heat, an evil heat, foul the way some air tastes foul or water tastes fetid. The choking smell of burning flesh coated the inside of my mouth and lungs.

I closed my eyes. Davey's words came back to me. *Please don't make me see. Please don't make me see.*

Those urgent, whispered words haunt me to this day. I hear them all the time. I think of them whenever some well-meaning person asks me about the war. I don't want to talk about the war. I don't want to even think about it. Let it lie. Don't make me re-live it.

Tell us about the war, Harry.

Please don't make me see.

Tell us what it was like.

Please don't make me see.

I sat in the snow for a long time with that foul heat pressing against me, staring into the flames, seeing nothing. My head hurt from trying to hold in my emotion; I could feel my levy of control beginning to give way under the strain. Twin screws twisted into both of my temples, clenching my face into a frozen sob.

Footfalls crunched the snow behind me. My one hand reached reflexively for my weapon in case it was the enemy and my other hand wiped at my eyes in case it was a friend.

It was Rebecca. She approached me slowly, almost cautiously, as if afraid I might shoot her. I've said before, it's embarrassing to be with a person when they show their weakness.

She didn't say a word. She didn't have to. She could see what I'd done and how it had cored out the center of my soul.

All the same, her presence alone was enough to bring my emotions to a boil. I couldn't fight them down anymore; I could taste something bitter in my mouth every time I breathed out and my throat clenched like a fist around my air supply. The last gasp Major Hayward had given me was now run out. Every breath I took felt like I was dragging water into my lungs.

Rebecca knelt down next to me and took me in her arms. Our arms wrapped around each other and she held me tight, squeezing the bitter feeling out of my body like I was a sponge. The wool of her overcoat scratched against my cheek. She felt warm beneath it, warm the way my wife felt when I hugged her on a cold morning after I'd gotten up early and she was rising late, still toasty from the covers like a coal kept warm in the ashes of the hearth.

It had been so long since I'd held a woman close. I never realized until then how much I'd missed it, and how much I needed it. I missed holding a soft, slim body. I missed the feel of the small of a woman's back, and the subtle sensuality of breasts pressed against my chest. I missed the smells, the touch, even the sounds of an extended embrace.

"When I am sad," Rebecca said at last, "I look up at the sky and try to think how small my grief is compared to the entire world, the entire universe. It makes me think my pain is not as big as I thought it was."

I sat back and broke our embrace, wiping at my eyes. The spasms of sobs that had raked me earlier started to subside.

"So many others have endured so much worse than us," she said. "We are fortunate to have as much happiness as we have seen."

"The world owes us nothing," I said.

"What?"

"Nothing." I said, shaking my head. "I miss my wife, Rebecca."

Air rushed into my lungs, without the impedance of a throat constricted with choked-off sobs. It was another last gasp.

More footfalls crunched the snow behind me. This time, it was Captain Powell, approaching reluctantly just as Rebecca had. His eyes were full of guilt for intruding on my moment of weakness.

"I need you," he said.

"Yes, sir," I said, with quite a bit of relief at the prospect of distraction. "What is it?"

"Kleg."

Andrew C. Piazza

60

"Two envoys came out of the woods with white flags about ten minutes ago," the Captain explained, as he led me back through the manor to the main foyer just beside the front entrance. "Kleg wants to meet."

Almost the entire company... what was left of it, that is... was gathered in and around the foyer, working the rumor mill furiously. GIs argued over whether Kleg was bluffing or if he actually had the entire Kraut army out there. We were in turn either saved or doomed depending upon whom you were listening to.

The rumors died out on the appearance of the Captain. "What's going on, sir?" one of the dogfaces asked.

"Sarge and I are going to go take a look," Captain Powell said. "I need one or two more men to go."

"I'll go," Major Hayward said. "I think it's about time I confronted my fears face-to-face. Besides, the more officers you have with you, the better."

He was right about that. The more uppity of the German officers hated talking to anyone but a fellow officer.

"What about me?" Wexler asked. "I mean, I am technically in command here."

"Actually, I would rather take Doctor Schmidt with us," Captain Powell said. "It'll let Kleg see we have some German prisoners. At least, that's what Kleg will think when he sees we have a German officer with us. He'll assume there's more. Doctor?"

Doctor Schmidt nodded. "If you insist."

"I'm afraid I do," the Captain said, then turned to the GIs. "Very well. The rest of you take up defensive positions. I want every machine-gun and mortar ready to go. We'll ride the meatchopper out to meet Kleg; it'll make him think twice in case he's thinking about breaking the white-flag truce."

"I'll ride shotgun," Tedeski said. "I want a look at this bastard."

Taking the meatchopper along made me feel a little better, but I have to admit, I was still a little sketchy about going out to have a face-to-face with Kleg. I kept thinking of Ryan's dying words, whispered through burned and blackened lips.

...he had a skull for a face and fangs...

I shivered once and checked the magazines in my ammunition pouch. All eight were fully loaded and ready to go. I also had three hand grenades hooked onto my gear, Ridley's .45 pistol, and a trench knife. I still felt poorly armed.

We climbed up onto the top of the meatchopper half-track and held on for dear life. Tedeski settled himself in the seat centered in the middle of the quad-fifties and moved the weapons around experimentally. It took a few minutes for the engines to churn to life, and then the big metal beast lurched and began clanking along the road toward the forest.

"What do you figure, sir?" I asked over the rumble of the half-track's engine.

"I figure he's running on empty," Captain Powell said. "From the reports we got over the radio, my bet is he's burned up most of his ammo and gasoline with his raid. That's why they targeted the arsenal. But they didn't get it, and they won't... I sent a squad out there to reinforce it."

"So he's bluffing."

"Not exactly. He's still got a force vastly outnumbering ours, and control over the only road out of here."

I noticed that the snowfall had died down significantly. It was still coming down, but nowhere near as much as earlier. Certainly not a whiteout, not even a blizzard; just enough to reduce visibility to one hundred yards or so.

One Last Gasp

"I don't really give a damn what Kleg has to say," the Captain continued. "I'm hoping to stall him, maybe bluff him, throw him off. If we're lucky, he'll let something spill that he shouldn't."

We were quiet for the rest of the ride to the edge of the clearing. I still felt shaky and tingly, like I'd been up for far too long. The meatchopper's quad-fifty machine-guns were right next to me, and I laid my hand on one of the massive weapons to try to steady myself. The steel felt strong, sturdy, reassuring; at over a hundred pounds of killing machine, it felt similar to what a suit of armor must've felt like to a medieval warrior.

To our right, I could barely make out the stables Kleg had turned into his makeshift arsenal. Dead bodies and trees torn up by the roots were scattered in the snow all around it. I couldn't imagine what kind of force could rip a tree up by the roots and throw it eighty yards or more. Then again, that same force had knocked around a seventy-ton Tiger tank like it was a water pail before it got inside and got to Goliath.

Keep it together, Harry, I told myself. *The Captain needs you.*

We saw them waiting for us where the road entered the line of snow-covered pines. There were three of them; two faced us and a third stood facing the forest, his back turned to us, as if he were studying the trees. They all wore the black uniforms and overcoats of SS officers.

"There he is," I said. "The bogeyman."

Major Hayward cocked the action on his submachine-gun and I followed suit. Captain Powell ordered the half-track to come to a halt about thirty yards shy of the three officers.

"Keep your finger on the button, Tedeski," he said. "And keep your eyes on the trees. Anything shoots, you blow it to the next world. There's no bonus points awarded for conserving ammunition."

"Hell yes, sir," Tedeski said.

We clambered down off the half-track and started toward the SS officers. None of them were armed, so far as I could see, with the exception of the pistols holstered at their sides. It didn't matter. Kleg's real weapon was the panzer battalion he had lurking out of sight in the woods.

The two officers facing us came to attention as we got close. They were both tall, blond-haired and blue-eyed; real Aryan bastards. The one on the left, a lieutenant with a good-sized scar running vertically over the left side of his mouth, stiffened slightly when he caught sight of Major Hayward. It only lasted an instant, until his cold eyes picked out Doctor Schmidt's Wehrmacht uniform.

They both saluted smartly and we returned it. They remained at attention; the four of us were far more casual. I rested my tommygun on my hip, mostly to remind everybody involved that it was there.

"Which of you is the commander of the Allied forces currently in the manor house?" the scar-faced lieutenant asked in rigid and accented English.

"I am," the Captain replied. "Captain Powell of the 101st Airborne Division."

"Captain," the SS lieutenant gave him a sort of chopping bow and nod, "may I present *Sturmbanfuhrer* Kleg of the 1st SS Panzer Division."

Our nightmare in human form turned to face us. My nerves crackled and snapped like a downed power line. Here he was in the flesh, face to face, almost close enough to reach out and touch.

And then, against all expectation, I smiled.

It was more than a smile; the smile was actually the tip of an undeniable iceberg of giggles suddenly brought on by a combination of fatigue and terror which now mixed with a sudden swell of relief. Kleg was no nightmare come to life, no demon with a skull's face. He was just a man.

He was of average height, perhaps a little shorter, with black hair and blue eyes. Ryan had said Kleg had a skull for a face. I could see how, in the dark, lit only by the distant flames of a burning farmhouse, the shadows could create such an impression on a dazed and shell-shocked man.

Kleg *did* have prominent facial bones, and more than that, he was gaunt; I mean *seriously* thin. So thin that his skin had stretched tight over his prominent facial features to create a ridged and sunken appearance that looked almost like a bared skull.

In the dark, the effect would be terrifying. Here in the light, though, he didn't look like a terror. He looked like he was sick, maybe even dying.

Once I saw that he was just a man, relief flooded into me and I simply had to laugh at myself. This was no super-human fiend we faced. It was another thug in a black uniform, and an ill-fed one at that. Of course, he was still a serious threat. He did have a panzer battalion, after all, but the point is, it was only a battalion of men, and I'd faced men like this more than once.

As I've said before, I've never been good at keeping my mouth shut when I need to. Considering the way my head buzzed with exhaustion, it took quite an effort to confine my relieved laughter to nothing but a wide smile and a huff of an exhale.

Kleg frowned and glanced at his scarred lieutenant.

"What is funny?" the lieutenant asked, eyes front and looking at nothing.

Whoops! I thought, and that only made things worse for me. It was like trying to hold in inappropriate giggles at church or a funeral; the harder you try to contain them, the harder they strain to get out.

"I'm... I'm sorry," I stammered, wiping at my face as if my smile was a stain I could rub off. "It's, um... I think I was expecting something else."

The SS didn't look too thrilled with my apology. "An enlisted man," Kleg said with distaste.

Hey, fuck you, buddy, I thought. *I squeeze my trigger finger just a little bit and this enlisted man is going to cut your officer's ass in half.*

"Captain Powell, you are trespassing on the property of the German Army," Kleg said, glancing briefly at Major Hayward. "You will surrender all American and British forces to me unconditionally. You will do this now."

Captain Powell and Major Hayward traded a glance.

"I think I can speak for all of the British forces when I say," Major Hayward said, "it will be a cold day in Hell before I surrender to you, Commander."

"It is a cold day in Hell already, Major," Kleg said with a smile, and I saw why Ryan had described him as having fangs. His teeth had been filed to points. They jutted out of his gums like the tips of long nails driven all the way through a thin board.

In those few seconds, everything turned around for me. Two minutes earlier, I had been a shattered, shivering, trembling husk of a man. But in that short period of time... I don't know what it was, but seeing him sneer down his nose at us like he already had us beaten began to form a solid steel core of resolve inside of me. After all, who the hell was he to come swaggering up to our camp, demanding we lay down and beg for mercy? He was just a man, like any of us, who would die under a bullet like any other man.

In his arrogant attempt to bully us into submission, he had created the opposite effect and provoked me into stubborn defiance. I think this was one way in which the enemy underestimated us. Hitler, toward the middle of the war when America stepped into the conflict, expressed his belief that the American Army was "the Italians of the Allies"... not a force to worry about. He was convinced that we didn't have the stomach for war; that once we got our hands dirty, we would bow out and give up in the face of the big, bad German Army.

It's a funny thing, though. Sometimes, when you beat a man down, take away everything he has and pound him nearly into submission, the worst thing you can do is flaunt your dominance over him. Sometimes, when you do that, the one who's been beaten down will decide he's got nothing left to lose and that he might as well go down taking you along for the ride. It was like that at Bastogne, when the Germans demanded our surrender and General McAuliffe replied with the now-famous "Nuts." I felt the same way. The hell with you. I'm not going to make it easy. I might go down, but I'll sure as hell wipe that lousy smirk off your face before I go.

"You are outmatched," Kleg said. "You have no armor to speak of and you are cut off from reinforcement. The weather is unsuitable to attempt any call for air support. You are on your last leg, as the saying goes. I repeat, you are outmatched."

Captain Powell's lips stretched into a ghost of a smile. "We were outmatched at Bastogne as well, Commander."

Kleg snorted and looked Doctor Schmidt over. "I also demand you hand over all German prisoners at once."

"Why is that?" Doctor Schmidt asked. "So you may feed them to your men, as you did with the Wehrmacht soldiers who were stationed here at Dom Caern?"

Captain Powell winced. "Doctor Schmidt..."

"Doctor?" Kleg hissed. "*Doctor* Schmidt?"

He traded a disgusted look with his subordinates.

"They know, *Sturmbanfuhrer*," Doctor Schmidt said. "They know everything that has happened here. Everything."

"Do they, now?" Kleg said, staring at Doctor Schmidt.

Captain Powell nodded. "In fact, you would be best off surrendering to us, Commander."

"Is that so?" Kleg said with a laugh. "And why is that?"

"We *know*, Commander," Captain Powell said. "And now everybody does. I've been in contact with both my Regiment and my Division. They know our position and therefore yours. They know what you've done and there's no escape from that road. Our reinforcements are on the way. There's no place for you to run. There's no place for you to hide."

Major Hayward cleared his throat. "And if by some miracle you should escape, it wouldn't matter. It wouldn't matter if you escaped the entire continent; after what you've done, they will hunt your sick, twisted carcass to the ends of the earth to hang you."

Kleg smiled. The points of his filed teeth pressed against his lower lip. "Hanging? After 'what I've done', Major, do you truly believe I am afraid of hanging?"

"I know your kind, *Sturmbanfuhrer*," Doctor Schmidt said. "You do not want to die like a criminal."

Kleg scowled at him, as if annoyed he was speaking at all. "I would be more concerned about the method of your own death if I were you, *Doctor*," he said. "You sicken me. No German soldier worthy of the name would ever aid the enemy in any endeavor."

"Enemy?" Doctor Schmidt said, gesturing toward the manor house. "The enemy is there, *Sturmbanfuhrer*! The enemy is that thing you call the

Geist. It is the enemy of everything that lives on this earth. If you ask why I help the Americans to deal with the Geist, it is because I know you are too much of a madman to be trusted with the task."

Kleg shook his head. "Madman. Courage is often called madness by cowards. It shames me to stand in the same air as you. You Wehrmacht have always shamed me. You should never have surrendered in that village. You should've fought to the last bullet and the last man. You murder Germany with your cowardice."

"Bastard! You dare speak for Germany?" Doctor Schmidt said, and for an instant, I thought he might strike Kleg across the mouth. "It is you who murders Germany! You and your filth murder my country, my people, with this love for conquest and killing that turns you into animals. This war has killed and maimed the best of our young men and turned more of them into monsters like you. You don't care about your people; you have love only for war. You worship it like a god, like you worship the Geist. You are all fools, stupid, blind fools, who worship a god that kills you and your kind indiscriminately."

"And your God is any better?" Kleg said. "He cares so much about you? Then why does he allow such evil to exist in the world? Why does he allow this war to go on? Why does he let men like me live? Why does he allow this? Hmm? Perhaps he has merely overlooked me."

The SS commander raised his arms and shouted up to the heavens. "Here I am, God! Do you hear me? I defy you! Strike me down! Send me back to the earth, if you can!"

Shoot him, I thought suddenly. *Just pull the trigger and end it here.*

I wanted to. God, I wanted to. A squeeze of the trigger, and that swaggering son of a bitch would drop like a stone. The look on his face alone would be worth it.

I couldn't, though. We were under a white flag truce. Besides, I could feel the pressure of unseen snipers drawing a bead on me from the woods. The instant I fired, they would cut me down.

"No?" Kleg asked of the sky, then returned his attention to us. "I suppose your God is not putting in an appearance today. I guarantee, however, that my god will. You say we worship the Geist like we worship war? The Geist *is* the war; it does not care who it kills because war does

One Last Gasp

not care. This is the nature of war. You bow before this God who you have never seen and who has never done anything for you. For all you know, he does not even exist. My god can be seen, touched, witnessed... and he provides gifts. Yes, his will is impossible to understand. Of course it is this way. All priests say the same of your God. Why should mine be any different?"

He nodded his head slowly, as if satisfied with his speech. "I tell you truthfully, when I was first given this command and this assignment, I was angry. All the Tigers and Panthers under my command, all to go to waste guarding some scientific installation when they should be crushing the British and Americans? Foolish. But I know now that my assignment here was an act of Fate. Perhaps the Geist itself somehow arranged for it. Who can say? But I was brought here for a reason. To bear witness. And now that I have done so, I will stand by the side of the Geist until I die. And perhaps, even after."

"Nobody stands by the side of the Geist," Major Hayward said. "The Geist is madness, and you have become madness as well."

Kleg looked Major Hayward up and down. "I've missed you, Hayward. You look good. The Americans have been fattening you up. So much the better."

Major Hayward stiffened, and Kleg grinned again.

"How many British troops are with you? I want to be able to prepare my kitchen staff."

"More than enough to send you to the hell you deserve," Major Hayward said.

"Oh, I have been to Hell," Kleg said with a shrug. "Many times. I took you there with me once, Hayward. Do you remember? I am looking forward to a repeat performance."

"Don't count on it," Major Hayward replied.

"I don't expect you to go willingly," Kleg said.

"That isn't what he meant," Captain Powell said. "He meant nobody is going down that tunnel. Ever again. And that... thing... you bow and scrape to is going to stay where it belongs."

Kleg's bright eyes narrowed. "What do you mean?"

"I mean," Captain Powell said, "you fire one more shot at us, and we'll blow the tunnel back into the earth. Boom."

Kleg stared at the Captain for a long moment. "You lie. You do not have sufficient explosive for this."

"Correction. I *did* not have sufficient explosive for this. Thanks to all of those stockpiled shells in that arsenal of yours, now I do."

Kleg glanced toward the outdoor entrance to the Rabbit Hole. "If you do this, if you destroy the tunnel, I will flay each and every one of your men alive. I will impale them all on wooden stakes. Do you know how this works? It is not through the belly like a spear. The legs are tied together and the point of the stake is put into the rectum as the victim is standing. Then he is pushed so he falls to a seat backward onto the stake. The point rips through the bowels. If it is done correctly, the person is propped up by the stake, which slowly forces its way further and further into the body. It takes days to die. I will see you this way, Captain. I will hear your screams echo through the halls of Dom Caern."

He turned his bright eyes on me. Disgust practically dripped from his fangs. "Is this more like what you were expecting, Sergeant?"

"I *expect* you'll have a hell of a time taking any of us alive, sir," I said.

Kleg snorted and looked through the snow toward the distant, vast shadow of Dom Caern. "That will not matter. The Geist has power over death. But you know this already, don't you?"

He shook his head. "You are the fools here. You see a god before you with limitless power, even the power to resurrect the dead, and yet you refuse to believe in it. You refuse to accept it. The God you worship is a lie, a pretty fairy tale told to children. The Geist is the true god, and you are fools to cling to your faith in an unseen deity."

"But enough of this," he continued. "Enough games. You say I have nowhere to run and no place to hide? I think the opposite is the truth. I give you until sundown to surrender. After that, I will come and kill you all. The survivors I will feed to my men, and then we will await your 'reinforcements' with the Geist at our side."

"So. Make peace with this God of yours," Kleg said, glaring at Doctor Schmidt pointedly. "All of you."

He turned on his heel and strode back into the woods. The other two SS officers followed him. The pines swallowed them up quickly, and even the sounds of their boots crunching in the snow was muffled by the snow-laden branches. They seemed to disappear like ghosts.

I wanted them to come back. I wanted to shout my defiance in their faces. I wanted the last word. As I've said before, Kleg's demands for surrender had the opposite effect on me. I was more set than ever on fighting him to the last gasp.

"What do you think of our situation now, Sergeant?" Major Hayward asked.

"I think I want to get that motherfucker Kleg under my sights, sir," I said. "Just once."

You had him under your sights, my mind reminded me. *Just now.*

"We've got a lot of work to do," Captain Powell said. "But I think you'll get your chance, Harry."

Andrew C. Piazza

61

"All the information we've got says Kleg has somewhere around fifteen panzers and maybe two or three hundred infantry," Captain Powell said, once he had all of us gathered in the dining room. "We've got Tedeski's three TDs and about fifty or sixty guys."

"It is hopeless," Doctor Schmidt said. "You cannot hold this position."

"We've been there before," I said.

"The doctor has a point," Captain Powell said. "It's an overwhelming force. We can't hold here. But there's nowhere to fall back to, either."

He shook his head. "Can't fall back. Can't defend the manor, especially with the Geist here."

"So, what then?" I asked. "Attack?"

"No," he said. "We'd be cut to pieces. Maybe... maybe it's time we started turning our liabilities into assets."

"Sir?" I said.

"Kleg wants the manor," the Captain said. "Let's let him have it."

Major Hayward nodded. "Yes. Let the Geist do some of our work for us."

"I'm not following," Tedeski said. "We let Kleg take Dom Caern?"

"Not quite," Captain Powell explained. "We fight him tooth and nail, but we draw him into the manor, or even better, into the Rabbit Hole. We've seen the Geist kill the SS just like our guys; it doesn't care who it kills. This crazy bastard Kleg wants to be close to it? Let him. We'll take out as many as we can and let the Geist take care of the rest."

"Yeah, but won't it kill our guys, too?" Tedeski asked.

"Yes, it will. But I'll tell you something. There have been times when I've called down artillery fire on our own positions because we were being overrun. Some of our guys got hit, but many more of theirs did, because we were in foxholes and they were out in the open," Captain Powell said. "There's no guarantee here, Tedeski. The Geist is a wild card element in this fight. But without that wild card, we're finished."

"Let Kleg's own madness consume him," Doctor Schmidt said.

"That's right. Very well. Here's Dom Caern," the Captain said, taking a hand grenade off his belt and putting it on the table. He set a clip of M1 ammo off to the side of it. "The road is at twelve o'clock. There's the arsenal at one o'clock. Tree line is up here; the road comes out here, right near the arsenal. Kleg's somewhere on that road. We don't know exactly where, but we will tonight when he attacks."

"Right where it comes into the clearing," I said.

"Exactly. He doesn't have a choice. If he wants to pounce those big, bad panzers on us, he has to get them off the road and into the clearing. So, here's what we do. We'll use a series of ambushes, hit and fade attacks, to take out as many of the panzers and infantry as we can as we fall back onto the manor. This will thin the herd as well as draw them in. Then, we get them into Dom Caern and the Rabbit Hole, get them tangled up with the Geist, and retreat into the woods to a pre-set rallying point over here around two o'clock. After that, it's make a run for it."

"Why don't we make a run for it now?" Rebecca asked. "Why the fighting?"

"Kleg's troops are all along that road right now and probably in the woods as well," I said. "If we try to run now, we have a huge force we have to fight our way through to get away. But if we draw them all here, the woods will be clear of his troops."

"That's right," Captain Powell said.

"I don't much like the idea of leaving Dom Caern in his hands," Major Hayward said.

"It won't be, for long," Captain Powell said. "Our reinforcements really are coming. They won't get here until tomorrow morning, which obviously is too late to keep Kleg off us. I've also put in a request for a bombing mission on Dom Caern. As soon as the weather clears, this place is nothing but a bad memory."

"But for now, we have to concern ourselves with staying alive long enough to escape. So, first ambush is on the road. We put men about a hundred yards into the woods, past the point where the road reaches the clearing. His column will be single file and easy targets. We nail the first panzer or two, turn them into obstacles for the others. Then we call on secret weapon number one."

"What's that?" Rebecca asked.

"Artillery," Doctor Schmidt said with a smile. "Of course. Kleg has been operating as a rogue unit for so long, he forgets you can call on help from other units. No ground troops can make it on time, and no airplanes can help because of the weather."

"But artillery works rain or shine and 'round the clock," Captain Powell said. "We've been reporting our situation via radio to Regiment this entire time. They've allotted us an entire battalion of artillery to call on when the time comes."

"105s?" I asked.

"That's right. Twelve of them."

The 105-millimeter howitzer was our workhorse artillery. Even though we were far from our lines, it didn't matter. The howitzers could throw a thirty-three pound bomb seven miles away. Their shells would destroy tanks and make fifty percent of any troops within twenty meters of impact a casualty.

"So we bottle them up and blow the hell out of them," I said.

"That's right. But they'll break through. There's too many of them," he said. "So we draw them to the arsenal for ambush number two. They'll overrun that position as well, and we'll let them."

"Sir?" Tedeski said. "Let them have all those shells, all that ammo?"

"Not quite," the Captain said. "We fall back to the manor. Once we're clear, and they have plenty of troops inside the arsenal, we blow it to hell."

"Nice," Tedeski said.

"After that…" the Captain said. "After that, it's a street fight. We draw them into the manor, fight them room to room if we have to, try to get as many as we can into the Rabbit Hole. Once it becomes clear that Kleg has committed all his troops, we can run for the woods. I'll blow a whistle and that will be our signal to get out. Once we're in the woods, we call artillery down on the manor house itself to cover our retreat through the woods until we find a friendly unit."

"Seems pretty tricky to pull off. Do you think it will work?" Tedeski asked.

"I think it's our only chance," Captain Powell said.

"What about the explosives in the tunnel?" I asked.

"Fictional," he said. "I made it up to see how Kleg would react. But I think we should make that fiction a reality. Either way, Kleg will draw some of his troops off the attack on the manor to take the Rabbit Hole quickly enough to keep us from blowing it."

"We'll divide our men evenly into three platoons. I'll lead 1st Platoon. Major Hayward, you take 2nd Platoon."

"Will your men be all right with that?" Major Hayward asked. "A British officer leading them?"

"You're the only other officer I've got," Captain Powell said. "I think they'll get used to the idea. We need everybody."

"Who's taking 3rd Platoon?" I asked.

"You," he answered. "All of my other platoon leaders are dead."

I almost protested at that. For the longest time, my place had been by the Captain's side. I might lead a patrol or something like that, but essentially, I was usually close enough to the Captain to look out for him. The fight that was coming was going to be the worst I'd ever seen; I knew that like I knew my own name. I didn't want the Captain to be off somewhere without me to keep him from sticking his neck out too far. It was stupid to think that way; in battle, there's no way you can really protect somebody close to you. You can watch their back, but a stray shell or bullet can easily kill them before you even knew it happened.

"So who's going to draw Kleg into the Rabbit Hole?" Tedeski asked. A look around the room answered that for him. "It's me, isn't it?"

"It has to be a tank destroyer," Captain Powell said. "Kleg's panzers won't bother with troops but they might chase a TD… especially one that's just given them a pounding."

"Well, then," Tedeski said. "Looks like I'm the guy."

"We'll try to send some troops down to help you out and draw some of the infantry down the tunnel as well."

Tedeski shook his head. "Don't bother. They'll only slow me down."

"Remember," Captain Powell said. "You don't need to take out all of the enemy. You only need to draw them into the village. After that, get the hell out of there as soon as you can. If, for some reason, anybody gets separated down there, use the cathedral as a rallying point. Clear?"

We all nodded.

"Very well. Let's get it done, then."

Andrew C. Piazza

62

As strange as it sounds, our preparations were completed with plenty of time to spare before sundown. We'd already dug in the day before, as soon as we reached Dom Caern; the foxholes and strongpoints were already in place, we only had to man them. Distributing weapons and ammunition took up more time than anything.

That was one thing we had going for us. We were short on manpower, but long on firepower. In addition to the thirty-cal machine-guns normally assigned to our company, we now had an extra boost of eight MG-42 machine-guns from the arsenal and as much ammo as we could possibly want for them. Twenty troopers traded in their M1s for *Sturmgewehrs*, and there were enough Panzerfaust rockets to hand out one to a man with extras to spare.

We had the tools for the job. Now all we had to do was stay alive long enough to use them.

Once the weapons were in the right hands and all the pieces were put into place, there was nothing to do but sit and wait. We still had a few hours before sundown, and there was no point in freezing all of our men solid, so we started to rotate some of them back into the manor to stay as warm as possible.

When my turn came around, I slung my Panzerfaust rocket and trudged through the snow back toward the manor. I ran into the Captain, Tedeski, and Major Hayward inside the foyer. Tedeski and Major Hayward were smoking; the Captain was describing how he wanted to conduct our falling back to the manor when the time came. Rebecca sat on a nearby chair, holding her carbine in her lap.

"Another glorious day in the Army," I said once I was among them. "Hurry up and wait."

Captain Powell smiled. "It's a good day to be alive, Harry."

"It's not a good day to be waiting anxiously, though," I said.

"Here, come on," Tedeski said, leading us further into the manor. "I got just the thing."

We followed him into a sitting room with a large table and a dozen chairs. Sweeping the surface of the table with his arm, he sat and promptly produced a deck of cards.

"You guys know how to play poker?" he asked.

I had to laugh. Here we were, in the worst of awful situations, trapped in a house of madness, waiting for a nightmare of a battle, and we would pass the time by playing cards. It was just crazy enough to be appropriate.

"What do we use for stakes?" I said.

Tedeski shrugged and shuffled the deck. "We'll play for matchsticks. Who cares? Hey, Doc! And Wexler… I mean, Major Wexler, sir."

Doctor Schmidt and Wexler stopped in the hall as they passed by our room. "What are you doing?" Doctor Schmidt asked.

"Come on in. We're having a card game," Tedeski said, waving them inside. "Join in."

The two men looked at each other. They seemed loathe to enter the room; I caught Doctor Schmidt's guilty glance at Rebecca before he said, "I, um, I am not sure that is a good idea…"

"Ah, come on," Tedeski said. "This is a non-discriminatory game in a non-discriminatory outfit. Black or white, male or female, soldier or civilian, Allied or German, enlisted man or officer; who the hell cares? We're all just card players, here."

"Well," Doctor Schmidt said, wiping his palms along his coat and stepping slowly to the table, "all right, then. Although I must admit, I am not much of a card player."

"Spoken like a true card shark," Tedeski said with a grin.

Doctor Schmidt frowned. "What is a 'card shark'?"

Tedeski's grin stretched even wider. "Also spoken like a true card shark."

"There's nothing to it, Doctor," Wexler said, settling into a chair between Major Hayward and Tedeski. "It's simply a matter of calculating the odds of getting one hand or another."

"A matter of calculating the odds, my ass," Tedeski said. "It's all about playing the other players; bluffing them when you have to, or convincing them you're bluffing when you're not."

"Do you know how to play, Rebecca?" Captain Powell asked.

"Are we playing five-card draw or stud?" she said.

The Captain grinned and looked at the rest of us. "I guess that's my answer."

"All right, all right. Enough jawing. Let's play some poker," Tedeski said, passing out cards with practiced ease.

I started off with a pair of eights and the King of Spades as a high card. My eyes explored the faces of each of the other players in turn, searching for any clue as to their standing.

Both Doctor Schmidt and Wexler arranged their cards from left to right. Tedeski stared at his hand and chewed his cigar stub relentlessly. Rebecca ran her fingers across the face of the cards and murmured to herself, as if reading Braille. Major Hayward raised an eyebrow and said, "Well, well," which I immediately took to be a bluff. The Captain, of course, showed me absolutely nothing at all.

"So, Major," Tedeski said around his cigar, "you ever figure out what the hell the Geist is?"

Major Wexler stirred once he realized Tedeski was talking to him. "Hunh? What do you mean?"

Tedeski tossed a few matchsticks onto the pot. "Well, you've been reading every scrap of paper the Germans left behind. Any ideas on what this thing is?"

"Plenty. That's the problem," Wexler said, pushing his glasses up on his nose and raking his hand through his hair. "I've got just shy of a million speculations and no definitive evidence to prove or disprove any of them. Is it my bet? I raise one."

"What I'm wondering is, why hasn't it wiped us out entirely?" Captain Powell said. "Why does it bother with this handful of killings here, some spooky games there? Why not just kill us all?"

"Toying with us," Major Hayward said. "Cat and mouse, you know. My bet? I call."

He's definitely got nothing, I thought, and tucked that away for later use.

"I'm wondering where it's been all day," I said, putting my matchsticks in as the bet came to me. "I call. I mean, ever since that thing with Davey and Goliath out at the arsenal, it's been quiet as a mouse."

"Maybe it's tired," Tedeski said. "I'll take one card."

"Maybe it was satisfied," Rebecca said. "It had its fun and was satisfied for a little while."

"Perhaps it senses the fight that is coming and is gathering its strength," Major Hayward said. "Three cards, please."

I drew two cards and got the King of Diamonds, bringing me up to two pair. Enough to make me feel confident, and when the bet came my way, I raised it three.

"I think it's a mistake to assign any sort of human motivations or characteristics to the Geist," Wexler said. "We have to remember that the Geist is an alien being, entirely alien. Concepts such as hate or anger or cruelty may not have any meaning to it. The notion of finishing us off may not ever occur to it. Maybe it doesn't even know why it does what it does. Maybe its psychology is that of a sentient form of chaos."

"Perhaps it does know what it's doing," Major Hayward said. "Perhaps everything it does is for a reason, and we simply don't know what it is yet."

"Maybe it takes its qualities from us," Captain Powell said. "From what it sees in us."

"Maybe it's like war," I said. "You know, how war kills indiscriminately, and the guys on the front line never have a clue about the big picture? They just get caught up in it. Hell, maybe the Geist's a general."

Tedeski, Doctor Schmidt, and Major Hayward folded and we laid down our cards. Wexler had a pair of aces and the Captain had three sixes. Rebecca showed the Captain her hand and asked him something in French.

Captain Powell scowled. "It's called a full house."

Rebecca's big eyes sparkled and her teeth flashed in a grin as she raked the little pile of matchsticks her way. I made a mental note to watch her more carefully as the game resumed.

"Okay, ante up," Tedeski said, as the cards came around again.

"I think perhaps Captain Powell has a good point," Doctor Schmidt said. "About the Geist observing us. I believe it must have some ability to see into our minds."

"What do you mean?" I asked.

"Well, it writes on the walls and makes the dead speak," he explained. "But how did it know our language to make this happen? It communicates in both German and English equally well, and sometimes switches between the two. It seems to know our names... Shorty called you 'Sarge' in the village, if you remember."

"I remember," I said.

"So it must be able to see into our minds, learn our ways in this fashion," he said. "This would also explain how it knows which nervous system pathways to activate when it animates the dead."

"But its control isn't perfect," Wexler said. "The language it uses is a little stiff, and the... dead... seem to be able to regain control of themselves, at least a little."

"Yeesh. That's the worst part of this whole thing," Tedeski said with a shudder. "Bringing the dead back to life like some sort of puppet."

"Even more disturbing to me is that some of them don't seem to mind," Major Hayward said.

I could tell he was thinking about the corpse of the SS trooper we'd killed in the kitchen. *The kitchen is open, Hayward*, he'd said out in the snow, and laughed. Maybe he didn't mind being under the control of the Geist. Maybe he'd given himself over to it willingly.

"Whatever it is, it's not the size of a zeppelin," Captain Powell said. "I don't know what those bomber pilots saw, but the shape I saw through the snow earlier today was more like the size of a house."

"Maybe it is a smaller specimen than those the bomber pilots saw," Major Hayward said. "Paul, earlier, when you said that the tunnel extends into the air as well as the ground… do you think collapsing the tunnel will keep the Geist in its place?"

Wexler shrugged. "It's hard to say. It could be that the tunnel provides a sort of guideline to our dimension. The Geist knows which way to go to get to us by following a tunnel cut through the earth. If that tunnel is collapsed, and the Geist finds nothing but a uniform pile of dirt when it comes looking for the tunnel, it may not know which way to go to get through."

It sounded like wishful thinking, but I didn't know what our alternative was.

"I don't understand how anyone could call that thing, the Geist, his god," Rebecca said. "How could anyone want to join it in its madness?"

"How could anyone want to join the Nazis?" Wexler said. "No offense, Doctor Schmidt."

"None taken. I am not a Nazi," Doctor Schmidt said.

"You fight for their Army," Rebecca immediately replied. "You keep them alive."

Doctor Schmidt fidgeted his chair. "It is not so simple. I am a soldier. I fight for Germany, not Hitler. I fight for my country, my home."

"Your country is run by Nazis," Rebecca said.

"Yes, but I cannot stop this," Doctor Schmidt said.

"You don't even try," Rebecca said. "Do you like what the Nazis do? How they kill and take everything?"

Doctor Schmidt shrugged helplessly. I almost felt sorry for him. "There are things the Nazis do that I do not approve of, yes, but…"

"But what have you done to stop these things they do?" she said. "Maybe something little, yes? Here and there, a small help to those your country murders or tortures, to ease your guilty conscience? But what do you really do to stop Hitler and his madness?"

"I am only one person," he said. "I cannot stop all of the evil in my country. I have a family. Even if I could do something, my family would be made to suffer."

"These are the things I always hear," Rebecca said. "I am only one person. It is easy to shrug off your guilt this way."

"What could I do? What? I did not vote for the Nazis, or join the Nazi party. They take power, that's it. I say anything, and I'm a dead man. My family is dead. What can I do?"

"Somebody has to do something," she said. "But bad enough you do nothing to stop them. You wear their uniform, fight with their guns."

"I said before, I defend my country. Ask these soldiers; as a soldier, are there some battles, some campaigns, that you can simply decide not to take part in because you don't like it? I am an instrument of policy, not a maker of policy. Besides, if a politician is elected that you do not like, do you immediately set out to overthrow the country? Of course not. Then you are a traitor to your country."

"This is different," Rebecca said. "Hitler and the Nazis are not just any politicians. They make you into monsters. You are a traitor to your country for not fighting them."

Doctor Schmidt shrugged. "You cannot choose your battles as a soldier. We all know this. I might as well ask Tedeski why he fights for a country in which he is treated as a second-class citizen."

"Oh, well," Tedeski said, "my daddy used to say, 'Everybody wants to go to the party. Nobody wants to clean up.' It's easy to get mad, want a revolution, demand change today, right this second... or else. That never works. Real change, lasting change, has to come in people's minds. You can't stop racism with a riot. You have to turn the racists' minds around, one at time if necessary.

"My great-grandfather fought in the 54th Maine, the first all-Colored unit in the Civil War. They were heroes. And for every white face that saw them fight, there was one less racist in the world.

"The same goes for me. 'The eyes of the world are on you,' my daddy told me as I left, and I fight like there's always a camera rolling. Because for me, there is. Colored folks fight poorly, then people will all say, 'See, just like I said... they're no good.' But we go out there and fight with honor, really kick hell out of Hitler... then guys like Cappy will see it. Maybe it even changes their minds. And that's one less man who will teach his kids to hate colored folk. And they won't teach theirs. And so on, until... well.

"That's why I like it over here. I do my job right, and it doesn't matter I'm Colored. Just as long as I do my job. That's all I ever wanted."

"But I've got a question for you, Doc," Tedeski said. "How do people like the Nazis take over a country, anyway? I mean, you seem like an okay guy, Doc. How is it that a guy like Hitler can get enough people behind him to lead a country, even when he does the things he does?"

Doctor Schmidt looked at his hands for a moment. "There are many reasons. Some of it is fear, and exploiting that fear. But I think much of it has to do with pride."

"Pride?" Wexler said. "What does pride have to do with it?"

"Pride is a wonderful, powerful emotion, one that can turn a beggar into a king... at least on the inside," Doctor Schmidt explained. "And like most wonderful, powerful things, pride can be corrupted and used by those who seek control for dark purposes."

"Hitler," I said.

"Yes. Can you imagine what it means to be German? Before Hitler, Germany was a poor country, terribly poor, crushed under the boot of the rest of Europe because of the Treaty of Versailles. So we were powerless, penniless, full of shame, held down in the mud."

"Then along comes a man, a man full of fire, full of spirit, so much of it that you think just by standing next to him you may catch some of his energy and run a thousand miles without tiring. Do you know the kind? And this man tells us we are not dogs, we are not beaten, that we can stand up and be proud to call ourselves German."

"Can you understand what this means? What it feels like to get up out of the mud and face down those who had held you there... and they *run*? This is how the German people feel when suddenly, Germany is no longer weak, is no longer the victim, but strong. Proud."

"And so it is easy to overlook many of the other things he does," Schmidt said. "It has always been this way. So long as the people are prosperous, there will always be sins the public is willing to ignore or disbelieve."

"This is your excuse?" Rebecca said.

"I didn't say I was proud of it," Doctor Schmidt said. "I said this is what can happen."

"And what about Kleg?" the Captain asked. "What makes him ally himself with a creature like the Geist?"

"Kleg?" Doctor Schmidt said. "Kleg is another story. His soul is twisted, and the SS have rewarded and encouraged that part of him until he has become nothing but cruelty. So it is not so surprising that when a man who is told that brutality is the natural order finds something like the Geist, he identifies with it. In the Geist, he sees everything he wants; power, mostly, but a perverse power, a cruel power, a power as a child or a madman would wield it. Every whim can be instantly realized without conscience or consequence, and so Kleg degenerates even further into madness."

"And as far as this 'alliance' between Kleg and the Geist is concerned… yes, it appears it created a great deal of weapons and munitions, but I doubt if it did this to gain Kleg's favor. Perhaps our killing each other amuses it and it gives Kleg weapons to continue doing the same. Kleg, like any other thug or brute, thinks that any man… or thing… that hands him a gun is his friend."

"That simple?" I said.

"Throughout the history of warfare, there have always been men who would fight simply for the love of violence, for bloodlust. Kleg is no different. First the SS encourages his darker impulses and gives him weapons and a command of troops and panzers. Now it is the Geist that takes him to the next level, allows him to fall into even greater depravity, and once again, Kleg believes he has an ally, when in truth, the Geist is tearing he and his men apart from the inside."

"Like the Nazis have done to Germany," Captain Powell said.

Doctor Schmidt shrugged. "Perhaps. And perhaps you are right, Rebecca. Perhaps I should have done something to resist the evil I saw around me when the Nazis took power. But at first, it seemed like it would all go away on its own, and then, they were so strong…" He shook his head. "Many times, I would hear a small voice in my mind, telling me to do something about it. But I did not. It was only a small voice in my mind, and easy to ignore, especially when the problem was so big and beyond the power of one man to change."

"It's hard sometimes to have faith in the face of evil," Major Hayward said, his eyes never leaving his cards. "I know all about it. It's easy to ignore what we know is right when there isn't any burning bush telling us exactly what God's Will is. If you believe in that sort of thing. Isn't that what Kleg said? His god can be seen, while ours cannot? It's easy to lose your faith in the small hours of the morning."

"Maybe God needs to come down off the mountain a little more," Tedeski said. "You know, like in the Old Testament? Come rolling down and tell people what's what."

An image suddenly popped into my head. Bodies lying in the snow, where the road met the tree line; Kleg's, mine, a few others that may or may not have been Captain Powell or Major Hayward. Kleg's SS panzer battalion, frozen in indecision now that their leader was gone, suddenly caught by our approaching reinforcements. And leaving Dom Caern, the rest of the company, all alive, all safe and leaving the Geist for our bombers.

"Damn," I said, and everyone turned to me.

All of the air squeezed out of my lungs. The silence in the room was like a thick fog; my voice didn't want to embarrass itself by trying a feeble attempt at piercing it with words that would have to be labeled as insane by everyone else in the room.

"Sarge?" Captain Powell said.

"When we were out there, talking to Kleg," I said, my voice small and uncertain, "and he was daring God to strike him down, I thought, shoot him. Shoot him dead, end it here, and damn the white flag. But I didn't. I told myself I couldn't break the truce, it wasn't appropriate."

I snorted. "Appropriate. Like the rest of war is. And I told myself I'd be shot down by snipers in the woods."

"You would have," Captain Powell said.

"But don't you see? What if... what if that was the voice of God, telling me what had to be done? What if I had killed Kleg, and that stopped his battalion long enough for the rest of you to escape? Wouldn't that be worth it?"

"That's just idle speculation, Harry," Captain Powell said. "You don't know it would've worked out that way."

"Don't I?" I said. "I can't shake the feeling that I had a chance to end it all and I blew it. I knew what I had to do, but I let fear and indecision and doubt make me hesitate long enough for the moment to pass. I blew it. So I know all about your little voice, Doc. I know how easy it is to brush it off as 'idle speculation' and ignore it. And it's like you said before, Major... now I think there's going to be a terrible cost."

The room got quiet. I felt stupid, like I'd gone too far. I felt like one of the drunks in my bar who blustered on and on about some damn thing or another, oblivious to the fact that everyone in the room was ignoring him. I wanted to take it all back. Just kidding, guys. I don't really think God is taking a personal interest in little old me.

"Kleg will kill you if he gets a chance," Captain Powell said suddenly, and it took a second for me to realize he was talking to Doctor Schmidt. "German or not."

Doctor Schmidt shook his head. "Germany does not matter to Kleg. It never has. Even before the Geist, he would gladly kill his own countrymen just to have somebody to kill."

"And now?" Captain Powell asked.

"And now? I would say he has given up his humanity, but that was gone long ago as well. Now he wears the uniform of my country, but it may as well be anything, any kind of clothing. It is meaningless to him. I see him for what he is. A warlord who obeys only death. He is as much my enemy as the false god he worships."

"And if you had a company of Wehrmacht here at Dom Caern?" the Captain asked.

Doctor Schmidt nodded. "I would resist Kleg to the last man and burn the house to the ground."

"What are you getting at, Jim?" Wexler said.

"Let's just say I'm following the small voice that's going on in my mind."

"Captain?" I asked.

His eyes never left Doctor Schmidt. "We're going to need everyone."

Doctor Schmidt let out a long sigh. He set his cards down on the table and folded his hands over them. Slowly, almost imperceptibly, he nodded.

"What, are you kidding me?" Wexler said. "He's a German Army officer, Jim!"

"Yes," Rebecca said. "He cannot be trusted."

"This isn't about the Germans versus the Allies anymore," Captain Powell said.

"No," Doctor Schmidt said. "It is about good versus evil, and it is about time I took a stand against Kleg and the Geist and all they represent."

"I'll take him in my platoon," Major Hayward said.

"Very well, then," Captain Powell said.

"I can't believe we're doing this," Wexler said. "A German Army officer."

"Hey, the hell with it," Tedeski said. "They didn't trust colored folks in the Army for a long time, either. We're in a crazy situation. I say, give the man a chance."

Doctor Schmidt looked up from his hands at last. "We must kill them all, Captain. Every last one of them. And throw their god back to the hell from which it came."

Captain Powell nodded. "My thoughts exactly."

Just then, Jack Pelosi burst into the room. He looked around the table once, perhaps wondering if he'd interrupted something, and then he dropped his bomb. "Captain.... The sun's going down."

I remember wishing he hadn't come into the room so soon. I wanted that moment, the seven of us talking and playing cards around the table, to stretch out into days and weeks and months. I could see the same feeling in the eyes of everybody there; even those of us who didn't like one or more of the others didn't want this moment to end. For all of our differences, we seemed to fit together; it seemed right that the seven of us should be sitting at a table and working through the problems of the world. And as we all felt that, I think each of us knew that this was the last time we would all be together; that some or most or maybe even all of us weren't going to survive to see the sunrise. Leaving that table was like getting out of a warm bed on a cold morning. I didn't want to go.

The Captain stood up first. "Very well, then. Let's take our places."

We left our cards and matchsticks forgotten on the table, and went out into the cold to meet Kleg and his god.

63

Captain Powell led 1st and 3rd Platoons to their places in the woods by the road. Major Hayward took Doctor Schmidt and 2nd Platoon to their places in and around the arsenal. Tedeski left to make sure his rigs were in place and out of sight… tank destroyers usually attacked by ambush.

I lingered in the manor house to make sure the handful of men that we were leaving there were in place. We had decided Wexler was best off sticking around with the 81mm mortar teams set up behind the manor. He'd be out of the way and less likely to get himself killed. Plus, having an officer around will often boost morale, even if you think the guy's an asshole, which is what most of the company thought of Wexler.

"Stand there by the sound-powered phone and tell these crews what we tell you to," I said, already shivering against the cold. The nervous jitters hadn't come on me yet, so I was aware of the light snowfall and accompanying frigid air worming its way inside of my wool overcoat.

"What if the line cuts out?" Wexler asked. He was watching the mortar crews setting their ammunition closer to hand. It wasn't much, unfortunately; one thing Kleg's arsenal lacked was ammunition for American mortars.

"Then we'll use the radio," I said. "Just be sure to have those flares ready to go. Once they break out of the woods, we'll need to see them to shoot them. They can see in the dark, remember?"

Wexler frowned up at the sky. "It looks like it's clearing up. With starlight, or moonlight…"

"Let's not count on that, sir."

"How will you call in that battalion of artillery for the attack on the road?" he asked.

"We've got pre-set artillery concentrations. Each one has a code. We tell them the code, they know where to shoot. We can adjust it by radio if we need to."

He nodded, and then shifted uncomfortably under the weight of the carbine slung over his shoulder. "What if, um, I mean, what if they get through to us, or, you know, what if…"

I put a hand on his shoulder. "There's no guarantees, sir. No sure bets. Just do the best you can."

Wexler blew out a breath, and nodded again. "I am… I am scared to death, Sarge."

I grinned and thumped him on the back before I left. "It's a good day to be alive, sir."

Rebecca followed me inside of the manor. "Harry? What should I do?"

I led her up to the second floor. Cappy had a spot picked out in a room with a view. The son of a bitch even had a sofa pulled over to his window of choice so he could wait for the enemy in comfort. A private from 1st Platoon named Barnes kept him company from behind a thirty-cal machine-gun. He'd decided a sofa was a bit much, so he sat on a simple wooden chair as he stared out the window adjacent to Cappy's. A pair of Panzerfaust rockets leaned up against the wall.

On a cot set against the far wall, Davey's unconscious body slept through the whole thing, still held in the grasp of the blue 88s. I envied him. He'd be spared the terrifying hours which I knew were sure to come.

"Stay here," I said. "Keep an eye on Davey."

"But…" she began to protest.

"Stay here and make sure nothing can come up behind them," I said firmly, with a glance at Cappy. He gave me an almost imperceptible nod.

"Harry," she said, laying a hand on my arm, "be careful. And take care of Jiim."

"I always do," I said. There wasn't much point in trying to explain that both of those activities would be impossible in the coming hours. Instead, I kissed her on the cheek and headed back out into the cold.

Tedeski had his tank destroyer hidden behind the arsenal, and I found him perched on top of the open turret, smoking his battered cigar and sitting behind a fifty-cal machine-gun like it was just another night. He waved at me as I approached, and I climbed up the side of the big metal beast and settled in next to him.

"What do you think, Tedeski?" I asked, getting a cigarette out and lighting it.

"I think we're gonna kill us a lot of SS sonsabitches tonight," he said with a grin.

His enthusiasm was infectious, and that was a big reason why I liked being around him. "How many do you think you can take?"

He shrugged. "If you guys bottle them up good so they come out piecemeal, in ones and twos, and those flares get up so we can see them… I figure I might be able to take as many as three or four before they get me."

"Don't take any chances."

"Sarge, I'm touched."

"Fuck you, sir," I said good-naturedly. "Remember, you're the bait to draw Kleg into the Rabbit Hole. Where are your other rigs?"

He twisted a bit and pointed back toward Dom Caern. "Hiding behind the manor. One behind the corner closest to us, the other on the far side. They'll engage the panzers as they come out of the woods."

"Three panzers each, at best," I said. "And another five or six on the road taken by the arty. It might be enough."

"It's a good thing we've got these TD's rather than Sherman tanks," Tedeski said. "The gun on a Sherman's too weak to punch through a Tiger or Panther tank's armor."

I nodded. "I once saw a Tiger tank get hit by five bazooka rockets and a 37mm anti-tank gun. Nothing. Just made little divots in the hull."

"Yeah, well, this baby will open them up like a tin can," Tedeski said, patting the tank destroyer's cannon.

"You don't have anywhere near as much armor, though," I reminded him.

"You can't have everything," he said. "Damn, it's cold! Nobody should have to fight in weather like this."

"I'm going inside to check on Major Hayward and Doctor Schmidt," I said.

"Hell, yes," he said, climbing down off the rig. "It's too damn cold to be sitting my ass on a big chunk of frozen steel."

Inside the arsenal, men readied and checked weapons by flashlight and the flickering glow of makeshift canteen lanterns. As if they weren't well armed enough, the GIs were making Molotav cocktails and Gammon bombs... improvised anti-tank bombs... and setting them near to hand.

"Hey, Sarge," Wayne said, waving me over. He was still armed with his M1, having expressed no desire for "any damn Kraut rifle" earlier.

"What's on your mind, Wayne?" I asked.

He leaned in almost conspiratorially and nodded toward Doctor Schmidt, who was filling the pouches of an ammunition bag with clips for the Schmeisser submachine-gun slung at his side. "We really letting that Kraut have a weapon?"

"It's like the Captain said," I answered. "This isn't the Allies versus the Germans anymore. This is us against Kleg and the Geist. We need everyone we can get. Including him."

Wayne frowned. "What if, you know, he turns and starts shooting us?"

"Kill him," Tedeski said. "But give the man a chance first. He deserves that."

"I guess," Wayne said.

"Well, I think we've got things well in hand," Major Hayward said, accepting a cigarette from me as well as a light. "Explosives are in place for when we fall back. Kleg won't risk using shells or grenades on this structure for the same reason he didn't earlier."

"Doesn't want to risk blowing it up," Wayne said.

One Last Gasp

"That's right," Major Hayward said. "He wants his munitions intact. So, a bit more level of a playing field. And there is that nasty surprise waiting for them in the wood shed."

Just to the side of the stables, away from the road, was a flimsy wooden structure about the size of a two-car garage. Major Hayward had dubbed it the "wood shed" for lack of another name. The thin wood construction made it a lousy defensive position, but it could and did conceal the "nasty surprise" Hayward spoke of.

"Are the men giving you any trouble?" I asked.

"No, no, none at all. Splendid chaps. Splendid," Major Hayward said.

"You seem pretty optimistic," I said.

"Not at all. I have no illusions as to our chances. However, there is a certain comfort one can find in taking definitive action, no matter how risky; and quite frankly, I am looking forward to the cathartic release of a good firefight."

Tedeski and I had to grin. Leave it up to Hayward to sum up an approaching battle in terms of personal growth.

I toyed with the idea of getting out to 3rd Platoon's lines and settling in, but the memory of the cold wind convinced me to have one more cigarette before I left. I'd smoked about halfway through it when I saw a GI named Elliot shuffle over towards Doctor Schmidt.

I took a few steps closer and watched, worrying that there might be trouble.

"Hey, uh, Doc?" Elliot asked almost shyly. "Is it Doc? Can I call you Doc?"

Doctor Schmidt closed the flap on his bag of ammunition. "Yes, of course. And you are... Private Elliot?" He read the name off of Elliot's jacket. "What can I do for you, Private Elliot?"

Elliot shrugged and looked down at his shoes. It was almost comical; I'd seen Elliot bayonet a man to death in the Hurtgen Forest while under heavy fire.

"I, um... I heard you were a psychiatrist. Or used to be one."

"Yes. I was a psychiatrist for approximately seven years before I was conscripted into the infantry," Doctor Schmidt answered.

"So… what'd you do?" Elliot asked.

Doctor Schmidt frowned. "What do you mean?"

"Well, I ain't never been to a shrink before," Elliot said. "I'm from West Virginia, out in the mountains, and you don't get much call for them out there. But I heard it's like going to see a priest."

"A priest?"

"Yeah, you know. They listen to your problems, or listen to you confess the bad things you done, and they make you feel better when you're beaten down or scared. At least good enough to get yourself through it."

Another GI stepped up next to Elliot. "Is it like that, Doc? What you do?"

I noticed almost a dozen GIs had congregated around Doctor Schmidt; not so close as to be noticed, but close enough that I could tell they were listening in.

Doctor Schmidt noticed it, as well. He looked around at their expectant faces, and in a moment that reminded me almost eerily of Captain Powell, he read all of their minds and said, nodding slowly, "I think you are right, Elliot. I think perhaps we should have a prayer."

And then, an already insane situation became more bizarre. The GIs, including Elliot, took off their helmets and bowed their heads, waiting for Doctor Schmidt's prayer. Doctor Schmidt frowned and hesitated, as if unsure what exactly he was going to say, and then he nodded to himself and began.

"Heavenly Father," he said, and I was dumbfounded as all around me, more GIs took off their helmets and bowed their heads. Tedeski followed suit, and nudged me with his elbow to remind me to do the same.

"Heavenly Father," Doctor Schmidt said in a clear voice, "for many days now I have allowed the enemies of Your Will to cloud my vision. I have failed to protect the weak. I have failed to fight the unjust. I have failed you in thought, word, and deed. I have done this out of fear and selfishness and pride.

"All I ask, Father, is that you allow me in the coming hours to erase the misdeeds I have done. Allow me to make up for my failures. Let me fight with honor and bravery.

"Do not let fear make me tremble before my enemies. Do not let selfishness enter my heart and keep me from sacrificing to help those in need. Do let not pride deceive me into believing that I am beyond Your Will.

"Let me stand strong with your Spirit, and I will not fail you."

"Amen," Tedeski said, and the other GIs murmured it in unison.

Maybe it wasn't the best prayer ever made up on the spot, but like Elliot said, maybe it would be enough to get us through this. It was quiet in the arsenal, and silently, I made my own addition to Doctor Schmidt's prayer.

Please God, give me one last gasp. And please, if I don't make it, keep my Kate safe and don't let her grieve for too long. And if it's at all possible, keep the Captain and Rebecca away from the Geist. Even if it means you have to take me instead.

"Thank you, Doctor," Major Hayward said softly. "Gentlemen, let's take our places."

"Yeah, I better get back to my rig," Tedeski said.

"I'd better get out to the Captain," I said.

"You watch yourself out there, Sarge," Tedeski said, holding out his hand. "Don't you take too much on yourself. There's a lot of us here to do the job."

I clasped his hand in mine. "You be sure to follow your own advice, Frank. You've got nothing to prove to me or anybody else here, so don't get reckless."

"See you out there," he said, and left the stables.

I've never liked good-byes, so I slipped out before Major Hayward or Doctor Schmidt could notice me leave. On my lonely walk out into the snow-covered pines, the sky itself seemed to press down on me like a heavy blanket, crushing the air out of my lungs and smothering me. I felt tired. It seemed like the enemies I faced were a vast ocean, and I was only a grain of sand on the beach. It seemed foolish to think I could stand in front of a power like that, that I might hope to survive in the face of Kleg and his god.

The Captain saw that in me as I approached his position, inside the forest next to where the road entered the pines. We'd argued over which platoon was going to take this position, closer to the manor, and which was going to take the position next to it, further into the woods and therefore in more danger. The Captain wanted the more dangerous position, of course, and of course, he couldn't have it. I insisted on that point. It was more than just the sound tactics of not putting your commanding officer out on the tip of the spear; I wanted to know I stood between him and Kleg. At least for a little while.

"How are you holding up, Sarge?" he asked. A half-dozen men were clustered closely around him, and others were scattered along the tree line next to the road. Machine-guns sat pointed toward the road, waiting for something to chew up.

"Sarge?"

"Peachy, sir," I said. "It's a good day to be alive."

The air still stifled me; I couldn't help looking around at the faces of my buddies and wondering who was going to get it. Maybe all of them. So many had already; Ridley, Lambourne, Shorty, Goliath.... I was running out of familiar faces. Sooner or later, I knew it would be coming for me, too. It was only a matter of time.

Inspiration comes in many forms. Captain Powell's wasn't as grandiose as Doctor Schmidt's prayer, but it was exactly what I needed.

"I understand the situation is normal, Sergeant Kinder," he said in a loud voice, which told me he was speaking for the benefit of everyone within earshot as well as myself.

"Sir?"

"I said, I understand the situation is normal. The enemy has us surrounded."

I smiled at the old Airborne joke and recited the punch line. "The poor bastards."

Like magic, Captain Powell's words put me in the right frame of mind, the infantryman's casual indifference to death and his stubborn defiance of the enemy. Hey, fuck it, we're all dead men walking, so what else is new? That sort of thing.

"I'd better get to my lines," I said, "out to 3rd Platoon."

The Captain nodded. "Check your phone lines and radio, make sure they're up and running. Kleg will probably make us sit for a while before he comes, but there's no sense in taking chances."

"Yes, sir," I said, and headed further into the woods, along the road, toward my new command. It was only after I'd gone a good thirty yards that I realized how abruptly I'd left the Captain. Once again, it was a slice of Captain Powell magic; he knew that to sit and talk and dwell on it all would only be counter-productive for me, so he built me up and sent me quickly on my way.

My platoon was already in place, in a vaguely L-shaped formation. The long side was arrayed along the road, ready to ambush the column when it came. The angle was at the far end of our line, away from the manor, with four guys and a machine-gun lined back into the trees to keep the SS from coming around our flank.

I made a couple of adjustments to individual positions and then settled into a shallow slit trench somebody had scraped out of the cold earth for me. I decided to pass the time by digging it... or chipping it, I should say, as the ground was still frozen on top... a little deeper as I waited for Kleg.

Jack Pelosi was in the next hole over with one of our captured MG-42 machine-guns. When he saw what I was doing, he came over to help out.

"What do you think, Sarge?" he said.

The physical effort of chipping away at the frozen earth made me feel better. The air didn't stifle me anymore; I didn't feel lonely or tired or like a tiny little insignificant speck. Doing something with real result, even if it was only as mundane as digging a hole a little deeper, reminded me that I could have an effect on my life, on my world. I wasn't powerless. I swung my shovel, dirt moved. It was a little something, but it was there.

"I said, what do you think?"

"I think we're going to kill us a lot of SS tonight," I said, and he grinned.

"Hell yes, Sarge."

We dug in silence for a little while after that, and my mind settled into enough of a lull that Kate could come to me, smiling and shining like the sun. There was more to this memory than those that I'd had of her before, though; in months gone by, Kate was mostly a numbing distraction, a drug to cover up the pain boring a hole in my spirit. That night, she was more than that. She was a reminder of a better world existing side by side with that of the war, as almost a mirror image of the Village of the Geist. Two sides of the same coin, and I was stuck in the middle, helping to decide which one landed on top. It was one of the very few times during the war that I actually realized what I was doing there. The first time had come months before, when we helped a French couple out of a cellar in a town we'd liberated. They had a baby girl that they told me had never seen the light of day before; she had been born while they hid in that cellar and they hadn't dared to venture out with the child for months since then. They wept as they carried her out into the sunshine for the first time. The last time I realized why I was there came months later, when I saw my first concentration camp. On that night, the Geist's night, I knew why I was there, freezing my ass solid in a dirty hole, waiting stubbornly to fight to the death against a nightmare of an enemy.

You can't have her, I thought, thinking of Kate, thinking of Kleg, thinking of the Geist. *You can't have any more of them. Not one more. It ends here.*

I remembered what I'd said to the Captain earlier. *I want that motherfucker Kleg in my sights. Just once.*

I whispered the final addendum to my prayer before settling back into my digging. "I won't fail you this time," I said. "It ends here. At all costs."

64

Almost the entire night had gone by before we finally heard the creaking of Kleg's panzers lumbering toward us in the dark. I knew why he did that; to make us shiver ourselves silly out in the dark, always tense, always wondering when he would come, exhausting ourselves with our long hours of silent vigilance. It's one of the advantages of being on the attack; you get to choose when the attack begins, and you can relax and rest while the defenders sit up all night out in the cold and wonder.

By that point, I'd been on the line long enough to dig my hole four feet deep. Hand grenades sat around the rim, ready for quick use. My Panzerfaust rocket lay close to hand as well. A sound-powered phone ran to my hole, and I tested the line often, to hear Captain Powell's voice as much as anything else.

I heard them coming as I was signing off on another of those line checks. "Hang on, sir," I said, and listened.

It was the sound of chains being dragged over pulleys, the sound of oily engines growling, the sound of frozen earth crunching under the weight of hundreds of tons of steel war machines. It was the sound of battle warming up its joints to hit us hard and fast.

The air coming out of my lungs seemed to tingle with electricity as I said into the receiver, "Here they come."

"Keep steady, Harry," the Captain's voice reassured me. "Get through to Division and our battery of 105s. They'll be ready for your command. Do it now."

"Yes, sir," I said, and disconnected so I could call Division.

They'll be ready for my command, I thought. *Great. Now all I have to do is see the enemy.*

The cold was instantly forgotten. My heart skipped its way around my chest, and once again, I felt the familiar crackle of nervous energy that turned me into a flickering light bulb before a battle. I was all sparking nerve endings and pulsing blood now.

You can hear the panzers now, but they're still a little ways off, I thought. *And they'll have a screen of infantry first… maybe thirty to forty troops… to try to keep us from knocking out the first tank in line and bottling the rest up.*

Infantry first, then. I got low in my hole and cradled my two most important weapons. One was the receiver to the sound-powered phone that would call down our artillery. The other was a detonator to our illumination for this portion of the evening's events. The other end of the detonator's wire led to a half-dozen jerrycans of gasoline buried in the snow next to the road. A twist of the detonator's trigger would blow apart and ignite thirty gallons of gasoline, lighting the area up with a massive bonfire. In theory.

I peered into the dark, keeping my head as low to the rim of my foxhole as possible. I had to fight down the urge to keep my Thompson submachine-gun in my hands; the gasoline bombs and the artillery were far more important.

It was even harder to resist when I heard the SS.

Some were on the road and some were spread out into the forest, to keep an eye out for us. They spoke in low voices to keep in contact with each other; the closest voice was perhaps fifty yards away.

We had to wait until the last possible second to spring our trap and catch as many of them in it as we could. So I waited, the phone to our artillery pressed to my face, and we let them walk straight into our lines. It was dark enough that I couldn't see them, and that meant they couldn't see me… only their vehicles had that experimental whiz-bang night vision equipment.

"Stand by fire mission," I whispered into the receiver, "Concentration Charlie Two-Zero on my command."

The guttural voices of the SS got closer and closer, and now I could hear their close flanking group coming through the forest towards us.

They were moving surprisingly well through the trees considering the dark, but there were still the snaps and crackles of occasional mis-steps. My shoulders began to shiver; maybe from the cold.

Do it. Call it in now, I thought, pleading with myself.

Not yet.

They're right on top of you, call it in now!

Not yet.

The oily clanking of the panzers became an all-pervasive low roar, like the air was filled with crushing tin cans, and finally, I couldn't take it any longer, I gave the command for our artillery to fire and twisted the trigger on our gasoline bombs to set the night aflame.

Nothing.

The big guns boomed far off in the distance, but our hidden jerrycans didn't blow. I twisted the plunger again and again, but the night stayed dark and quiet.

"Shit!" I whispered, and the night exploded.

Gunfire, shouts, screams, flashes of light, grenades exploding, the whip-cracks of close rounds zipping through the air, and then, in the midst of sudden madness, the whistle and crash of our artillery landing on the road. The night was a black curtain lit at pinpoints by muzzle flashes or explosions.

I shouted to Pelosi, "Jack! It didn't blow!"

He couldn't hear me; he was working his machine-gun overtime and the close explosions of the artillery were deafening. I gritted my teeth and checked the wires leading to the detonator to make sure they were connected. A flash and boom that rattled my teeth came from the road, and an instant later, a treetop twenty meters to my right front blew apart. The panzers were moving up.

Somebody fired a Panzerfaust blindly at the tank and the rocket exploded harmlessly in the trees. The lead panzer in the column fired another shell into our lines, blowing another tree apart. Dirt and shrapnel and wooden splinters flew through the air. A GI started screaming in pain off to my left, but there wasn't any time to worry about that.

Come on, baby, I thought, practically caressing the detonator before I twisted it again. *Don't let me down.*

A half-dozen bright orange blooms of flame erupted over the icy road and into the far trees like firecrackers lined in a row. In an instant, the night was lit in a hellish strobe flash. It was like lifting the curtain on a stage where the play is already in progress. The dark had hidden everything from me, but now, in the flare of those fireballs, I could see so much it was impossible to take it all in at once: the panzers lined up on the road, the SS infantry rushing towards our lines like madmen, and the impact of our artillery shells blowing the world apart around them.

The lead panzer was a Panther tank, and at the same instant that the jerrycans blew in their spectacular display, an arty shell scored a direct hit on the tank. The turret blew up and off the rest of the hull, but the tank clanked its way forward a few more yards before stopping, like a decapitated corpse that didn't know it was dead yet.

The infantry fared far worse. The gasoline blew up and outwards like geysers of flame, and many of the SS were covered in it, the fire clinging to their clothes and skin. Some of them rushed at us anyway, as if unaware they were burning alive, and others flailed about on the ground in agony. It didn't matter. We shot them down all the same, now that we could see them easily and they were caught out in the open on the road. In fact, as I joined in on the killing, I distantly appreciated the irony in our killing them in the same way they'd executed our prisoners not too long ago.

The artillery shells falling amongst the tanks and infantry did as much damage as we did... maybe more. The shells were falling very close to our lines; if I hadn't been so preoccupied with tearing the infantry apart with my tommygun, I would've told our guns to back off a little bit before our guys got hit by friendly fire. As it was, I fired burst after burst into the SS, gunning them down remorselessly, stopping only to reload.

One of the SS I shot was burning from head to foot, but still he charged into our lines. I hit him with two bursts from my tommygun, and he still kept coming on, until a 105 shell hit right behind him and threw his burning body into the branches of the pines.

One Last Gasp

The SS had nowhere to go but forward, so they charged directly through the maelstrom, heedless of the bodies of their comrades being blown to pieces and tossed through the air like sacks of grain. At first it seemed like none of them would survive, but they pressed forward in a tidal surge, relying on the flesh of those in front of them to stop our bullets long enough for the next in line to reach the trees. They were relentless, stomping over the bodies of their fallen and then into the tree line, laying down a fearsome barrage of fire as they advanced.

There were too many of them. A few of them trickled into the tree line piecemeal and were shot down almost immediately. The trickle soon became a stream, however, and the pressure of our small arms wasn't enough to stem the tide.

Pelosi had stopped firing and I dashed to his hole, firing at the shapes in the trees as I went. This was no time for Pelosi to quit; we had to keep our machine-guns going if we were going to have any chance at holding the SS back.

"Damn it, Jack," I said as I slid into his hole, but I stopped cold. Pelosi was slumped over his weapon, a foot-long wooden shard skewering his neck.

I reloaded his machine-gun as I tried to take stock. It was difficult to tell what was going on; everything was a mish-mash of dark and shadow and sound and light, like a madman's kaleidoscope. The fire from the jerrycans had died down somewhat. Between it and the burning Panther tank, the road was fairly well lit, but the trees were still mostly cloaked in darkness. Three parachute flares opened up over us... a gift from Wexler and our heavy mortars... and that helped, but the trees were still a haunted house full of shadows dancing devilishly in the firelight.

More panzers came up the road; one of them pushed the burning Panther tank off the road with its larger bulk. It was a big Tiger tank; somebody fired a bazooka at it, and I saw the rocket hit the hull, but it bounced off that heavy armor plate like a skipped stone. The Tiger responded with a withering barrage of machine-gun fire that tore the snow-laden branches off the pines, and then, the big cannon swiveled around far enough to blast a hole in the forest right where the bazooka had fired from.

At least two more panzers followed the Tiger. One actually maneuvered off the road and into the forest, crushing the trees remorselessly under the weight of its steel. Its machine-guns blazed continuously and its cannon fired point-blank into one of our foxholes. The ground itself seemed to leap underneath me. I hoped the GIs had gotten out of that hole before it was obliterated.

The artillery still fell like heavy rain, but the infantry accompanying the tanks continued to rush through the barrage. It was like trying to hold back a river by throwing rocks at it. I tore ragged holes in their line with bursts from Pelosi's machine-gun, but for every one or two that I hit, another three made it into the cover of the trees. Soon the incoming fire became so great that I didn't dare stand up to fire; instead, I threw grenades and waited for the gunfire to die down a bit before climbing out to crawl back to my hole.

Something fell into Pelosi's foxhole and a second later, I was lying face-up on the ground, wondering what had happened. My ringing head pieced the last few seconds together enough to come up with a vague theory about a German grenade in Pelosi's hole, with Jack's body absorbing most of the impact.

I needed to get up and move, but my mind and body were dazed and shaken, so I ended up staring dumbly into the treetops instead. The battle roared and raged and exploded all around me, but it seemed a distant reality, like a storm raging on the ocean when you're a few feet under the surface.

My eyes tracked the lazy arc of a descending parachute flare. It left a trail of smoke behind it, and I wondered idly why flares didn't burn through the strings holding it or through the fabric of the parachute itself.

Burning through the fabric, my dazed mind thought. *The fabric is thin. We know all about burning through the fabric around here. They burned right through the fabric of reality, let the Geist out, and now we're all going to die.*

The flare tracked past something burning in the branches halfway up one of the pine trees. After a few seconds of staring, I realized it was the SS trooper who had been set alight by our gasoline bombs and thrown into the trees by an artillery shell. His limbs were splayed out

One Last Gasp

among the branches in a grotesque and unnatural manner, bent at right angles where they shouldn't be able to.

He looks like a human swastika, I thought, and almost laughed out loud. *No shit, he really does. Heil Hitler!*

Next I noticed the mist of air streaming out of my mouth and into the cold night. I experimented with blowing it in front of the flare to see if it blocked out the light.

Harry, a voice that I didn't recognize but definitely wasn't my own said, *get up*.

No, come on, my shell-shocked mind complained. *It's cold.*

HARRY! the voice insisted. *GET UP NOW!*

The world swirled back into me and I came up to the surface of that stormy ocean. Bombs and shells were exploding all around me; men shouted and fought and died in the midst of a thundering hailstorm of lead.

I rolled over onto my stomach. My weapon was missing; as soon as I felt the strength returning into my limbs, I began to push myself up onto hands and knees to look for it.

Something slammed into my ribs on the left side and then hit the snow hard on my right. Some trooper had been running like hell and tripped over me.

"You asshole, watch where you're..." I began to say, and turned to come nose to nose with a sprawled SS stormtrooper.

He shouted and tried to get his rifle around for a shot at me. I grabbed his weapon by the barrel with both hands.. thank God I was wearing heavy gloves... and held on for dear life as it rattled lead past me and harmlessly into the trees. An elbow to the face distracted him long enough for me to knock the rifle out of his hands, but he was on me the instant thereafter, tackling me backwards into the snow.

He was heavy and probably could've crushed me underneath him given enough time. Steel flashed toward me in the uncertain light and I barely got my forearm up in time to block the downward thrust of his arm. The SS trooper growled and pressed one hand on top of the other, getting his weight behind his blade. His eyes glittered red in the light of the parachute flare floating lazily above us, and spittle fell from his snarling lips onto my face.

My free hand pulled the trench knife from my leg sheath and I stabbed him in the hip until I hit bone. He screamed and twisted away from my knife, and I used the leverage to throw him off me. My knife went with him, still stuck into his hip, so I clawed desperately for my pistol as I rolled away from him. He lurched towards me, wildly stabbing his knife. The blade missed me by inches and buried itself into the snow.

Ridley's .45 came free from my holster and I fumbled with the hammer and safety catch as the SS trooper struggled back to his knees for another lunge at me. The big pistol bucked once in my hand just as the SS trooper straightened back upright; the round hit him in the shoulder and he fell onto his side a few feet away from me. I shot him again, and again, and a fourth time, and even after he was still, I put another slug into his back to make sure he'd stay down.

My tommygun was on the ground nearby so I scooped it up as I dashed back to my foxhole and jumped in. Muzzle flashes from small arms fire were all around me, as close as twenty yards away, and the panzer smashing its way through the forest was only another ten or fifteen yards past that. Two more panzers were burning on the road… victims of our artillery… but this position was a lost cause.

I ducked into the hole and put the phone receiver to my head. After repeating myself several times in a shout to be heard over the gunfire, the artillerymen acknowledged that I wanted them to drop the next barrage directly on my present position.

At the top of my lungs, I shouted, "3rd Platoon! Fall back! Fall back!" and threw my last two grenades before scrambling out of my hole and dashing through the trees back toward the manor.

65

I counted at least six GIs rushing back through the trees with me, and once we were in the relative safety of 1st Platoon's lines, my platoon rallied at the Captain's CP. Of the seventeen of us originally on the line, I had eleven left, two of whom were walking wounded.

"Wounded head back to the manor," I ordered, only now realizing how out of breath I was. "Four of you stay here as reserve. The rest of you, get out to the line and pair up in foxholes with the Captain's platoon."

The Captain waved me into his foxhole. "How'd you do?"

I snorted. "How do I look?"

"Like hell, Harry."

"That's about right, then."

I was still a little shaky from my hand-to-hand contact with the SS, and my body had begun to tremble when the rolling thunderstorm of gunfire hit the outskirts of 1st Platoon's lines. Our troopers answered back with a thunderstorm of their own, but the Captain and I both knew it would be a temporary reprieve.

Oddly enough, the shakes disappeared as soon as the battle flared up again. I took stock of my ammunition magazines and reloaded Ridley's pistol.

"Can you estimate their losses?" Captain Powell asked.

I shrugged. "I saw three panzers get blown to hell by our arty. There may have been more I didn't see. Between the 105s and our weapons fire, maybe fifty or sixty troops."

He shook his head. "We're going to have to do some serious damage before we fall back again. Get Wexler on the sound-power and call for more flares."

Wexler's voice sounded shaky even over the phone, and I could practically see him pushing his glasses up onto his nose and raking his hand through his hair. "What's going on up there?" he asked.

"What the hell does it sound like, sir?" I answered. "We're pounding the shit out of each other. Keep those flares coming. Tell the guys we've collapsed onto 1st Platoon's position and will have to fall back to the arsenal shortly."

"Any sign of the Geist?" Captain Powell asked.

"Any sign of the Geist?" I relayed to Wexler, then gave his response back to the Captain. "No, sir."

"Can't be long, now," the Captain said.

I didn't know if he was talking about the battle or the Geist, but if he meant the battle, he was right. Crackles of gunfire started up on our right, in the trees, and in front of us, the road waited to be crushed under the steel of their panzers' tank treads. The old smell floated to me, cordite, and it made my heart skitter-step with the recent memory of the melee I'd just escaped. I'd been given one last gasp to get my ass out of there, but my feet were still in the fire.

"I'm going to need one more," I said to myself.

"What?" the Captain asked, but before I could answer, the firefight came close enough to pull us in and we began firing into the trees at dark phantoms barely lit by the glow of red parachute flares.

Their advance stalled out and the incoming fire petered out to almost nothing. "This is nowhere near as bad as before," I shouted to the Captain over our gunfire. "They've lost their momentum, I think."

"Let's take advantage of that," the Captain said, and he got on the sound-powered phone to contact the arsenal.

We had our sixty-millimeter mortars set up behind the arsenal, and under Captain Powell's direction, they began dropping shells amongst the SS, blowing holes in their stagnant line. We had four machine-guns going as well, and when the incoming fire tapered off to nothing, I thought that maybe we'd routed them.

The Captain called for the mortars to cease-fire in order to conserve ammunition. "This is too easy," he said.

"Should we counterattack?" I asked. "Throw off their momentum, spoil their assault?"

The Captain held up a hand for silence and listened for a moment. "They haven't lost their momentum," he said, shouldering his weapon, "they were waiting for the panzers to catch up. Panzerfausts! Ready!"

GIs began scrambling for their anti-tank weapons and I suddenly remembered I'd left mine forgotten at my old foxhole. Soon, I heard the tanks, clanking down the road toward us. They opened fire with a few cannon rounds before we could even see them, blowing apart trees and sending shrapnel whizzing through the air.

A sudden flurry of small arms fire drove the Captain and I below the rim of our foxhole. A group of SS infantry was firing from directly across the road, and from the sounds of it, there were maybe seventy or eighty of them over there.

"Where the hell did they come from?" I shouted.

"Kleg must've sent them wide through the forest around our arty to flank us," Captain Powell said.

Our light mortars and machine-guns began to answer back to their barrage. Tracer bullets lanced back and forth in both directions across the road and into the trees, seeking out victims. Every now and again, they would find one and a man would scream or simply slump onto the ground.

Kleg's panzers came into view on the road. The first in line was hit in the track with a Panzerfaust rocket, and it answered back with a few weak bursts of machine-gun fire before another rocket hit it and set it afire. Almost simultaneously, three more Panzerfausts hit the next two panzers in line, setting them on fire as well.

"Wait a minute. Those aren't tanks," I said, peering at them through the half-light as they burned. "They're self-propelled artillery pieces."

"Kleg's using them as decoys," Captain Powell said, pausing to adjust the fire of our light mortars onto the road by radio. "He's hoping we'll burn up our anti-tank weapons and mortar shells on them and not his panzers. Those big artillery guns are probably out of ammo anyway."

Two GIs rushed toward us, retreating from the front line, and joined up with the four guys from my platoon I'd kept close as reserve. "There's a tank coming through!" one of them yelled. "We can't stop it! We're out of rockets!"

We could hear it then, crushing its way through the pines, stopping to blast away the parts of the forest it couldn't run over. Its machine-guns fired continuously; we didn't hear any response from bazookas or Panzerfausts.

The Captain gritted his teeth. After a moment's deliberation, he grabbed the Panzerfaust sitting outside of his hole and growled, "Follow me."

"Captain!" I shouted, but he was already off into the night, running like a madman with a rocket slung over his shoulder and his tommygun in his hands.

There was nothing to do but run after him. "Four of you, stay here," I shouted to the cluster of GIs I'd designated as our reserve. "You two, follow me!"

It felt like I was trying to run between raindrops in a monsoon, except the rain was lead and flying sideways. How none of us got hit, I'll never know. The Captain led us away from the road and further into the trees where the fire wasn't as intense so we could flank the panzer to the right.

There wasn't much action where we were... it was amazing what a difference a mere forty yards made... and we slowed our pace to keep an eye out for any infantry between us and the tank. We were behind a thick row of pines and couldn't see anything to our left, where the action was, but when the branches shook and snow fell off of them, all four of us spun and leveled our weapons at what came out of the trees.

It was a half-dozen SS, trying to slide their way around our right flank. We opened up on them with everything we had, tearing them to pieces. They never knew what hit them.

"Come on!" Captain Powell said, charging into the trees from which they had emerged. I ran blindly after him, and we surprised another dozen SS who were just beyond the row of pines.

One Last Gasp

With a wild yell, the Captain fired on them, and the rest of us followed suit, screaming like banshees. To our surprise they turned and ran, which was lucky for us, because our weapons went dry after a burst or two.

We could see the tank now. It had stopped in a cleared out area a little larger than itself, and was taking advantage of the open space to rotate its cannon freely. The barrel pointed away from us, off to our left, but I still tackled the Captain to the ground when the big gun boomed. Snow shook from the pine boughs and the ground jumped beneath us. Dirt and wooden splinters flew through the air.

"It'll tear our lines to shreds if we let it keep firing," the Captain shouted over the gunfire.

Bullets dinged off of the tank's metal hide and were answered with a hail of machine-gun fire. A GI ran across to the far side of the tank, a Panzerfaust in hand, but tracer bullets and small arms fire tracked him down and tore him up. The SS infantry were starting to crowd in close to the tank to use it as a shield. There were only some on the far side from us now, but more advanced through the trees towards us.

"Henry! Pin them down with your B.A.R.! Mike! Sarge! Cover me!" the Captain shouted, and rushed further to the right, away from that cannon barrel and the machine-gun mounted next to it.

I sprinted to keep up, firing a long burst into a pair of SS troopers coming towards us from the tank's direction. They retreated behind the panzer and out of sight.

We came to a halt and I emptied the rest of my magazine at the infantry trying to come around the tank. It drove them momentarily behind the tank's steel hull for cover, but as I reloaded, I could hear somebody banging on the hull of the tank with a rifle butt and then shouting commands in German. A second later, the panzer's turret began to swivel towards us with an evil whine.

Mike threw a grenade but it exploded harmlessly next to the tank. He might as well have thrown a rock, for all the good it did against that heavy armor.

"Captain!" I said, watching the big cannon barrel come towards us. "Hurry!"

Captain Powell knelt behind a tree, the Panzerfaust rocket already to his shoulder. He aimed unhurriedly; it was as if he were oblivious to the certain death swinging in our direction.

"Captain…" I said again, and he fired.

The rocket punched through the tank's armor and set it aflame in a fiery orange plume. The infantry scattered around it dropped to the ground, felled by shrapnel or fire or both. My guess was the Captain had hit either the gas tanks or the ammo supply to make the tank go up like that.

He dropped the spent tube to the ground and unslung his tommygun. "Let's go."

We headed back the way we came toward the hailstorm of fire the SS were laying down from across the road, when the Captain brought us to a halt. "Hang on," he said, staring into the pine trees further into the forest, away from the fighting.

"What is it?" I asked.

Without a word, he took a grenade off of his gear, pulled the pin, and threw it into the trees. A few seconds later, it went off, and instantly, the air was filled with a barrage of small arms fire that filled the air with angry hornets. Mike was hit with multiple rounds outright and was dead before he hit the ground. The rest of us dropped and scrambled away from the firing as quickly as we could.

"Go! Go!" the Captain shouted, and we low-crawled past another row of pines and climbed to our feet as eight or ten potato-masher grenades began to twirl out of the dark trees to land where we'd just been.

They went off a few seconds later, shaking the trees and the ground beneath us, but we'd already hotfooted a short distance away. The Captain led us further into our lines and brought us to a halt once we found a brief pause in the action.

"We've got to get out of here," he said. "Henry, pass the word. The Sarge and I will slow them down as best we can."

"Captain?" I asked.

"They're throwing another flanking move around behind us," he explained. "One is across the road, the other is what we just bumped into. It's a pincer move; they'll trap us in a bear hug and wipe us out."

"Shit!" Henry swore, looking around him as if he could see the pincer happening.

"Go now," the Captain ordered him. "As soon as you get to the arsenal, tell Major Hayward to shift the artillery to this position."

"Captain?" Henry said.

"We'll be right behind you," the Captain said over the gunfire crackling in the woods around us. "Go!"

"How are we going to slow down that many guys?" I asked.

"We only need a few seconds," Captain Powell said. "We'll get a machine-gun and shoot like crazy, make the SS slow up long enough for our guys to get out."

"Then how will *we* get out?"

He didn't answer me; instead, he ran to a nearby foxhole with a captured MG-42 machine-gun in it and picked it up after checking its belt of ammunition. The GI who had been assigned to it was dead, most of the left side of his face and skull caved in. I recovered two belts of ammo and a Panzerfaust rocket, and the Captain led me off towards the rear of our lines, back towards the flanking group we'd run away from.

We could hear them running through the woods, and the Captain hit the dirt, taking cover behind the trunk of a felled tree. He began firing into the dark even before I dropped to the ground beside him. Tracer bullets poked fiery fingers into the close rows of pines, reaching out for our unseen enemy.

Captain Powell burned through an entire belt before the return fire came. It was tremendous. Bullets thudded into the tree trunk we cowered behind and into the pines all around us. It came from everywhere; from our left, from the front, even from our right, which was our way back to the manor. We tried to reload the machine-gun and shoot back but the air was too heavy with lead to do anything other than press ourselves low behind our tree trunk.

A group of SS came charging through the trees to our left. The closest weapon I had to hand was the Panzerfaust, so I fired it directly into the charging mass, blowing a hole in their line. Captain Powell laid down a long burst with the machine-gun, sending even more scrambling for cover, but it was clear that we were seconds away from being overrun.

"Come on!" the Captain shouted, hoisting the machine-gun to his shoulder. "We're out of time!"

We ran through the forest like madmen, stumbling over roots and bouncing off tree limbs in the flickering half-light of the parachute flares. The SS were still shooting all around us, at foxholes and positions already abandoned. They would figure out soon enough that those positions were empty and then they would rush forward like a tidal wave.

I hoped that Captain Powell knew where he was going, because I had no idea which way was up. The pines were in close rows where we ran, and it was like being in a giant cornfield… visibility to the left and right was a few yards at most.

We could hear dozens of the enemy moving past the trees to our left and right. Some even ran through our row and then disappeared back into the trees, but we didn't fire on them. Instead, we ran like hell and hoped that in the uncertain light they would assume we were on their side.

We kept up that charade until we hit the tree line. There we found a machine-gun crew setting up behind a tree to fire on the arsenal. We shot all three of them before they could spot us and then ran out of the trees at top speed.

Two red parachute flares still floated through the air, but it wasn't exactly sunlight, and to the GIs in the arsenal, we were just two dark shapes rushing out of the trees. Scattered rifle shots snapped the air around our heads and we dropped to the ground, skidding forward along the downward slope in the snow. My helmet fell off and tumbled down the hill towards the arsenal.

"101st!" the Captain shouted at the top of his lungs. The fire zipping around our ears died out, and we scrambled to our feet and began running forward.

The snow kicked up around our feet. The SS had reached the tree line in force and were blazing away. I tackled the Captain to the ground again as tracers lanced out of the trees and zipped by mere inches over our heads.

"Move!" the Captain shouted over the din, crawling forward on his elbows. One of the trees torn up earlier by the Geist was close by, so we scrambled over it and pressed down into the snow. Bullets thumped into the wood and chipped splinters off the top of the trunk. Machine-gun and rifle fire from the trees crisscrossed with small arms fire from the arsenal, until it felt like my overcoat might get singed by the tracer bullets carving up the air.

"We're sitting ducks out here!" the Captain said.

Then, with a sudden surge of an oily engine, Major Hayward's nasty surprise knocked down the wall of the wood shack and lurched forward. It was the meatchopper half-track, and its quad-fifty machine-guns threw heavy rounds from one end of the pines to the other and back again, tearing apart the trees and the SS hiding behind them.

"Go! Go now!" Captain Powell said.

We hotfooted it all the way to the arsenal, never stopping until we'd skidded around the corner of the building and into the waiting arms of our comrades. Wayne was there, waiting for me with my helmet in his hand.

"Rolled all the way down the hill to me, Sarge," he said. "I can't believe you guys made it out of there!"

He disappeared as the parachute flares went out and the night closed in. I took another last gasp and put my helmet back on my head. The night was far from over.

Andrew C. Piazza

66

The meatchopper's heavy fire drove the SS back from the tree line only long enough for us to catch a quick breath. Soon, they were back in force, and bullets sang their lethal whine through the air. The metallic creaks and clanks of panzers began coming close enough to hear, and the Captain sent a runner to Tedeski's nearby TD to warn him to get ready.

Our 105s began dropping amongst the trees, blasting them into clouds of wooden shards that thudded home in the flesh of the exposed SS infantry. Between the arty and the meatchopper, we were holding back the tide of the enemy, but once Kleg's panzers rolled in, that stalemate would be broken.

The runner returned from Tedeski's TD. "Lieutenant Tedeski says he needs more flares, Captain," he said. "He said he can't see a goddamn thing, his words, sir."

"Yes, why have the flares stopped?" Doctor Schmidt asked. He had ammunition belts for our thirty-cals slung around his neck, and was running them out to wherever they were needed. "We cannot see to shoot like this."

"But the SS can," Captain Powell said, "with the night vision equipment in their vehicles. Very well. Sarge, get on the sound-power to Wexler and tell him to send up more flares. Doctor Schmidt, take Wayne and get to that thirty-cal over there... they need your ammunition."

I went inside the arsenal with the Captain and found the sound-powered phone. A couple of spins on the crank, and I began shouting "Wexler! Wexler!" so I could hear myself over the gunfire echoing though the stables. The smell of cordite was worse indoors; I found myself grimacing at it and yet inhaling it through my nose in quick, stuttering sniffs, as if I wanted to torture myself with the unpleasant odor.

There wasn't any answer on the sound-power, so I spun the crank and tried again. "Wexler! Goddamnit, we need more flares, Wexler! Now!"

There was an answer over the phone, but it was drowned out in a sudden hail of gunfire that drove me to cover behind a handful of sandbags stacked up as protection inside of the arsenal. "What? Say again!"

"Harry!"

It wasn't Wexler's voice. The voice over the phone belonged to Freddie Howard.

"Let's play some ball, Harry. Let's play some ball."

The phone slipped from between my nerveless fingers to fall to the dirt.

Captain Powell took one look at my pale face and read my mind. "The Geist."

It was more of a statement than a question. I nodded weakly.

He looked around the stables for a moment or two... the only time I'd ever seen him indecisive... and then said, "We can't stay clumped up here for long, then. If it decides to roll through here rather than through the SS, we'll be wiped out."

"I'll make sure the explosives are ready to go," I said.

"No. I'll do that," the Captain said. "Get outside and help Major Hayward direct the defense. Be ready to pull back quickly."

"Yes, sir," I said, and grabbed a nearby Panzerfaust rocket before darting outside and behind the stables.

Major Hayward was back by the sixty-millimeter mortar pit. "Sergeant? Where's our flares?"

"There aren't going to be any flares, sir," I said. "The Geist has stepped into the ring."

He stiffened and looked at the snowy field around us, as if expecting to see the creature bearing down on us right then.

"What about these light mortars?" I asked, then added, "Sir?" when Major Hayward didn't respond.

"Hmm? Oh, um, no, no good, Sergeant, we're out of ammunition for them."

"All right. You guys," I said to the mortar crews, "destroy the tubes and then get your rifles to join in on the fun. Back up that meatchopper..."

A sudden boom cut me off in mid-sentence. A Panther tank had emerged from the trees and foolishly fired on the manor house. The muzzle flash from its cannon drew fire from a half-dozen Panzerfausts... none of which hit... and two of our tank destroyers. One of the TDs scored a hit with their big 90mm guns and blew the Panther into junk.

"The panzers are breaking through!" I said. "Move out! Now!"

"Wait!" Major Hayward said, snapping out of his momentary daze. "You men, go inside and get yourselves a supply of Molotav cocktails. When the panzers break through into the open, hit them with the Molotavs."

"They'll just burn on the surface," one of the GIs said.

"We'll use them to mark the panzers so our tank destroyers can see to hit them in the dark," Major Hayward explained. "Now go. Go!"

"Rally 2nd Platoon on the right side of the arsenal," I said. "I'll get 3rd Platoon on the left and spot for Tedeski's TD. You keep the SS away from that meatchopper. It's the only thing holding them back."

Major Hayward slapped me on the back and nodded. "Go!"

I ran to the left side of the arsenal and shouted for 3rd Platoon to rally on me. Tedeski's tank destroyer fired its cannon again, practically blowing out my eardrums with the report. Incoming rifle and machine-gun fire dinged off the TD's steel hide. One of Tedeski's crew fired back with the fifty-cal mounted on the TD's turret.

I counted seven men left in my platoon. We set up a thirty-cal in a foxhole at the corner of the arsenal and a bazooka team nearby. Panzers were starting to push their way around the burning Panther tank, both on the road and through the trees. Our TDs fired at them but without parachute flares for illumination they were firing blind. The moonlight on the snow was insufficient to hit a moving target.

Tracer bullets streaked across our position and tracked down the turret on Tedeski's TD. Slugs thudded loudly into the tanker firing the machine-gun up there. He slumped forwards over the rim of the turret.

"Shit!" I waited until the tracers left to find other victims before climbing up onto the TD and into the turret. Our cannon boomed again, and I wondered how any of Tedeski's men weren't deaf by now from the repeated ear-splitting thunder of their guns.

"Tedeski!" I shouted down into the hull of the TD.

"Where's my goddamn flares?" Tedeski shouted back, sticking his head up into the turret.

"The Geist," I answered. "We lost our mortars. Be ready to fall back!"

"Fall back, hell!" he said. "I'm just getting warmed up!"

A cannon's muzzle flash flared from the trees on the far side of the road, betraying another pair of panzers rolling into the open. The shell smashed into the tank destroyer on the far side of Dom Caern. It burst into flame with a brilliant fireball that licked at the walls of the manor house.

"Shit! They just nailed one of your rigs," I told Tedeski.

"Son of a... get that bastard! Wait! That one! Get that one!" Tedeski barked at his crew.

The turret began to turn with a low whine. This time, I plugged my ears with my fingers before the big cannon boomed, blowing apart another panzer which was lit up by the light of the burning Panther tank.

"They're going to try to mark some panzers with Molotav cocktails," I told Tedeski. "Watch for it."

Right on cue, a half-dozen troopers scattered into the snow toward where the dark shapes emerged from the road. The GIs around the arsenal laid down heavy fire to cover their frantic advance, but one of the troopers fell almost immediately.

Flickering spots of light flared in the dark as they lit their Molotavs with Zippo lighters. The SS used the lighters as beacons to direct their fire. One trooper was shot to hell as soon as his Molotav was lit; a slug burst the bottle and the trooper was instantly engulfed in flame. Another managed to throw his before getting machine-gunned by the tank he'd just hit.

"There! One o'clock!" I shouted down to Tedeski, and the turret began to turn toward the Panther tank covered in burning gasoline.

The other GIs retreated toward the manor, dragging the wounded back with them. The SS infantry in the trees began to reach for them with tracer bullets, but the meatchopper threw a blaze of fire into the trees in response and quieted them down. I worked the action on the TD's mounted fifty-cal and lent a little fire support of my own.

The tank destroyer's cannon boomed beneath me, hitting the lit-up panzer. Another shell hit it a second later from the other TD positioned on the near side of Dom Caern, adding another burning metal shell to the two already on the road.

"Whew! That got him!" Tedeski whooped.

I couldn't quite share his enthusiasm. We couldn't keep this up. We'd already lost one TD and couldn't keep sending GIs to rush out into the open to mark tanks with Molotav cocktails. The SS were taking severe casualties, but they seemed to have limitless numbers to replace their losses. We didn't. Every man we lost was a key position left unmanned.

Suddenly, there was a *Thoomp!* from our heavy mortar pit behind the manor and a few seconds later, a red parachute flare opened up over the battlefield. I was too thankful to wonder where it had come from.

That thankfulness died quickly. In the bloody light, I spotted two tanks and about thirty troops advancing on our left flank about two hundred yards away on the other side of the road. The tank destroyer by the manor fired on and hit one of the panzers, disabling it, but the TD was immediately blown apart by return fire.

"Tedeski!" I shouted down into the hull. "We're getting flanked and we lost another TD! I have to go tell the Captain!"

"Hurry!" Tedeski shouted back.

I clambered down off the TD, keeping the steel between myself and the sudden influx of fire from our left flank, and ran for the inside of the arsenal. Inside, Doctor Schmidt was kneeling next to the door and firing at the advancing SS. Near his feet was Wayne with a gunshot wound in his leg.

"Doc!" I said. "Take another man and get Wayne back to the manor. We're getting flanked."

"Don't leave me," Wayne said, grabbing at Doctor Schmidt's leg. His face was pale and he was trembling from head to foot. "Don't leave me."

"Nobody is leaving you," Doctor Schmidt said, reloading his weapon before he knelt and pulled Wayne to his feet. "Come on, my friend. We will go together and find you a medic."

He waved another trooper over to help him and they half-led, half-carried Wayne toward the manor. I thought about getting help for another downed GI but a second glance told me he was already dead.

Our guys fired from foxholes dug into the stable's dirt floor. They had knocked holes in the wooden wall in front of their positions to provide firing ports of a sort. The Captain was in one of those foxholes, directing the fire from the thirty-cal manned by Elliot, his new foxhole buddy.

"Captain!" I said, scrambling over to his hole and crowding in; the wooden walls didn't stop rifle bullets and stray rounds snapped through the air all around us. Wooden splinters chipped away from the inside of the wall and rained on top of us like heavy snow.

"What is it?"

"They're flanking us in force on the left… two panzers and thirty troops. We've lost two TDs."

"The Geist?" he asked.

"Haven't seen it yet."

"Very well. We're falling back," the Captain said. "Tell Hayward to fall back immediately with 2nd Platoon. You take 3rd Platoon and Tedeski's TD and head for the Rabbit Hole to lure them in. We'll cover."

A sudden flurry of machine-gun fire ripped through the wooden walls of the arsenal, driving us to cover. Elliot didn't duck down fast enough and caught one in the head that rang his helmet like a muted bell as it punched through and blew his brains out.

One Last Gasp

Captain Powell grimaced and stole a peek out of his hole. "Tiger tank right in front of the arsenal," he said, "and a large force of infantry accompanying it."

A thunderclap and flash came from the Tiger's cannon, followed a second later by the meatchopper bursting into flame. GIs scattered away from the burning half-track, and some of them were tracked down and torn apart by machine-gun fire.

I stared at the burning hulk of the meatchopper, a little outside of myself. It had been the levy that had held the flood of infantry back... until now.

"We're almost out of time," Captain Powell said, raking the bolt on the thirty-cal and firing it at the troops around the Tiger tank. "Get moving!"

I scrambled out of the foxhole and found a runner to relay the message to Major Hayward. A few seconds later, I was back in the TD's turret, shouting for Tedeski to fall back.

"A Tiger tank has broken through in front of the arsenal! They're getting overrun! We have to fall back!"

As if to punctuate my order, 2nd Platoon began retreating toward the manor at a full run, carrying whatever weapons they could salvage. The SS on our left flank fired on them but the distance was enough that only one or two GIs were hit.

"Forward!" Tedeski ordered his driver, and our TD lurched forward violently.

"What are you doing?" I screamed. "We have to get out of here!"

"Just one more!" Tedeski answered. "I just want one more of these bastards!"

I swore and manned the turret's fifty-cal again, spraying bullets into the SS accompanying the Tiger tank as we pulled forward from behind the cover of the arsenal. Small arms fire splashed across us; there were at least forty or fifty troops surging forward out of the trees.

"Tedeski..." I said.

The tank destroyer's cannon boomed, once again shaking my spine and rattling my teeth. The high velocity shell smashed into the side of the Tiger tank, tearing the armored hull open and disabling the vehicle.

"Yeah!" Tedeski shouted. "Master race *that*, you son of a bitch!"

The Captain ran out of the arsenal as we backed up. A half-dozen men followed him out.

"What are you still doing here?" he shouted at me. "We are *falling back!*"

"Move it, Tedeski!" I said down into the TD's hull. "We're out of time!"

I waved for the remnants of 3rd Platoon to climb up onto the TD. They scrambled up onto the rig's hull and held on for dear life as Tedeski turned us around and drove us toward the Rabbit Hole.

"This is it?" I asked. "Only five of you?"

"This is all of us, Sarge," one of them answered.

A shell exploded near us and threw snow and shrapnel into the air. The second panzer rolling up on our left flank… the one that hadn't been knocked out… was firing on us.

"Move it, Tedeski!" I said, as another shell hit off to our left side. I fired the fifty-cal behind us at the onrushing SS, in vain hopes of stemming the tide for at least a few seconds, as the TD's churning treads sped us toward the Rabbit Hole.

The black shapes of SS infantry swarmed around and into the arsenal, firing at us as they went. The ground shook and the air seemed to push at me with unseen hands as the arsenal exploded, hurling wooden planks and debris for a hundred yards. A fireball rose up into the night sky. Secondary explosions from the shells inside the arsenal boomed and flared and flashed. It was better than the Fourth of July.

That's right, you bastards, I thought, watching the blown-apart bodies of the SS burn. *Harry Kinder was here.*

"Oh shit!" one of the troopers on the TD's hull screamed.

I started to turn towards him, back toward the manor, when a sudden strong gust of wind blew over me from the passage of a massive object rushing close by me. It was like standing near the edge of a subway station when the train blows past, or next to a highway as an eighteen-wheeler speeds by you, missing only by inches.

It wasn't just the wind; it was the feel of something massive hurtling by me at great speed. I recoiled reflexively and ducked away from the rushing mass that brushed the metal skin of the tank destroyer. One of my troopers screamed as he was knocked off the TD's hull and sent flying; the scream was cut short and there was the wet, sloppy sound you hear when you hit a deer or dog with your car on a dark road. The entire tank destroyer lurched to the side underneath me like it was a toy bumper car knocked around the amusement park.

"What the hell was that?" Tedeski shouted up to me. "It just shook a twenty-ton rig!"

For an instant, I didn't look. An illogical fear kept me from it; I kept remembering what Rebecca had said about the Geist... *If you see it, you are already dead.* For that hesitant moment, I felt that if I looked at the Geist, I would be doomed like Lot's wife.

Then, curiosity took control, and I spun the fifty-cal toward the massive bulk speeding away from us. The parachute flare above me winked and burnt out, but not before I got a few seconds' worth of a look at the Geist.

A lot was lost to the wavering half-light of the flare. At first, all I could make out was that it was vast and... shifting is the best word, I suppose. Vast and shifting are the two words I seem to cling to when I try to describe what I saw. It was about the size of a two-story house, but it was stretched out into an elongated ovoid shape that rippled and changed even as my mind made a feeble attempt to categorize it. Its movement was vaguely reminiscent of that of a snake; it glided across the ground effortlessly, directly into the GIs retreating from the arsenal.

Its vaguely ovoid shape underwent an instant transformation... like oil in water, as Major Hayward had said. It seemed at first glance to be smooth but as the parachute flare died out, I spotted spiny projections extending themselves from the main mass of the creature.

That's all I saw. The rest was lost to the dim light and the far distance; all I really got was the vaguest of vagaries before the sky went dark again.

Screams began to arise from our men. The panzer on our far left flank fired at us again, but the shell went wide and kicked up snow close to the creature. In an instant, the dark mass sped from the retreating GIs toward the panzer that had foolishly fired a near miss at the creature by mistake.

It's unnerving to see something huge move that quickly. When we see film of massive creatures like whales or elephants, we see them lumber along slowly, wielding their heavy weight like a cumbersome club. But when something that big moves with the lightning speed of a charging leopard, our eyes want to rebel at the sight.

The panzer and its accompanying force of infantry didn't have a chance. I could see flashes from rifle barrels as the SS fired uselessly at the creature; the gunfire was replaced quickly by screams and the deafening metallic crash of the Geist's impact with the tank. I could hear what was happening more than I could see it; at that range in the moonlight, it was only large, dark shapes colliding for my eyes. My ears picked up the shriek of metal rending and tearing like paper.

I'm not a fool. I wasn't about to shoot at it and draw its attention. Instead, I stared vainly into the dark for any scrap of a visual clue as to what was going on until our tank destroyer slid down into the Rabbit Hole and we got a temporary reprieve from the battle.

Why did it slow down when the Captain fired through the door back at the library? I wondered. *Especially when it looked like it could shrug off machine-gun fire just now?*

Maybe it was because we only fired at a small piece of it and the SS were firing on the massed creature. Or maybe its shifting body structure was in turns vulnerable or impervious to gunfire. Major Hayward had told me that when he stabbed a piece of it in that bar in the village, he hit something rubbery and yielding, and yet, that same creature had torn apart a Tiger tank to get to Goliath.

It was impossible to figure out. I didn't have the time to try anyway. The TD churned its way down the Rabbit Hole, lurching to a sudden halt at the point where the tunnel intersected with the stone room leading back into the manor.

My guys started to climb down off the vehicle, and I waved them back up. "You guys stick with the TD," I said. "Help keep the infantry off it."

One Last Gasp

Tedeski stuck his head into the turret as I climbed down. "Where are you going?"

"Up into the manor. See what's going on," I answered. I was suddenly aware of the choking fumes coming from the TD's engine. "Is that thing okay?"

Tedeski frowned, as if he didn't understand me, then his face brightened into a smile. "Don't worry, Sarge. She always smells like that."

"All right," I said. "Just remember, you don't have to kill everything down there. Just wait until the SS are inside the village, then haul ass back up to the surface so we can blow the tunnel. Ditch the rig if you have to."

"Over my dead body!" Tedeski said with a grin, dropping back down into the TD's belly. "Good luck, Sarge!"

"Good luck, Frank," I said quietly, watching his steel monster roll down the tunnel and toward the village of the Geist. There were real monsters down there, and I hoped Tedeski would be nimble-footed enough to tap-dance around them and back up to the surface again.

I gave myself long enough to watch the tank destroyer drive out of sight before I ran up the stairs and into the manor. The battle was still on, and was about to take an even greater turn for the surreal.

Andrew C. Piazza

67

I found Wexler crumpled into a ball in a corner of Rebecca's old cell. He had his arms clasped around his knees and he was crying hysterically.

"Wexler! Wexler!" I said, darting into the cell and grabbing him by the arms.

He shrieked and if he had been armed, he might have shot me. As it was, he tried to wave me off feebly and buried his face back in his knees.

"Wexler, what happened? Where are the mortar crews?"

"Dead. They're all dead," he moaned into his knees.

"Wexler," I said, lifting his head up, "Get a hold of yourself. Tell me what happened to the mortar crew. We called for flares."

He shook his head. "We were back there and firing them off. I... the Geist came for us. It... it was everywhere. It killed them all. There were dead men... I'm sorry. I'm sorry. I ran away."

"Who sent that last flare up?"

"I did. I hid for a while and then sneaked back there, looked out a window to see if it was still there, if the dead... they were gone. So I fired off the one flare they had ready and hid again. I'm sorry. I'm sorry."

"Wexler." I had to pull his head up by the hair to look into his face. "You did okay. Now come on."

Wexler blinked his bleary eyes a few times. "I... I did?"

"You did. You went back to where you'd seen the Geist to fire off that last flare. It helped us hold Kleg back a little longer. So come on. It's not over yet."

He looked around the cell like leaving it was sheer madness. "But..."

"Sir, there is no safe place now. The SS are coming, and the Geist could show up anywhere, including here, and if you're all alone..."

That was all it took. Wexler scrambled to his feet, clinging to my arm like a lifeline, and I led him at a run through the dark hallways of the basement and then up the stairs.

We found Doctor Schmidt leading a pair of troopers down a hallway. He waved them on and then stopped for us, checking his ammunition pouch.

The rattle of gunfire shook the floorboards all around the manor. It seemed to come from everywhere at once; as I opened my mouth to ask Doctor Schmidt what was going on, a cannon shell smashed into a far-off section of the manor, rattling my teeth and skipping my heart's beat. The whole house shook as if there had been a brief earthquake.

"The SS are storming the manor," Doctor Schmidt explained breathlessly. "We cannot hold them back. They charge us like madmen."

"Fanatics," I said. "They want Dom Caern."

"They want to get away from the Geist," he said. "How is your ammunition supply?"

I checked my bag and groaned when I saw it was empty. The magazine in my tommygun only had a handful of rounds left. "Shit."

"Back in that room is a supply of weapons," Doctor Schmidt said. "I will hold here until you can arm yourselves."

"Come on, Wexler." I dragged the Major into a nearby study where piles of M1 Garands and carbines had been left by troopers who had armed themselves with *Sturmgewehrs* instead. I handed Wexler one of the carbines.

"Remember how to use this?"

He nodded weakly and worked the action.

"Here, take these," I said, stuffing four German potato-masher grenades into his belt and two more into my own. I debated briefly with myself on whether or not I wanted a carbine or a full-size battle rifle until my eyes picked out the flame-thrower lying off to the side.

"Fuck it," I said, and hauled it onto my back.

One Last Gasp

"What do I do?" Wexler asked, wringing his hands around his weapon.

"Watch my back," I answered. The starter cartridge on the flame-thrower lit on the first try, and a tongue of flame danced around the end of the sprayer. "Anything SS or inhuman, blow it to hell."

I led him out of the study, my movements clumsy and awkward from the heavy tank on my back. Doctor Schmidt glanced at the weapon in my hands and gave me an appreciative shrug. "Careful you do not burn me with that, please."

I would've smiled but the close gunfire all around us turned me into a live wire once again. My body was all crackling nerve endings and pounding heartbeats and panicked breaths. I could practically feel the electricity snapping and crackling its way along my nervous system.

"Let's go," I said, trying to keep my voice from trembling.

We headed down the hall at a trot, with no idea where we were going, when a sudden chorus of shouts was cut off by a flurry of gunfire in one of the rooms up ahead. "Oh, God!" Doctor Schmidt said. "The wounded!"

Fresh energy surged through me. The weight of my flame-thrower was forgotten as I followed Doctor Schmidt at a run up to the open doorway leading to the thundering gunfire.

The sure knowledge of an imminent death struggle dumped adrenaline on top of adrenaline into my veins until the universe seemed to pop. The walls of Dom Caern seemed to radiate energy until they washed out all of existence in their brightness; everything seemed unreal and distant and separated. I felt set outside of myself. The next few seconds came in flash-bulb snippets of reality, like time was an old record and the needle was skipping across it.

I saw:

Doctor Schmidt reach the door before me. Him shouldering his weapon. The open doorway and then the room beyond as I reached it at last. Inside the room, five SS changing magazines on smoking rifles. Wayne and three other GIs shot absolutely to pieces on the floor.

The thunder and crash of Doctor Schmidt firing his weapon shook me out of my almost hallucinatory experience. He raked the SS back and forth with his weapon, punching holes through their bodies. Just before I hit the trigger on the flame-thrower, I thought, *Burn, you bastards.*

The room became an instant inferno. The SS not killed outright by Doctor Schmidt's barrage shrieked like banshees and danced out their deaths, colliding into each other until Doctor Schmidt's submachine-gun searched them out and put them down.

Heat radiated through the open door as from an open oven. Everything in the room was on fire; the bodies, the furniture, the walls. The memory of what they'd done two nights ago burned through my mind and I thought, *How do you like it, you sons of bitches.*

Doctor Schmidt pulled me away from the intense heat. "Careful, Sergeant. You are setting the manor on fire."

"Good!" I said.

Behind us, Wexler shouted "Sarge!" and began firing his carbine as quickly as he could pull the trigger. Doctor Schmidt and I turned and saw the hallway behind us was filled with dead men walking.

Wexler's panicked shots carved holes and blew pieces out of them, but they continued to stride forward, oblivious to the wounds. Both dead GIs and SS stomped forward inexorably, some holding rifles at the waist almost as an afterthought.

"Run!" I said, and turned the flame-thrower on them as they began to shoot.

Bullets bit chunks out of the wall next to me. Plaster showered over me and stung my eyes. The dead fired their weapons from the hip, without aiming, as if unsure how a rifle worked. The fire from my flame-thrower quickly engulfed them, but still they came on, unstoppable.

Doctor Schmidt pulled me out of the hall and into a side room. As soon as I was out of the line of fire, he plucked two potato-masher grenades out of Wexler's belt and tossed them down the hall into the midst of the animated corpses.

The walls shook when the grenades exploded. Bits of fiery human wreckage flew past the doorway. We didn't stick around to see what was left of the dead men; there was a door on the opposite side of the room leading to another hallway and we took it at a run.

"Wait! Wait!" Wexler said, bringing us to a halt. "Where are we going?"

"How the hell should I know?" I said. "This is a free-for-all, now!"

Shouts and rifle fire erupted into the hallway dead ahead of us. Two GIs ran backwards out of a side room, firing their rifles non-stop back through the doorway from which they came. One turned and bolted, his face a mask of terror, and in the next instant, Death came through the door.

It happened within seconds. A large, spiky, monstrous shape flew out of the doorway and into the hall. It looked to be part spider, part praying mantis, and part starfish, and it moved with a terrifying speed for something so large. Its black carapace smashed directly into the first GI. He was thrown against the far wall and immediately skewered by a half-dozen barbed limbs which twisted and tore him apart.

The second GI only managed to take three running steps toward us, screaming "Help me!" before the creature was on him as well. Its hindquarters melted like warm wax and formed into what started out looking like a scorpion's tail with a large scythe of a blade on the tip. The tail-like appendage slashed down and cut the fleeing GI from right shoulder to left hip. The blade-tail melted back into the creature's body before the split halves of the GI's body hit the floor with a wet thud.

The three of us were struck numb by the inhuman speed of the Geist's attack, long enough for the creature to charge us. It didn't turn to face us; its body didn't seem to have a back or front, and as it charged, the spiny limbs facing us sprouted a forest of six-inch thorns ready to tear our flesh apart.

Doctor Schmidt fired on it first, joined quickly by Wexler, but it came on too fast for their fire to have much effect. It moved with the speed of a Major League fastball; I don't know to this day how I ever got my unfeeling fingers to clench down on the trigger fast enough.

A stream of flame erupted from my weapon and reached out to engulf the creature not ten yards away from us. It kept coming; I flinched involuntarily away from the lethal impact of that nightmarish body, but it never came. The creature seemed to shatter like glass into a thousand shards, which then split into sand-like grains which subsequently disappeared. The entire transformation was done in an instant.

A cold gust of wind blew over us.

I shook from head to toe, blinking stupidly, amazed I was still alive. All I could do was stand and stare unbelievingly into the air that had held my onrushing death until a split-second ago.

"Is that it?" I finally whispered. "Did I kill it? Did I kill it?"

"I don't know." Wexler's voice trembled as badly as mine.

"It was only a part of the creature," Doctor Schmidt said. "Come on. We must keep moving, before it returns."

The door through which we'd entered the hallway burst open. Smoke billowed into the hall, closely followed by burning corpses that walked purposefully toward us with outstretched arms dripping flaming bits of flesh.

Doctor Schmidt brought up our rear as we ran, firing his submachine-gun low to cut the legs out underneath the first of the dead men. They may not have felt the pain, but a shattered bone won't support weight, and two of the corpses fell to the ground, tripping up and slowing down the rest of the mob.

We took another turn, pausing briefly as four SS troopers rushed across the far end of the hall and into another room.

"We can't go that way," Wexler said, as close gunfire echoed from that direction.

"Well, we sure as hell can't go back," I said. "Any bright ideas, Doc?"

Doctor Schmidt changed the magazine on his weapon. "I do not know… wait. Rebecca."

I suddenly became cold. "Oh, shit. Let's go."

"Hold it," Wexler said, holding us back as we started off toward where the SS had disappeared. "The SS are down there."

"The SS are all over the place, Major," I said. "That's the only way I know of to get upstairs… unless you want to go back and face those dead men."

"Make sure you have a full magazine of ammunition in your weapon," Doctor Schmidt said to Wexler. "Be ready for contact to be close, and follow me. You will be fine."

He led us off at a run, down the hall and toward the main entrance to Dom Caern, where the stone staircase was. At least, I hoped it was still there. I hoped the Geist wasn't changing the architecture of Dom Caern as the battle raged.

A sudden flood of SS troops surged into the hallway twenty yards ahead of us. They looked to be running away from something rather than charging forward; I think that was why they didn't instantly cut us apart. They looked as surprised to see us as we were to see them.

Their weapons came up. My nervous system shorted out in a spasmodic heartbeat; there was nowhere to go and no cover to save us from their rifles.

A barrage of gunfire blasted into the SS ranks from the rear. Stray rounds punched through their mass and zipped past us. Wexler screamed and fell to the ground, and Doctor Schmidt dragged me down before a slug could hit me as well. The flame-thrower's starter cartridge burned my arm as I fell on it, but I got it out from under me in time to look up and see the last of the SS shot down.

Beyond the pile of bodies, Captain Powell shouted for a cease fire from the four GIs by his side. I pulled Wexler to his feet and ran forward, thankful beyond words that the Captain was still around to try to get us out of this madness.

"Are you all right?" he asked us once we stepped around the SS bodies to join up with him.

"Oh, yes sir. It is a good day to be alive," I said, stammering through trembling lips. I was shaking again, all over; it seemed as though Death were all around me, always behind me, and I could never turn around fast enough to keep it from stabbing me in the back.

"Wexler's hit," Captain Powell said.

Wexler looked down at the hole punched through his forearm. His eyes became dinner plates. "Holy shit, I'm shot. I'm *shot*."

"Captain! Over here!" Doctor Schmidt said.

He was looking through the doorway the SS had poured out of, his weapon at the ready. Screams echoed off the walls beyond.

A sudden anger surged through me; I'd been kicked around and shot at and terrified so much, and now my briefest of lulls in the fighting was once again taken away from me.

Leave us alone, I thought as I pushed my way over to the doorway. *Leave us ALONE, you bastards!*

I crowded into the doorway next to Doctor Schmidt and then Captain Powell crowded in next to me. Inside the room, we saw what made the SS flee into the hallway. Their own men.

For some reason, none of us fired into the dozen or so black uniforms milling around the room, which I now recognized as another dining hall. Perhaps it was because none of them had rifles. Perhaps it was because it was obvious that they had no immediate interest in us, only in the figure they had pinned down on the long table in the center of the room.

Perhaps it was because that figure they had pinned down on the table was Kleg.

He was on his back, each of his arms and legs pinioned by one or two walking corpses in black uniforms. Kleg's face was locked into a scream; he thrashed about with the strength of a drowning man, but the weight of the dead men was too much for him to fight.

We watched in stunned horror as an SS trooper climbed up onto the table. Most of his face was a blasted tangle of red and white and scraps of flesh; in his left hand, he held a SS dagger. With deliberate slowness, he pushed the point of the dagger into Kleg's chest, below the neck and to the side of the sternum.

Kleg's thrashes became even more desperate. The faceless SS trooper had only pushed the point in an inch or so, enough to cause intense pain but not enough to kill. We continued to stare in grim fascination as the faceless SS put his right hand on the back of the knife blade and with the same slow deliberateness, used both hands to drag the dagger blade down along Kleg's ribcage, carving through the cartilage connecting his ribs to his sternum.

His screams were hoarse and high-pitched. I could see his hands clenching and unclenching and his legs twitching spasmodically as the dead slowly carved out his heart.

One of the dead SS turned his head and looked right at us. A second later, he and two other corpses not directly involved with holding Kleg down took a few steps toward us.

"Sergeant," the Captain said, and I swept the room with flame.

One of the dead SS corpses lying at our feet in the hallway twitched. At first I thought it just to be death throes, but when his eyes opened and he sat straight up, we nearly tripped over ourselves trying to get out of the midst of the bodies.

"We have to get out of here," Captain Powell said. "Right now. How's Wexler?"

"He'll be okay," one of the GIs said. "In and out, not bleeding too bad."

"Keep pressure on it," Doctor Schmidt said, helping Wexler to his feet and leading him down the hall. "I will help you. Come on."

I lingered long enough to sweep the SS corpses in the hall with the flame-thrower before rushing to catch up. The bodies continued to struggle to their hands and knees in spite of the flames engulfing them.

"We were going to get Rebecca," I told the Captain once I caught up.

"That's where we were going," he said. "We're out of time here; once we get Rebecca, I blow the whistle and anybody left alive gets the hell out of Dom Caern."

"There's a radio up there too. We can contact Tedeski, tell him to pull out and blow the Rabbit Hole," I said.

"Very well," Captain Powell said. "And before we leave, you expend any fuel left in those tanks inside of the manor. I want this place burned to the ground."

Andrew C. Piazza

68

"Captain Powell! Over here!"

Major Hayward shouted to us from the main entrance's foyer over the rattle of intermittent gunfire. He and three other troopers were throwing a lot of fire down a hallway splitting off the main chamber. Stray rounds snapped past them around our heads; return fire from the enemy.

"What is it?" the Captain said, gesturing for us to move into support positions.

"Seven or eight SS, giving us some trouble," Major Hayward answered. "We can't break the impasse and we're running low on ammunition."

"Sarge," the Captain said, and a second later, I set the entire hallway ablaze with a burst from the flame-thrower.

"It's almost empty," I said, testing the tanks' weight by shifting it around on my shoulders.

"Very well. Major Hayward, hold this position with these men. Sergeant Kinder, you, Doctor Schmidt, and Major Wexler, come with me."

"Don't take too long!" Major Hayward shouted after us as we headed up the staircase.

The gunfire inside the manor was now intermittent and sparse; little flashpoints of thunder and death scattered far and wide. Still, my heartbeat was fast and furious all the way to the room where I'd left Rebecca in Cappy's care.

Cappy was in the doorway, firing an M1 calmly at a pair of SS troops who rushed into the hallway from a side door. Pop, pop, pop, and both SS fell dead to the floor as Cappy's rifle went dry and ejected its spent clip with its distinctive *Ping!* sound.

"Where's your Springfield?" I asked.

"Inside the room. Figured this was better for close up than a sniper rifle," Cappy said. "What are you guys doing up here? Where's Rebecca?"

The Captain shot him a look. "What do you mean, where's Rebecca? She isn't here with you?"

For the first time in my life, I saw Cappy nonplussed. "Well... no, no sir, she took off after you. We got that radio message..."

"What radio message?" Captain Powell said. "How long ago did she leave?"

"I... I'm not sure. A while ago. We got a message over the radio from the mortar crews telling us you were caught down in the Rabbit Hole, in the village, and that you were in trouble. She took off before I could stop her. Barnes went after her and I took over on the thirty-cal until it went dry. I didn't want to leave Davey."

I looked over and to my surprise, Davey was awake and huddled into a ball on his cot. He had a carbine cradled in his arms like a toy, but he mostly stared straight ahead at nothing.

"The mortar crews are all dead, Cappy," I said.

"But I talked to them. Chris O'Keefe, I recognized his voice. It was him."

"I was there," Wexler said, swallowing hard on a dry throat. He still had a hand clamped over the wound in his arm. "The Geist killed them all. Nobody escaped but me."

Captain Powell closed his eyes to think for a moment. "You're sure she went down into the Rabbit Hole?"

Cappy didn't have to answer. The radio did it for him.

"Harry," a voice crackled over the radio receiver. "Harry Kinder. Come down here with us, Harry. Come play ball."

"Do you recognize the voice?" Captain Powell asked.

"I'm not sure," I said.

"Jim. Jim Powell," the voice said. "Come down with us, Jim. We're all down here. I missed Rebecca."

"That's Barnes," Cappy said slowly. "That's his voice."

Captain Powell reached up to his neck and took off the whistle hanging from a string. Wordlessly, he handed it to me.

"Sir?" I said.

"Blow that after you link up with Hayward's men downstairs. Get everyone out of here."

"But you can do that..."

"I'm going after her," he said.

His expression told me an argument was useless, and it didn't take long to realize that I wasn't going to let him go alone. "Wexler, take this."

Wexler took the whistle from me with a frown and looked at the Captain.

"Harry," the Captain said, shaking his head.

"Cappy," I said, ignoring him, "take Wexler and Davey and get everybody to the rallying point. Doctor Schmidt as well... and he is not to be harmed. Understood?"

"I am coming with you," Doctor Schmidt said, relieving Wexler of his remaining grenades.

"Nobody is going but me. That is an order," Captain Powell said.

"Fuck your order. Court-martial me if I live," I said, shrugging out of the nearly empty flame-thrower and picking up a B.A.R. left leaning against the wall.

"Then I'm going too," Cappy said.

"You can't," I told him. There was an ammo belt covered in pouches with B.A.R. magazines, and I strapped it around my waist. "Wexler's shot and Davey is in no shape to go anywhere unattended."

"He's right," Captain Powell said. "You must get the two of them to the rallying point. Hold that position and cover us when we cross the open field toward the trees."

The Captain looked me over as I checked the B.A.R. "Sarge, I really..."

"Sir, let's not argue about it. Let's just go," I said.

"Cappy," the Captain said. "You give us fifteen minutes. After that, call down the artillery right on the manor house. Everything we've got."

Cappy looked down at the ground and nodded. He knew what that meant.

"Tedeski," he said. "That dark... that guy took out a lot of panzers, him and his TDs. Don't forget about him."

"Right," Captain Powell said, and got on the radio. "Tedeski. Tedeski, what's your situation down there?"

Tedeski's voice crackled over the radio. "My situation is very goddamn extreme! All hell's breaking loose down here! I hit a Panther tank on its way out of the tunnel, but a Tiger pushed its way through and we had to haul ass. It's cat-and-mouse down here now."

"Understood," Captain Powell said. "We're coming down there."

"Not a good idea, sir."

"No choice. Rebecca's down there. Keep an eye out for her. And Tedeski... fifteen minutes until Dom Caern is history. Understood?"

"Understood, Captain. We'll keep an eye out for Rebecca. I'm out."

"I will take the flame-thrower. My weapon is empty," Doctor Schmidt said.

"Very well. Let's go," Captain Powell said.

Wexler and Cappy helped Davey to his feet. Doctor Schmidt strapped the flame-thrower onto his back and familiarized his hands with the controls.

"I don't wanna go out there," Davey said drunkenly. "It's out there. Leave me here. Leave me here."

"Davey," Wexler said. "We are leaving the manor house. We are leaving Dom Caern. Do you understand?"

"Leaving?" Davey asked. He swayed on his feet. "Really? For really real, we can go? We can go home?"

"Straight home, Davey," Wexler said, slipping an arm around Davey to help support his weight. "Come on. Those drugs aren't all out of your system yet, so hang on to me."

There was a sudden hailstorm of gunfire unleashed on the first floor just before we reached the stairwell. The Captain waved Doctor Schmidt and I forward, while the others took cover in a nearby room. My breathing started to come fast and shallow again as we rushed to the banister overlooking the foyer.

Pandemonium ruled below us. Our guys were firing in all directions, sometimes hitting each other, sometimes hitting the three shape-shifting forms swirling among them and tearing them to pieces.

One of the shapes looked very much like a wide drill bit; it spun like a top and crashed into its victims, slicing their skin to ribbons with its whirling edges. Another was a vaguely ovoid blob with multiple limbs crushing and piercing its way along the floor; it looked a bit like an octopus or squid. The third was nearly indescribable. The closest thing I can relate it to is a metallic and crystalline latticework which turned into a more solid, organic form bristling with fanged mouths and crushing, lobster-like claws.

Major Hayward and two other GIs poured fire into the octopus-like creature; it seemed to shatter into a thousand pieces and disappear. An instant later, the spiraling drill carved the two GIs into mincemeat. Hayward ran for the stairs, but a lance-like limb shot out of the crystalline creature and severed his right arm at the elbow.

"No!" I shouted, and fired two long bursts into the creature.

Pieces of it chipped off and disappeared. It flew up into the air, right at us, and both Captain Powell and I blazed away into the center of its mass. It was a long burst from the flame-thrower, though, that made it dart back down to the first floor.

The third creature also leapt into the air, suddenly transforming into what looked like a flying serpent with wide wings and a long tail that ended in a tangle of barbed steel. Doctor Schmidt sprayed a quick burst at it, enough to give it pause, before he ran off down the hallway and away from us.

"Go!" he shouted. "I will draw them off! Go!"

The Captain pulled me into the room where Cappy and the others were hiding as the winged creature landed on the second floor. Its wings melted away and became a dozen spiny legs that scuttled the creature off in pursuit of Doctor Schmidt. The crystalline creature seemed to melt into a jelly-like substance and went after him as well, looking like a snake swimming through water.

I reloaded the B.A.R. and stepped into the hall to open fire but the Captain stopped me.

"No. You'll only draw attention to us. We can't help him now," he said. "Down the stairs. Fast."

Major Hayward was the only survivor. We found him at the base of the stairs, staring numbly at his severed right arm that still clutched his Sten submachine-gun. Blood pumped out of the stump in steady streams.

"Get a tourniquet on that arm," Captain Powell said. "And hit him with some morphine and get him the hell out of here."

"My arm," Major Hayward said softly, as Cappy knelt down next to him and tied a tourniquet above the grisly wound.

"We'll take care of it," Wexler said to us. "Go find her."

Smoke was starting to choke the hallways of the manor from all of the fire we'd been spreading around. We heard some grenades go off on the second floor, which I hoped meant that Doctor Schmidt had given the Geist the slip, but there wasn't any gunfire between us and the stairway leading to the basement. Without a word, the Captain dashed down the hallway leading toward Rebecca, disappearing into the smoke after a few yards. Without a word, I followed.

Behind us, the shrill shriek of Wexler's whistle told anybody left alive in the manor to run like hell. Captain Powell and I, on the other hand, ran straight down into the midst of madness to face the Geist on its own ground.

Okay, you son of a bitch, I thought grimly. *Let's play some ball.*

69

The Rabbit Hole was pitch dark and for our entire mad sprint down its depths, I felt like our waving flashlight beams practically begged to get us killed. We clicked them on and off at irregular intervals, leaving them on long enough to insure that we weren't about to run face-first into a stopped tank in the next twenty yards.

Then, at last, we saw the massive doors ahead of us. They were lit in the ambient glow of a nearby fire, and once we crept up to them, we saw a Panther tank burning beyond the doors. It almost blocked the entrance. A handful of dead SS lay blown to bits around it.

"My God," Captain Powell whispered, at his first glimpse of what lay beyond the doors.

The Village of the Geist was burning.

It was nighttime in that place, a pair of moons shining brightly in the dark alien sky. Their light reflected off the snow and turned the houses into dark, hulking shadows separated by strips of white. Many of the buildings were ablaze, throwing off heat and smoke and brilliant orange light that danced across the snow like fairy fire.

We could hear the clanking and creaking of tank treads off in the distance, but it was impossible to tell if it was Tedeski or the Tiger tank he'd warned us about. Gunfire crackled here and there amongst the dark and burning buildings.

"We have to stay out of the open," Captain Powell said, his eyes still fixed on the surreal scene. "This is incredible. When you said it was down here… it doesn't matter. If she's here, hopefully she's at the rallying point. The cathedral."

"It's over there," I said, pointing to our front right. "But it's right on the main road."

"Very well. We'll use the buildings and alleys. There may be close contact. But Sarge... this is a low-key operation. We are not here to engage the enemy. If they don't notice us, don't draw attention by firing. Understand?"

"Yes, sir."

"Let's go."

We darted off to our right, toward a building whose front half had been smashed into rubble. Small fires burned inside, and in their dim light, we could see some American weapons and equipment lying scattered nearby. There were bloodstains as well, large ones, but no bodies.

The Captain slung his submachine-gun and picked a discarded bazooka up off the ground. "Get some extra rockets," he said, and then led me into the shattered building.

After what I'd seen the Geist do, some extra rockets sounded like a good idea. I recovered a bag of them from the ground and scurried inside the blasted house as there was a sudden increase in the tempo of gunfire to our left front.

The Captain waved me to the left side of the house, where the windows looked out onto the street. I thought I could see dark shapes dashing between houses in the distance, but with the uncertain light, it was impossible to tell.

A cannon boomed in the distance. The shell hit a far-off building a split second later, shaking the remaining windows of the house in which we hid. Machine-gun fire started up in that direction as well, putting it thoroughly in the Do Not Approach column.

"Out the side," Captain Powell whispered. "Into the back alley."

We crept out into the alley but there wasn't any way into the next building. The Captain waved me around to the rear of the house... the side away from the gunfire... and thankfully, the back door was empty.

We leap-frogged five buildings in this fashion, each time dreading what horror we would find inside, each time finding nothing. The firefight in the distance petered out to nothing, which made me nervous.

As long as the enemy was shooting over there, they couldn't be sneaking up on us over here.

"This is taking too long, Captain," I said.

"I know," he said. "Very well. We'll run along this alley behind the rear of these buildings, keeping them between us and the street. You lead."

We ran as quietly as we could, slowing down each time our alley intersected with one that led to the main street. The clanking of tank treads came closer and soon filled the air, which is why I never heard the SS before they were right on top of us.

They came out of a side alley two buildings ahead of me. I froze absolutely still, counting five shapes that crept into the alley and headed away from us. Luckily for me, the pale moonlight made me blend in with the pile of rubble I happened to be crouching next to, so the SS simply moved up a few buildings and disappeared into a house.

"Move up into the side alley," Captain Powell whispered loudly, to be heard over the tank.

The next building was some sort of two-story shop with a wide alley leading to the main street. The shop was intact and dark, and its alley was a perfect place to hide for a few seconds, so the Captain brought us to a halt. We hugged the wall and waited for the creaking steel monster to roll past us. It would be either Tedeski or the Tiger tank, and make our lives either easier or tougher.

Of course it was tougher. I could tell as soon as the front slope of the tank's armor rolled into view that it wasn't ours. A pair of SS infantrymen walked beside the tank, speaking to each other in German. They couldn't seem to look around fast enough; they each tried to cover 360 degrees at all times.

"Get ready," the Captain said, kneeling and aiming the bazooka.

"Can't we just leave it go?" I said. The front of the tank had rolled past and now we had a perfect broadside on its flank. However, Tiger tanks were heavy on the armor, so there were no guarantees with a bazooka, even on a side shot.

"It's headed for the cathedral," he said. "Ready?"

I gritted my teeth and shouldered my weapon. "Do it."

Flame spat out of the back of the bazooka, lighting the alley for an instant. The rocket smashed directly into the track of the creaking war machine, which subsequently pulled its treads to hell and rumbled to a halt.

The two German sentries on our side of the Tiger tank shouted and covered their heads as flying shrapnel from the rocket flew over them. I cut one down immediately and sent the other limping for cover with a long burst. The Captain heaved a grenade at the tank to scatter any other infantry and we retreated behind the shop.

"Reload," Captain Powell said. I got an extra rocket out of my bag, pulled the arming wire, and shoved it into the tube.

"Ready." I patted him on the helmet.

"That tank is immobilized but it can still shoot," he said. "Its turret won't be able to traverse far enough to fire down side streets, but we'll have to be careful if we use the main road."

Rifle fire suddenly snapped past us and bit chunks out of the brick wall nearby. Something cut my cheek and the Captain shoved me back into the side alley and away from the incoming fire.

I came back around the corner shooting. The five SS who had walked right by us now fired from the house into which they had disappeared. I raked the entire building until my weapon went dry and then ducked back into the alley to reload.

"This is no good, Captain," I said as I changed magazines. "If the guys from the Tiger tank see us, they'll have us in a crossfire."

"Get ready to move," he said, and knelt down next to the corner of the shop.

Again, fire whooshed out of the back of the bazooka, and the rocket smashed into the first floor of the house from which the SS were shooting. As soon as it hit, the Captain ran for the steps leading up to the rear entrance to the shop, with me on his heels. We were inside of the shop before the dust settled.

"Now what?" I asked once I'd reloaded the bazooka.

"Fire off that clip at them and then meet me in the front of the shop," he said, already up and moving.

Muzzle flashes sparked in windows across the alley. They came feebly at first, and I was able to answer back in kind, but soon the incoming fire became too intense to compete with. Bullets blew the floor and walls into a flying cloud of wooden splinters and chips of brick and stone. I had to scramble on hands and knees to the front of the store, where the incoming fire couldn't hit me. The Captain was knelt down next to a window and watching the immobilized Tiger tank.

I pulled myself up to a kneeling position to get a look. In the fiery light from several buildings completely ablaze nearby, I could see the disabled tank straining to move on a broken tread. Three troops stood on top of the tank, pointing in our direction and shouting into the Tiger's open hatch. The turret began to turn in our direction with a slow whine.

"This isn't good," the Captain said, and then added, "Oh *shit!*"

I craned to look at what had pulled that out of him. It was the Geist, rushing in to attack the Tiger tank.

It loomed up over them in vaguely the same form as had leapt onto the second floor landing of Dom Caern to chase after Doctor Schmidt: wide and flat, with bat-like wings that made it look like a manta ray that had a heavy tail or appendage hanging down with a scythe blade on the tip. But this time, it was enormous; at least the size of a city bus.

The battlefield was instantly forgotten. The Captain and I stared in dumb fascination as the SS on the outside of the tank shrieked and turned too late to bring their weapons to bear. One was cut in half by that terrible tail as the Geist leapt up into the air; the others were crushed flat beneath its bulk as it impacted on the top of the tank so hard that the entire steel chassis shuddered.

It drew its flattened shape upwards, like a handkerchief lying flat on a table picked up by the middle. As soon as the tank's hatch was exposed, the scythe-tail smashed against it, finally changing shape to clamp onto it and twist with impossible strength. We could hear the thick steel armor rend and whine as the Geist twisted it like an aluminum can.

The turret whined to a stop, blocked by the bulk of the Geist's body. The cannon boomed with thunder; panic fire that sent a shell uselessly into a building a block further up the street. The machine-gun mounted next to the cannon rattled and spat fire, but the Geist merely drew the endangered portion of its body out of the way of the bullets. The machine-gun couldn't twist far enough to track it.

At last... I say at last, but it was only a few seconds... the hatch ripped off. The scythe-tail reached up into the air and then dove straight down into the hull of the tank. Screams that matched the shrieks of the tank's rending armor came from within; the scythe-tail came up briefly to fling an unidentifiable red mass of body parts out of the tank. It had changed shape again: the scythe blade was now a series of tentacles arranged in a ring around the tip, each with a swirling tangle of blades rotating on the end.

The tail rammed back into the hatch and the screams soon died out, ending in gurgles and then nothing.

I only had time to blink before a deafening explosion blew dirt and debris over the Captain and myself. A grenade had gone off in the rear of the shop; I had to shake my head to clear it of the ringing caused by the close concussion.

"They're coming in the back!" I shouted as a hailstorm of rifle fire chewed up the rear of the shop.

"Follow me!" the Captain said, rushing out of the front door and kneeling on the stoop.

"Are you nuts? The Geist is out there!" I said, but when he aimed the bazooka, I had to get out there and next to him or the backblast would cook me alive.

He fired as soon as my hand touched his shoulder. The rocket hit dead center in the mass of the creature, right in the midst of the flat body draped over the tank. Huge chunks of it blew into the air; I cringed involuntarily, thinking I might be hit by some. There was a shrieking sound unlike any ever uttered on Earth and then the Geist shattered into a thousand pieces and disappeared.

The Captain glanced back into the shop. The bazooka's backblast had set the entire front of the building on fire, but the SS on our rear flank continued to pour rifle fire into the shop.

"Come on!" he said, as the SS stormed into the rear of the building.

"Where are we going?" I said, as he led me across the street and past the torn Tiger tank.

"Any place away from that!" he shouted back to be heard over the ringing in our ears.

We made it about fifty yards down the street when the SS reached the front of the shop. Bullets began to snap and whine around us, thudding into wood and chipping away the brick of the buildings on our left. I pushed the Captain into an alley and spun to return fire...

... as a cold gust of wind blew past us.

Our eyes went wide and we followed the passage of the wind back the way we'd come. Two of the five SS troopers ran out of the front of the shop, rifles blazing, dead-set on catching us and cutting us down. Their comrades fired from the windows to cover them.

I've described how the Geist seemed to shatter like glass into splintered fragments, each of which then split again and disappeared. Now I saw the reverse; what seemed like a hazy portion of the air suddenly filled with particles of dirt or stone, all flying in the same direction in a cloud. The particles then joined together to form larger pieces, each perhaps the size of a pebble or so, and then these melded together to form the body of the Geist.

It happened in an instant, so quickly that it dared the eye to believe it. One instant, there was nothing; the next, a cloud of dust integrated into what I guessed to be the entire mass of the Geist. It was as big as I'd seen it in the clearing outside of Dom Caern; as large and heavy as the buildings on either side of the street. Its form was impossible to describe; there were too many shapes and appendages and variations going on for my eye to process them all, but the overall effect was that of an amoeba sending out countless extensions.

"Go," I whispered hoarsely, pushing the Captain further into the alley as the SS screamed and shouted and died. "Go!"

We ran in a dream-like haze through the dark streets of the village. I had no idea where the alleys that we took led; I only guessed at the general direction of the cathedral and stumbled towards it as best I could. Thoughts swirled and fought and collided in my mind, each of them desperate to make sense of what I'd just seen, but none would come through clearly.

We bumped and careened off brick walls and doorjambs; we felt none of it. My mind was shattered worse than the heaviest shelling could ever inflict on me. It was as if my mind tried to protect my sanity by convincing me I was in the midst of a hallucination.

And then, against all expectation, we stumbled back out onto the main road across the street from the cathedral. The Captain and I stared at it stupidly for a second, as if not quite believing it was there, and then I took a drunken step toward it.

"Hold it," Captain Powell said, grabbing my arm. "Harry, take a second, okay? Let's pull it together, here."

Staying still for a few seconds helped me come back into myself a bit, and the night lost a little of its hallucinatory quality. I took a couple of deep breaths and shook myself like a dog to wake up out of my walking dream.

"Okay. Okay," I said. "Are you okay?"

He nodded in reply and gestured toward his bazooka. "Any more rockets?"

I checked the bag. "Just one."

"Load it and let's go."

We took enough time to reload the bazooka before dashing across the street and to the steps of the cathedral. It was lighter here; three buildings a bit further up the street blazed out of control. At the top of the steps, I could see that more and more of the village was burning. The flames created a wide orange glow over the village that seemed to mark the fire's future territory. Candlelight from within the cathedral shone through the stained glass windows. Occasional rifle shots punctured the still air in the distance.

"Ready?" the Captain asked.

I took a deep breath, nodded, and we went in.

70

The cathedral was on fire.

What I had taken from the outside to be candlelight was actually the flames from heaps of books burning around the aisles of the cathedral. The flames licked at the pews; several had already started to burn on one end and the carpet was smoldering and burning. Several pews had been piled up at the altar and turned into a bonfire. The flames sent dancing shadows across the lunatic stained glass set into the walls.

Five dead men... three SS and two GIs... unceremoniously tossed hymnals one at a time onto the bonfire. They didn't notice us at first; we were able to walk slowly up the main aisle to within ten yards before one of the dead GIs spotted us.

It was Barnes. The left side of his ribcage was opened up from top to bottom.

The Captain slowly took the bazooka off his shoulder and leaned it against a pew as the dead men forgot their books and shuffled towards us. Without a word, Captain Powell unslung his submachine-gun, checked the magazine, and shouldered it as the dead men got close.

He aimed carefully before he shot them, letting them get close enough so that he knew the first burst would blow out the base of their skulls and put them down. The first was Barnes. Then an SS trooper. Then another. I stepped up next to him and shot the second GI... one of my 3rd Platoon men who had come down here with Tedeski... and Captain Powell got the last SS.

When it was all over and there was only the two of us in the burning cathedral, the Captain let his empty weapon fall to the floor with a clatter.

He reached out a hand for the nearest pew, as if for support, and sank slowly to a seat.

He stared straight ahead at nothing. I looked around the empty cathedral, watching it burn, desperate for something to say to get the Captain up and on his feet again. There was a hymnal on the floor, dropped by Barnes, and I picked it up and opened it.

"It's in English," I said. "Nursery rhymes."

If Captain Powell heard me, he didn't show it. He simply leaned forward and rested his face in his hands.

"Captain," I said as gently as I could. "Captain, she's not here."

He didn't move.

"Captain, we can't stay here."

"I know," he said softly.

"We have to get Tedeski if he's still around and get out. We have to blow the Rabbit Hole. Captain…"

"I said, I know," he said again, and lifted his face out of his hands.

He looked slowly at the cathedral burning around him, at the trappings of religion warped into madness by an alien mind. For a second, I thought he would refuse to move from that spot, preferring to die there rather than face failing to find Rebecca.

"She could still be all right, sir," I said. "She could've linked up with Tedeski or gone up the Rabbit Hole… we don't know yet, sir."

"Let's just go," he said, and without another word, he stood, picked up the bazooka, and led me out of the burning cathedral and into the street.

"How's your ammunition?" he asked once we were outside and in the street. He sounded tired.

"Um, this magazine and three more," I said.

"I have this rocket and then my .45," he said. "Very well. We stay small and out of sight. Stick to the buildings. We're almost out of time before the arty strike hits the manor."

There was a sudden flare-up of rifle fire far off in the distance, and then, from deeper within the village where it was dark, we heard a voice call out to us.

"Jim! Jim!"

One Last Gasp

Relief flooded into Captain Powell's face. "Oh, thank God! Rebecca! Over here!"

"Jim, don't leave! Don't leave me, please!"

"She must've seen the cathedral was compromised and hid nearby where it was dark and she could still watch for us," he said with a grin. "Clever girl. Come on!"

Something tickled at the back of my mind.

"Jim, please, I'm scared. Don't leave me alone over here."

Harry, I want you to teach me how to shoot a gun. Jiim will not show me. You and Jiim are both the same way with this.

You and Jiim.

Jiim.

"Hold it," I said, grabbing the Captain's arm.

"Come over here, Jim," her voice called out again. "Jim, please don't leave me."

"What the fuck are you doing?" he snarled, trying to shake me off. "Let go!"

"*Listen!*" I hissed, holding his arm even tighter. "Where's her accent?"

I felt the tension in his shoulders melt away as he stopped fighting me. The muscles in his face loosened as well; his relieved grin melted into a long, open, unbelieving O.

"Oh no," he whispered. "No, no."

In that moment, I realized what was happening. The entire mass of the Geist was off in the distance, where we'd heard gunfire... too far away to catch us if we'd left right away. So it used her to stall us long enough for it to get within striking range.

"Captain," I said, pulling on his arm, trying to keep my weapon shouldered with my free hand. "Captain!"

We stared into the silent dark, waiting for something to show itself and praying that it didn't. Soon, sounds came from the dark; not words, but the desperate grunts and moans of struggle. This time, when Rebecca's voice came, it sounded as if someone was grinding the heel of a boot into her stomach... pained and tortured.

"Jiim!" Her voice floated to us true and clear, accented and trembling. There was a pause, only a second or two, but it seemed like an eternity before she shouted with what sounded like her last gasp.

"Jiim... run! *RUN!*"

The skin tightened and crawled all over my body and electric bolts shot down my spine. I spun on my heels and bolted for the Rabbit Hole before the echoes of her scream had finished bouncing off the gray walls of the village.

The Captain wasn't moving and my hand reached out by reflex to grab him and drag him along behind me. He fought me, dragged me down like an anchor, and I came within a hairsbreadth of letting go and leaving him there to die.

"We can't leave her!" he said.

I grabbed him by the jacket and shook him hard. "Captain, she is *dead!* Do you hear me? She's already dead! Now *come on!*"

He came along with me when I pulled this time, slowly at first, then gaining speed and keeping up with me once the instinct for survival began to come back to life inside of him. Soon, I didn't have to drag him at all; he ran with me down the street and past the torn-open Tiger tank.

"How far to the Rabbit Hole?" he said breathlessly.

"I don't know!" I shouted back. "Too far!"

There was the sound of something heavy hitting the ground far behind us and...

(*sledding, it sounds like sledding, Davey told me it sounds like sledding*, I thought)

...sliding through the snow. We poured on the speed as best we could, legs pumping until our muscles burned like the buildings in the village, but I knew we couldn't outrun that thing.

"We have to get into the buildings!" I said.

"No, it'll come in after us!" Captain Powell shouted back.

There was a loud, clanging impact behind us. The Geist had hit the disabled Tiger tank and was moments away from getting us as well. I wanted desperately to look back but I forced myself to keep my eyes front and concentrate every ounce of energy on running top speed.

A large shape loomed out of the dark streets in front of us, coming straight on. *Oh, fuck*, I thought, my body sagging in resignation of my doomed fate. It had split a piece of itself off to cut off our retreat.

My legs went out from under me as Captain Powell shouted "Down!" We fell heavily into that fake, dry snow, and I closed my eyes shut and pressed as hard into the ground as possible, thinking somehow it wouldn't hurt as much when the Geist killed me if I was pressed hard into the ground.

The world exploded around my ears. The earth trembled beneath me and my eardrums exploded with the sound. Another explosion, this one muted, and a second later, I opened my eyes and realized I wasn't dead.

Twenty yards in front of me, the hatch popped open on Tedeski's tank destroyer with a loud clang and his head popped up. "What the fuck are you guys waiting for?" he shouted. "Let's get the hell out of here!"

Andrew C. Piazza

71

The Captain and I scrambled to our feet and bolted for the TD. It hadn't been my certain death coming on after all, then; it had been my salvation.

"What happened to it?" I said down into the hull of the TD after Captain Powell and I climbed up. "What happened to the Geist?"

"Nailed it with the cannon," Tedeski said. "It disappeared into thin air."

"It'll be back," Captain Powell said. "Haul ass for the Rabbit Hole."

"No shit, sir," Tedeski said. "Hang on!"

Captain Powell lowered himself into the hull of the TD and I got on the fifty-cal machine-gun mounted in the turret. One of Tedeski's TD crew lay slumped over the edge of the open turret; there were bullet wounds punched out of his back.

"Tedeski, you've got a man down up here," I said.

"I know. I couldn't leave him down here, not with what that thing does to you," he shouted back up to me as the TD lurched forward and sped down a side street to turn back toward the Rabbit Hole. "Man, you wouldn't believe the shit I've seen down here!"

"Yes, we would," I said. There was a clatter of metal beneath me; the Captain was helping Tedeski reload the TD's cannon. I hoped we wouldn't need it; I had a feeling Tedeski had scored a lucky shot and I didn't want to have to rely on that again.

"Did you find her?" Tedeski asked after giving his TD driver some directions.

The Captain just looked at him for a second. "Turn this turret around before we go into the tunnel," he said. "If we have to shoot, it will be behind us."

"Rabbit Hole, dead ahead!" I shouted, keeping the fifty-cal aimed ahead of us as the turret rotated with a whine around me to aim back into the village. It was hard to believe; all that time for the Captain and I to creep our way to the cathedral, and we'd driven back in under two minutes.

Tedeski's driver brought the TD to a crawl so we could maneuver around the burning Panther tank outside of the massive double doors. As soon as we were through and into the tunnel, our forward lights switched on and the TD kicked into high gear again.

I spun around to watch back down the tunnel. It was dark, but the TD still had its small floodlight mounted on it from when I'd gone down into the tunnel the first time. I had to lean over the edge of the turret to switch it on, but after a couple seconds' worth of fidgeting, the floodlight mounted coaxial to the cannon switched on and lit up the tunnel behind us.

The engine rumbled and greasy exhaust choked my lungs. No matter how fast the TD drove, it wasn't fast enough; I wanted to *fly* out of that tunnel.

"Stop up ahead at the storeroom," the Captain said. "Where the platform used to be."

We lurched to a halt and the Captain and Tedeski climbed out, followed by Tedeski's driver. "Sarge, stay on the fifty and keep a watch down that tunnel while we check the charges," Captain Powell said.

"Hurry," I said. The floodlight wouldn't give us much warning before the Geist came at us, and I didn't know if even the fifty-cal would have much effect on the entire mass of the creature.

The storeroom was dark and they had to use flashlights to find the timer for the explosives. All the same, it was a matter of seconds before they checked to make sure it was rigged and ready to blow.

"Let's go," the Captain said, leading them back to the TD. "Fuse is set and running. We've got five minutes to…"

One Last Gasp

Rattling thunder filled the storeroom, sending lances of terror straight through my heart. Bullets snapped the air and dinged off the tank destroyer's skin.

It was submachine-gun fire, coming from the far side of the storeroom and directed straight into the three men climbing back onto the TD. There were meaty thumps as bullets found their way into flesh and bone. All three of them fell from the vehicle; the Captain, Tedeski, and the TD driver.

I would've screamed but rounds clanked off the metal turret and buzzed past my head. Something bit the inside of my right arm. More slugs thumped into the dead body slumped over the turret as I ducked down below the rim until the gunfire died out.

Rage poured through me. Not now, not after we'd come so far. I spun the fifty-cal toward the storeroom and blazed away relentlessly, firing blind at first and then using the flare of the big machine-gun's muzzle flashes to track down the dark form that rushed forward towards the TD with a Schmeisser submachine-gun in its hands.

I didn't hit him. It was too close and the fifty-cal wouldn't tilt down far enough to get him. For a second, I thought I was dead meat, but the figure dropped his empty weapon with a clatter and yanked an SS dagger from its sheath before falling on the TD driver.

The thick wet sounds of the blade driving home sent needles through me. I vaulted over the rim of the turret, dragging my .45 pistol out of its holster as I went. An instant later, my boots hit the floor of the tunnel and I leveled my pistol at the SS who'd shot the Captain and Tedeski.

It was Kleg. Even in the half-light spilled off from the floodlight pointed down the tunnel, I could see it was his corpse come back to life. His charred skin was cracked and split open; his eyelids and lips were gone, and his hair as well. Now he truly did have a skull for a face, a leering, burnt skull that grinned fangs as he turned and came at me.

I got off two shots before he jumped me. The first thudded home in the hole in his chest where his heart used to be; the second blew a chunk of burnt flesh out of the side of his neck.

It didn't slow him down. His heavy body crashed into me and knocked me into the side of the TD and then to the ground. I hit the edge of something metal and felt a rib crack from the impact. He stabbed down with his dagger but I got a hand up and grabbed his wrist before it could get me; his free hand grabbed at my gun and held it away from his head.

"You will never leave me," he croaked through scorched vocal cords. "Never!"

The smell of burnt flesh filled my lungs. It felt like it would suffocate me.

We wrestled around on the tunnel floor, each trying to get the advantage. He was on top of me and I was weakened from my cracked rib, but the damage his body had endured couldn't be wiped away by the Geist's control. I pushed him against the tread of the TD, to my left, and that gave me enough leverage to jam my pistol up underneath his right armpit.

The gun's report was muffled by Kleg's body. Again and again I fired, five times, until the gun was empty. Bits of charred flesh flew about and over my face. Kleg didn't so much as flinch; in fact, he bit down into my arm as I fired. His filed teeth drove into my skin and drew blood. I screamed and tore my arm out of his mouth, finally heaving him up and off me.

We both scrambled to our feet. Kleg took a step toward me and tried to swing his dagger, but I'd shot into his right shoulder for a reason. He may not have felt the pain, or maybe he felt it and the Geist's control pushed him on anyway, but nothing could make that arm work again. The .45 rounds had pulverized his shoulder and his right arm now dangled uselessly from a scrap of tissue.

Kleg went to transfer the dagger into his other hand, and I saw my chance. Bolted onto the side of the tank destroyer's hull were racks for pioneer tools; standard issue for any tracked vehicle. The pickaxe was gone, but there was a twelve-pound sledgehammer, which was just as good.

I got it down as Kleg switched his dagger into his left hand. My cracked rib flared in white-hot pain, but I was lost to rage again and

One Last Gasp

heaved the sledgehammer up over my shoulder. I didn't care what happened to me anymore. I only knew that I had to destroy Kleg once and for all.

He came in with his dagger. I swung the hammer in a low arc and used it to side-step his attack. The sledge smashed directly into the side of his left knee; the joint cracked audibly and gave out beneath him. Kleg fell forward against the raised stone floor of the storeroom, catching himself with his arm.

He was facing away from me and never saw it coming. I swung the sledgehammer again and smashed down on his remaining forearm, shattering it into charred bits.

Kleg twisted and fell to a seat on the tunnel floor, propped up against the raised floor of the storeroom. He looked up at me and tried to struggle to his feet, his shattered limbs waving about uselessly.

The pain from my rib was forgotten. I adjusted my grip on the sledge.

"Stay in Hell this time, you son of a bitch," I said, and swung the sledge over my head like I was splitting wood.

Kleg's skull crushed under the impact of the hammer, leaving a gory pink mess in the midst of a tangle of burnt skin and bone. His body slumped over and onto its side. His charred skin still twitched spasmodically.

I dropped the sledge and fell to my knees next to the Captain. He lay face-up on the tunnel floor; there were bullet wounds in his left leg and side.

Don't be dead, I prayed quickly. *Don't be dead. Please don't take him too.*

"Captain?" I said, shaking him a little to rouse him. "Captain?"

Tears had started to cloud my vision when his eyes fluttered and then opened. "Ah," he said, gritting his teeth against the pain. "I'm hit. I'm hit."

"You've got one in the leg and one in the side. They don't seem like they're bleeding too bad but we've got to get out of here before the tunnel blows or the Geist comes or both."

"The others?" he asked.

"The TD driver's dead. I haven't checked Tedeski yet," I said. "Can you get up?"

"Leg wound feels numb. Like somebody hit it with a baseball bat," he said, still gritting through his teeth. His hands were pressed over the wound in his side and his body was starting to tremble. "This one in the side hurts like hell. I don't know if I can walk. Go check Tedeski. Do it now."

I scrambled over to where Tedeski lay. He was worse off than the Captain; one bullet had only clipped him but two slugs had gone into his back and punched out the other side. His eyes were open and he was breathing, but I couldn't tell if he was aware of what was going on or not.

"Tedeski?" I said.

"W-was that Kleg?" he said. His body shook much worse than the Captain's; his wounds were bleeding badly and he seemed like he was barely holding on to himself. "Did you g-get him?"

"He's gone," I said. "But we're out of time. The Captain's hurt and your driver's dead. We've got to get out of here and get you to a hospital fast."

"I, uh, don't think I can walk," he said. "Can't really... feel my legs."

I buried my face in my hands. I couldn't carry them both. With only minutes left before the explosives went off, I didn't think I could carry even one of them. And it couldn't be long before the Geist came calling.

"Sarge?" the Captain asked.

"He's... he's pretty bad, sir," I said.

"Do you think you can carry him?"

My pained silence was my answer.

"Very well," the Captain said, struggling to keep his voice steady through the pain. "You get going then, Sarge."

"Sir?"

"You heard me. Go on and get going. We'll see if we can slow the Geist down for you."

"No, no way, sir," I said, returning to his side. "Absolutely not. There is..."

"Harry," he said softly, looking at me with sad eyes. "Just go."

One Last Gasp

I couldn't stop the tears then. They spilled down my cheeks and cut clean tracks through the dirt and the grime and the blood. Now it was my body's turn to tremble; my hands clenched and I shook like I was naked in the cold.

"Just go, Harry," he said again.

"No!" I shouted, grabbing him by the arms. "God damn you, Captain, don't you give up on me! Not now! There is no way in hell I am going to leave you here to die! No, sir! You are going to *live!*"

Some inner reservoir of strength opened up. I lifted the Captain up by his jacket lapels, manhandling him to his feet somehow and propping him up against the TD so his leg wouldn't give out.

"Stay there," I ordered the Captain. "You're going to have to help me with Tedeski. Tedeski!" I said, kneeling by his side. "If I get you into that TD, can you drive it? It's our only chance. Can you do it?"

"You can bet your ass I'm going to try," he said.

I got his trembling body over my shoulder in a fireman's carry and got him over to the TD. The pain in my rib was a distant entity; I was lost in a haze of adrenaline and a stubborn, unthinking will to live. Somehow, some way, I got him up on the TD and down into the hull. I don't really remember it. It was like I was in some sort of fugue or trance.

The next thing I knew, I had Tedeski propped behind the controls of the tank destroyer with the Captain by his side to help him. Tedeski started to pass out for a second, but I managed to bring him back around. There was a box of cigars on the floor near his feet and I jammed one into the corner of his mouth.

As badly as he was hurt, he still managed to smile. "I'm okay."

"Then let's go. Let's go!" I said.

The TD's radio crackled and a voice came over it. "Tedeski!" it said loudly. "Tedeski! You should not have shot me, Tedeski."

"Oh, shit," the Captain said.

"I will never let you leave," the voice said. "I am going to make it hurt this time. It will take a long time for you to die. All of you are going to die. I am coming for you. I am coming for you *now*."

"Go, Tedeski, go now," I said.

"What can I do?" the Captain said, looking helplessly over the controls as he would the console of a spaceship.

"Help me with that," Tedeski said, pointing to one of the levers.

We lurched once and then began grinding forward, slowly gaining speed as we clanked and creaked up the tunnel. I stuck my head out of the turret and checked our progress. The TD churned along at about a man's running speed.

There was a loud sound far off below us at the other end of the tunnel... the doors to the village being smashed off their hinges. "Tedeski!" I shouted down into the hull. "Faster!"

"I'm barely hanging on here," he said. "I go any faster and I might send us crashing into the tunnel wall."

"How long until the explosives go off?" I asked.

The Captain checked his pocket watch. "Less than a minute."

"We're not going to make it," I said, and got on the fifty-cal. I couldn't see the Geist yet but I knew it was coming; I rattled off a long burst down the tunnel. Tracer bullets lanced beyond the reach of the floodlight and disappeared into the dark depths of the tunnel.

"You cannot stop me," the radio crackled and warbled. "I am going to KILL YOU ALL!"

"Faster!" I shouted again. "Jesus Christ, go faster!"

The TD began to speed up; first to fifteen miles an hour, then twenty, then twenty-five, then thirty. It started to track back and forth, scraping up against one wall of the tunnel and then the other as Tedeski struggled to keep it under control.

"I can't hold it!" he said. "I can't... help me, goddamn it!"

The Captain struggled to help him maintain control of the vehicle as we continued to gain speed. I rattled off another long burst down the tunnel; panic was taking over and I laid down on the trigger until the machine-gun ran out of ammunition.

"Shit!" I shouted, and then I saw it.

The Geist loomed up out of the dark like an onrushing subway train; it filled the tunnel completely like water forced up a pipe. The front was smooth like the tip of mercury rising in a thermometer; it shimmered with shades of silver and gray.

One Last Gasp

It gained on us by about thirty miles an hour, closing the distance at a terrifying rate. As it got closer, two long appendages extended out of its mass to reach out towards the tank destroyer. The tips opened up like fingers to form whirling blades.

"The cannon!" I screamed, dropping down into the hull of the TD. "How do you shoot the cannon?"

"That!" Tedeski said, pointing to a trigger by my right shoulder.

"Harry!" the radio boomed. "Let's play some ball, Harry!"

I grabbed the trigger and fired without aiming. The cannon thundered and the tunnel was suddenly filled with dust and dirt; it fell from above us and choked the air. The shell's concussion had started some sort of cave-in. I couldn't see a thing. I didn't know if I'd hit the Geist or not, but it should've impacted with us already and it hadn't.

"Time's up!" the Captain shouted.

The explosives piled in the storage room detonated a split second after our TD shot out of the Rabbit Hole and into open ground. The ground shook beneath us; I actually felt the twenty-ton tank destroyer lift beneath me and almost skid out as a bright light blinded me.

Shit we didn't make it, I thought breathlessly, and then I realized that the blinding light was sunlight reflecting off the snow. We'd made it after all. We'd escaped the Geist.

I stood up in the turret and looked around at the clearing in a daze. It was morning; the sun had come up and sat low in a blue sky. The tank destroyer clanked forward toward the trees and our rallying point; behind us, Dom Caern burned in a fiery inferno. The hole we'd just shot out of seemed sunken in and smaller; the tunnel had collapsed.

The cold air stung my lungs and I suddenly realized how tired I was. The sun was almost too bright to stand; after days and weeks of dark nights and gloomy skies, the morning light was like a piercing searchlight aimed directly onto my retinas.

I slumped against the side of the turret and shielded my face with my hand. Black smoke rose into the sky all around me; from the burning hulks of TDs and tanks and the splintered remnants of the arsenal as well. I turned around and looked at Dom Caern, watching it consume itself for a while before finally turning my back on it. Shells began to whistle overhead and then smash into and around the manor.

"There's our artillery strike," I said to nobody in particular. We were far enough away from the manor not to worry about a short round hitting us, so I leaned back and enjoyed the show, watching our 105s blast pieces of the manor to junk.

The tank destroyer began to slow down as we approached the tree line. I saw Wexler and Cappy come out of the forest, waving to us, and then we suddenly came to a lurching halt about thirty yards away from them.

"All right, Captain," I said, lowering myself into the TD's hull, "let's get you out first so Cappy and I can pull Tedeski out. Tedeski? Hell of a job, man. Hell of a job."

The Captain raised his face out of his hands and reached over to close Tedeski's eyes for him. "He's dead, Harry," he said, eyes full of tears. "He's dead."

I closed my eyes and let my weight sag and slump against the steel of the tank destroyer's hull. He'd held on long enough to get us out, and then I guess he couldn't hold on any longer.

The sound of Wexler and Cappy climbing up onto the TD shook me out of my haze. "Come on, Captain," I said, then shouted up into the open turret, "Get some bandages and some morphine! The Captain's been hit!"

We dragged the Captain out of the TD and sat him next to it. "Who else made it?" I asked, as Wexler and Cappy started bandaging the Captain's wounds.

"Davey is keeping an eye on Major Hayward in the trees," Wexler said.

I waited for him to go on, and when he didn't, said, "That's it? Nobody else made it out?"

"Just you two," Cappy said. "And Tedeski. Is he still inside the TD?"

"He's dead, Cappy," Captain Powell said, shivering a little bit with the cold and the pain. "Bled to death while getting us out of there."

One Last Gasp

Cappy sat back into the snow and looked at the TD as if he could look into it. His shoulders slumped and for the first time I'd ever seen, he let his rifle slip out of his hands and fall into the snow.

"Did you recognize the voice that spoke to us? Just now, I mean, as we came up the tunnel?" I asked Captain Powell.

He nodded. "Doctor Schmidt. With no accent."

It became very still. The wind blew across us, but it was only fresh air and not the Geist come for us. The snow in the clearing swirled in circular eddies across the ground, completely oblivious to the artillery shells smashing the manor to pieces. We all sat there for a while and listened to Dom Caern die, when Wexler suddenly jumped to his feet.

"Oh, my God! Rebecca! She made it!"

I twisted and looked before I could stop myself. I should've known better. She was there, standing among the columns by the front entrance to the manor, oblivious to the shells exploding around her. Somehow, she'd made it up the Rabbit Hole and into the manor during our lunatic flight from the village and the Geist, before the explosives turned the tunnel and the basement of Dom Caern into rubble.

"We have to get her out of there before she's killed by the artillery," Wexler said. "I can't believe she made it!"

I looked at the Captain. "She didn't, Major."

"What are you talking about?" Wexler said. "She's right there."

The Captain didn't meet my gaze; he stared at Dom Caern and let the tears stream down his cheeks. He murmured something under his breath, something that was lost beneath the explosions of the shells pounding the manor house.

"Cappy," I said, turning to face Dom Caern once more, "is your rifle loaded?"

He looked at me for a second, and I returned his gaze long enough to see the horror of understanding spread across his normally stoic features. He unslung his sniper rifle and chambered a round slowly, almost reverently.

I watched until the end. She stood among the pillars as the manor burned and the shells burst around her, and as I waited for Cappy to take her pain away, she lifted an arm and beckoned for us to come back to Dom Caern and join her.

After an eternity of waiting, Cappy's rifle thundered, and she fell at last.

72

The story doesn't end there.

We carried Major Hayward to the road as best we could and traveled along it, back toward our lines, past the still-burning hulls of the war machines we'd destroyed the night before. The road was pockmarked with impact craters from the artillery. We had to pick our way carefully around the scattered bodies and body parts.

A half-mile back from the last of the charred panzers, we found a couple of German supply trucks abandoned on the road. They were empty. It took a little effort to get one turned around and pointing away from Dom Caern, but the trailer gave our more seriously wounded some shelter and we started a little fire in there to keep them from going into shock from the combination of cold and their wounds.

Of course, we only had to drive about a mile before we bumped into the reinforcements scheduled to 'rescue' us that morning. Our truck was instantly turned into an ambulance; we picked up a medic from the 3rd Armored, who hooked Major Hayward up to some plasma and re-dressed his arm, and then we drove back to an aid station to get him some more serious attention.

Wexler stayed behind to supervise the destruction of Dom Caern, "the complete and utter destruction", as he put it. We could hear heavy artillery firing on the house, and before we left, Wexler was on the radio to confirm our bombing mission on the manor was on the way.

"It's not coming back," he told me. "Not ever."

That was the last I ever saw of him.

The aid station also treated the Captain and myself, and after loading another half-dozen wounded GIs onto our captured truck, sent us to a rearward area to get everybody to a hospital. Hayward was unconscious the entire time, through the benefit of morphine; the Captain and I lay close on either side of him, a blanket stretched across us, to make sure he didn't get too cold. I kept the plasma bottle under my arm to make sure it stayed warm enough to keep flowing.

We didn't talk. There was nothing to say, and besides, the touch of morphine we'd each been given kept us pretty out of it all the way back to the rear. At some point, the drug wore me down enough that I passed out in the back of that bumping, canvas-covered German truck.

I woke up in a field hospital with nothing but strange faces around me. I asked about the others, but nobody seemed to know anything, and I had to sit and bite my lip and go crazy with boredom and ignorance for two days until I found anything out.

On that day, Colonel Davis showed up with another staff officer I didn't recognize. He grilled me on what had happened at Dom Caern, and then about all of my combat experiences all the way back to Normandy. I didn't understand it; I thought maybe I was in trouble or something.

"Well, Harry, here it is," he said at last, using his Now Hear This tone. "You're going to England for a little while, until you get over these wounds. The docs tell me you should be back within a month or two. When you do, you'll be 2nd Lieutenant Kinder. Congratulations, Harry."

A field commission. The Captain had taken the time to put it through even as we waited for Kleg to come for us.

"I... I don't know what to say, sir," I said.

"Don't say anything. You just heal up quick and get back here to win this war for me."

"What, um... what happened to the others? Davey and Cappy? Captain Powell?" I asked.

"The others?" Colonel Davis said, as if that were an unusual question. "Um, let's see..."

He looked at his staff officer for a second, as if the sight of him would remind him of the facts. "Well, there was the battle fatigue case..."

"Davey," I said.

"Okay. He's going to spend a few days in the rear before we send him back out on the line. The other one, the sniper, he has been reassigned to another battalion. 1st Battalion, I'm sorry to say, has been deactivated."

That wasn't much of a shock, as we only had four men left.

"All right, Harry," he said, patting me on the shoulder. "I want you to know I think you boys did a hell of a job out there at that manor house. You sure as hell showed that Kleg son of a bitch what was what. Hell, an entire SS heavy panzer battalion, completely wiped out by a half-strength company! There's going to be decorations for this, you can count on that. Major Wexler has personally recommended both you and Captain Powell for the big one, the Medal of Honor. That may be a stretch, but I'd say Silver Star, definitely."

Give it to Shorty, I thought. *Or Goliath. Or Tedeski. Or somebody else that died so I could live.*

"What about the Captain, sir?"

"Hmm? Oh. Captain Powell has already been evacuated to England. He'll get his promotion. I want that man on my staff."

I groaned inwardly. "A staff position? You're taking away his command?"

"Taking away? Son, this is a big step up! Besides, it'll be safer for him back at Regiment with me. I think he's been through enough."

It was useless to try to explain to Davis that a staff position was worse than a death sentence for the Captain. Captain Powell was born a combat commander; it was what he was made for, he was a natural for it. Leading men in combat was where he belonged, not stifling in a rearward area under mountains of paperwork. He'd go crazy there, imaging himself back in a meat packing plant with a clipboard in his hand, imagining himself out of the loop and shuffled aside. I closed my eyes and thought of him staring at mountains of paperwork, with nothing to distract him from that final haunting image of Rebecca's corpse beckoning to us from the front door of Dom Caern.

I didn't even notice Colonel Davis leave.

By late March, the German Army was shattered and beaten. Somehow, though, Hitler convinced them to fight on, fight and die in a doomed cause for an increasingly skittish madman. While some German units capitulated by the hundreds, there were fanatical units of SS and Hitler Youth who made suicidal attacks on Allied units until the very end.

On March 27th, Cappy Johnson was riding on top of a Sherman tank with seven other GIs on a small road through the German countryside when a twelve-year-old Hitler Youth fired a Panzerfaust at point blank range from behind some rubble. The rocket damaged the tank, but didn't knock it out; the shrapnel wounded four GIs and killed two, including Cappy. There were a dozen of the Hitler Youth waiting for that column. They knocked out two half-tracks and a truck before the GIs flushed them all out. None survived to be taken prisoner.

On April 1st, 1945, I returned to the front line. I'd been discharged weeks before; it took that long to find a platoon for me to take command of. I ended up in a strange company in a strange regiment in command of men I'd never met before. It felt wrong. I felt like a fraud. I kept looking for Captain Powell. Whenever there was nothing to do, I took off my helmet and stared at the single bar painted on it signifying my status as an officer. It didn't look right. Somebody would shout "Sarge!", looking for my platoon sergeant, and I would straighten up and look around for a few seconds until it dawned on me that I wasn't "Sarge" anymore.

They were good guys, and took to me well enough, I guess, but it was never Charlie Company of the 518th. My new company commander was Captain Wythe, a recent graduate of OCS, and he tended to leave me to my own devices, which was fine by me. I kept to myself a lot in those days.

Two weeks into my first command, I was ordered to investigate reports of a "work camp" near our position. We'd been running into slave labor working in civilians' homes for some time now; Poles, Slavs, anybody and everybody the Nazis had taken control over and shipped back home to use as cheap labor. But we hadn't seen anything like this before.

The "work camp" turned out to be a "death camp". It was the first we'd seen of concentration camps; some other units had found some already, but news of them had yet to trickle down to the GIs in my outfit.

So you can imagine my shock when I walked up to the barbed wire gates and found hundreds of walking skeletons standing and staring at us with vacant eyes and expressionless faces. For a second, I knew, I *knew*, they were dead, dead and come back to life. Nobody could look like that and still be alive. And knowing that, and what it meant, I suddenly found it hard to breathe; the world shimmered before me and became a hodgepodge of terrified thoughts.

I almost passed out. My platoon sergeant later told me that I was crying and whispering, "Jesus Christ, not again, not again, let them go, you bastard," and saying something about a "Geist" and the walking dead. I convinced him it was just exhaustion and shock that tipped me over. The reality, of course, was that I thought the Geist had escaped to set up shop once again.

It wasn't the Geist, though. Just the good old fashioned evil that men do.

On August 17th, 1945, I returned home. The Silver Star I'd received from our trip to Dom Caern gave me enough points to be among the first to go back to the States. They asked me if I wanted a commission in the Regular Army, make a career of it. I told them to go to hell.

I can't ever describe what it felt like to walk into my home and hold Kate in my arms for real, for really real this time and not just a trick of my mind. I held her so tight I thought it might kill her; she never complained. There was a lot of crying and a lot of kissing and I remember wanting the rest of my life to be held in that moment, standing there on my front porch, warm, clean, safe, with my wife held in my arms as tight as my arms could squeeze. It was an actual dream come true.

For the first time in forever, I was able to breathe easy.

Two years later, Kate was pregnant and I began thinking that I needed to take my choice of career up a notch now that I was going to be a daddy. The Army was generous enough to pay for college, so I enrolled and got my degree in History. I figured that since I had been a part of history, I would have a leg up on the other students.

I ended up teaching at a high school back in Allentown, Pennsylvania, and life was good. Baby One was followed quickly by Two and Three, I liked my job, and Kate never asked me to tell her about the war. It was getting so that I thought I might be able to leave those days in the attic of my memories.

It didn't work out that way.

73

I couldn't stop thinking about the Captain, and how he dreaded the end of the war and his subsequent return to what he considered to be a small and insignificant life. His face, long and forlorn, haunted my dreams. In those dreams, I saw him in those final moments outside of Dom Caern, staring at Rebecca's beckoning corpse before Cappy ended it for her and the artillery smashed the manor to pieces.

In my dreams, I could hear what he whispered under his breath at that moment.

You should've left me.

After school, before I left for the day and while the classroom was quiet, I would stare at my desk and see him walking numbly through life, wishing he'd died at the manor so he'd never have to suffer what he would think of as a humdrum existence. I remembered our talk at the kitchen table in that nameless village outside of Dom Caern. I wanted so badly to go back in time and say something to make it right.

There was more to it than that. Wexler had gone back to insure the manor house was obliterated, wiped off the map; but until I saw it with my own eyes, there would always be that tunnel leading to Hell, at least in my mind.

It got to be an obsession. Thoughts of Dom Caern consumed my every thought, day in, day out, and finally, I told my wife I was going back to Europe.

"I've got to close the door on some memories," I told her. "Actually, I have to make sure the door is closed. It's hard to explain."

I sent letters to everyone who survived the war: Davey, Wexler, Major Hayward, and especially Captain Powell. The rallying point was set in a hotel near Bastonge, several months from the date of the letter to insure everyone could arrange their schedules accordingly. I picked August, so it would be warm and there wouldn't be any memories of the dreadful cold and snow we'd suffered the first time around. Major Hayward responded immediately, confirming he would be there. The others didn't write back.

The days until August passed in a blur. It was all I could think about; my lesson plans suffered terribly. I rehearsed what I would say to the Captain over and over, turning it around a thousand times until I was sure I'd gotten it right.

He didn't show. Neither did Wexler.

I almost didn't recognize Davey when I saw him in the hotel lobby, nor did he recognize me. We'd never seen each other cleaned up and in civilian dress before. It took about five seconds of uncertain staring before we mutually grinned and caught each other in an embrace.

"Damn, Sarge," he said, and over his shoulder, I caught sight of Major Hayward strolling amicably into the hotel. He had a pipe in his mouth and his right jacket sleeve was pinned up to his shoulder so it wouldn't swing about.

"My Goodness," he said with a smile, and we shook his left hand and clapped him on the back.

"It's good to see you, Major," I said. "Can I help you with your bags, sir?"

"It's Jonathan, now," he said. "And I can manage, but thank you, Sergeant."

"Harry."

"I'm still Davey," Davey said, and took one of Major Hayward's bags anyway. "Let's get these stowed and hit the bar. I want to know *everything*."

Major Hayward had left the Army and now taught at a military college. His daughters were rapidly reaching the age where every boy over twelve became an immediate threat in the eyes of their father.

"I thought losing *this* was a trial," he said, tapping the stump of his right arm with the stem of his pipe, "but try corralling two fourteen-year-old girls sometime."

I'd always feared losing a limb more than death when I was on the line. Some guys prayed for a foot to get blown off, so they could go home, but me, I always thought living with the loss of an arm or a leg would be worse than dying. And yet, Hayward seemed to take it in stride, joking about how he still reached for a pint glass in the pub with his stump every now and again, having forgotten his right arm was no longer there.

"Makes for an awkward moment with the lads," he said, "so I just shout 'I say! Can someone lend me a hand?' and we all laugh it off."

It was good to see Davey had come out okay, as well. Like me, he'd taken advantage of the GI bill to get some college behind him, and now, he had his dream job... university librarian.

"Librarian?" I asked.

"It's the best!" he said. "It's quiet and whenever things are slow I can read as much as I want to. You wouldn't believe how much I've learned about!"

He proceeded to regale us with bits of trivia from every known sector of human existence, from Egyptian mummification to the latest in submarine advances to the fossil record of the dinosaurs. Major Hayward and I did our best to be enthralled.

We left for the manor early in the morning, to keep the bad dreams of that place at bay with the promise of long hours of sunlight. The little village was still there... I still never bothered to discover its name... and it was child's play to find the logging trail leading to Dom Caern. It was blocked off with a chain stretched between two upright logs. It wasn't locked or secured; I think the chain was there just to tell people that the road was no longer in use.

That was readily evident. The trail was overgrown with grass and weeds, and as we stood and stared at it, a deer trotted out of the trees and crossed the trail about a hundred yards into the forest.

"Well, if the deer are back," Davey said, and that seemed to puncture the latent fear keeping us from driving down that trail.

We had to drive carefully, to be sure we didn't get stuck in any muddy spots, and just as I was thinking we were getting close to the scene of our final battle with Kleg, a deep pothole in the road prevented us from driving any further.

After we climbed out of the car we could see that the 'pothole' was actually an old impact crater from artillery. There were a lot of them; this was where I first called in our 105s on Kleg's column. I pointed out the ditch where we'd hidden our jerrycans of gasoline; further up the trail, we could even see a rusted-out hulk of a tank lurking in the trees.

"Captain Powell got that one," I told them, and we walked on.

"What do you hear about the Captain?" Davey asked.

"I have an address, but he didn't respond to my letter," I said. "The place where he used to work told me they haven't heard from him since he left for the war. They don't know if he's even working at all. I'm afraid that he might've just given up."

"Damn shame," Major Hayward said. "He was a top-notch man, your Captain. Top notch."

"Still is," Davey said. "He's not dead."

"Somebody needs to tell him that, I think," I said. "That's why I was hoping he would come here."

"I saw him once," Davey said. "I mean, while the war was still on. I ended up as a runner for my new company commander and I had to go back to regiment one day. I found him in an office they had set up in a house, and... I wish I hadn't. He looked miserable. He smiled when I came in, but it was almost like he was embarrassed to have me see him there. That's all he talked about, was how he was stuck in the rear, how he wanted to be out front with us on the line again. He said he felt like he was slowly disappearing back there."

"There it is," Major Hayward said, and the trees came to an end.

It was gone. Out in the clearing, there was no sign that Dom Caern had ever stood; the ground was flat and green, and no rubble betrayed the resting place of the manor. Wexler hadn't just had Dom Caern blown to bits; he must've had them bulldoze it under. Even the outbuildings, the stables and the wooden shed nearby, were nothing but mounds of grassy dirt now.

"Gone. It's all gone. Buried under," Davey said, and suddenly, his face choked up and he buried his face in his hands. "Shit. *Shit.*"

"Davey?" I said, and immediately felt stupid. Didn't I see Shorty's shade out there where the manor once stood? Didn't I see him buried under in the tunnel we called the Rabbit Hole, trapped in that creature's fabricated village?

Davey sniffled and wiped at his eyes. "It's... I still have trouble sometimes, you know? Like I think of Goliath and... just... why couldn't he have made it, you know? Why me and not him? I don't know. I miss my friend."

"Take a look around you, Davey," Major Hayward said. "Tell me what you see. I'll tell you what I see. Green fields and free people. That, my friend, is not a small thing. There was a great evil in this place, and make no mistake, had we not stopped it here thousands more would have died. Thousands, and each one with friends and family and dreams for a rich life. We stopped it. The cost was great; some lost their lives, and others lost a part of themselves... and I don't mean just this," he said, tapping his right sleeve with the stem of his pipe. "All of us lost those we love. But it had to be done."

"Always remember that the world owes us nothing. Every day we're given is a gift. We know that better than anybody else. Your friendship with Goliath, however brief, was a gift. Some people never have a friend like that for their entire lives. You were blessed to have known him at all, just as I have been blessed to have known each of you."

Davey wiped at his eyes once more. "Thanks, Major."

Major Hayward nodded and led us back toward the car. "Come on, now. Let's leave this place behind us. It's the past, and we should look forward more than we look behind."

The drive back to the hotel was quiet, and I've never been good with quiet times. "I wish Captain Powell had been here," I said in order to fill the empty air. "To hear what you said back there, M... Jonathan."

"Tell him," Major Hayward said.

"I don't know if he'll listen," I said.

"Nonsense. Tell him what you've seen here," he said.

"Seen here?" I asked.

"Stay for a few days," Major Hayward said. "Trust me on this. There's more you need to see than a dirt mound out in the forest."

We spent the next three days in Belgium, and we were treated like royalty by the locals once they found out who we were. They were especially taken in with Major Hayward and his missing arm. I don't think we paid for a drink the entire time, and everywhere we went, we were among friends.

The last night I was there, I found myself sitting and watching the people around the pub. Not just the ones chatting away with Major Hayward and Davey… who didn't let a language barrier keep him from trying to explain the intricacies of mummification to the locals… but each of the little throngs of people clustered around the place. I saw free people, safe people, smiling people free from the weight of conquest and oppression and death. I saw people free to live their lives the way it was meant to be lived; not in last gasps, but in slow and easy breaths.

It's a good day to be alive, I thought.

We kept in touch after that, Davey and I especially, and after a while, I finally broke down and wrote once more to Captain Powell. Major Hayward was right; somebody needed to tell him what we saw on that August trip to Belgium. There were things he needed to hear that I was leaving left unsaid. So, at last, I took pen to paper and wrote:

Dear Captain:

I can't help addressing you as "Captain", even though I heard you got your promotion to major after we left Dom Caern. To me, you'll always be my captain and company commander; it seems the natural way to think of you.

I guess you think that way too, from what Davey told me. He and I and Major Hayward met up in Belgium to revisit Dom Caern. I wish you had come as well. It opened my eyes up to a lot of things, and as I put it to my Kate, it closed the door on a lot of memories.

Except one. I keep remembering that conversation we had in the little village outside of Dom Caern, with Rebecca sleeping in the chair nearby. You told me how your life was meaningless before you came to the war; how in the midst of all that madness, you felt that you could make a difference in the world at last. I didn't know what to say then, but I do now.

You don't need to lead men into combat to change the world. You don't have to fight, kill, and die to make a difference. And you don't need to be a company commander in a combat zone to meet a woman and fall in love.

I make a difference every day in my life. I do it in my job... I'm a schoolteacher... and I do it as a husband and father. I do it as a friend and neighbor and any other thing I need to be during the course of my wonderfully ordinary life. The differences we make don't have to be vast or violent in order to be profound. There's plenty of good that needs to be done out there in the world... you don't need a uniform or captain's bars to be a part of it.

I know it's more than that, too. I know losing Rebecca must have been shattering, as losing Goliath shattered Davey. But Davey's doing fine now. Great, actually. I've come to realize that Major Hayward was right when he said that the world owes us nothing... that every day and hour and minute we get is a gift we haven't earned. Your time with Rebecca was a gift, even if it was too brief. Better brief than never at all.

You should've seen Belgium this time around, Captain. Green fields and free people, Major Hayward said, and it was beautiful. I've come to think we were blessed to be a part of making it that way.

It's a good day to be alive, Captain. They all are, I think, even the dark days, even the days in which you think God is a madman and the world is nothing but misery. I'm proud to have been under your command and I thank God that I was there to be a part of what needed to be done. But it doesn't end there.

Every day is a challenge worth taking. I really believe that's true. The challenges may not be so grand as liberating towns and villages from the Nazis, but like those in the theater say, there are no small parts... only small actors. The only trick is finding a role that fits you. There's lots of parts to play, Captain, and I can't think of anyone better than you to play any one of them.

He never replied.

Major Hayward died in 1982 of a stroke. It was quick and he went in his sleep. Davey and I flew to England for the funeral. We met his daughters, and his grandchildren, and I felt a little more secure about the future of our species when I saw that something of that man still lived on. The world is woefully short of men like Major Hayward.

In 1993, Davey sent me an obituary of a Major James Powell from Chicago. Never married, no kids, and a life filled with public service… local politics. He never ran for any office other than those on a city or county level, despite multiple offers for state-level appointed positions. I guess he didn't want to lose his company and become a rear-echelon staff officer again. He belonged on the front lines, and that's where he stayed.

I like to think that the letter I sent him made a difference. I like to think he took some of it to heart. But then I read the part again where he died alone and with no children and I wonder if he ever recovered from the sight of Rebecca beckoning to us from the front doors of Dom Caern.

Some wounds never heal.

Late last year, just after my eighty-second birthday, I got a call from Davey's family asking me to come to his house in upstate New York. He was dying, and asking for me.

"Sarge," he said, smiling weakly when I reached his side. I'd seen him since he turned old and gray, but he'd lost a lot of weight and I could see he wasn't long for this world.

I took his hand in mine. "You know, Davey, you can call me Harry. We haven't been in the Army for a long time now."

"You're Sarge," he said. "You'll always be Sarge, whether they pin lieutenant's bars on your collar or not."

"How are you holding up, Davey?" I asked.

"I'm dying," he said. "And I'm a little scared about it. But a little excited too. Did you know there's a lot of religions that believe you get reincarnated again and again, so your soul can learn all the lessons it needs to learn? I like the sound of that."

"Me too," I said.

"Sarge," he said, and I had to lean in close to hear him, "what we saw... in Belgium, I mean... it was all real, wasn't it?"

I nodded.

He shook his head. "You don't think Rebecca was right, do you? That you go to that other place and become like the Geist when you die?"

We were too old and too good of friends for me to lie to him. "I honestly don't know, Davey. I don't think so. I hope not."

"Me too," he said. "Stay here with me?"

"I will."

"I'm going to be cremated," he said.

I nodded. "So am I."

It was Kate's turn six months later. I had her cremated too.

They're all gone now, even my shining Kate, who I can still see standing in the late September sun of my mind if I close my eyes and concentrate hard enough. Nobody is left. I am the only surviving member of 1st Battalion, 518th Parachute Infantry Regiment, 101st Airborne Division, Army of the United States. Soon it will be my turn.

But I've left something out, something that I had been hoping to sweep under the carpet of my memories and keep from view. Now that I've aired all this out, though, I suppose it's only right that I include everything, even that one terrible day that still keeps me up at night starting at shadows and twisting the covers in my hands.

Andrew C. Piazza

74

On a muggy Saturday in May, 1954, a package arrived in the mail with no return address. This being long before the era of the Unibomber, I shrugged and slit it open with my pocketknife, thinking that maybe Christmas had come early.

Inside was a metal canister containing a spool of film from a hand-held camera. It had a serial number stenciled on the side.

At the time, I didn't think anything of it, other than that it might've come to the wrong address. I checked the writing on the package... it was meant for me, all right. No note, no identification, nothing. As that particular day was full of concerns regarding three young Kinders making a terror of themselves, and as I didn't have a movie projector to play the film, I simply stuck it in a drawer with a half-hearted promise to solve the mystery sometime when the kids weren't burning the house to the ground.

Four days later, I answered a knock at the front door to find two expressionless men in spit-shined uniforms on my front porch. There was an inexplicable moment of complete terror, until I reminded myself that the Army didn't own me anymore and I could relax.

"Harold Kinder?"

No one who addressed me as "Harold" was to be fully trusted. "I'm Harry Kinder."

"Mr. Kinder, I am Captain Donaldson and this is Captain Jackson. We're with the Air Force."

"Air Force? Sorry, fellas, I only ever jumped out of planes; I never flew them."

They didn't smile.

"Have you received any communication from a Lieutenant Colonel Paul Wexler in the past few weeks?"

So Wexler made light colonel, I thought. "Communication?"

"A phone call, a letter… a package?"

It started falling into place for me then, but I'd played poker before, and knew how to keep a straight face. "No," I lied.

"Are you sure?" Captain Jackson asked, eyeing me carefully.

"Major… *Colonel* Wexler and I were not particularly close," I said. "What I mean is, I only knew him for a few days."

"So he hasn't sent you anything?"

"Nope," I lied again. "How is Colonel Wexler?"

They looked at each other. "Colonel Wexler took his own life with a .45 caliber pistol eight days ago."

The exact date of the postmark on the package. I didn't need to ask to know that Wexler hadn't put the barrel to his temple in order to blow his brains out; he'd put the gun in his mouth to blow out the base of his skull.

"Did he ask to be cremated?"

They looked at each other again. "How did you know that, sir?"

I shrugged. "Something we once talked about."

"You know, we could get a warrant to search your house," Captain Jackson said.

"Get a whole stack of them," I replied. "Won't change the fact that I don't have anything to find."

They seemed to accept that reluctantly and turned to leave.

"We don't need to tell you that the activities at Dom Caern are classified and not to be discussed with anyone," Captain Jackson said.

"Captain, anyone I told about what I saw at Dom Caern wouldn't believe me," I said. Something in their faces made me add, "*You* don't believe it happened, do you?"

Their pause betrayed them. "We believe *something*…" Captain Donaldson began, but Captain Jackson cut him off.

"Good day, sir."

I waited ten minutes before rushing out to my car. It was normally a fifteen-minute drive to my school; I think I made it in seven.

One of our janitors let me in. He didn't bother to ask why I was there. One look at my hollow eyes convinced him to mind his own business.

We had a lot of movie projectors in our A/V room. I picked out the one I always used for my classroom and spooled the film onto it.

There wasn't any screen set up in there, so I took the projector into my classroom to watch it there. I closed the blinds and kept the lights out, and even before the film started rolling, the old feeling was back. Tingling energy crackling from my spine out to my fingers and toes; nervous anticipation, the same kind I got before I would go into battle.

I knew what was going to be on there but I bit my nails in anticipation anyway as the first few seconds rolled by with nothing but the visual static preceding any of those old-time movies. Then, abruptly, as abruptly as the jerk on your harness when a parachute opens and catches you out of a free-fall, a picture leapt onto the screen.

It was the charred bodies from the first night it all started, when the SS put a flame-thrower onto our men lined up as prisoners. Wexler must've taken it as soon as he got there; it was daylight and the detail was uncomfortably precise.

The picture shifted to that of the charcoal drawings, both the Crucifixion and Kleg's rendition of the Geist. Soon thereafter, the picture shifted to an image of Dom Caern, taken from where the road first emerged from the trees.

It got worse after that; the kitchen, and then Freddie, still alive and mutilated, and after that, the basement of Dom Caern. It would be a gross understatement to say it was eerie to watch it all played out on the screen in black and white. All those men I had known... Shorty, Cappy, Goliath, all of our company... walking around alive when I knew that they were dead made the small muscles in my back start to shudder. It was too much like what the Geist had done. They were gone. They shouldn't be walking around, even if it were only on a movie screen.

There wasn't any sound to the film, which somehow made it worse. I never have liked Quiet Times.

The part I was dreading began. The screen showed the tunnel we called the Rabbit Hole, lit by our floodlights and flashlights. I could see Doctor Schmidt, Goliath, and Tedeski, and when the picture shifted, I saw myself as well. We held our weapons at the ready and there was terror on all of our faces.

I watched the rest in numb, horrified fascination; the doors, the village, the cathedral, everything. Only when Shorty's walking corpse came on the screen did I realize I had shoved a fist in my mouth and was biting down hard on it.

I switched off the film just as Warnal and Peterson's mangled bodies shambled onto the road. My hand was shaking and when I looked down at it, I saw it was bleeding from where I'd bitten it.

I replaced the film in its metal canister and walked home in a daze. It took two hours to get there. I don't know why I left my car at the school, but in my condition, it was probably best that I didn't drive.

My mind was still swimming in a dull haze when I got back to the house. Kate was upset with Becky, our three-year-old terror, for drawing on the walls. I was actually pretty impressed. Along with the flowers and suns, she had managed to reproduce most of the alphabet as well.

I wasn't in any shape to deal with that chaos just then, so I wandered out back to where my two sons were playing. They had a few neighborhood friends over and most of them were playing Army in the yard with little green plastic soldiers. The younger of my sons was set away from the group with another boy, staring at the ground with a magnifying glass.

I walked over to see what he was looking at. James, my oldest, interrupted me with an insistent question. "Dad! Dad!"

"Hunh?" I asked, still unfocused and dazed.

"Bobby says our name means 'kid' in German," James said. "Does it? He says that's where 'kindergarten' comes from... a kid's garden, a kid's place."

I saw then that my other son wasn't examining the ground with his magnifying glass, but instead was burning a daddy long-legger insect that he'd pulled the legs off of.

In that instant, everything fell apart for me. The world suddenly tilted and whirled in on itself, and with a choked cry, I sank to my knees, trying to hold onto my sense of reality with slipping fingers.

There are seemingly innocuous things that when put into the correct context, become terrifying. A child writing on the walls is a nuisance. A young boy playing Army in the dirt, gleefully knocking over plastic soldiers and tanks, is a perfectly natural sight. So is a child torturing bugs, even if it is a bit macabre. But put together, they became an explosive mixture, lit by the memories of Dom Caern dredged up by Wexler's film.

Bobby says our name means 'kid' in German... that's where 'kindergarten' comes from... a kid's garden...

Harry Kinder, the Geist had spoken to me through the mouths of the dead, *I should be in your garden.*

If the Geist knew how to communicate in our language by reading our thoughts, then if it was presented with two languages at once... German and English... it might confuse similar words. Or perhaps even mix them together.

I should be in your garden.

Kinder's garden. Kindergarten.

It wrote on the walls. It killed us in gruesome ways for sport. It created piles of weapons for Kleg in order to spark battles between us, and then gleefully rushed out to knock us over like little plastic green men. The bomber pilots had seen specimens as large as a zeppelin, but ours was only the size of a house when concentrated into a single mass.

The Geist was a child among its kind.

That was the realization that turned my legs to water on that muggy afternoon in May. As unstoppable, as inscrutable, as terrifying and lethal as the Geist was, it was merely an infant among the countless numbers of a formless race living on the other side of reality.

It's still there. *Here*, really; Wexler said that their reality coexists with ours, so those things are all around us, inside of us, watching us with longing, waiting for a chance to break through where the fabric is thin.

I don't pretend to have all the answers, or even any of them. I only caught a glimpse of the Geist, just as I only caught a glimpse of the war. I don't have any answers about that, either. Some things are too large to be dissected. Some truths are too complex to be realized. If there is such a thing as truth at all.

So I still don't know exactly what the Geist is. A malevolent spirit who found a doorway from Hell to Earth, or an alien being from an unfathomable reality. Maybe they're the same thing.

What I do know is, some damn fools are still trying to rip open the fabric to that other place. Wexler's suicide and the sudden arrival of the film told me that.

Maybe they'll never figure it out. The only documents we recovered from Dom Caern were that poor doomed Wehrmacht soldier's letters, and I have those. And maybe collapsing that tunnel will keep the Geist where it belongs; Wexler had mentioned that the holes in reality were self-sealing, so maybe the Geist has lost interest.

Or maybe... maybe the Geist will grow up one day and have a desire to go back and re-visit the sandbox of its youth. If it does, as Major Hayward said, I fear there will be a terrible cost, measured in brave souls who will be lost and shattered in order to buy the human race one last gasp.

AUTHOR NOTES

Thank you, Gentle Reader, for allowing me to share my daydreams with you. I hope you found the time well spent.

If you enjoyed this novel, there are a number of ways you can support it. You can leave a review on Amazon or wherever you bought the book, and letting me know what you liked about it. That's a big help.

You can let any friends who you think might like to read a book like "One Last Gasp" know about it, whether through sharing a link on social media, via email, or just good old fashioned word of mouth. Finally, you can follow me on Facebook:

https://www.facebook.com/andrewcpiazza/.

Know that any support you choose to offer, and any feedback you choose to give, is greatly appreciated.

If you'd like a little more of this story, I have a prequel short story available, exclusively for the members of my reader's email list. It's free to join. The story is entitled "Flying Fortress", and tells the tale of the doomed B-17s that Major Wexler mentions as having disappeared in the area of Dom Caern. You can get it by following this link: https://dl.bookfunnel.com/dog919rgy7

This novel was a labor of love. It took about a full year to complete, and required a huge amount of research into the historical period, which was fine by me, because I'm a bit of a recovering World War II history addict. Writing this novel allowed me the excuse to indulge my habit to more extreme levels... I actually now own a large hardcover reference work entitled "Encyclopedia of Weapons Of World War Two", amongst many, many other similar volumes.

When this novel first started germinating somewhere in the dark recesses of my brain, it began as a rather simple experimental idea...

could I mash up a World War Two war story, with a horror story, and make it work? There were horror novels written before with a similar setting; F Paul Wilson's "The Keep" is one example.

But Wilson's book isn't really a war story; it's basically Evil Wizard Vs. The Nazis, and really, you could pluck that story straight out of World War Two and set it in the modern day with the evil wizard killing off paranormal researchers instead of Nazi occupiers and nothing would substantially change. I wanted to create something different.

I wanted the war to be an integral part of the story, including big, splashy battle scenes, and a discussion of how it looked and sounded and felt to be an infantry solider in the middle of the largest battle ever fought by the US Army, smack dab in the especially brutal winter of January 1945. And, I wanted the horror to mesh with the war story, in such a way as one informed the other, so as to become inseparable.

Of all the points in time and space to set the novel, The Battle of the Bulge quickly took center stage. I considered some other engagements, such as the Hurtgen Forest, but one of the quirks of the Bulge that I found fascinating was that, even though it was such an enormous battle spread out over such a colossal area, a lot of the stories shared by the soldiers read more like individual, small-scale engagements. This could provide for the more intimate setting required for a horror story… things aren't nearly as scary when we all can share and discuss them in the light of day.

Over and over again, I read about the snow-covered pines in the forests of Belgium, that were so deep and dense, that the descriptions reminded me of descriptions of the densest jungles of Vietnam, where entire units could get swallowed up and lost. Perfect. That's where it all started.

A lot of the characters and details of the novel were born from all of that obsessive research. I discovered that any large manor houses in the area were designated by the abbreviation "Dom." on Allied maps; that stuck in my head, and led to the creation of Dom Caern, a manor house out in the middle of this dense forest, tucked away in the middle of this massive conflict, just out of sight enough to be the focal point of the horror element of the story.

The horror element. Let's talk a little about that. Why The Geist, instead of vampires or werewolves or some other convenient, ready-made horror trope? First off, I don't like ready-made. That's not as fun as making it all up myself.

Further, I cut my teeth reading the horror of HP Lovecraft, who wrote a very particular, peculiar brand of horror that I find very compelling. "Cosmic terror", it's often called, and it's based around this idea that the human race is a small, infinitesimal, meaningless accident, spinning helplessly through space on this rock called Earth, surrounded on all sides by colossal, ancient, terrifying forces of such power that the only reason they haven't wiped us all out, is that they haven't noticed us... yet.

It's an extension of the basic terror of existence and the knowledge of eventual oblivion that holds all of us in its grip from birth to death. It's that sinking feeling, that deep suspicion that we all have, that we aren't all that special, that the human race isn't so exceptional, that other species have risen and fallen before us, and we're destined for the same fate. As the soft platitudes of religious faith that tell us our spirits will live forever begin to lose their luster in the light of scientific inquiry, we are left with a hollow, dark nihilism in which we began to doubt the supremacy and value of human life.

Which is very, very similar to what many combat veterans have written about their experiences in war; that you start off thinking "it can't happen to me, I'm too smart, too good-looking, too all-around awesome to get killed", and then, after watching people die all around you for no apparent reason, those thoughts morph into "it *could* happen to me, but I'm too well-trained and too careful to get killed", and then, finally, to "there's nothing special about me at all, and it *will* happen to me". The same existential crisis that lays at the heart of Lovecraft's terror... the same crisis that lurks within all our psyches... is accelerated and amplified in the awful crucible of war.

So. Now it didn't seem like such a strange match-up, to write a war story that was also at its heart, a Lovecraftian horror novel. As the novel began to take shape, so did the Geist... an essentially unknowable, unstoppable, cruel creature of otherworldly origin, toying with us like dolls… and the epiphany of the ending, which is also very, very Lovecraftian… the realization that no matter how horrifying you thought the problem was, it's really much, much worse.

I also liked the idea of a new explanation of the classic "haunted house" or ghost story… that rather than dead spirits inexplicably hanging around just to watch us eat and sleep and take the occasional crap, instead, these spirits might be beings existing in another dimension able to influence ours in areas where "the walls are thin". And so Dom Caern became a haunted house, of a very different sort than what we're used to seeing.

More and more historical details begged to be added to the story. I would discover odd little quirks unique to that particular conflict and felt compelled to include them. As an example, the tank destroyer… a vehicle that only existed in World War Two. Never before, never since… an experiment in sticking a really big gun on a (relatively) lightly armored vehicle with the express purpose of hunting down other tanks. I had to have one (or four) in my novel.

Which meant that I needed to reference an armored unit in the area where I had set the novel, and lo and behold, there was another bizarre quirk of that war that immediately came to light when I discovered the 761st Tank Battalion: racially segregated combat units.

It can be difficult to remember that a short seventy years ago, we were still dividing up combat units on the ludicrous basis of skin color. And so Tedeski, who originally was an American of Polish descent, became African-American, and a new minor sub-plot of race relations was born in to the manuscript.

Many of the characters serve to act as focal points of discussion on the war. Our narrator, Harry, is the Everyman who serves as our eyes and ears, and varies from being exhausted and spent and terrified, to defiant and brave and practically rampaging with violence. I wanted to point out that bravery and cowardice can and do exist in the same person; the same man who receives the Medal of Honor charging machine gun nests can find himself hiding paralyzed with fear in a hole the very next day. What makes bravery special is that it is found co-existing with fear, not in the absence of it.

Harry needed to be the company sergeant, because as our eyes and ears, he needed to be able to be present both where the officers were making decisions, and also where the enlisted men were dealing with the consequences of those decisions. He needed to be everywhere. And his rank began to inform his character; as Captain Powell was the father figure, Harry became a sort of eldest son, subordinate to the father (and somewhat worshipful of him as the father), but also expected to be the big brother to the company and capable of making it run.

Captain Powell represents the best of us. He always knows the right thing to do, the right thing to say, how to lead men and inspire them, and how to direct them to be the best version of themselves. A capable warrior, he knows the value of mercy and restraint, but is far from a pushover. We see in him that desperate situations can bring out the best in a person… and also shatter them. Captain Powell's loss of Rebecca and his subsequent descent into despair represents the awful truth of how sending our best and brightest off to war is an exercise in ruination; so many of those best and brightest are damaged irreparably by the experience.

Rebecca represents the civilian population caught up in the war. So often, war stories focus on the soldiers and the battles, when I also find it fascinating to contemplate the experience of a non-combatant stuck in the midst of all of that madness, blown this way and that way like a leaf in the wind, by forces hopelessly beyond their control. The soldiers have weapons to defend themselves and companions to guard them; the civilians are raw nerves exposed to the whims of massive, heavily armed, sometimes poorly restrained groups of young men who have been encouraged to perform violent acts on a regular basis. I cannot imagine how they coped.

Doctor Schmidt is the German Captain Powell; an essentially good man, very capable, decent, and a good soldier, who happens to find himself in the terrible position of being asked to defend the country that he loves by a government that he despises. He stands in for the Germans who had the complicated position of being patriots who wanted to see their country thrive, but who also had no love for the Nazis or their genocidal agenda. Exactly what does one do in such a situation? Doctor

Schmidt is a good man trying to navigate an impossible situation as best he can.

Kleg, on the other hand, is Doctor Schmidt's opposite; a cruel, sadistic man who doubles down on the evil he sees around him. He very obviously represents the Nazis and the SS, and more deeply, he represents those among the human race who love war, who crave having all the restraints of civilization removed so that they now have license to exercise the worst depravities lurking in the primitive areas of their brains. Kleg worships The Geist, because he worships war. Madness, destruction, and depravity are his gods.

Major Hayward, that magnificent Brit who demonstrates the extraordinary stoicism of his countrymen, seems the best equipped to handle the terrible misfortunes of war. He is the one who reminds us, "The world owes us nothing", and although he has moments of weakness, he does what is necessary and endures the consequences with aplomb and dare I say it, style.

His attitude and story arc are a homage to the incredible endurance of the people of Great Britain during this conflict. It's easy for Americans to forget that World War Two didn't start with the bombing of Pearl Harbor; the British (and others) had endured years of war and unbelievable levels of suffering and sacrifice before the US got around to joining in on the conflict. Hayward is there to remind us that even in the face of despair, there is hope, and even in the face of loss, there is a bright and shining silver lining to the sacrifices of the soldiers in those snow-covered pines. Green fields and free people, he says. Yeah.

It's a good day to be alive.

Other Books By Andrew C. Piazza:

Strange Days (short story collection)
Mage Hunters series (urban fantasy action adventure):
Shards Of Glass
Resurrection Day
The Intron Code

Made in the USA
Las Vegas, NV
02 January 2023

64751479R10282